Bears in the North

By Alistair Hall

Raven Fell Limited *Publishers*

First published in 2021 by Raven Fell Limited

A CIP catalogue for this book is available from the British Library.

ISBN 9781916299726

Edited by Kat Harvey, Athena Copy

Graphics by Room for Design, Northallerton.

Printed and bound in Berwick upon Tweed, Great Britain by Martins.

Raven Fell Limited, Bedale

books@ravenfell.co.uk

Then Talhaearn, 'Father of the Muse' was renowned in poetry; and Aneirin and Taliesin and Blwchfardd and Cian who is called 'Wheat of Song' were illustrious all at the same time in British Poetry.

Historia Brittonum

BRITANNIA 412AD

HIBERNIA

● Hill of Tara

Drumanagh ●

LOCH NEAGH

DUMNONIA

SEGONTIUM ●

YR WYDDFA

● ISCA DUMNONIORUM

ALAUNA ●

MAGLONA ●
LUGUVALIUM ●
UXELODUNUM ●

● ISCA AUGUSTA

THE EDGE VIROCONIUM

DEVA ●

BANNA ●

VILLA WRIKON
OCTAVIUS HILL

BREMETENNACUM ●

REGED

DURNOVARIA ●

● LINDINIS

MAMUCIUM ●

GLEVUM ●

CORSTOPITUM ●

CORINIUM ●

LETOCETUM ●

VINOVIA ●

SORVIODUNUM ●

CATARACTONIUM ● PONS AELIUS ●

BADON DERVENTIO ●

ELFED

● ISURIUM BRIGANTUM

CLAUSENTUM

CAMBODUNUM

VECTIS ● VENTA BELGARUM ●

CORIELTAUVORUM ●

DANUM ●

● EBORACUM

LACTODURUM ●

● LACTODURUM

Gainnion ●

● NOVIOMAGUS

CAUSENNIS ● Ypwines Fleot

● LINDUM

VERULAMIUM ●

LONDINIUM ● DUROBRIVAE ● ● Creeganford

● Wippeds Fleot

● CAMULODUNUM

DUROVERNUM ●

● RUTUPIAE

● VENTA ICENORUM

● BONONIA

GAUL

CALEDONIA 412AD

LOCH NEAGH

DUNNAD

ALT CLUT

CANDIDA CASA

CRUFFEL

DIN EIDYN

PICTS

FORTRIU

ORCADES

To the south of the Antonine Wall

Early Autumn 412

Ninian encouraged his pony up the steep hill toward the solitary figure of King Coel. Mounted on his black stallion, the great king, the Bear of the North, was ready for battle. In the half-light of a crisp breaking dawn, his old Roman cavalry armour glowed, and the bearskin hood worn over his helmet enhanced his warlike appearance. The bishop's summons from the camp to meet privately with Coel had been unexpected so close to the advance, but curiosity and duty had brought the earnest young man regardless of any trepidation. Soldiers and cavalry were everywhere, forming into their units and tensely awaiting their deployment. Their fear was so tangible that Ninian could almost have reached out and touched it as he rode through their ranks. The king was staring into the distance but turned when he heard the approaching hoofbeats.

'Ah, bishop, thank you for joining me, I should dismount to pray with you, but time is pressing.'

'I am told you now intend to attack these Picts, my king?'

'It ends today, Ninian. It is eighteen months since Talorc brought this seething mass of heathens south – and twelve months since they overwhelmed our defences at Pons Aelius, ravaging the countryside far to the south and sacking Eboracum. In the end, we must be grateful to the mountains, forests and rivers for succeeding where our soldiers could not, for it was the land itself that eventually stopped their advance, and now the famine they created has starved their own army forcing its return. Our God works in mysterious ways.'

Ninian bowed his head in reverence to the Lord. 'So why do you attack today, my king? It is not difficult to see you are sorely outnumbered and the Picts only days away from their homeland.'

'Once this army is fed, it will once more be a threat to all. The Romans called this region Valentia; it is Christian and was garrisoned for thirty years, but now the Empire has abandoned Britannia, it is left to us to protect our cives from Pictish ambition. Tell me Ninian, how does your Christian mission in this region fare?'

'Slowly, my king. There is a minor kingdom just north of here, ruled by a King Tuduvallus. He and his people are converts, but he is terrified of Talorc and worships in secret.'

'So, the progress of your mission would improve greatly should Talorc be defeated?'

'That is so my king, you are indeed helping in the Lord's work.'

'I am encouraged that Myrddin has foreseen a great victory here, a massacre. This latest incursion by the Picts was no raiding party – it was almost an invasion, Talorc's entire tribe moving through our lands like a plague of locusts. I am minded of the Goths, who harried the Romans in similar fashion as they moved across the Empire in tribes so large they could not be stopped. We must not succumb to the same tactics. If Talorc reaches his homeland with his stolen booty, he will be hailed a hero, and without doubt, he will attract sufficient support to return time after time. We must kill them all now or cower before heathens for decades to come.'

'I have heard that the Christians of Eboracum were martyred alongside their bishop.'

'It was worse than that. Lord Crannog tells me that when the Picts sacked the city they broke into mausoleums and desecrated graves, hoping to find the Roman trinkets that so satisfy their lust for treasure. For centuries, they watched the Romans with resentful envy, and the withdrawal of the legions has provided the opportunity the Picts have been waiting for, but King Talorc is a warrior, not a campaigner. He has not fed his army, preferring to use his carts for booty instead of

2

supplies. He is over-confident, believing we will not attack him so close to his homeland and that he is protected by his numerical superiority, but we have set a trap. Our allies from Alt Clut and Din Eidyn have cut off his path north; the Picts will find themselves fighting on all fronts with empty bellies.'

'I see. So, what do you wish of me, great king?'

'I want you to pray hard for victory. There will be many dead, including women and children, but we can show no mercy. After this day is over, bishop, you must press on with your Christian mission. Only our Lord can truly show them the error of their ways; swords and spears will only serve to inflame their resolve.'

The sun was nearly risen over the hills as a group of horsemen approached them.

'My king, it is time. Edern and Cinhill will commence their attack soon, and so must we if our plan is to succeed.'

Coel wheeled his mail-coated stallion around and rode away down the hill.

'God be with you, King Coel,' Ninian muttered under his breath as the sounding of horns echoed across the valley, calling all soldiers to arms.

*

Crannog heard the signal.

He had spent over a year skirmishing with Picts, containing their ambitions to the north-east of the Cwmry territories, well away from the grasslands and cattle herds of the Pennines. He had scouted after the large force, following their loot-laden wagons as they trundled northward through the wasteland they had created themselves. At the outset, the Pictish force had been two to three thousand strong. Talhaearn, his commanding officer, had been unable to prevent them breaking through the wall near Pons Aelius and had been unhorsed and badly injured in the fighting. Now Crannog was in command, and it was down to him to lead the charge on the left flank and link up with King Cinhill.

The Pict army had been diminished by disease and starvation, making their return to Pictland inevitable. But even though they were weakened, Crannog knew the Cymry were still outnumbered four to one. He consoled himself: God was on their side and a well-trained cavalry horse was equal to five infantrymen. Sword in hand, he signalled to his men who surged forward.

The two turmae broke cover with the sound of the horns still ringing in their ears. Not yet engaging the enemy, they rode hard up the left flank, maintaining a safe distance from the javelins thrown by the swarming Pict infantry. King Cinhill, with about one hundred cavalry, was already engaged, axes and swords flashing in the bright, early, autumn sunshine. The sound of battle now filled the valley, and Crannog deployed his archers to the rear before leading the charge on King Cinhill's right flank. The terror in the emaciated faces of the enemy betrayed an army stretched beyond desperation, so nearly home but too weak to fight. The Cymry, all fed and furious, were making light work of their hated adversaries – it was like scything corn. Crannog's archers easily picked off the fiercest warriors from a safe distance as if it were target practice, and the fear that had knotted Crannog's stomach all morning was forgotten as he hacked his way through the throng.

Coel's forward cavalry charge had initially withstood a stern challenge from Talorc's best men, but now the enemy had realised they were surrounded and looked to the rear for their best chance of breaking out and heading for home. Suddenly, Cinhill and Crannog found themselves overwhelmed by the mass of Picts that had turned to flee. The archers were forced to hold their shots, frustrated by the enemy's close contact with their own troops, and so, the ferocity of the combat intensified.

After a further hour, Coel's bear hood could be seen finally closing on their position. King Cinhill dropped to the ground, a javelin penetrating his chest. But his sons closed up and bravely fought on with great skill. Bodies piled on bodies, screams filled the air, and the cloying scent of butchery pervaded Crannog's senses. He was covered in blood, exhausted, but his sword arm kept swinging until, finally, Cymry surrounded the remaining Picts who threw down their weapons.

'Which of them is Talorc?' Coel asked his son-in-law.

Edern of the Gododdin pointed to a powerfully built, grey-haired Pict at the centre.

'That is him there. I have fought him before.'

'Disarm them and bind their leaders,' ordered the king.

At spear point, the remnant put up no resistance.

'Centurion Alwyn.'

'Yes, my king.'

'Recover our dead and collect up the weapons and booty. Dispatch the enemy wounded to Hell. Hold their men prisoner and send the women on their way. We shall make camp by the Clyde and wash away the blood of our enemies so that we are cleansed of its taint before we give thanks to God. Bishop Ninian awaits our return.'

*

The following morning brought a light rain. The gentle patter of drops on the tents complimented the sound of rushing water from the shallow river, a soothing sound after the cacophony of war. Crannog had awoken from a deep, dream-filled sleep and looked outside to check on the royal prisoners. Each was bound and tied to an individual stake driven hard into the ground. It was apparent they were all Pictish nobles, warriors much like himself, and still proud enough to hold their heads high.

'See their proud bearing, Crannog,' said Coel, who had walked across to join his comrade.

'Yes,' he replied. 'It will make it easier when we come to remove their heads.'

'Perhaps the sons of Cinhill will accept that task. They fought bravely alongside their father and continued to do so after he fell – they are due their revenge.'

'Do we yet know which men are Talorc's sons? They are so difficult to tell apart,' said Crannog.

'Edern knows,' replied Coel. 'Go and find him and Ninian, and let's put an end to this.'

Crannog returned quickly with both Edern and Ninian. Prince Cynloyp, the eldest son of the fallen King Cinhill, had also been summoned and arrived with a mighty battle-axe.

Edern pointed out the sons of Talorc who were led to a rock and beheaded. The king of the Picts looked on as his family and nobles were executed. Edern pointed to the youngest remaining noble.

'He is Drest. His father was a strong enough rival to Talorc for our captive king here to have the man murdered.'

King Coel rose to his feet.

'I know you understand our language, Talorc. I admire you as a warrior but not as a king. You have brought nothing but death to the Cymry and your own people, and now it is your turn to suffer that fate. Cynloyp, avenge your father.'

Talorc was led to the bloody execution stone where, with a single swing of the axe, Cynloyp removed the head of his enemy.

'We will take the severed heads of Talorc and his sons to Banna where we will mount them on the wall facing north. Now, Ninian, take the boy called Drest to the river and baptise him at sword-point. Tell him about our Lord and, when that is done, bring him to my tent. Do not release his bonds and keep him under close guard.'

Crannog saw Edern give Coel a quizzical look. 'What is your plan?' he asked.

'I will release him if he swears to remain a Christian and leads the remnant of his people home in peace.'

'I doubt that will discourage future attacks.'

'I know, but he will remember what he witnessed on this campaign, and so, he will begin to see what I see. The Romans have left, and there is no longer any treasure to seek. Prosperity comes from trading, not raiding, and we are all tribes of this island. We should try to live side by side as good Christians. If we do nothing at all to change our ways, we will be at war again within a generation.'

'And what of the Saxons and Scotti, my king?'

'With the Picts quelled, we can turn our focus toward those raiders. Our militia can cope with their kind of threat.'

Coel looked around at his victorious allies and commanders.

'Raiders not invaders. I shall ask Talhaearn to incorporate that line into one of his poems.'

Crannog could not suppress his humour.

'Perhaps he would be better practising staying on his horse, my king.'

The gathering laughed heartily. It had been some time since humour had graced the court of King Coel.

II

Gaul

Winter 427

Palladius had travelled a great distance to meet Bishop Germanus at the abbey dedicated to St Cosmas and Damian by the River Yonne. The frost that had formed overnight had seeped into his bones during morning prayers – Rome was so much warmer at this time of year – and it was a relief to be moving his limbs as he climbed the steps to the bishop's private quarters. The Holy Father had insisted that he consult with Germanus before Easter, a sign of how shocked his Holiness was by the news from Britannia.

The bishop was sat at a table piled with scrolls where he was reading with the assistance of candlelight. Palladius remembered Germanus from when he had attended the investiture of Pope Celestine, although it was unlikely the bishop would remember him – just a lowly young deacon, even if he was from a noble family.

'Ah, Palladius.' Germanus looked up. 'I have just read the Holy Father's request for your audience. How was your journey?'

He looked older than Palladius remembered, reflecting the challenging years the Empire and the Church had endured.

'God was merciful, your Grace. The sea was calm and the journey overland free from trouble.'

'These are good omens for your mission – travel can be difficult these days and particularly so at this time of year. Come, sit by me.'

Palladius sat on the bench to the side of the table.

'I was sorry to hear of your father's death. We were acquainted in the Imperial service during his time in Armorica; he was a fine soldier. His promotion under Johannes was justly deserved.'

'And sadly sealed his fate, your Grace,' Palladius added quickly.

'These past few years have been difficult for us all,' Germanus said, 'but now, perhaps we can look ahead with some hope. General Aetius is successfully defending Gaul, and Galla Placidia holds the reins of the Western Empire.'

'Which she does with great competence,' added Palladius.

'She is blessed with a keen intellect and remarkable determination. Her long list of personal tragedies gives her much experience to draw on. The suffering and sacrifice she has endured has forged the Empress into a leader to be reckoned with.'

'The Holy Father holds her in high regard.'

'That is good to hear. So, tell me, how may I help the Bishop of Rome?'

'By lending your influence to ensuring orthodoxy prevails in Britannia, your Grace – it is a grave worry. The Holy Father has received a request for help from Vodinus, the recently ordained Bishop of Londinium, and I have brought you a copy of the missive to read.' Palladius reached into his satchel and pulled out a scroll, passing it to Germanus. He watched the bishop carefully read the letter, imagining the renowned legal mind sorting through the ramifications and solutions. After several minutes, Germanus placed the letter on the table, his gaze distant, deep in thought.

Palladius cleared his throat. 'The Holy Father requests that I travel to Britannia to confirm these claims and report back to you, so that we may consider a strategy.'

'Yes,' said Germanus, his attention coming back to Palladius, 'that would be wise. It would be premature to adopt measures before we have proof of these claims. What is your view, Palladius?'

'God knows no boundaries, and the Empire of the Lord reaches beyond the Empire of the Romans. Wherever there is a Christian, there should be an orthodox church.'

'But is this drift toward Pelagianism endorsed by the leaders of the Britons? Can we rely on Roman law to prevail, even though their territory is no longer part of the Empire?'

'It is my belief that Roman law is still upheld, but I shall make it part of my mission to discover if all Britons hold true to it. Pelagius was excommunicated for his heresy, his teachings forbidden by the Church. That is straightforward enough, but there seems to be more at stake. The situation appears to have been exploited by one leader of the Britons known as Vortigern. He has partitioned the vast estates that Melania gifted to the Church in the time between the passing of Bishop Fastidius and the election of Bishop Vodinus. The newly elected Bishop of Londinium is most put-out.'

'The letter mentions a Pelagian bishop called Agricola?'

'He is the son of Bishop Severianus of Carthage, a convert who travelled to Britannia in search of fellow heretics, but it appears he is nothing more than a puppet of this Vortigern. As you can see, Vodinus even questions the validity of Agricola's ordination, an extraordinary claim which the Holy Father wishes me to investigate.'

'Does Vodinus have no other loyal servants of the Church he can call upon for support in resolving this problem.'

'Ninian is the only other bishop in Britannia. He administers to his flock of Britons in the North where King Coel's army defends the border. He carries the word of God to their enemies – the barbaric tribes known as the Picts and Scotti. He is somewhat occupied…'

'King Coel? There was a respected tribune called Coel… but that was more than twenty years ago. It can't be him though – surely he is dead?'

'Apparently not, your Grace. His army still defends the old northern frontier.'

'What about Galla Placidia? Is she likely to send her warhound, Aetius, to recover this part of the Empire?'

'Aetius is ambitious and may yet consider a campaign, but the Empress has not disclosed any such plans.'

10

'Then I shall write to General Aetius and seek his opinion whilst you undertake your visit and enquiries. When we have a complete picture, we will seek the Holy Father's guidance. Tread carefully, Palladius – there are powerful forces at work, and beyond Gaul, you represent only the Church, for the Empire no longer holds authority there.'

Palladius bowed his head. 'Then God will protect me.'

III

Banna on the Roman Wall

Winter 427

The old warrior watched the embers burning blue in the bitter, icy draft that blew in beneath the door. He drew his woollen cloak around him, warming his chilled bones. Myrddin sometimes saw the future, but Talhaearn could not, and his mind struggled to guess what might occur when the king died. What did God expect of him? Would the slaughter begin again? More death – he had witnessed so much already. He closed his eyes and exhaled through gritted teeth. Would it ever end?

Not for the first time, he tried to remember the faces of his murdered parents; still, he couldn't see them. He had only been three at the time of their death, but he felt sure he'd know them in Heaven. There were so many he would recognise in that blessed place...

Coel and Strawdawl had become his guardians when he was very young. A king and queen, no less, taking an orphan and raising him alongside their own. Memories danced back and forth. Young and strong, fighting for Rome. Loyalties sorely tested by the Empire, until the Roman overlords deserted Britannia's shores. Hard years standing with the northern tribes, defending the Wall, enemies coming from all directions – the Scotti from Hibernia to the west, the Picts from Caledonia to the north, the Saxons from across the Oceanus Germanicus to the east.

Talhaearn leant forward to be closer to the embers; his face was hot, but his back felt the cold that leached into his hut. Curse the weather – so much snow. It was easy to lose himself in the flickering embers, drifting... The North would not be defeated that much had been proven, but the game had changed... He leant back. Now it was

Saxons raiding the south, Britannia's soft underbelly. Talhaearn's gaze was drawn to the rattling door and beyond, to where his ailing king lay abed. Once the most important general on the entire island, now Coel's forces could do no more than defend the northern frontier with regional militia. The Romans were gone, and no amount of hoping and cajoling by the Britons to the south was going to encourage them back. The Empire's frontiers had collapsed, and the Britons faced their future alone.

He drained the last dregs of his evening cup of mead and threw several logs on the fire. The embers flared and flames licked upward; a heavy sigh escaped his pursed lips. With the king gravely sick, how long before their enemies sensed weakness and came probing the North? Who would stand against them now? He stretched out his tired, aching legs. If only Ceneu had survived. The young prince should have stayed closer to his bannermen – that was their training – but the enemy had seized the opportunity, isolating him and cutting him down. Taly squeezed his eyes shut as if that would stop him witnessing it all over again. If he had seen the breach, he could have covered, could have come to his adopted brother's aid… but instead, the king's only son had bled to death in his arms.

Heaven… so many were waiting for him there. After his parents, his own beloved wife Tara and precious son Bewyn, along with Coel's wife, daughter and mother, all slaughtered on one dreadful day in a chance raid by the hated Scotti. And now… now, the central pillar of his life, King Coel, lay dying. It was the old king's wish that his two grandsons, Gorwst and Mor, should inherit the kingdom equally. Fine nephews both, but were they ready? Their grandfather's boots would be hard to fill. He had taught the boys everything he knew, but King Coel was not only a great warrior – he was also a clever statesman. Myrddin had seen the future, and Coel had listened, leading the Cymry away from Rome's crumbling empire, saving them from destruction. For twenty years, laments for the dead had been replaced with songs in praise of the heroes who had secured freedom for the North, the Cymry no longer fighting out of duty or fear but as warriors who fought for their king in defence of their homeland.

'Heroes and widows,' he toasted aloud to himself – they always came in equal measure.

Taly looked to the wall where his mail coat and polished shield reflected the flickering fire. He no longer rode with the militia, having taken on the important role of secretary to the court. Educated like a Roman and capable of writing a little verse, he was now the king's bard too. It was his voice that could be heard over the crackling fire in the great hall, exalting heroes on long winter's nights, making humorous toasts… but not in this dour mood.

A sudden movement to his side caught his attention.

'Can you hear something, Plato?'

His wolfhound's ears were pricked, eyes on the doorway. Getting up, the big dog padded across the room. He ran his snout along the base of the door and then returned to his place by the fire, lying down and placing his jaw on his paws after an exaggerated yawn.

'All's well then, lad,' said Taly, giving the dog a rough stroke around the ears.

The blizzard outside would keep the enemy at bay until spring, but he felt his melancholy would last forever. His eyes drifted to his sword. Together, they had taken many lives, and it was his bed companion, his only bed companion. Not since his wife and infant son had been murdered had anyone shared his bed. He slipped his sword beneath the covers now as he climbed stiffly into his bed. All those years of fighting since their deaths had not succeeded in sending him to Heaven, to be by their side. Coel would see them first – the lucky sod – but only God should determine when it was his turn. Taly would not forsake his oath to fight until his last breath. He closed his eyes once more to say his bedtime prayer.

> *Dear Lord, keep this place safe. Deliver Coel Hen*
> *from his sickness and give strength to Brianna.*
> *Protect Gorwst and Mor and speed their return.*

*Goodnight, my sweet Tara, and hunt well in Heaven,
Bewyn. I will join you both soon enough.*

He listened as the wolves began howling in the forest beyond the Wall – *Ah! That's what Plato heard.*

He drifted off to sleep.

*

It was a cold, wild night. Taly stirred in the early hours at the height of the blizzard when his wolfhound joined him on his bed. After a fitful sleep, he arose before dawn, stoking the fire, stiff, wincing at old pains earnt in many battles. His left arm, shoulder and hip still hurt from the fall from his horse, a slight limp his daily reminder. As long as he could grip a shield and swing his sword, it did not matter. His limbs felt worse in the cold though walking off the stiffness always made him feel better. He unlatched the door but could only push it halfway. A foot's depth of snow had fallen, drifting against the door. In the half-light, he took a brush and began clearing the obstruction, watching as Plato patrolled around his hut.

This weather will make all journeys difficult, he thought. Would Prince Mor's meeting with King Vortigern have taken place yet? Eboracum was a strange location to choose. In decay, it had suffered from a recent plague and only the legionary fortress within the outer walls was likely to still provide safe shelter. A strange choice and a difficult journey overland for Vortigern. Brianna had sent two messengers to advise Mor of the king's health, but Taly had sent two more as a precaution and to ensure Mor knew the king was deteriorating. He hoped they had found the prince quickly – the brothers should arrive together to avoid any power plays. Gorwst was stationed west at Alauna and could easily return in less than a day, but the snow had surely undermined Taly's attempts to co-ordinate the princes' return.

Doorway cleared, Taly glanced up to see Bryn struggling across from the great hall in the driving snow. Her hooded cloak was pulled around her – hopefully, concealing his breakfast.

'Good morning, Taly,' she said, revealing the fresh loaf and hot gruel.

'Come in and warm yourself.'

She shook the snow from her clothes and stood as close as possible to the fire.

'How is the king this morning?' he asked

'His fever is high; he is still delirious and struggles for breath. He is very poorly.'

'How is Brianna?'

She raised outstretched hands to the fire for warmth. 'She is tired but keeps vigil by the king's bedside, placing cool rags on his brow.'

Bryn pulled back her cowl, revealing her dark auburn hair and striking brown eyes. After all his grim thoughts and the bleakness of the weather, she was a tonic to his morning – a sharp contrast to her mother, a rather stern, rotund woman renowned for efficiency and a sharp tongue.

'How is your student Cian?' she asked, her eyes avoiding his.

'We shall know soon enough – he's assigned to me this week.' The slight colouring in Bryn's cheeks reinforced his sense that he would be seeing more of Bryn than her mother in the forthcoming days. 'Please let Brianna know that they are both in my prayers.'

Bryn lifted her cowl to cover her head and scurried out into the snow, heading for the kitchen at the rear of the great hall. Cian was a lucky young man. Taly felt the corners of his mouth lift; he enjoyed training the promising young soldier, in much the same way he had Gorwst and Mor.

He devoured his breakfast watching the dawn break slowly, revealing the full effect of the overnight storm. Snow had banked up against several buildings, including the great hall and the granary. The western gate was open, but the drifts were as high as the men trying to shovel a way through it. Taly put on his red cape and sheepskin boots and stepped outside his hut. The cold air cut into his lungs like a knife.

'Foul morning, sir,' said one of the soldiers when Taly approached the gate.

'I can't remember snow this deep,' Taly replied as he entered the door to the gate tower and climbed the steps. The view from the wall was limited by the driving snow, but the entire region looked to be completely shrouded, even trees were barely discernible. Returning to the shovelling party by the gate, he encouraged their labours.

'Keep at it, lads.'

'Aye, prefect. Looks like we'll be cut off for days, mind.'

Taly felt himself stand a little taller at the use of his rank, even though he gave few orders these days. Plato was by now covered in snow and had adapted a leaping style to cover ground, making Taly laugh. Too much reflection had brought on his melancholy, and the burst of genuine mirth spurred his resolve to think about life not death.

'Let's get back to that fire, Plato,' he said.

As Taly tramped and Plato leapt through the snow, they met Cian making his way across from the barracks.

'Morning, prefect.'

'Good morning, Cian,' said Taly, holding the door to his hut open. 'Please step in.' They removed their capes, shaking off the snow. 'Come sit with me by the fire, lad.'

Cian had the look of his father, a deacon of the church at Maglona. The man had done well, teaching his son to read and write and follow the Creed of the Lord. But Cian was his own man – when pressed to join the Church, he had voiced his preference for life as a warrior. It was a decision Taly fully supported.

'How are your parents?' Taly asked as he watched his student remove his sword and place it alongside his own.

'It'll be a struggle to look after the stock in this snow, but my sister is now fifteen and my brother twelve, so reckon they'll manage. They're all just so pleased I've been appointed your aide.' He made

17

himself comfortable on the roughly hewn chair. Plato inspected the lad and settled by his feet.

'I'm pleased they approve. Education is so often overlooked these days, and you should be careful not to squander yours on the battlefield.' It might have sounded like a rebuke, but Taly had seen too many promising students die on the tip of a spear to hold back. 'We live in dangerous times,' he added, qualifying his comment. 'And I hope you appreciate that King Coel and the princes have approved your appointment. It is a sign of the great trust they put in you that they would have you work as their secretary.' The lad's pleasure would have been hard to miss – honest through and through, that one. Taly continued. 'This role requires skill in language, reading, writing… and a talent for muse is useful.'

Cian was sat forward, drinking in everything Taly had to say. A swell of warmth for the lad rose through the old warrior.

'Loyalty, integrity – necessary virtues if you are to be useful.' Taly paused, purposefully adopting a more serious expression. 'You will not always agree with the royal family's decisions or their actions, and what you hear and see may prove uncomfortable for you at times, but it is not your role to criticise!'

Cian nodded, his expression rapt.

'You may well witness the best and the worst of humankind, but you must never seek to influence, nor proffer your opinion unless it is sought, and even then, use great caution! Do you still want the position?' Taly asked sternly.

It was unlikely that lad had ever been asked a more important question. Taly watched the young soldier intently.

'I will do my best, prefect, but I will need your wise tuition and direction if I am to succeed.'

'Yes. You will, indeed,' said Taly, grinning. 'Now, tell me, what are the men talking of in the barracks these days?'

'Fears for the changes that will come should the great king die,' said Cian. 'The more ambitious war-mongers hope there might be campaigns to conquer other regions, that war will yield lands, booty and greater opportunity. They think there is a good chance that Prince Mor and Prince Gorwst might follow such a track. In truth though, it's mostly just heroic bluster. They know nothing of the world beyond the lands they defend… neither do I for that matter.'

Taly nodded. 'As secretary, you will have to understand the politics of Britannia and perhaps even those of the lands beyond our shores. But we should begin with your own king's policies, policies which I expect will continue even after his death.

'It was through wisdom and military prowess that the king overcame the North's struggle to defend the frontiers. He learnt from the Romans that prosperity is the answer to ending continuous war, so even though soldiers' pay has become an issue, he would never advocate solving this problem through the aggressive raiding and pillaging of our neighbours. Prosperity comes from peace not war. The Romans are gone from our shores now; their military failure has left us with the responsibility for our own defence but also for our own prosperity. Many citizens only remember the security that the Romans brought us, and they think the only solution to the cycle of war is to tempt the Romans back, offering them the glorious recovery of Britannia.' Taly stretched out a leg, feeling his old joints click from hip to ankle. 'Make no mistake, no good will ever come of this. The North belongs to the Cymry. There was a time when we would have thanked God if a legion had appeared on our flank, but not anymore. Magnates, traders, clerics and tutors may lament the apparent loss of security, but they forget the cruel slavery inflicted by the Romans and the burdensome taxation. We may have to fight harder now, but our first duty after our faith is to our own prosperity, for our region and then for our province.'

Cian shifted in his chair. 'My father considers faith above everything else and believes the Second Coming is imminent, perhaps even in our lifetime. He sees the sacking of Rome by barbarians as a portend of the doom we must first expect to endure, the so-called Sixth Seal of the Revelation.'

'And what do you believe?'

'Religion and Rome confuse me, prefect, but I cannot believe that the past is our future. Even though I understand the Church feels vulnerable without its powerful patron, I agree with your view – without being able to mount our own defence, there is no chance for prosperity or religion to flourish.'

Taly nodded. The lad had a sharp mind. 'Our heroes died for our freedom and would rise from their graves if a Roman legion set foot north of the Humber. It is our duty to defend the North from everyone – Picts, Scotti, Saxons, Romans and even the Antichrist if it comes to that. If you know how our kingdom was founded, it will help you understand why we must maintain our independence. What do you know about the history of the Carvetti and the Brigantes?'

'Only the legends about Myrddin, the sword of Venutius and that Coel is descended from mighty northern kings who defeated the Romans many times.'

'Aye, lad, there's some truth to that. Coel's father was a Roman governor of the northern provinces who married Tancorix, a princess of the Carvetti. At that time, Rome was seeking to expand its frontier beyond the Wall. Rianorix, her young brother who was recognised as "Bear" of the Brigantes following his father's death, colluded with the northern tribes who then attacked and defeated all the Roman armies in Britannia. It was known as the Great Conspiracy. Picts, Saxons, Attacotti, Scotti and northern rebels attacked together, but the co-operation fell apart, degenerating into chaos. Coel's family was besieged by Attacotti at Uxellodunum but held out and did not come to harm. Rianorix was considered a traitor by the Romans, since he had betrayed both the army and his family. When the Romans returned in huge numbers, he was captured, tortured and later executed. Tancorix yielded on behalf of the tribe, but her son, Coel, was required to join the Roman legions as part of the treaty, almost as a hostage, to distance him from the tribe and the rebels. Donatus, Coel's father, wisely placed him with the general, Magnus Maximus, who had strong links with Britannia and had himself married a Cymry princess. For a while, Coel was stationed in the North where he married Strawdawl of the Gododdin, the bride to whom he was betrothed by his parents. In two years, they had two children, but then he was snatched away from his young family, posted overseas for eleven years with Maximus and the legion.'

Cian looked surprised. 'He fought on the Continent?'

'Yes, in a twist of fate, Coel helped to train and then lead the unit of Attacotti the Romans captured in the Great Conspiracy. Under the overall command of Magnus Maximus, they gained a fierce reputation fighting the enemies of Rome along their northern frontier in Germania. He became a friend of Maximus and Elen, but despite this Roman influence, he never lost his loyalty to our tribe. Do you know the significance of the Bear to the North?'

'The battle leader of the northern tribes. He remains so until death, unless challenged and defeated?'

'Precisely, this title is passed generation to generation. It is a great honour with huge responsibilities, because the duty of the Bear is to the tribes not the state. Rianorix was no traitor.'

Cian was clearly enjoying his history lesson. The lad was transfixed, hanging on every word.

'Myrddin persuaded Coel to visit Rianorix prior to his execution, whereupon the prisoner disclosed the ancient riddle to his nephew, conferring the status of the Bear upon Coel. Coel would have been condemned a traitor had this been discovered. He later collected the badly tortured body of his uncle, and in secret with Myrddin, they buried him by the River Eden. He commissioned a tombstone in his uncle's memory, and it is there to this day.'

Cian's eyes were wide with wonder.

'Is Myrddin a supernatural being?' he asked, his voice a reverent whisper.

'Myrddin is a seer who knows secrets about the tribes and studies the old ways. Some say he has magic powers. I don't know about that, but he certainly has "the sight" which can lead him into dark places. There have been two Myrddins in Coel's lifespan, and he is respected and feared by all tribal chiefs. They say that the bear goddess Artio protects him and appears to him at times of change. The Church fears his influence but does not dare seek to destroy him, although they loathe his interference. It is said that he predicted the rise of our kingdom and the fall of the Romans. He lives in a secret cave in the mountains where the next Myrddin, an apprentice like you, is training.'

Taly heard Cian's stomach growl and felt his own grumble in sympathy. It had been a long morning session, and lunch was overdue.

'Let's take a walk for some fresh air. Was it Plato who said, "Educating the mind without educating the heart is no education at all"?' The dog stirred at the mention of his name.

Cian stood up to follow. 'I think that was Aristotle.'

Taly opened the door to the latest blizzard, snow once again covering the path he had cleared.

'Quite so. Well, neither philosopher was aware of our God nor benefited from the education of a Christian cleric like your father, so what did they know?'

Cian laughed. They headed across the yard in easy companionship, leaving Plato asleep by the fire. They made their way to the rear of the great hall and, on opening the kitchen door, ran straight into Bryn's mother Lyn.

'And what do you want?'

'Food, woman, and some agreeable company,' quipped Taly.

'Well, you'll get neither from me, so I suggest you retreat to your hut and wait until something is ready.'

This was a standard exchange with the widow, but he knew her heart was warm even if her exchanges were cold.

'How's the king?'

'Very sick. Now be off so we can get on; we've enough to be doing for those who deserve it without having to run around after you two.'

On turning to leave, Cian was visibly amused at the way Taly had been dismissed.

'I see you carry influence in the kitchen, prefect,' he said.

'And I hear you have romantic interests in the kitchen,' Taly replied.

His suspicions that Cian and Bryn were fond of each other were confirmed by the flush in the lad's cheeks. They had just arrived back at his hut when Taly suddenly realised he had a good excuse to make himself scarce.

'I'm going to take Plato up to the top fields to see that the horses have been fed. I think it might be wise to bring them in in these conditions. Will you wait here for the food? – I will only be a short while. Plato!' he commanded.

The dog bounded out, and Taly ploughed through the snow once again, heading for the east gate. The lean-to wooden stables erected all along the east wall were empty, but horses were only brought into the fort to be put to work. Beyond the gate were railed fields full of the king's horses. The stable boys were hard at it, distributing hay. Plato bounded off to start his usual patrol, once again delighting in the deep snow. Taly scooped a handful of barley oats smeared in honey from the stables then whistled. A proud black stallion tossed its mane and, peeling off from its companions, trotted in Taly's direction.

'Good afternoon, Jet, did you think I'd forgotten you?' The horse pushed his head against Taly's cloak to find the oats which he duly produced. 'No exercise today. You keep an eye on the king's horses for me.'

On the way back past the stable, he saw one of the many stable hands.

'Everything in order?' he shouted.

'No, it's chuffing not, prefect. Feeding this lot in this weather is chuffing hard work.'

'Well, keep at it. Do you need extra help?'

'Nah, we'll chuffing manage.'

'Good lad.'

There were just too many horses to bring in. He could see the entire garrison had been deployed around the compound to cope with the weather. The guards at the gate were walking up and down stamping their feet to keep them warm in the worst winter conditions for some years. Plato reached the door first, and as Taly entered, Bryn and Cian sprang back, startled from their deep conversation by his arrival.

'Ah, food has arrived, I see,' said Taly, ignoring the couple's embarrassment.

'Yes, prefect,' Cian said briskly. 'Thank you, Bryn.' She headed for the door and slipped out into the snow.

The plate of mutton, bread and pickle looked appetising.

'Bryn is a lovely girl,' Taly said, tucking into his food.

'She is that prefect.'

Nothing else was said until the meal was finished. Cian stoked the fire, and they settled back in their seats. Before Taly could speak, there was a loud knock on the door. Cian stood up quickly to open it.

'May I speak with Taly?'

Taly recognised Brianna's voice and stood up, answering from within his hut.

'Come in, come in, Brianna,' he said. 'Cian, take my hound and check feed is being distributed to our precious stock – you have to watch the farmhands in these conditions. Plato!' he commanded. 'Go with Cian.'

The young soldier grabbed his cloak, and Plato dutifully bounded out the door. Taly and Brianna sat together by the fireside.

'How is the king?' Taly asked gently.

'His fever is worsening, and he is very weak... I fear his heart will give up.'

'Is he conscious?'

'No, he is still delirious, calling out for Strawdawl, Ceneu, and yes... you, Taly.'

'He is just lost in time, Brianna.'

'I don't know what to do. Both the priest and Myrddin are requesting to be at his bedside, but I have so far declined their attendance.'

'Quite so, we must wait for Gorwst and Mor to return.'

'Taly, what if he dies?'

'God will take him when He wants him; our duty is to protect the succession. We don't need bedside influencers or dream interpreters muddying the waters – the boys must sort it out between themselves.'

'Should I recall Gorwst? He was travelling back to Alauna, though the snow may have delayed him.'

'Yes, but send a message tomorrow so that his return coincides with that of Mor. I think we should spread the word that the king is over the worst and on the mend.'

Brianna looked surprised. 'Why?' she asked.

'To calm the intrigue,' he replied.

'That will ease everyone's tensions, apart from mine.'

'We can only try to keep him in this world by giving him the best chance of survival. He is a fighter, and somewhere in his dream world, he is fighting his enemies – he will not give up easily.'

She reached for his large hand. 'Thank you for your wise counsel. I must get back to his side.' Her sweet smile belied her worry. Taly's heart hurt to see her looking so wretched and worn out.

She left quickly in the direction of the hall. The weather had deteriorated, and the howling wind was once more bringing dense, grey clouds from the north. Taly thought more snow was looking likely, and he hoped Mor would be setting off from Eboracum soon, perhaps arriving in three or four days. Cian returned with Plato who headed straight for his place at the fireside.

'The horses and stock are fine and fed, but this snow will soon cover their feed. How is the king?' he asked.

'He seems to be improving, and I suggest you tell your commander that when you report later. I've decided to keep vigil at the king's bedside this afternoon and evening. Brianna needs some rest, and I should be present at his recovery. Let's continue your briefing tomorrow at dawn.'

'Thank you, prefect, I expect I shall now be shovelling snow for several hours.'

Taly smiled at Cian's light-hearted comment, but his mind was filling with a tense apprehension. The family needed to be together at this time; instead, they were scattered across the country, facing dire and difficult journeys.

IV

Eboracum

Winter 427

Already a day late and every chance Vortigern would take *another* day, now the snow was coming down. Prince Mor had arrived with his troop of thirty cavalry one day early. That's what you did when you knew the weather could be a hindrance. Since arriving and discovering Eboracum was not the welcoming city it used to be, he had confined his men to the decrepit, cold barracks within the old fort, and they were becoming restless. Gundad assured him the Dobunni king would arrive today, but a glance at the steadily falling snow once again raised Mor's doubts.

He had risen early, prayed, breakfasted and decided to work off some of his impatience with a walk along the riverside on his way to visit their host. Was Flavius Gundad to be trusted? The self-styled governor of the city was tolerated by Grandfather because he paid a tribute to operate in the city. Mor ploughed on through the snow. How was it Taly had described the merchant? Ah, yes – *a tricky, corpulent man in his middle years, a Frank of the Gaini tribe who had been settled on the River Trent by the Romans*. The tribe were all sailors and well-connected traders, and it was known that most vessels on the River Ouse and those that embarked from Petuaria were either owned by Gundad or working with him. He had certainly gained the trust of Vortigern and the rest of the Council, and Mor had been told that Friothulf, King of the Angles of Lindsey, was his friend and close associate. No doubting that Gundad was a powerful man, but was he a trustworthy ally?

He looked across the river at the dilapidated palace on the west bank that his troop had passed on their way from Isurium. The city's streets were deserted except for debris, pulled-over statues and even some corpses. Mausoleums had been smashed and graves re-opened when the Picts had sacked the city, and the western bank had never been reoccupied. It seemed as if the River Ouse had risen, undermining buildings and wharves on both banks, and the bridge had become so dilapidated it had been treacherous to cross. Why had Gundad not repaired it? Did he want the city cut in two? Mor could see that the eastern bank was better maintained. New timber wharves had been erected on the banks of the Foss, a tributary to the Ouse where Gundad's trading barges were moored. Grandfather had told him many times that he loathed Eboracum. But then, in the old king's opinion, *all* Roman cities were disease-ridden and full of criminals, so he had left Eboracum to its own devices. Clearly, this suited Gundad who treated it as his personal domain. All Mor's knowledge of Roman culture came from what Taly had taught him. What should a Cymry warrior care either way for the cities of a collapsed empire?

And then there was King Vortigern. He was known to consider himself a high-born Roman, and Grandfather had cautioned Mor to expect arrogance. Mor had never visited the south-west of Britannia, but it had seen little of the wars endured by the North, its towns and cities made soft by peace. It was still possible to live like the Roman elite in these places behind the shield of the North, and all the generations of Vortigern's family had apparently done so. The southern king was married to a high-born Roman noblewoman renowned for her beauty.

Mor reached the end of the river path, now almost invisible beneath the snow, and headed for Gundad's townhouse complex that stood between the fortress and the northern city walls. The merchant knew more than he was saying about the purpose of Vortigern's visit, and Mor would have answers before the king's arrival.

Gundad had adapted a house that had once been the residence of the commanding officer. When Mor arrived, the merchant's servants were at work everywhere, stacking wood for the fires, setting up tables, sweeping the floors. The air in the house carried both the smoky smell of roasting meat and the sweet scent of baking. Gundad was stood in the middle of the dining hall issuing instructions like the captain on a vessel when he caught sight of Mor.

'Ah, Prince Mor, good morning to you. How may I be of help?'

'Forgive me, Gundad, I can see you are busy, but I have some questions in advance of King Vortigern's arrival.'

Gundad ushered Mor into a side room.

'Please, ask me anything.'

'King Coel has instructed me to request his tribute. I believe you owe him for two years? I presume you will have it ready for our departure?'

'Coinage is a little short, so we have supplemented that with a quantity of gold and silver plate. I have a list of the weights though, and yes, it will be ready for your departure.'

Gundad looked agitated, but he had clearly been expecting the demand, so what was bothering him?

'Our thanks. Now, on to more pressing matters. I require advance notice of the reason for this meeting with King Vortigern. Secrecy is all very well, but time is short, the weather bad, and I need to have time to prepare my own response.'

'Great prince, there really is no secrecy; I merely wished to give King Vortigern the opportunity to lay his proposal before you himself. But I see the error in that reasoning, so I shall attempt to give you the relevant details. It seems that we are all victims of your success. The Picts, unable to breach your northern defence, have turned themselves into sailors and marines. They are tearing the heart out of the provinces to the east and south. The Angles who provided naval support for the Romans are no longer able to counter these attacks. They are not paid mercenaries anymore, but settlers, their interests having shifted over time to trade and farming.'

A fair point, though the switch had undoubtedly been aided by Gundad's quest for profits.

'King Friothulf of the Angles has suggested to the Council that they make a treaty with the Jutes, a ferocious maritime tribe, and employ them as mercenaries to counter these marauding Picts.'

'Jutes? Are they not Saxons?' exclaimed Mor. 'The same Saxons who we know already raid the east and south.' Where did Gundad's interests really lie? 'Are not all Germanic coastal tribes Saxons – even yours, my friend?'

'That is not strictly true,' replied Gundad, bristling. 'We Franks know that raiding Picts pretend to be Saxons and that there are brigands in the Great Forest who claim to be both Saxon and Pict. If you recall, Friothulf's tribe was originally settled under the direction of the Roman Count of the Saxon Shore, and he is loyal to the Council. We have both traded for many years with a Jute called Whitgils whose tribe has come under pressure in their homeland both from rising seas and Huns moving in from the east. These Jutes earn their corn as mercenaries rather than raiders.'

Mor could not help raising his eyebrows at some of these outlandish claims, but he remained silent to allow Gundad's explanation to continue.

'We are assured that in exchange for a new homeland and supplies, Whitgils will defend our shores and estuaries from the Picts.'

This was too much. Mor roared with laughter. 'So, they just happen to have a great fleet sitting around with nothing to do, which they will put at our disposal, and we have land that doesn't already belong to anyone to give them? Presumably, this fleet isn't the one already raiding our coasts, pretending to be Picts?' Mor paused, giving Gundad a hard stare, but the merchant refused to make eye contact, his manner shifty. 'I can't believe King Vortigern would agree to deal with the devil.'

Gundad shrugged and, still avoiding Mor's gaze, delivered a barbed reply.

'King Vortigern considers it a much better proposal than the one put forth by the southern provinces – that we invite the Romans to return.'

That old threat again. It didn't merit a response. Clearly irritated that the veiled threat hadn't had the desired effect, Gundad continued to press the point.

'King Vortigern will explain to us when he arrives how the Roman general, Aetius, is reported to have recovered most of Gaul, and he will also brief us on the activities of another Roman, Ambrosius Aurelianus, son of Sebastianus from Venta Belgarum, which have him worried.' Gundad switched back to his usual fawning tone. 'He wants to work with you, great prince, because you share common purpose.'

Mor's distrust of Gundad was growing. Yes, both he and Vortigern had no wish for a return of the Romans, that much was true, but every indication was that the Roman Empire couldn't muster enough military strength to defend its existing borders, let alone recover old territories. If anyone could be trusted to make a call on such a thing it was King Coel, and Mor knew his grandfather was certain that they had seen the last Roman legion to set foot in Britannia.

'We shall see, but don't think to try and manipulate the North like a Roman. It will not go well for anyone who tries. Vortigern will be here today?'

'I believe so.'

'Then I will leave you to your preparations.'

*

Mor wrapped his cloak around him as he trudged back to the barracks through the lying snow. What was Gundad's game? What did he gain from fulfilling an ambassador's role for Vortigern? Had Gundad's ambitions got the better of him, making him think he could manipulate the visiting king? Mor's mind raced through the options. East of

31

Eboracum was the domain of the Parisi, mostly farmers who had much in common with the Franks and Angles. The Humber estuary had become the domain of many sea-going tribes, so perhaps... Was this Gundad's attempt to carve out a kingdom for himself? The dilapidation and decay of the west bank of the city and the lack of enthusiasm for repairing the bridge might suggest Gundad was discouraging contact with the southern Brigantes, perhaps creating a border? Mor found difficulty suppressing the thought that the best solution might be to run his sword through Gundad now, before he could follow through on whatever he had planned. Taly had warned true – the corpulent merchant was full of trickery. Grandfather had always focused on the Picts and the Scotti as his chief enemies, but were the increasingly ambitious Saxons now becoming a more urgent threat?

He entered the barracks and went in search of Padell.

'Have you seen Captain Padell?' he asked a young soldier who was oiling his sword.

'Boats have been spotted, my lord. He's on the wall watching the visitors arrive.'

Mor stepped outside and caught sight of his captain on the south wall. He walked to the steps that led up to the viewpoint and joined Padell. Three boats were making steady progress up the river.

'Did you discover much from Gundad, my lord?' asked Padell.

'Yes, there is a proposal to use Saxons as mercenaries to resist raiding Picts.'

'Raiding Picts?' questioned Padell. 'Surely it is the Saxons who are raiding south of the Humber?'

'Those are my thoughts. There is much more to this than we yet know.'

Gundad appeared on the wharf below with a reception party of staff and slave porters, but only one boat at a time was able to disembark at the wharf. He ran run up and down the quayside, fussing and bowing a lot – it was a slow but amusing process. First came four soldiers, presumably the king's bodyguards, then the king, followed by the queen with her two young children. Maids, servants, advisors and secretaries also disembarked. Gundad led the entire procession past the front of the fort to his townhouse complex beyond. Each boat carried twelve passengers and twenty crew with a captain at the stern. The second boat held a further nine soldiers and also three men and a youth dressed like Saxons. This party lingered on the quayside with Vortigern's commanding officer whilst the final boat of twelve soldiers disembarked.

Padell nodded toward the three Saxons. 'I'm thinking we should find out who they are,' he said.

'They look like leaders and one has brought his son,' said Mor.

The crews and Saxon guests headed toward the timber-built huts outside the eastern wall, but Vortigern's soldiers, equipped much more like Romans, walked toward the fort and joined the Cymry men in the barracks. After some sizing up and good-humoured banter, Mor was greatly relieved that they were all allies. Gundad's city militia, which Mor knew existed, were nowhere in evidence. In good spirit, it was decided that half of each unit should visit the city's taverns and become acquainted whilst the rest kept guard; they would change over duty the following day.

Mor left these arrangements to Padell along with his counterpart from Vortigern's unit, a captain called Viracus. It had not escaped Mor's notice that though there were several taverns in the city, the church had burnt down at some point leaving no Christian presence. Gundad was not a convert, seeming only to worship commerce. The city had the feel of belonging to a foreign country, but then Roman cities had been designed to represent the Empire and not their region or local population.

One of Gundad's servants presented himself to Mor. 'Prince Mor, King Vortigern and Flavius Gundad request your presence for dinner at dusk.'

'Please tell them I am looking forward to the occasion,' he replied.

Only a few hours to wait before he discovered more.

V

Banna

Winter 427

Taly made his way across the snow-covered yard to the great hall. The storms had ceased, replaced by an eerie silence, nothing moving, no voices or animal calls. He wondered if God had thrown a huge white blanket over the world out of respect for the old king's final days.

He opened the large, wooden door then closed it quietly behind him. Brianna was sat at Coel's bedside at the far end, Bryn looked to be darning to the side of the large hearth. He walked quietly, past the dining table and crackling fire, acknowledging Bryn as he drew closer. Brianna seemed to be sleeping, in spite of Coel's rasping and gasping, struggling for breath even in his sleep.

Taly placed his hand gently on Brianna's shoulder. She opened her eyes and placed her hand over his. Her look held such deep sorrow.

'He's getting worse,' she whispered.

'Go lie down and get some rest; I will sit with him for the rest of the day.'

'Thank you, Taly. Call out if you need me.'

She walked toward her curtained bedchamber, and Taly got comfortable on the large, wooden chair she had vacated.

He looked at the ashen face of the king, almost as white as his long, matted hair. Seeing the fever was still raging, Taly wrung out a cloth in the pot of water at his feet and placed it on Coel's brow.

'We need to get you better,' he said softly. Then with a wry grimace, 'Forgive me, my king, nobody was ever better.'

This man had been his guiding light for half a century. From that first meeting, the bond had been strong. Coel had just returned to the

North with the XX legion led by Magnus Maximus. Neither Ceneu nor his sister Peithien had seen their father since they were infants; their excitement had been nearly as great as Taly's apprehension. He had hidden so as not to interfere with the family's joyful reunion, but Ceneu was sent to find him, dragging him to the day-room. Coel was sat on his campaign stool in his ornate Roman officer's uniform surrounded by his staff and family. Ceneu had pushed Taly, wide-eyed, in front of Coel, and he had bravely tried not to lower his gaze. To this day, his stepfather's words rang clear in his mind.

'Talhaearn, I have heard much about you. My wife tells me you are a scholar. Come shake my hand.'

Taly had stepped forward, holding out his hand, proud that he managed to keep it steady. Coel had grasped it and scooped him onto his knee.

'Your father was my friend, and you are welcome, scholar, but we shall have to make a warrior of you too. Can he fight, Ceneu?'

The elder boy had flushed with pride at being consulted.

'Better than most of his age, Father.'

'That is good to hear, because the Picts don't write, they only fight!'

Taly had loved Coel and Strawdawl from the start. They had made him one of their family, never once making him feel slighted, his bond to Ceneu and Peithien always that of a brother. He had been a similar height to Ceneu, despite the two-year age difference, so they had done most things together. Coel had been eager for them both to ride and fight well, even taking them on campaigns, much to Strawdawl's disapproval. Much later, Taly had realised that Coel had been trying to make up for his enforced eleven-year absence.

Shortly after the king's return, the elder Myrddin had come to tell the family of his recurring dream about a bear, an eagle and a fish. Myrddin was convinced the bear in his dream was Coel and that he was destined to recover the lands of the northern tribes. Within days of this visit, Taly had found himself sailing with Coel and Ceneu to Seguntium for a secret meeting of the Cymry chieftains and the mighty Magnus Maximus. How seasick had he and Ceneu been? But as they approached the snow-capped peak of Yr Wyddfa and navigated through the Afon Menai, all thoughts of sickness had passed. The gathering they had witnessed had been unforgettable. The quayside had thronged with soldiers, officers and horses. Later, they had listened as the proud Magnus Maximus outlined his plans, interpreted into Cymry by his beautiful wife Elen. The meeting had bristled with excitement as the chieftains were given authority to defend their own lands – 'Protectors' of their people. Their father was leader of the northern tribes, and the youths had burst with such pride when Maximus, now hailed as Emperor, had chosen Coel to be Dux Britanniarum, the position Maximus had previously held himself.

Taly sighed, grasping the cold, sweating hand of the old warrior now struggling even to breathe. 'That was some achievement... a Cymry warrior becoming the most powerful Roman soldier on our island.'

Lynn approached with a cup of mead.

'Did I hear voices?'

'I was just speaking with the king, but I don't think he hears me.'

'It is so sad, but death comes to us all.'

She turned, heading for her kitchen. Lynn never minced her words thought Taly as he sipped the drink she had warmed for him. Much like every warrior, the king kept his weapons and armour close to hand – on a bench next to his bed even now. The elaborate officer's equipment reminded Taly of the glorious early days. He and Ceneu training together, vying with each other for the most senior commissions. With Maximus as Western Emperor, the army had enjoyed a period of recovery, and the North had been well-garrisoned and secure. Then came the happiest of times, when Taly and Ceneu married two sisters on the same day. Tara and Brianna. What a celebration. How beautiful Tara had looked, and within a year, the children began to arrive. First, his son Bewyn, then Gorwst followed by Mor a year later. His precious peak of happiness – high times that fate could not wait to crush. There was only one place for his thoughts to go from there, so he lingered in time for a moment, remembering the family days, everyone together. Sadly, they were too few.

Were there rational explanations for what followed? There had to be – for without reason, how could there be sanity? Which evil spirit had set out to destroy his life, stirring him into a cauldron of despair, gleefully watching him drown? Surely, his Christian God could not be so cruel, could not stand back and watch a faithful servant suffer such anguish? Taly, head bowed, squeezed the old king's hand. Coel had suffered equally. In their combined grief, they had sought refuge in revenge, becoming formidable warriors. It was a lifetime ago, but the pain was still as sharp as if it were yesterday.

First had come the news that Emperor Maximus had been defeated then executed. The many Britons who had rallied to his standard never returned, either lost in battle or resettled around the Empire. Those cursed Picts had pressed their advantage, pushing forward over the northern frontier, isolating the northern allies in their strongholds at Alt Cult and Din Eidyn. They had quickly reached the Wall, destroying forts and killing Taly's people. Coel had made good use of his cavalry, holding the Picts in the Southern Uplands but unable to push them further north. Two years of cat-and-mouse raids... Rome, under Theodosius now, finally agreed to send an army to relieve the beleaguered militia, appointing a Comes Britanniarum to assume command. The fool of a new commander had clashed with Coel, instructing all garrisons to abandon the Wall and push the enemy north again. King Talorc of the Picts had retreated to the northern frontier, and the army had followed, leaving the north-west defenceless. As Coel had predicted, the Scotti came in force, raiding and pillaging Cymry homelands. Tancorix, Strawdawl, Tara and Bewyn... they'd died together, trapped in a church set alight by raiders, the roof collapsing... They should have been safe in Maglona. They should have been safe...

They were found all huddled together, Taly was told. A sight spared him at the time, though pictured many times in his nightmares.

The Scotti were long home by the time the army of the North returned to discover the painful loss and bury their loved ones. Spurred on by grief, Ceneu and Coel spent the next ten years travelling throughout the North, developing defence plans with their allies, the Britons of Alt Clut and the Gododdin. Family ties were strong since Gwawl, Coel's sister, had married the Gododdin king, Edern, and the couple's son, Cunedda, had garrisoned Deva on the instruction of Maximus. Taly had been posted east to Pons Aelius and promoted to prefect. Once again, the Pictish king, Talorc, had brought his army south, but this time, the Cymry militia were able to stall his advance and summon the Roman mobile army from the south. A better defence this time, but with one notable casualty.

Taly screwed up his eyes and sighed heavily as he pictured Ceneu unhorsed and slashed across the neck, bleeding to death in his arms… He had carried his brother's limp body to their father. Coel's grim sorrow was so intense he did not speak for days. Eventually, Taly had told Brianna… Oh God, it should have been him. Why had God not taken him instead?

Then the Romans withdrew – Rome left vulnerable by a Goth invasion, soldiers' pay ceased, two years' wages owed, the Empire in chaos. The remaining garrisons in the south had rebelled, but Coel and Taly had wanted no part of it. What was that soldier called again? Ah yes, Constantine. Taly never met him, but the man thought they could grab the Empire from the Romans, encouraged by that powerful Briton, Gerontius, the Trinovantes' leader – he'd sought Coel's support but been refused. Constantine and Gerontius had misjudged both their strength and each other, their defeat inevitable. Everyone then agreed enough was enough, and the Cymry had stepped into the aftermath, expelling all the Roman officials and tax collectors from Britannia.

As ever, Talorc saw his next opportunity in the unrest, thinking the Cymry distracted. The Picts crossed the northern border for a third invasion, and they would wish they hadn't. The northern tribes who rallied behind Myrddin and Coel were fighting for their own freedom from tyranny this time. The war was bloody, vicious and vengeful. Coel had led them past the wall eventually, murdering every Pict his army could find. They had put Talorc and many of his sons to death, but Drest, one of Talorc's rivals, had sued for peace, promising to convert his people to Christianity. A resounding victory that left Taly empty, and Coel had felt the same. After decades of fighting there was no one left to savour the spoils with; they were just the last men standing. It was a sin, but Taly longed for his own death... He felt tired and was drifting... He thought he heard Coel's voice, *Protect the family; it is an earlier Heaven*. No, he didn't speak, just words in Taly's swirling reverie and, yes, ensuring the succession would be his responsibility soon, but whilst Coel still breathed, he served only his king. Taly fell asleep, finding respite from the painful past in oblivion.

*

It must have been hours later when he woke himself up by accidently kicking over the pot of water. Now it was Brianna's turn to touch *his* shoulder. He stood up with difficulty, his legs numb.

'Age,' he whispered, kissing her on the cheek.

As he crossed the yard, he looked up at the cold, night sky bursting with stars. 'Which one is you, Ceneu? You should be here in my stead.'

VI

Eboracum

Winter 427

It was dusk when Mor entered Gundad's house. The long corridor was lined with staff, Viracus guarding the inner door. Mor handed his cloak to a servant and stopped to speak with the captain.

'No tavern for you tonight?' he asked.

Viracus smiled. 'Padell and I will be inspecting them tomorrow night.'

Mor laughed. 'Be careful, captain, they say the women in this city marry you before you are sober.'

Mor entered the same room in which he had earlier located Gundad. The merchant and King Vortigern were deep in conversation. Warmth spread from two large fires at either end of the room, silhouetted against one was a beautiful woman talking to two young children. The tables were set in a V-shape with benches for seating, and they were laden with all manner of foodstuffs.

Vortigern strode across to Mor.

'Prince Mor, how splendid to meet you. It is some time since I last saw your grandfather – a great man and a mighty warrior. I see you have his build.'

'King Vortigern, I too am pleased to meet you. King Coel sends his condolences for the death of your father Vitalis. The Council will miss his great wisdom.'

Vortigern was a stout man, perhaps ten years older than Mor. He was dressed in fine Roman style and spoke with precision. He did not look like a warrior, but his manners were impeccable, and he certainly had the look and gravitas of a king.

'Please forgive my rough uniform; I brought no finery and have rather misjudged this occasion,' Mor added.

'Think nothing of it. Tell me, is your grandfather still in good health? He has done well to survive so many decades of war.'

'He still knocks me to the ground in the practice yard; he shoots the straightest arrow out hunting, and he has a charming way with the serving girls that I have yet to master.'

'My father was the same. How are we ever to compete with such heroes?'

'I would not seek to try! Your journey was difficult, I hear?'

'Indeed, it was. I will never again travel by boat at this time of year.'

'Were you avoiding the Great Forest?'

'No, Prince Mor, I had Saxons to meet with, settlements and territories to see. It was a mistake to bring the children, but I was unable to dissuade them from such an adventure. We have only just warmed up now. Come sit down, we must make a start if we are to eat all this food.'

'Good evening, Gundad.'

The merchant had been shuffling past them and paused to respond.

'Good evening, Prince Mor. I hope you enjoy our little feast.'

Gundad's hospitality looked impressive. The Roman ghosts haunting the city would surely approve. Gundad, his wife Fortuna, Vortigern and a lady-in-waiting sat at one arm of the V, whilst Mor, Vortigern's wife, her children and a nanny sat opposite.

Vortigern's wife leant toward him. 'Prince Mor, may I introduce myself? I am Sevira, and this is Vortimer and Catigern; they are excited to see the jugglers and magicians.'

'Juggling looks so difficult – I can't imagine how they do it, can you?' Mor said, smiling at the children.

Gundad clapped his hands in a theatrical manner, and entertainers suddenly outnumbered the guests. The children loved it, participating

42

whenever invited. There were disappearing apples and tumblers as well as jugglers. The wine was already flowing, and the meal began. Seafood and every sort of meat and poultry adorned the tables. Catigern was three or four and sat on Sevira's knee. Vortimer, who looked to be at least seven, had taken an interest in Mor and squeezed in between him and the queen. Unlike his elder brother, Mor had not yet married, but the family scene he had inadvertently become a part of made him long for his turn. Young Vortimer was already developing the regal bearing of his father and showed no shyness which was entertaining.

'Is it true you are a great northern king with a large army?' he asked Mor whilst the queen was occupied with Catigern.

'I am,' he replied.

'Why is your army so big?' he persisted.

'Because we defend the northern frontier,' replied Mor.

'Is your army bigger than the Romans'?'

'No, but it is better than the Romans'.' This answer seemed to satisfy the lad's curiosity.

'I want to be a soldier when I grow up,' he said, admiring Mor's uniform with small fingers.

'Then one day, we shall face the enemy together.'

Vortimer looked pleased with this reply.

After the jugglers, the children were ushered off to bed by the nanny. Just as Mor was about to turn back to the adults, Vortimer turned and saluted Mor with his fist to his chest, saying, 'Goodnight, soldier.'

'Goodnight, soldier.' Mor saluted in reply. 'Sleep well.'

Once the children had left, the queen relaxed. She moved closer to Mor. 'Do you have children?' she asked.

By God, she was beautiful, and she was dressed in Roman elegance, wearing a toga – a short fur jacket her only concession to the cold. There was a heat to her, and her perfume had an intoxicating effect.

'I am not yet married but hope to be soon,' he replied.

Dancers trooped in and performed in a style Mor had never seen before. From the East, he was told. It was exotic, fast and thoroughly enjoyed by all. The food kept arriving, and Mor marvelled at Gundad's generosity and resourcefulness. He had clearly been planning this for months, marking this as an occasion that mattered a great deal to Gundad. But what did he expect to gain from his investment?

Gundad continued to ply his guests with wine, and servants stood in the shadows ready to replenish every sip that was taken. Vortigern was drinking heavily, clearly distracted by the ample charms of Gundad's wife. He was becoming more than a little familiar with Fortuna, yet her husband seemed delighted by the king's attentions, and he continuously signalled to servants, only joining the conversation if he was addressed. Sevira suddenly spoke to Mor in his native tongue.

'Do you have a sweetheart?' she asked softly.

Where had he heard that accent before…? Ah yes, the Cornovii, that was how their allies from Viroconium spoke.

'Not yet, but I hope to have a family like yours one day. Your accent interests me; are you Roman or Cymry?'

She laughed. 'Both, but is that all that interests you, Prince Mor. I was hoping you were a man for the ladies. As you can see, my husband certainly is – though he takes it to the point of embarrassment.'

Vortigern's interest in Fortuna had intensified whilst Gundad was away from the table organising his servants.

'It's just as well it is so cold, or we may have been obliged to watch one of his floorshows,' she said bluntly.

Gundad's fires were well fuelled, and there felt to be underfloor heating too, but the cold still pressed against their backs. It seemed the rumours of Vortigern's lascivious reputation were not unfounded, and Sevira's comments betrayed her disgust and humiliation.

'He does seem rather over-excited.'

They both laughed, but Vortigern's attentions continued. Pointedly choosing not to watch, Sevira turned to Mor.

'I was told by my mother that King Coel was a friend of my father's.'

'What was your father's name?'

'Magnus Maximus.'

He hadn't been expecting that! 'Surely, you are too young to be the Emperor's daughter?'

'Sadly, I never met him; my mother was carrying me when he died.'

'He is still held in high regard amongst all Cymry; he set us on our path to freedom. A great emperor.'

'Coel also knew my grandfather, King Octavius of the Cornovii.'

'These were great men, Sevira; you come from a strong lineage.'

'They were men with vision and integrity, few such men survive.' She cast a disdainful glance in the direction of Vortigern. 'Are you coming to the Council meeting when it is held at Viroconium in the summer?'

'Yes, I believe it will be me who my grandfather sends.'

'Then come and stay at my villa. I want you to meet Igerna, my cousin. She is young, beautiful, and I have yet to find her a suitable husband.'

'With my grandfather's permission, I'm sure that would be in order.'

Though Sevira's eyes sparkled in the candlelight, there was a deep sadness to this beautiful, regal woman.

'All the men in my family are dead. In marrying Vortigern, I have forced the Cornovii to accept a Dobunni overlord. It has been hard for them. As some small recompense, I maintain my home in Cornovii territory – I am their queen first and Vortigern's second.'

Interesting. It seemed dynastic friction was not just reserved for Mor's own family where the ambitions of his brother's wife Marchell were becoming ever more ill-disguised. Sevira's happy family impression was not as secure as he had first thought.

Vortigern banged the table and stood to make a toast.

'To our host for his generous entertainment, and to this lovely woman for her delightful company. What say you, Mor?'

'Yes, indeed, Lord Vortigern. May God watch over us all and keep us safe.'

He raised his cup of wine in reply. To his side, Sevira did not move. As her husband sat down and continued his carousing, she kept her gaze steady, looking only at Mor.

'My mother was a devout Christian throughout the best and worst of times. I miss her wisdom and guidance.'

Sevira looked tired, perhaps the cause of her melancholy.

'The river journey must have been arduous and cold, my lady. Do you regret accompanying the king?'

'Yes, but only because of the weather. Vortigern and Gundad have plans for the Trent region which neither of us had visited before, but in truth, it was impossible to inspect – forest screened the banks for much of the trip, and then there were endless muddy banks bordered by flat plains, not at all like the countryside around Viroconium.' She smiled at Mor. 'Still, I have at least met a handsome man. Please, forgive me, but I must away to bed; I am tired, and the children will not sleep well in strange surroundings.'

So that's their intention – new plans for the old Roman Colonae

'Of course, my lady, I too must rejoin my men. Tomorrow will be challenging.'

They both stood. Sevira said goodnight to Gundad and walked away without interrupting her husband. Vortigern was clearly very drunk, and Mor had to clear his throat several times to announce his presence.

'King Vortigern, what time is our meeting tomorrow?'

Vortigern looked blankly at Mor, before turning, bleary-eyed, to their host. 'What say you, Gundad?'

'I will keep the fires burning, and we can meet here.' He hesitated then looked Vortigern up and down. 'I think midday will be soon enough.'

*

As Mor walked down the corridor, Sevira stepped out of the shadows.

'Thank you for your company and kindness to the children.'

She held his hands, stood up on her toes and kissed his lips.

'My husband always seems determined to embarrass me. I regret my tiredness and look forward to sitting together again tomorrow. Sleep well.'

'Goodnight, my lady.'

She slipped away.

Mor couldn't go straight back to barracks after that, so he took himself for a stroll by the river before entering the east gate. Sevira's perfume lingered with him, the excitement raised by her closeness and candour had not dissipated at all. Slightly drunk himself, he relieved himself against the wall of the fort and entered the barracks.

He lay down on his bed on the wooden floor in his sparce cubicle. It was very cold, but extra furs had been laid out for him. Instead of his usual bedtime prayer, he allowed his imagination to take him on a heated sexual encounter with Sevira, before he fell into a deep sleep, oblivious to the cold.

*

He rose early, before dawn. Suffering the effects of too much wine, he took himself on another walk to clear his head. The winter storm had returned, and in the early-morning, biting wind and driving snow, he felt a little ashamed of his attraction to Sevira, his passions now overridden by deep pity for her sad story. There would be opportunity to speak to her again this evening, but for now, he pushed such thoughts firmly out of his mind. It would make better use of his time to exercise his horse, carefully, in the snow. That's what he would do – ride out around the city's perimeter, taking Padell so they could discuss what they had both discovered from the previous evening.

*

Though the ride proved refreshing, the conditions were not conducive to much conversation. Even with the poor weather, Padell agreed that it was strange how deserted the city seemed.

On returning to barracks, two messengers, sent from Banna, were waiting. The men were tired, wet and cold from travelling through the night. Taking the message they had brought, Mor read it, dread spreading through him with a cold more bitter than the weather. Grandfather had been in rude health when Mor had left. Surely, this was a mistake? But the men shaking from the cold confirmed that they had heard the king was gravely ill. They had other disturbing news, providing a welcome distraction from the first message.

They spoke of how the going had been difficult in the blinding snow, so the militia at Isurium had recommended that they abandon the road and follow the river on its east bank. There was less flooding on this route, no rivers to cross, and the Ouse did not meander on this section making it easy to follow. The advice had proved good, until they had approached the confluence with the Nidd where they spied several campfires on the western shore and many keels moored alongside the riverbank. Suspecting that the ships belonged to Saxons or other brigands, they had used the cover of the forest to pass without alerting the sentries. Altogether, they had seen five ships and at least as many campfires. Concerning news indeed.

'Do not mention this to anybody and go get some warmth, food and sleep,' said Mor. He turned to Padell. 'Ships moored upstream? They must have passed through this city to get there, so Gundad knows about them and, I'd wager, knows the identity of their occupants.' They walked outside together. 'It is almost time for my meeting with Vortigern. In light of all this news, we should prepare to leave tomorrow at first light. I'll inform them at the meeting that that is our intention, that we're not waiting for the weather to improve. Send two fresh messengers to Cambodunum. They are to find a Brigantes leader called Lord Crannog and ask him to meet Prince Mor by St Helen's Ford at midday tomorrow, and for him to bring as many men as he can muster. They should be prepared for a fight, but I will compensate them.'

'You consider the ships pose a threat to our journey then?' asked Padell.

'I'm not certain, but I have been wondering where Gundad's own militia are billeted as we haven't seen sign of them. My guess – it's them camping upriver. But why are they hiding out on the west bank of the Ouse?'

'It would explain why we saw little activity on our ride around the city. Do you think they plan an ambush?'

'I hope not, but it seems a strong possibility. Five ships could amount to as much as one hundred and fifty men, which is why I'm sending for Lord Crannog.'

With midday approaching, Mor retraced his steps to Gundad's dining hall. He acknowledged Viracus who was now in attendance in the same corridor where Mor had met with Sevira the night before. Light snow flurries had followed the morning's storm, so he brushed the snow from his cloak before entering the dining hall where the warmth from the fire provided a welcome contrast to the frigid air in the barracks.

'Ah, Prince Mor,' Vortigern exclaimed. 'Come and sit with us.'

'Good afternoon, gentlemen,' Mor said, taking his place at the table. 'Did you sleep well, King Vortigern?' he asked.

'Too well. Gundad's hospitality was most welcome after several days spent trying to keep warm on those river boats.'

Mor cleared his throat, steadying himself to ensure his voice would not crack. 'Gentlemen, I have received a message from Queen Brianna this morning. My grandfather is gravely ill, so I must return to Banna. I intend to depart at first light tomorrow, but I will have to visit Isurium along the way, a day's delay which I cannot avoid.'

'This is sad news,' said Vortigern, 'but we can deal with all pertinent matters quickly. We will be hosting the meeting of the Council at Viroconium this summer, and my queen is insistent that you come to her villa as our guest.'

'Please convey my respects to Queen Sevira; of course, I accept,' replied Mor.

'To business,' said Vortigern. 'Our families were appointed guardians and protectors by Emperor Maximus, a duty we have fulfilled for over forty years. Our fathers and their comrades all confederated against the Roman usurper, Constantine, so delivering the Patria into the safe hands of the Council, but we have never returned to cordial relations with the Empire. We have, nonetheless, many Gallic friends, which has allowed us to watch from a distance and witness civil war undermining an empire now overrun by heathen barbarians who covet wealth but not laws or religion. Those of our people protected by Cymry militia hold no fear, but the cives of the south and east are terrified – there is no longer a mobile field army to rescue them, and their defences have become weak in the face of a bolder enemy. In the autumn, I was canvassed by a deputation from cities and towns of the east demanding that the Council appeal to the Romans for help. Our fathers would never countenance such a step and nor should we. Do you agree, Mor?'

'I do, Vortigern, but I sense other pressures which our existing resources may not be equal to, so we must plan accordingly. The Romans are in disarray, any commitment from them would be too great for them to bear, especially since there is no longer the advantage of a standing Roman army in Britannia.'

Vortigern looked to be listening carefully. The Empire's woes were not news to any of the homeland's ruling class; they were well-informed through the Church, thanks to the constant contact between bishops and clerics who regularly updated each other with news.

'I agree, but are you acquainted with Ambrosius Aurelianus?' asked Vortigern.

'I am not,' replied Mor. 'Who is he?'

'He is the son of Sebastianus of Gaul, a defeated usurper. He fled to Venta Belgarum for safety after his father was executed and family murdered. He is a Gallic noble who owns much of the land to the south of Sorviodunum. He is developing a militia to defend his interests.'

'This would seem good news,' said Mor. 'Surely, that will take some pressure off your southern borders.'

'Quite so,' replied Vortigern, 'but he holds a Roman appeal for those on the Council who represent the southern cives, and they want me to include him on the Council. I have so far declined.'

Such arrogance. Vortigern might have styled himself as High King of the Patria, but it was the Council who should decide its members.

'That is harsh,' Mor replied. 'Surely the powerful Theodosian regime are no lovers of Gallic nobles. May I suggest that he could be groomed as a particularly useful ally? I may be wrong, but I doubt he will align himself with the Romans who murdered his father.'

Vortigern nodded, but it did little to disguise his irritation at being asked to tolerate a rival on his border.

'No matter, our chief threats are those coming from our eastern and south-eastern coasts, and more cavalry to the south of my lands does little to solve that. Some say these raiders are Picts, some say they are Saxons. Whatever they are, they manage to land their ships undetected and unopposed, murdering, plundering and laying waste but vanishing before our militia are able to find and engage with them. In the west, we both seem to have the measure of the Scotti, but the eastern and southern raids are a threat compounded by so many vulnerable coastal estuaries.'

Mor knew the problem well. The Cymry had firm control of the Tweed, the Tyne and the Tees, but the Humber was a small sea, impossible to patrol even with cavalry. A fleet of ships might be one answer, but it was a vulnerable coastline impossible to patrol sufficiently on land.

'May I join this debate?' Gundad interjected. 'I am convinced that you should employ mercenaries to defend your shores. The Romans have, for some time, recognised the merits of mercenaries, and marine tribes co-operate with Romans in every province.'

Vortigern flicked an impatient hand in Mor's direction. 'Yes. Explain my plan.'

'Prince Mor, Whitgils the Jute will agree to defend our eastern shores from Picts and other raiders, provided he is given a substantial landholding, a tanet. His sons are warriors not farmers, so they will require payment as well as supplies.'

'How many ships do they have?' asked Mor.

'His sons, Hengist and Horsa, can muster at least forty ships and a thousand warriors. They will not just defend our shores; they will also take the fight to the Picts.'

'And what do we do if they attack us instead?' asked Mor.

'We will ensure we have an agreement in place to confederate our armies to crush any attempted Jute insurrection. This is why your support is so important, Prince Mor,' said Vortigern.

'King Vortigern, my grandfather will consider this, but it is a high-risk plan, and we already have our hands full resisting attacks by land and sea in the north. Whereabouts is the land you would be granting them?'

'Ah yes, well this was the reason for braving the cold trip by river. To the west of the Trent is an area of land known as Inkle Moor, and further south, there are large areas of land on river islands, all of which are devoid of settlement. The Angles and the Gaini were settled by the Romans in the Colonae along the eastern bank of the Trent, but between the western bank of the river and the Great Forest, there is a vast area which is all part of the old Roman province. I have spoken with the local tribal leader, Gwyranfon, who has agreed to a Jute settlement. Gundad and his ally, King Friothulf, will co-ordinate supplies and payment. This is an opportunity to turn potential enemies into allies.'

'And who is to pay for this opportunity?' asked Mor.

'Well, this is for the defence of the entire Patria, so the cost should be shared between all regions.'

'I don't think my grandfather will agree to that. As things are, the North can barely fund the militia which defends the northern and western borders against the Picts and the Scotti… so perhaps we should be getting paid too?'

Vortigern laughed. 'Prince Mor, I hardly think that would be an appropriate request from a Protector.'

Mor held his tongue and turned to Gundad. 'Are you and Friothulf not able to raise a marine militia and fight the Picts using your own ships?'

Gundad shifted uncomfortably in his chair. 'We have no resources for such a venture. Our men are commercial sailors not warriors, but we will help where we can.'

Gundad's uneasiness was palpable and understandable – after all, the Angles had been given their land by the Romans in exchange for doing exactly what they wanted to employ the Jutes to do.

'King Vortigern, if the cives of your kingdom wish to pay for their enemies to defend them, then that is their choice. The North cannot participate in this risky venture. My chief concern is having a potentially hostile army stationed just across the Humber from my southern Brigante cousins. Forgive me, Gundad, but barbarians are mostly untrustworthy, and if your gold runs out, they will seek recompense elsewhere. The Humber estuary is a vital artery that leads to the very heart of the Patria. You will be giving a potential enemy the keys to the gate.' Gundad and Vortigern looked displeased. That was fine by Mor. 'Let me be clear,' he continued, 'this proposal is unlikely to be authorised by the Council unless there is also a treaty in place to control these heathens. There will need to be some robust safeguards, and speaking personally, I think you are exacerbating the problem not solving it.'

'Why do you think that?' asked Vortigern.

'I have some serious doubts as to the real identity of the Patria's raiders. We believe that they are mostly Saxons. Be sure, if I hear reports of incursions or mistreatment of the Cymry, I will bring the army from the North and destroy them, whoever they are.'

Gundad bristled, looking toward Vortigern for a defence that was not forthcoming.

Mor continued. 'I know that many think King Coel has become weak with age and weary of conflict. I have even heard it said that he may be more concerned with his purse than his principals, but I should warn you there are still bears in the north who will defend their dens. Do not interpret our tolerance of Saxons as weakness. We do not seek more power or to subjugate our neighbours, only to fulfil our sworn duty as Protectors.' Mor looked directly at Vortigern. 'I sense danger in this proposal, and my grandfather will too, but we will not oppose decisions reached by the Council. Though we may reinforce our southern borders to protect the Cymry's interests... as a precaution...'

There was an awkward silence, but neither Vortigern nor Gundad seemed surprised by Mor's words. The knowing looks that passed between them spoke volumes.

'With danger everywhere, we have few choices, Prince Mor. I can see that you and your grandfather are prepared to gamble that Rome will never return, whereas I dare not. I fear them far more than the Picts or your bears,' Vortigern said. 'I have no choice but to appease the southern cives. Please do not misunderstand our objectives. I envy your sense of purpose and strength, but the world our fathers left us is changing, and if we are to protect our gains, we must be creative and make decisions as bold as the Roman emperors – we should co-operate with the Saxons.'

'Well said, King Vortigern.'

Gundad's very vocal support for Vortigern seemed to indicate that he no longer considered himself a vassal of King Coel. Tolerating Saxon settlers was different to co-operating and paying them. How firm a grip did Coel really have on Eboracum? Mor could almost smell the stench of Gundad's ambition. As for Vortigern, it seemed he had already discounted the North from his plan before presenting it. There was little doubt that Mor's response had been anticipated, and there was no intention of heeding his warning. It was becoming clear to Mor that Vortigern already considered himself the most powerful king in the Patria. The Council was weak because most other leaders and kings were influenced by him. Vortigern's wealth was rumoured to be as great as that of a Roman senator, allowing him to dominate the Patria. Only the northern army had the military strength to challenge him, but it was known that they had no real ambition outside of defending their own freedom. It was easy to see why Ambrosius Aurelianus was considered such an unwelcome neighbour. A return of the Romans would certainly ruin Vortigern's ambitions. No, Mor had no doubts – it was best to detach himself from this plan, even if it made the North appear weak and insular.

Vortigern and Gundad were now busily discussing terms, making it clear that Mor's presence was no longer required.

'Gentlemen, I must prepare for an arduous journey tomorrow. I will look forward to hearing the terms you have secured at the Council this summer. Gundad, is King Coel's tribute ready?'

'It is, my lord, and already at your barracks with your captain. Safe journey north.' He did not make eye contact.

'Yes, indeed,' said Vortigern. 'I hope your grandfather recovers. The queen will miss your company this evening.'

And I will miss hers.

'Till the summer then.'

Vortigern and Gundad looked relieved to see Mor make for the door. He encountered Viracus in the corridor.

'It has been good to meet you, Viracus. We leave at dawn tomorrow.'

'It has been a pleasure to meet you, Prince Mor. The king has indicated that we should leave tomorrow too, and I will be pleased to get him underway now that you and Padell are leaving. There are far too many Saxons hereabouts for my liking.'

'There are more than I would have expected, Viracus, and I suspect more than we see. Safe journey, my friend – we will meet again.'

Night had fallen, but the sky was clear, the moon now visible after the passing of the storms. The meeting had raised much to think about. It would seem that Vortigern was unaware of Gundad's militia waiting upriver, that the king's familiarity with the merchant was not collusion, just arrogant over-confidence and misplaced trust. Viracus would ensure his king's safety – an important consideration despite their opposing views – but Gundad needed watching. Vortigern was right about the changing world, but he was being misled into believing he could pay off an enemy in the manner of a Roman emperor. It would only encourage the Saxons to secure further gains. An enemy had to be defeated; it was the only answer. In one respect though, Vortigern's solution might at least mean that the Saxon threat would now be brought out into the open, in plain view, instead of appearing and disappearing like ghosts in the night, pretending to be Picts. Vortigern was no warrior, and in his arrogance, he made poor decisions, trusting heathens. Aye, there was trouble to come from this.

He arrived back at the barracks to find Padell inspecting his men to ensure readiness for their departure. Pulled through the doorway was a very large chest containing gold and silver coins along with a great deal of silver plate and domestic items. Mor inspected the contents. There was less in coinage than was usual, and the edges had been clipped. A sign of the times – no coins had been minted for at least twenty years. The plate was all of Roman origin. Mor turned to Padell.

'This looks much like stolen booty.'

'You're likely right. It's a lot of weight, my prince. We have been given an ox and a cart to carry it. It seems they want to slow us down. Should we switch it for a sleigh?'

'No, we will need to ride quickly. Hack the plate to pieces as quietly as possible. Give each of your men an equal number of coins and pieces of hack silver to place in their feed bags. Make sure they know to protect it on pain of death. Tomorrow, we will leave at dawn, slowly pulling along the cart loaded with an empty chest, travelling in the direction of Isurium, but once we are beyond view of the fort, we will ditch the cart and ride cross-country to St Helen's Ford to meet up with Crannog. Did you keep watch as I left the meeting?'

'I did, my lord. My men saw two of Gundad's men leave, travelling along the eastern bank of the Ouse. A further two were seen rowing a coracle upstream.'

'As I suspected. If you were planning to ambush us, where would you wait?'

'Between the two river bridges. That way we could attack the enemy after they crossed with their back to the river.'

'I agree. They will expect us at one of those two bridges that cross the Nidd.'

'What is your plan?'

'To travel with all speed and meet Crannog, then try to gauge how best to tackle this threat.'

There was a loud knock at the door. Padell opened it cautiously. 'It's Viracus, my lord… with Queen Sevira.'

Mor walked briskly outside.

'Queen Sevira, it is very cold; is everything as it should be?' He glanced at Viracus who had taken several steps away. She removed her cowl and looked into Mor's eyes. She was even more beautiful in the moonlight.

'You were going to leave without saying goodbye.' She spoke again in his native tongue.

'My grandfather may be dying; I must return straight away.

'I had heard. I pray God he recovers. I have also heard of a disagreement with my husband?'

'It is a difference of opinion rather than a disagreement.'

'He will need your assistance in future days, of that I am certain. Please come and stay when you travel south for the Council meeting. I do so want you to meet my cousin.' She added the last in a slightly louder voice. Gently, she pressed a lock of hair into his hand, whispering, 'And keep faith with me, even if you cannot keep faith with my husband.'

Sevira turned to leave, and Viracus stepped up to her side. Mor raised the lock of hair to his nose, the colour and perfume betraying it as hers.

Back inside, Padell looked inquisitive.

'What was that about?' he asked.

'I'm not really sure.'

The excitement tingling through him was not unwelcome, but he could not allow it to distract him.

VII

Alauna

Winter 427

The guards on Alauna's parapet fell silent. Good, they'd finally heard the royal party's approach.

'It's the prince, open the gates,' shouted one.

The riders filed into the fort, every one snow-covered. They looked like ghosts until they dismounted and shook the snow from their cloaks.

'You look frozen stiff,' said Silvius.

Gorwst looked at the captain responsible for his cavalry detachment and managed a grim smile.

'Help us with the horses and get these men blankets and a roaring fire,' he commanded.

'We did not think you would attempt Shap in these conditions; you are hardy men.'

'We were already committed when we saw the indications that the weather might turn for the worse, so we rode hard and fast. There was little shelter until Brocavum, but by then, we all agreed our own firesides were beckoning and chose to press on.'

Silvius took the reins of Gorwst's exhausted horse.

'I have two pieces of news, the most important being that the king is gravely ill. As yet, we have only heard this from travellers to the port today – perhaps a messenger will arrive soon with more information. The other news is that Bishop Ninian was unable to embark to Whithorn so is staying in the chapel until the weather clears. He invites you to pray with him.'

'I will prepare to leave for Banna in the morning, messenger or not. Tell Ninian I will pray with him at dawn before I begin my journey. I will need a fresh horse and a revived guard – I have already put these men through a gruelling journey, and they will not thank me for another.'

'I will choose men capable of keeping up in this weather. They will be ready to leave as and when you require. There have been no reports of Scotti in your absence, but we have not been able to view across to Criffel for at least a week.'

'This weather seems set to continue and should protect us from our enemies. How is my wife?'

'Eager for your return, no doubt. In your absence, she received a message from her brother and dispatched one in return.'

Gorwst left the fort and climbed the whaleback hill toward the timber compound that surrounded the hall he had built himself. The snow made the ascent slippery, a reminder of how difficult it had been to drag the pagan altars, taken from the fort, up to where they had been used as post foundations for his hall. No one need know that the feigned sacrilege to the pagan gods was to provide all at the hall with protection from evil. It never hurt to keep all options open.

The unrestricted views in every direction were shrouded by the weather, giving him little distraction as he trudged up the slippery slope. Dusk had fallen, but the snowstorm had not abated, and the wind tore at his clothing. As he drew closer to the compound, the excited barking and howling from his dogs within reached fever pitch. The guards at the compound opened the gate, and he was mobbed by the pack. Each dog knew its specific duty and had its own ways, but his favourite, Hercules, was always first to him before standing back to allow the others a share of his affection. The best hunting dog Gorwst had ever raised, the mutual understanding between this dog and his master needed no extravagant gestures of affection.

As he entered the hall, a welcome but suffocating heat met him. He had completely lost the feeling in his limbs on the ride, now the sudden heat brought a tingling that was almost painful. He rubbed his hands and stamped his feet to speed up the process. His wife of nearly one year, Marchell, was standing, silhouetted by a roaring fire at her back, her fair hair braided loosely. It was a greeting to unnerve any man. She was a couple of years older than Gorwst and so beautiful. He loved and desired her beyond measure, of that he had no doubt. Their marriage had come late, but with her being not only beautiful but also the sister of King Coroticus, it had helped to secure a continued alliance with Alt Clut.

'Husband,' she exclaimed, holding out her arms.

He went to her, calming the dogs with an abrupt command. He removed his cloak, and even though he was soaked to the skin, she pressed close, giving him a long, lingering kiss that warmed his very soul.

'Come to the fire and change out of these clothes. I have food ready.'

Settled by the fire, the storm was relegated to no more than a distant howling which intermittently buffeted the building in impotent rage.

'How was the journey and how are your relations, Ceretic and Einion?' Marchell asked him as he devoured the food.

'They were in great spirits until the snow curtailed our meeting. Their return journey over the mountains will have been difficult. Ours was less so because we made it up Shap before the snow took hold. It's just as well because the horses could hardly cope as it was. We took the route past Bassenthwaite to take advantage of the landmarks, but if we had delayed even an hour, we might not have made it back.'

'I prayed that God would bring you home tonight; there is much news.'

'I have heard that Grandfather is gravely ill,' he said between mouthfuls. 'Only gossip from travellers, mind – but a concern, nonetheless.'

'Yes,' replied Marchell. 'We will discuss that in a more private moment, but I have other news,' she said playfully, with that glint in her eye he found so hard to resist.

'Well, tell me, woman.'

'I am carrying your child.'

Gorwst gave out a mighty roar, threw his food to the floor and hugged her a little too hard. This set the dogs off barking, and he howled with laughter.

'Hear that? We are all delighted.' He picked up his drink and swallowed a large measure of mead. 'It's about time, woman. I've been expecting a result from all that effort I have been putting in!'

She hit him playfully.

'Well, don't think I'm finished with you yet,' she said. 'Let's send the servants to their quarters; I yearn for privacy with you, husband.'

Marchell summoned her chief maidservant, Cara, and told her to send everyone to their quarters. Gorwst finished off his meal as the servants began to leave, all except for Cara who was never far from her mistress. Whilst they left, Gorwst stared into the fire, losing himself to the flickering flames. Truly, he had never been so content, but this news about Grandfather was rubbing hard on him. The old man had always been there for him. Not just the dominant force who had defended the Cymry, he had been a father to him after the death of his own. Coel had taught him to fight. 'Get up,' he would shout, every time he knocked the young Gorwst to the ground, time after time with painful blows from a practice stave. There had been no mercy, not until the day Gorwst had parried and struck back. He started from his reverie when the heavy door slammed behind the last of the departing servants.

'Are you tired, husband?' Marchell reached across and refilled his cup with the sweet mead she had warmed by the fire for him.

'Never with you, Marchell, but I must away before dawn. I am to pray with Bishop Ninian at first light, and then I leave for Banna.'

'We have not yet heard from your mother that the king's illness is serious, and I was hoping to come with you...' She turned away from his watchful eyes, clearly upset by his plans.

'Surely your condition and the weather are at odds with such a notion?'

He could not risk her safety.

She turned to look at him, and with steady resolve said, 'I can ride a horse as well as any man. You need me with you – especially if his time has come.'

Gorwst did not reply. The journey would be harsh; he would not see her suffer. Marchell filled his cup again.

'Who will be king?'

'Probably me,' he said casually.

'Probably?' Marchell repeated slowly. 'I married a king in waiting. My brother expects you to be king. Why only probably?'

'We should pray for my grandfather's recovery; he is not yet dead,' Gorwst said.

Marchell pursed her lips in that way she did when she became frustrated with him. 'No, husband, we should plan!' she said, her voice rising with her anger. 'Do you think I can't see you are strong in arm, but weak in resolve. You say probably, and I can see why. The rumours say he is unconscious and rambling. What do you think others are doing in this moment whilst we are marooned on this hill with a handful of men? Do you not think they might be seeking to steal your birthright from you?'

'Who would do such a thing?' He sat upright, all sense of languid relaxation gone.

'Gorwst, don't be a fool,' she said forcibly. 'Whosoever commands your tribe's militia can make himself king of the North. You and I and our unborn child surely murdered to make way for your rival!'

'No, no, that will never happen!'

'Husband, I watched Coroticus kill both of our stepbrothers. Christian piety always comes second to the lust for power. He killed

63

them not on the battlefield, but when they were at prayer. If we do not go to Banna together then expect to lose your kingdom. Gods, old and new, watch these events. It is but a game to them – the throw of a die or a cruel, unforeseen twist can change events forever. This storm is a celestial challenge – it tests us, to see if we are worthy. It is clear to me now – we must go together, tomorrow.'

Gorwst remained silent. He had learnt to value Marchell's intellect and her uncanny ability to foretell events. Her experience was unquestionable, his trust in her judgement unshakeable.

'Who will Talhaearn support? His influence will sway any decision.'

'He has always been fair.'

'Who do the army captains support?'

'Both myself and Mor, but there are elements who think we should attack and raid like your brother.'

Marchell paced up and down in front of the fire.

'Talhaearn and your mother love each other, do they not?'

'That is the rumour, but I think their love for my dead father weighs heavy on them both.'

'The men respect Talhaearn, and *his* mother was a Carvetti princess, is that true?'

'I believe so, but he has no designs on the kingdom, and he is crippled by grief.'

'Are you sure? He is a hero, he saved all your lives, the army support him… He has only to marry your mother, and your future is, at best, delayed, at worst, given away to Mor.'

'Why would he do any of those things?'

'He is too canny for it not to have crossed his mind, and he favours Mor – I know it. Your brother is handsome and educated, much more like his uncle than you are.'

Hearing her voicing his private fears made his stomach churn with a sudden anxiety.

'I love these people, Marchell.'

'But do you trust them, Gorwst? I married a future king; our son is meant to be a king. You must act in our interests.' She placed her hand on her belly, including their unborn child in the discussion. 'We trust you, husband. Do not forget my brother expects me to be a queen.'

At the mention of Coroticus, Gorwst suddenly remembered the messenger… Ach! He would ask her about that tomorrow on their ride to Banna. When had he accepted that she would not be dissuaded? Probably the moment she raised her voice in protest.

'You will need to be ready at dawn. We leave after I have prayed with Ninian.'

'Bring Ninian. I will speak with him, and he will support our cause.'

Marchell stood up and stepped in front of him. She released the cord that secured her robe, revealing her beautiful, naked body.

'Now, husband, come to bed and show me that you are the strong man I married.'

She clasped his large hands in hers, drawing him in the direction of their bed. He dutifully followed.

VIII

St Helens Ford

Winter 427

Mor and his troop set off an hour before dawn, crossing the bridge by torchlight. As planned, they rode slowly until out of view of the fort then hid the cart with the empty chest in a copse, releasing the lumbering oxen into the surrounding countryside. Quickening the pace, they rode south-west for seven miles to meet the River Verbeia where they turned north toward St Helens Ford which lay opposite the now deserted fort on the south bank. They arrived well before the agreed time of midday to find the two messengers with Crannog and fifty or so horsemen already waiting for them. Though they had only met once before, Mor recognised Crannog instantly. The burly man sat a good head above his men, raising a hand in glad greeting when he too recognised Mor. He rode up to meet the new arrivals.

'Well met, Lord Crannog. Thank you for this timely assistance.'

'We are pleased to see you, young prince. You have been too busy fighting Picts and Scotti to manage a visit to us for some time, so we have much to discuss later.'

'There is more going on in these parts than my family had appreciated, Lord Crannog. It seems that the Saxons are no longer content with their allowances under the Romans and are ambitious to acquire new homelands.'

'They creep up the rivers like parasites. They despise our language, our laws and, most of all, our religion. If they enter our territory, we kill them!'

'That is good to hear, because it is for just such an opportunity that I have summoned you.'

'You have been in Eboracum attending a gathering with them I'm told?'

'Not intentionally "with" them. But now I am suspicious that they plan to ambush my troop to recover a tribute they have reluctantly surrendered to me. I will explain it more fully later, but for now, we require safe passage to Isurium. We suspect a force awaits us at the Nidd crossing.'

Crannog smiled broadly displaying the gaps left by several missing teeth. 'So, you want us to ambush the ambush?' He laughed, enjoying his own wit.

'Well, if you could outflank them by crossing upstream, we will turn the surprise in our favour. If, however, they are not gathered to attack us, we will still need to ride to where they are camped on the Ouse and move them off the west bank.'

'How many keels?' asked Crannog.

'My scouts saw five with many men.'

Crannog whistled in surprise. 'That's a lot of Saxon scum to have made it this far along the river unnoticed.'

'Aye, all camped in our territory. How long will you need to circle behind the bridge on this road?'

'No more than two hours.'

'Then we will wait two hours by this ford before continuing our journey. God willing, we will dine with you in Isurium tonight. Good luck.'

*

The weather was improving, and the snow had melted a fraction, which would make both journeys less difficult. Crannog and his troops had set off at a quick pace whilst Mor, Padell and their cavalry lingered.

'He seems a good man,' said Padell.

'Crannog fought alongside Talhaearn and my father until he retired back to his family's lands in Elfed. His father was one of the chieftains forced to work as a slave in the mines. My grandfather released him from that slavery; we can rely on his loyalty without question. Gather the men.'

Mor stood amongst his troops and found he had no difficulty summoning the sincerity he required for what he had to say. These were good men.

'Before this day is done, we may find ourselves facing an enemy superior in number but inferior in skill. We must use our advantages to best effect. Our friend, Crannog, and his men will be positioned behind the expected ambush site. We will have no say over exactly when they will deem it best to reveal their presence and engage, so we must cross the bridge two by two with our shields held high. The enemy will not attack until we have crossed, but it pays to expect the unexpected. Once across, they won't wait long; they may well create some form of diversion. The bridge opens onto a clearing, but we will be surrounded, make no mistake about that.'

He paused and looked around. His men were listening intently, their faces apprehensive at the prospect of riding into a trap but showing no signs of doubt.

'Expect them to move troops in to cut off our retreat across the bridge, so our best tactic will be to charge in tight formation up the road and punch a hole through their line allowing us to turn and engage them from their rear. They will be expecting us to be hauling the cart and silver, so they will not be prepared for such an immediate and swift reaction. Once over the bridge, form into lines of four. When the last two have crossed, be prepared to charge upon my command.'

Dusk was approximately three hours away, when Mor commanded his troop to mount up. They followed the old Roman road to Isurium. The bridge where they expected the ambush was eight miles distant. As they drew within view of the river, Padell called a halt. He performed a quick inspection of the horses' girths and his men's readiness. Mor ran his eye over his troop from where he sat upon his horse. They all showed signs of nerves and trepidation, but each man had seen action against Scotti raiders, and they were well-armed and well-trained. They would not let him down. He considered a brief prayer to dispel grim thoughts and raise spirits, but quickly dismissed the idea – there was no time for that.

Padell climbed back on his horse and drew alongside Mor.

'We are being watched,' he said quickly, under his breath.

Mor nodded, gave his mare's neck an encouraging pat and set off at a slow trot. The bridge over the Nidd, built using simple stone pillars and timber planks, was not very wide. On the approach, his troop drew into tight formation as instructed and crossed with as much haste as possible, doing well not to betray their suspicions about what awaited them. Once over, rustling and movement could be heard coming from behind. The Saxons were springing their trap, and when Mor's men reached the top of the bank, they were confronted with a line of men armed with spears, positioned maybe fifty paces across the clearing.

'Charge,' Mor shouted immediately. Horses whinnied and snorted as heads-down the troop accelerated to a gallop. Arrows flew past them from the surrounding forest, Mor grateful that the suddenness of their attack had frustrated the archers' accuracy. Their attackers were in disarray, caught unprepared. Mor and Padell hacked through the centre of the enemy line, swords swinging left and right. His troop burst through in an instant, pounding up the road until they were beyond accurate range of the archers in the treeline. As they wheeled around, a whistling salvo of arrows passed over their heads coming from behind, felling men in the enemy line.

Mor looked around wildly. Relief rushed through him when he saw Crannog and his men ride out of the forest to join the attack.

'We meet again, Lord Crannog,' said Mor, as the two troops joined up.

'Just in time to save you from embarrassing yourself, young prince,' said the old warrior.

Mor grinned; he was enjoying himself now. Another salvo of arrows flew over their heads, and they charged at the enemy again. Their would-be ambushers were now in complete disarray, fleeing east, heading for their keels. Mor slashed with his sword, taking another Saxon down. He drew his horse to a halt, leaving his battle-hardened cavalry to cut down the fleeing Saxons.

'They won't get far!' Crannog shouted. 'I have archers waiting for them along the path they'll take to get back to their keels. Their tracks were obvious in the snow.'

Men were shouting, screaming and dying, but the rout proved mercifully brief.

'How many Saxons left alive?' Mor shouted across to Crannog, the clearing now empty of all living Saxons.

'Difficult to tell,' said Crannog. 'I want to say none though.'

'Then none it shall be,' said Mor. 'Padell, follow them along the bank and kill all you find. Crannog, you and I will make for the Ouse with great speed and either secure or destroy their keels. I don't want news of our victory to reach Eboracum until after tomorrow.'

*

Within half an hour, they reached the pool at the confluence of the rivers. The Saxons had left only a handful of sentries who wisely surrendered as soon as they saw the large cavalry force. Amongst them was a nervous youth who looked familiar. Mor couldn't quite place him, but he was sure the lad's identity would come back to him.

After a further hour, Padell and his men came out of the forest, dragging along a bloodied prisoner.

'Crannog's archers got most of them as they fled and some drowned trying to cross the river. Very few escaped. This one seems to be their leader.'

'Don't kill him yet; we need to discover the purpose behind this outrage.' Mor couldn't keep the triumphant grin off his face. He looked around at the men who had fought for him and raised his sword in the air. 'The day is ours.'

A great cheer went up. They had done well, and their casualties were few. That first salvo of arrows had inflicted some injuries, but it was the horses who had taken the main brunt of it. Once they had organised the prisoners and the wounded into separate ships and put the sound horses to work pulling the ships upstream along the tow path to Isurium, Mor and Crannog left Padell in charge and rode ahead with a small guard of six riders to secure their lodgings for the night.

*

The pink limestone walls of Isurium Brigantum rose before them in the early dusk. It was good to see those solid walls that had protected the once important city and port of the Brigantes from raiding Picts and, later, Saxons. By the time Mor and Crannog arrived, the gates were already closed. The rose walls contrasted against the snow, giving the city a dreamlike, fairy tale aspect; Mor's poetic musings were soon shattered by Crannog's hammering on the gates with the pommel of his sword.

'Open up, it is Lord Crannog, and I bring Prince Mor. What kind of hospitality is this?'

Every hound in the fort began barking. Two guards peered sheepishly over the wall before scrambling to a more alert position and calling, 'It *is* Prince Mor. Quickly, fetch the decurion.'

The gate was opened with little delay. As soon as he saw who stood in the opening, Mor leapt from his horse and clapped an old friend of Taly and his father's on the back.

'Alwin, you have missed some excellent sport not far from here today.'

'Forgive us, Prince Mor, we could hear the fighting on the wind, but did not venture out to find out more. We brought the country folk into the fort for their safety and shut the gates.'

'You are all safe now, Alwin. Our troops will soon be here with Saxon prisoners, the wounded and several Saxon keels. The men will be hungry and thirsty… I presume you have supplies of meat, ale and wine we can purchase? We are about eighty strong with almost as many horses which will also need feed and good stabling.'

Mor was happy to see the look of relief that crossed Alwin's face at the offer of payment for the hospitality. He had calculated correctly then – with it being so long since Isurium had needed to feed such a host, they were ill-prepared. Fortunately, the presence of so many families from the surrounding lands and their livestock would make the task simpler, especially if there was some coin to be made.

'Prince Mor, two riders arrived just before dusk. They were intent on delivering a message to you in Eboracum, but reluctantly agreed to interrupt their journey upon my advice. I doubt they have finished tending to their horses yet. They will be pleased to see you.'

'Thank you, Alwin. I will speak with them once we have stabled and fed our horses. Some of our brave steeds have taken injury; do you have someone skilled in healing animal injuries?'

'We have two such men who have a particular understanding for horses. I will have them summoned immediately.'

Alwin took Mor, Crannog and the six riders to the stables where they met the messengers sent by Taly. The men looked relieved to have completed their mission so early.

'Greetings, Prince Mor. We have an urgent message for you.'

As the soldier reached inside his clothing, Mor felt a sudden apprehension. Had Grandfather passed? Was he too late in returning? He opened the message and smiled with relief.

'It's from your old comrade Prefect Taly.'

'Is it bad news?' asked Crannog

'Sadly, my grandfather is very sick. This message encourages me to hurry back. Crannog, let us go and sit by Alwin's fire. We will eat with the men later. For now, we have much to discuss and little time before I must return north.' He turned to the messengers. 'When Padell returns, send him to me.'

Isurium had burst into life. Fires were lit, hay and feed laid out in the stables; the cives were rising to the challenge of providing hospitality for eighty guests, and the sounds of preparation rose as the sun set behind the distant Pennine hills. It was still very cold, and the cloudless sky threatened a severe frost. At least Padell would have some moonlight to help him find his way to the gates.

Settled by the fire with cups of mead, Mor studied Crannog. He was about the same age as Taly though he looked younger, more carefree. Life had been kinder to him, providing him with two sons who had accompanied the troop that day, fighting bravely.

'Today has provided considerably more excitement than is usual for around here,' he said with that famed twinkle in his eye, and Mor found it easy to laugh with him. 'How fare the wars with the Scotti and Picts? Surely, there is little to tempt them south now the Romans have gone?'

'True,' replied Mor. 'Our allies grow stronger, and the Scotti are more likely to trade with them than raid them now. The Picts have a powerful new king, Drest, who is wiser than his forebears. He knows that the Romans no longer threaten his kingdom. My grandfather killed the former king, Talorc, who was Drest's rival. The new king is busy consolidating his power amongst his immediate neighbours. It makes no sense that he'd be responsible for the raids to the south.'

'Hmmm, I agree,' said Crannog. 'We see no Picts around our region, although there are brigands in the Great Forest who have come from near and far. Saxons, Franks, escaped slaves from the Empire and even some Cymry traitors and criminals, but no Picts that I know of. These brigands do not bother us for fear of reprisals, but their attentions are easily drawn to the rich pickings further south. It is this combined with the mounting threat from the east that really concerns us.'

'How so?' asked Mor.

'The Humber is an open door to the Continent. All manner of people now inhabit its shores, and many are skilled sailors. The Empire brought them to these regions, and the Parisi welcome them. The Gaini and the Angles were both settled here by the Empire and still think of themselves as Roman cives yet behave so much like Saxons that it is difficult to tell them apart.'

'I'm sure there were Angles amongst the enemy today,' said Mor, an image of the young lad amongst the sentries guarding the keels coming to him, thinking he might know where he remembered him from. 'What is your opinion of Gundad of Eboracum?'

Crannog spat on the floor. 'That bastard! We have no dealings with him. He prefers to throttle our trade, even though he is the principal merchant in the east. Our cattle and crops no longer travel in his direction – our only markets are to the west and north now. It is no longer safe for our people to live close to the Humber – whole families have disappeared. Gundad is a powerful man with a private militia, although I cannot say if he is responsible for the brigandry in the Great Forest. Our men patrol as far as the rivers but not far beyond, and Danum has become a fort for ghosts.'

These were developments that Grandfather knew nothing about. How had they been so blind to the mounting threat on their southern doorstep?

'We have assumed our back door was secure for too long. I am sorry, my friend, that we have neglected our southern cousins.'

'I would say not. You have had good reason to look north, and these changes follow the Romans' departure. After all, it is not long since I was fighting alongside Taly in defence of the Patria. Though I should tell you that the regional tribes now believe Gundad is paying King Coel to turn a blind eye to him mistreating loyal subjects.'

'The king will be furious when he learns about that,' said Mor.

'You take your eye off a dog, and it will readily snatch your food!' said Crannog with a smile.

A flustered looking Alwin entered the room.

'Padell is back with all your men; it's chaos out there.'

'We will be sure to book in advance for the next ambush,' quipped Crannog.

Mor suppressed his laughter when he realised that Alwin was not joining in.

'Alwin, be still a moment; I have some questions.'

74

'Can they wait, Prince Mor? I've a thousand things to do.'

'They cannot, Alwin, I won't keep you any longer than necessary. Do you know Gundad of the Gaini?'

'Gundad of Eboracum? Only by reputation. The metal merchants left Isurium long before I took this command, and no one visits that city from here anymore, not since the plague. Our local farmers trade with northern and western tribes. We have no keels moored here for there is nowhere for them to ship to.'

'Well, tonight we have brought you five which you must keep safe for the king.'

Alwin paled and became even more agitated. Perhaps it had been a mistake to bring up yet another new responsibility so soon? Better let the decurion get back to work.

'Please go about your business, friend. My men are at your disposal.'

Alwin turned to leave and bumped into Padell coming the other way.

'Alwin, my old friend, how are you?'

He pushed past. 'It's chaos,' he shouted over his shoulder as he marched away down the corridor. 'Just chaos.'

'He's usually in bed by now,' Crannog joked as the captain entered.

'Now I have you both with me,' said Mor, trying not to laugh at Alwin's expense yet again. 'Well done today. How many men did we lose, Padell?'

'Two, both to arrows. We have recovered their horses.'

'And the enemy?'

'There are corpses strewn from the bridge to the Ouse.'

'There will be recriminations; we would be wise to act swiftly to shore up our defences. I must leave with all speed tomorrow, though I will need only four companions with five spare horses. Padell, collect the tribute together. Give each of our soldiers two silver siliquae in gratitude for their bravery. Pay old Alwin what he asks for his services and award twenty siliquae to Lord Crannog. Give our dead heroes a Christian burial.' Mor turned toward the older warrior. 'Lord Crannog, I ask only that, early tomorrow before the ravens pick at their corpses, you strip the enemy of their weapons. Keep these for your own security. Use the tribute you have earnt wisely and be wary of attack, for it will surely come. We need to bolster our eastern defence. Gentlemen, a change is upon us. The North must now defend frontiers, that until this week, we did not know existed. I will counsel with King Coel and my brother about how best to counter this problem. Padell, only return north when you are entirely satisfied with Isurium's security. Now, the prisoners?'

'They are chained in the forum. Shall we deal with them before we eat?'

'Yes. We need to know more about their leaders. I'm not sure, but one had the look of someone I saw during my stay at Eboracum.'

*

Arriving at the forum, Mor spotted the prisoners chained to a column which afforded them a little shelter. He addressed them as a group.

'Who here speaks Latin?'

The men looked frightened, and only the youth replied.

'I do.'

'So, tell me who you are and what your purpose was.'

'Why should I tell you anything?' replied the youth without lifting his head.

Mor heard his voice rise with his fury. 'Don't doubt our resolve, young fool. We have no need for slaves, and this is not a game. Men died today.'

Mor grabbed the hair of the wounded prisoner with the most senior appearance.

'Is this your leader?'

There was no reply, and Mor had no time to indulge them. He drew his sword and slit the prisoner's throat before casting him aside.

The man convulsed and died at his feet. The other prisoners looked terrified. Good.

'I see you are not content that you have made enough widows for one day.' He walked toward another prisoner and grabbed his hair. This one screamed and recoiled, struggling violently, but Mor retained his grip, lifting his sword toward the man's throat.

The youth was pale with shock. 'Wait,' he cried, his voice quavering with fear.

Mor let go and looked at the youth expectantly.

'I-I am Freuleaf, s-son of Friothulf. These men are-are Angle sailors, and the warriors were Saxon m-mercenaries.'

'Why did you attack us?'

'Gundad wanted to recover his tribute. He said that, at the sight of so many warriors, you would throw down your weapons, and leave the chest behind when you ran for your lives... We were to pretend to be Picts.'

Crannog howled with laughter. 'Gundad should know that Prince Mor can tell the difference between a Pict and Saxon. Do you know how many of both kind we have killed?' he hissed viciously.

'So we can thank Gundad and your father for the deaths of so many. The North doesn't take prisoners'—Mor raised his sword once more—'unless, Freuleaf, you come to Banna as a hostage and swear an oath of loyalty to me on pain of death. Do this, and I will release these sailors in the morning so that they can recount to their master and your mercenaries' widows the consequences of this foolish attack. The Angles were once Roman cives, but now they bring nothing but shame upon the Patria. Will you comply?'

The youth nodded.

'Gundad's greed clearly outweighs his common sense. He has become over-confident and underestimates the North. Merchants should never be allowed to make military decisions.' Mor wiped the blood off his sword on the dead Saxon's tunic. 'Padell, put this boy in the guard house but ensure he is ready to ride with me in the morning.'

He turned to leave. 'And release these prisoners on the eastern bank tomorrow but remove all their clothing before you do, so their shame can be known to all.'

Crannog laughed. 'Running from the wolves should keep them warm!'

As they strolled back to Alwin's quarters, Crannog gave Mor an intrigued look. 'You guessed he was Angle royalty?'

'I wasn't sure, but I thought I recognised him. It's a good outcome. A high-value hostage gives us leverage, and the boy will provide evidence to my family of the mounting Saxon threat.'

Bonfires were burning, and meat sizzled sending sparks flying up into the night sky. Some men sang, others just drank. Mor had asked for meat and drink to be sent to his room, planning to retire early, but instead, he lingered with his brave comrades long into the night. A hard ride the next day was unavoidable, but with God's help, the skies might clear and enable them to ride through the following night by moonlight to arrive at Banna the following day.

Gorwst would listen to what he had to say, but the north-west was surrounded by Scotti who were now considered the northern army's primary threat. Taly might understand better that these settlers posed a greater threat than raiders. As for Vortigern… well, he was arrogant and clueless, mindlessly facilitating a barbarian invasion akin to those the Romans had spent years staving off. No doubt about it – there was trouble ahead.

IX

Banna

Winter 427

The morning air was cold and sharp in his lungs when Taly drew his first breath of the day outside his smoky hut. The snow crunched as he walked to the latrines whilst Plato, frost-deprived of his usual scents, skulked around the edges of the walls and huts. It was still dark, but a bright moon shone out of the clear sky; the storms had passed for now.

In the latrines, he sat next to Primus, decurion of the guard at Banna.

'A cold seat this morning, Primus, but the stars fill the sky which gives hope that there might be some sun to melt this snow.'

'Then there will be flooding and mud, prefect,' Primus replied, cheery as ever.

'How fare the men?' Taly asked.

'They are cold in the barracks, cold at their posts and many worry about their families and stock in these conditions. Most are convinced our enemies are sat by their firesides and think we should be doing the same.'

The complaint registered, but the fort was undermanned, the king was sick and both the princes were away. Whether Primus liked it or not, Taly was in command, and relaxing the guard because of a bit of snow was not his idea of mounting a diligent defence. When you trained as a Roman soldier, you learnt that discipline counted above all else.

'Better keep them moving then! You are free to raise this complaint with whichever of the princes returns first, but until then, we continue to mount a full defence. By the end of today, the snow should have melted enough for you to reinstate regular patrols.'

Primus did not look enthusiastic at the prospect of another cold day at his post. 'The Picts have not attacked in numbers for many years, prefect. Yes, there are raiders and rustlers, but it is the Saxons and Gaels who threaten the Patria from the sea, and they usually aim further south. The Scotti and Picts now fight each other, and both are further contained by our allies the Gododdin in the east and Alt Clut in the west.'

'The weather will abate, but the Picts will not. We shall continue this discussion another time in warmer and less odorous surroundings.' Taly stood to leave but added, 'Never forget the danger we guard against – we are only two days ride from Pictland. And it is through mutual respect that we retain our allies. We are at least equal to them all but only if strict discipline is maintained. You were promoted for your leadership qualities, Primus; have they been frozen by winter?'

The decurion lowered his head, unable to meet Taly's eye. 'No, prefect.'

Taly nodded and limped out, not heading for the stables as usual, satisfied that Jet would have already been turned out. Plato set off in the expected direction then stopped when he noticed his master's uncustomary direction. Taly answered the hound's questioning look with a tip of his head toward where Cian was already stood waiting by Taly's door in the half-light. At dawn, as requested. The lad had good discipline. Plato bounded up to greet his first visitor of the day.

'Good morning, Plato, and good morning, prefect.'

'It certainly is and look at this clear sky, perhaps the snow will melt a little today.'

Their greeting was interrupted by the sudden sound of raised voices and the crash of furniture falling. They turned just as the door to the great hall was flung open. A man staggered forth a few steps before falling in the snow.

'Quick, Cian, come with me,' said Taly as he ran toward the collapsed figure of King Coel.

'Hurry, we must get him back inside.'

As they lifted him, the king looked blankly at his surroundings. Straining to speak, he mumbled, 'Ceneu, where is he? I must tell him.'

Brianna rushed outside.

'I tried to stop him, but he knocked me to the floor.'

'We heard the commotion. Are you hurt?'

'I'm fine, but we should get him back to bed quickly before the whole fort knows what has happened.'

Taly and Cian supported the king between them and helped him back into the hall where they placed him back on his bed. It was hard to look down at the great king, the man who had been father to him, and see him looking so limp and lifeless.

'Cian, please go and attend my fire; I will join you soon.'

Taly waited until the door had closed then held Brianna's hands. 'It seems Coel believes he is close to his death, so he is desperate to discharge his most solemn duty before it is too late. He is seeking out his heir so that he might disclose the talisman of the tribe.'

Brianna managed a faint smile, communicating her gratitude for his support by squeezing his hands, unable to speak thanks to the tears rolling down her cheeks. Without opening his eyes, Coel spoke.

'Taly, is that you, boy?'

'It is Coel. You are very sick and must rest.'

'Ceneu has gone, hasn't he?'

'He died in my arms long ago.'

'I remember now. Where are my grandsons?'

'They will be here soon. Now rest.'

Brianna wiped away her tears and immediately set about straightening the bed.

Taly stood to leave, picking up a fallen chair as he passed.

'What progress, Brianna?' he said. 'Did you send a messenger to Gorwst?'

'Yes, he has left already.' She turned to look at the king. 'I have prayed to God that He will bring Coel back from his sickness, but I fear the Lord has other plans for us.'

*

When Taly got back to his hut, he was met with an anxious Cian.

'How is he?' he asked.

'On the mend. We have just spoken for the first time since this fever gripped him.' Taly sat down by the fire. 'Gorwst and, hopefully, Mor will arrive tomorrow, which will relieve some of our anxieties. I expect we will have many secretarial duties to fulfil. You look anxious, Cian; what worries you?'

'I had very little sleep. The barracks were bitterly cold, and when I did manage to drift off, I dreamt I was in battle with the Antichrist and his barbarians.'

Taly smiled. 'I take responsibility for placing that in your thoughts. Next time, better to dream about Bryn,' he teased.

'I cannot, prefect,' Cian said glumly.

'How so? She is, I suspect, prettier than the Antichrist.'

'My parents consider me betrothed to one of their friend's daughters. Their disappointment would be unbearable. Bryn is the daughter of a German soldier—'

'A brave man who died in defence of the Patria,' interrupted Taly.

'I know, but... they are proud, and I am their eldest son.'

'I think Bryn's disappointment may be the greater.'

'And mine also,' added Cian, hanging his head.

'So, let's continue your training. Where did we get to yesterday?' But before Cian could answer, Taly caught sight of someone making their way across from the hall through the window. 'Speaking of Bryn, she's heading this way with our breakfast.'

Cian leapt to open the door.

'Good morning, prefect, and to you, Cian,' she said as she entered the hut.

'I presume you heard the disturbance from the king?'

'Yes, but is it not a good sign? A sign that he is recovering his wits? I thought we had lost him.'

'Sit with us a while before venturing back out into the cold.' Taly motioned her to sit.

'I cannot, my duties,' she replied.

'Blame me. You know how your mother enjoys any excuse to chide me.'

Bryn smiled in acknowledgement of this well-known truth and sat between them whilst they started to eat their food.

'We were just discussing dreams Bryn; do you have many?' Taly asked, avoiding eye contact with Cian.

'I dream a lot. I dream about my brave father leaving but not returning, and then sometimes, I dream I am in my own home with many children around me.'

Bryn shot a glance at Cian who was staring fixedly into the fire.

'Ah well, let's hope there is an element of prophecy to that. Can you still speak your father's tongue?' Taly asked.

'I can, although I am out of practice and to hear it reminds me of his loss.'

'Try not to lose that skill, Bryn. Perhaps it would help you to feel less of a loss if you were to pray in his language, so that he might hear you better.'

'Thank you, Taly. I have never thought to do that. He always admired you.'

'For what, I can't imagine. He was a very brave man; the whole Patria owes him a debt of gratitude so great it could never have been repaid in this life, but I'm sure it has been in the next. If it had not been for Agiluf's courage, Brianna and her sons would have been taken from us.' Taly held her hands. 'It was the darkest of days which has bound us all together forever; none of us will ever forget.'

Bryn nodded, clearly too overcome with emotion to speak. She stood to leave, and Taly embraced her.

As the door closed, Cian gave Taly an insightful look.

'So, it was her father who defended the bridge with you?' The lad had a quick, sharp mind; he would go far. 'I had heard the stories in the barracks about your bravery against a band of marauding Scotti who attacked Banna whilst the garrison was engaged further north.'

'It was, and I will tell you about that in due course. He was a very brave warrior.' Taly fell silent whilst he gathered his thoughts. Poor Bryn, she deserved some future happiness. It would have been better if he had died instead of her father, but God had once again decided otherwise. The Almighty's plan was as impossible to decipher as ever.

It had been that night after Agiluf's death, when Brianna had tenderly bathed and dressed his wounds, that they had given in to their feelings. They had made love with a passion that had shocked them both, but in the aftermath, they had sobbed over the loss of Agiluf and then Ceneu, Tara and Bewyn. For all the depth of love they had for each other, their joint grief was too great a burden for them to ever consider sharing a bed again. He still felt shameful now, though it was such a long time ago...

Cian's voice drifted gently into his memories. 'I think we were at the point where Ceneu and you were training to be cavalry officers?' The lad was tending the fire, allowing Taly time to return to the present.

Taly lifted his head. He knew better than to reflect on his time with Brianna. There had been too much water under that bridge since then.

'Yes.' He took a deep breath. 'Maximus and the legion never returned, and Coel, as Dux Britanniarum, was in an impossible position. Raiding from the Scotti intensified, and they took advantage of our limited military resources – we may well have been trained Roman soldiers, but Rome itself was in a civil war and only sent limited assistance. Coel remained a Roman general for a time, then Emperor Theodosius sent his own man, a Comes Britanniarum, with a task force, but Rome was still trying to apply old methods to new problems. Punitive raids against the Picts brought only temporary peace to the northern frontier. Coel's cavalry units were effective but overworked, and after years of brutal attacks and desperate defence, Coel decided to resign his post with the Roman legions, preferring to offer his services as a mercenary. The Romans were furious, because it meant they no longer had the resources to defend the frontier. Coel's cavalry troops became a private militia – a northern army. This gave him the freedom not only to decide his own strategy but, more importantly, who and what to defend. He had turned himself back into the regional Protector of his own people.'

'Did that fulfil Myrddin's prophecy?'

'The elders of the tribes thought so, but the seer has always indicated to the king that there is much more to it.'

'Do you know the details of the dream?'

'I can remember the gist; it was the significance of the Bear to the tribes that resonated most. Since ancient times, the Bear has been the name for our nominated battle leaders. Venutius is particularly remembered, but the obligation goes back much further. Coel has fulfilled the role with distinction, but during Roman days, it was a secret appointment. The talisman that is passed between Bears gives clues to the location of a cave full of weapons hidden from the Romans by the tribes. It apparently conceals the sword of Venutius – a weapon of renowned quality, sometimes called Caledfwich – as well as his gold torc. They say that the Myrddins know the location of this hiding place but are sworn never to disclose its whereabouts because leadership must always be earnt.'

'My father has always warned me not to involve myself with prophecies and omens. I try to be a good Christian, but there is much that remains a mystery. My friends all believe in omens and the old ways, and there is a lot we don't understand. Cocidius, god of war, is still secretly worshipped by many of my fellow soldiers. Also, there are patterns to the stars which influence the future, and I am keen to know what message they hold for me.'

Taly smiled. 'It is *my* prediction that you have much learning to complete which the god of war will not help you with. Your father is wise, but the kings we serve look for omens to assuage their many vulnerabilities. Now, the details for the dream of the bear…

'A very young bear wandered across a frozen sea in search of food before becoming lost and hibernating in a deep forest. Come spring, the bear could not find the sea but made friends with an eagle who guided him back to the shore. The eagle warned him that the water was full of serpents for one hundred miles in each direction. This meant that, though the bear could see his homeland, he could not cross, and he sat on the shore in great sorrow. Suddenly, his sorrow was interrupted by a fish who swam to the shore. The fish explained to the bear that each day, at precisely midday, the serpents all slept for one hour, and that if he swam swiftly and followed the fish, he would get home safely.

'Next day, when the sun was at its highest point, the bear plunged into the sea and followed the fish, reaching the opposite shore just as the serpents awoke. Whilst the exhausted bear lay on the shingle, the fish magically transformed into a beautiful maiden who offered him a sword. She told him that the sword would kill all his enemies including the serpents. The young bear declined saying that he knew not how to hold or use a sword, whereupon the maiden told him to return should he ever have future need of it. She then vanished beneath the dark water.'

Cian looked fascinated. 'I have heard of this dream but never in such detail.'

'Well, the tribes interpreted it is as heralding Coel's return, when he was released from the imperial eagle, and they consider the weapon to be the sword of Venutius. Myrddin's dreams are considered prophetic, but their interpretation can lead down many paths.' Taly laughed. 'I dream often, but mine are strange mixtures of past events to which I attribute little meaning and no message. Indeed, the older I become the more I realise that practical thought and planning outweigh the power of omens.'

'I hope you will not consider this an impertinent question, but can you tell me a little about Bryn's father?'

The lad had Bryn on his mind, but there could be no harm in indulging his curiosity, and it was unlikely the poor girl would ever bring herself to recount to him the tragic loss of her father.

'Agiluf came from a country north of the Rhine frontier. He was a Roman soldier who chose to stay here when Rome withdrew its troops. He married Lyn, one of the king's junior maidservants at the time, and joined Coel's militia. Coel was once again campaigning in the far north, but I had experienced a bad fall from my horse and could not ride such a great distance. We had just accompanied Brianna and her children to a local wedding when we were ambushed by Scotti. It was a lightning raid, taking full advantage of the garrison's absence. We attempted to fight them off, but more raiders were turning up all the time, so we managed to break away and rode as fast as possible for Banna which was not far. We made it to the bridge below the fort, but the Scotti were at our heels. Agiluf and I dismounted to face the raiding party. We had to give the king's daughter-in-law and her children time to get to safety; the raiders were intent on their capture, knowing well how valuable they would be as hostages. We held the bridge and the steep bank long enough for Brianna and the boys to make it inside the fort, but by the time our cavalry came down the hill to relieve us, Agiluf was dying from his many wounds. I held him at the end and promised I would look after his family.'

'A brave man,' said Cian.

'One of the best,' Taly replied. 'Beware of heroic tales though – you will hear songs sung about the bravery of Cymry warriors who fell on the battlefield, but they do not tell you what you really need to understand. The Patria is now divided. The south, for so long the beating heart of Roman Britain, is under attack from many seafaring raiders who no longer fear Roman retribution. Gaul is no longer a secure Roman dominion, and in Coel's opinion, the Empire is a dying animal that can still lash out but has no strength left for recovery. Cives and some churchmen hope the Empire will recover, and that one day, we may rejoin it, but the many tribes from north of the Rhine and Danube are taking over the world, so if we invite the Romans back, these barbarians are certain to follow and take over our lands. Under Coel's protection, the North is more secure than the regions of our fellow countrymen, so that encourages them to try to draw us into their schemes and plans. Vortigern of Glevum's family, in particular, attempts to influence events, citing our seat on the Council of Protectors as acceptance of joint responsibility for southern security, but they have never stepped up to help us fight the Picts and the Scotti, so that puts an end to that argument!' He paused to emphasise the point. 'Now it is *their* way of life that is under threat, their cries are loud but their justification mute. Coel's legacy is his people's hard-won security in this Christian kingdom. What we are witnessing is a transfer of the pain and misery that we endured for decades to those cives who sat back and enjoyed the riches of the Empire. Maybe it is God's retribution for their sins of greed and sloth. Some clerics certainly think so, particularly since these events have been accompanied by a severe plague that has ravaged many Roman cities.'

Cian's father held similar views which he had shared with Taly on occasion, though he was less strident in their delivery.

Suddenly, shouting was heard from the direction of the hall. Taly heard footsteps running across the yard, and Bryn flung his door open.

'Come quickly,' she shouted, 'the king is convulsed in agony.'

They sprinted from Taly's hut to the hall where Brianna was trying to calm the king, his body arched in pain.

'Taly's here, Coel.'

She beckoned Taly to the bedside, and he put his arm around the old king's shoulders trying to comfort him. Coel's eyes were rolling, and his legs were kicking spasmodically. With what looked like a great effort, he stared directly into Taly's eyes.

'My adopted son, it is you who I choose to be the Bear. Listen to this riddle, but never speak it until it is needed.'

He whispered the rhyme of the talisman into Taly's ear then slumped back, exhaling deeply, seeming much calmer now that his duty had been fulfilled. There were a few more short breaths, but then no more.

Brianna wailed and wept, whilst Taly took a long look at the man in his arms. The man who had been everything to him. King, Protector, father and guiding light. Coel Hen was dead.

By now, servants and other attendants had begun to gather. Framed in the doorway of the great hall was a figure in white holding a stave. The bright light from sunlight reflecting off the snow threw shafts of light around him, penetrating into the dark hall. Taly squinted to identify the spectral image.

'The king is dead,' he pronounced in a loud voice.

'I know,' Myrddin replied. 'I felt him leave us.'

The seer did not enter the hall. Instead, he turned away, leaving the household to grieve.

After a while, the local priest was called to say prayers for the dead king, and Taly summoned Primus to officially inform the garrison.

'A sad day, Primus, our king is dead. I suggest you cancel patrols and double the guard. We must remain alert whilst we await the princes.'

'Yes, prefect. Who will be king now?'

An honest question that Taly could not yet answer.

'We await the princes,' he repeated.

*

Taly had asked Cian to tend to his fire whilst he dealt with everything, and he was surprised to see the young soldier back so soon.

'You have a visitor,' said Cian, pointing back toward Taly's hut. 'Myrddin requests a meeting with you.'

Taly frowned, but after a brief word with Lyn, he went to his hut. The king had always shown the seer great respect, but conversations with Myrddin were never about anything trivial. Taly tried to hide his apprehension as he entered his hut.

'A sad day. Though you must be hungry from travelling in such cold weather, so I have arranged food for you,' Taly said, taking his seat next to the seer by the fire.

'Thank you, Talhaearn. This is a faithful and wise hound, you have here.' He stroked Plato. 'He senses imminent change.'

The hound was at Myrddin's feet, watching the guest intently.

'He has been my companion for many years,' replied Taly.

Bryn arrived with bread, cheese and meat, nodded at Taly but left immediately without speaking.

'Will you stay?' Taly asked Myrddin. 'I can arrange some quarters for you.'

'Again, thank you, but I already have lodgings only a short distance from here.' Myrddin spoke whilst he ate. 'Coel has recited the riddle of the talisman to you.' It was not spoken as a question. 'You are now the Bear, official leader of the Brigantes confederation.'

'I neither expected it, nor want it,' replied Taly.

Myrddin continued to eat. 'So, did you delay informing Gorwst of his grandfather's condition?'

'Not so that he would miss speaking with his grandfather. I didn't think the king would die so quickly, and Coel has always said the princes should jointly reign, so I thought it better they arrive together.'

'The riddle of the talisman can be shared with only one leader; the tribes must never be divided.' Myrddin put down the plate and looked directly at Taly. 'Take the throne yourself or choose Coel's successor.'

'My only intention is to fulfil Coel's wishes and protect his legacy. Have you seen something, Myrddin?' he asked cautiously.

'Much death in the Patria,' the seer replied, adding, 'whoever is king.'

Taly could see the sincerity in Myrddin's eyes.

'I have already seen too much death, but if it is mine you speak of, then it is long overdue, and I do not fear it.'

'It is not your death I foresee, brave Talhaearn, but the death of our people. A fearsome serpent will come from the east. If it goes unchecked, it will devour the entire island. Our people will be slaughtered and our culture crushed. One leader from our tribes will contain and then crush this threat, but you must choose correctly, or division will be our defeat.'

'Coel's wishes were that his grandsons be considered equal. I will not break a solemn oath by choosing one over the other.'

'It is unavoidable, Talhaearn. You must make your choice or the consequences I have foreseen will follow. The throne and the tribes are different matters. The southern Brigantes acknowledge the Bear, and they are many.' Myrddin stood. 'I cannot control events, Talhaearn, but I know the Fates favour both Coel's choice of you and your ability to choose wisely when you eventually decide. Now, I must go.'

'Stay longer; I have so many questions.'

'The answers are in your heart, faithful soldier. I have foreseen that one of the whelps brings a bishop to support his claim, so I must away. The followers of the new god believe I am their enemy, but they are wrong, naïve and cannot see the future.'

When he strode out of the door, Plato whimpered as if he had been released from a spell. 'I know, Plato,' said Taly, 'I'm relieved that he is gone too.'

Taly had never expected to be anything more than a spectator at this succession. In contrast, he had been left with an almost impossible decision. He needed to seriously consider which path to take, because it seemed that his people's survival depended on him choosing well.

For now though, honouring the king was his first priority amongst the many duties he had to fulfil. He walked briskly toward the hall, noting that the snow was beginning to thaw, but a severe overnight frost seemed likely. As he approached, the large door opened. Primus, with five comrades, carried the king through the doorway at waist-height, before raising him to shoulder-height. They bore him reverently toward the bath house. Brianna had dressed the king and combed his long, white hair. He looked at peace, but it was still a sad sight – such a potent force reduced to an inanimate husk. His great age had never diminished his authority, but his death would encourage their enemies to press against their defences, and the likes of Drest, the king of the Picts, would almost certainly set out in force to test the Cymry.

Uncharacteristic anger made Taly want to curse aloud that fate had contrived to burden him with such a difficult choice. Why could the king's grandsons not have been at Coel's bedside? Surely then, the old king would have made the right decision? Perhaps fate had deliberately intervened to put him in this position? He shuddered at that prospect though, for fate had never been on his side.

*

Brianna looked worn out, her face still red from the tears shed all day for Coel. They sat at a table by the fire.

'I am weary, Taly, weary with age and weary with heartache.'

'We are entering a new era, Brianna. Soon, there will be grandchildren to tire you.' He smiled at the thought of Brianna as a grandmother.

'You always manage to say something uplifting, Taly. You are just the tonic I needed.'

'Myrddin thinks the boys will quarrel,' he said, unable to stop himself from sharing his burden.

Brianna looked concerned. 'I fear that he is right, but what is to be done?'

'Coel and I discussed this but never reached a conclusion. True leadership is earnt, it cannot be gifted. But a choice has to be made, and whatever the outcome, they will need to agree, or our enemies will exploit our divisions.'

Taly was on dangerous ground here. Brianna loved both her sons and would not wish either to be disadvantaged at the expense of the other. They both knew Gorwst to be faithful and strong but slow-witted – he had been so since birth. Mor, by contrast, had the intellect and charm of his grandfather but had not yet shown drive or leadership, possibly because it had not yet been required or perhaps because it was easier to defer to his elder brother who had bullied him as a boy.

'I have some ideas, Brianna, a compromise which I will put to them both.'

'When do you think they will arrive?'

'Gorwst may arrive tomorrow, but Mor... I can't be sure – he may be two or even three days yet.'

Brianna looked at Taly.

'Perhaps we needed this change; it could mean more time for ourselves?'

Lyn arrived with some bread and wine.

'Thank you, Lyn. I see you are hard at work.'

The housekeeper looked at Taly and pulled a face, commenting, 'And when has that ever been any different?'

They all laughed for the first time that day.

Brianna continued.

'I'm sure the boys will need your help more than ever now, but Lyn and I are planning to plant vegetables by the fruit trees in the spring, and we could use some help?'

Taly looked at her. It seemed Brianna was searching for her future now the king was dead.

'I think I might like that,' he replied, 'but first, we need to present a strong and united front. Myrddin raised the prospect of a split in the confederation. The southern Brigantes are loyal because Coel freed them from slavery, but we must seriously consider their interests in any plan for the succession.'

Brianna looked blankly at Taly. The emotional stress of the last few days had really taken its toll on her.

'Have you ever grown vegetables?' she asked.

Either her mind was elsewhere, or she was refusing to engage on the subject of the succession until her sons arrived. Taly, by contrast, was unable to think about anything else.

X

Luguvalium

Winter 427

Gorwst had not made the progress he had hoped. Marchell had decided to bring Cara and extra luggage on their journey, then the bishop had proved reluctant to accompany them to Banna. It had taken a considerable amount of persuasion by Marchell to change his mind, and by the time they had all set off, they were three hours beyond dawn with only five hours of light left. With such little time, they would only get as far as the town of Luguvalium. Even with the snow, if Gorwst had been travelling by himself, he would have reached Banna in one day.

In a temper, he led the party slowly along the snowbound route, not trusting himself to speak. Marchell was pointedly ignoring his petulance whilst riding alongside Ninian who now seemed more positive about his invitation to support a future king. Gorwst listened to their conversation whilst he ground his teeth and stubbornly held his silence.

'Your brother, King Coroticus, is kind to us. He has even visited my foundation, the Candida Casa at Whithorn.'

'He is a devout Christian, your Grace, but the responsibilities of maintaining authority amongst the northern tribes present him with many challenges to his faith.'

'As a young man, the Lord sent me a vision of Christian churches in every town across the north of the island, even into the domain of the Picts; it is a difficult task, but that is my mission.'

'My brother and Prince Gorwst will help you, and I know that the Gododdin wish for the same. Three kingdoms bound together in

95

Christian brotherhood, for the glory of God. You trained in Rome I am told?'

'A long time ago. It was a wonderful city, although I hear it has since been sacked and desecrated by heathen Goths. I was a follower of Martin of Tours until he died; that's when I returned to the Patria to fulfil God's bidding.'

'I'm sure you have noticed that our Christian God is too often associated with Rome and the legions. Old ways and old gods have enjoyed a resurgence since the Romans left.'

'I agree. It is unfortunate, but we must all strive to admonish those who undermine the true God.'

'There is a seer called Myrddin who influences Coel's family. He is not a believer. Do you know him?'

'Our paths have crossed, and I am aware that our faith is yet to convince him.'

'They say he sees the future.'

Ninian laughed. 'The future comes, with or without Myrddin.'

What was Marchell doing discussing Myrddin with Ninian? Gorwst swung around in his saddle.

'Be careful in this snow; the horses need guiding carefully. That messenger from Alt Clut will have struggled on his return journey in these conditions.' He paused then added. 'What message did he bring from your brother?'

'Coroticus had heard rumours that Coel had passed. He expects me to be queen soon.'

Gorwst returned to his thoughts. Marchell was close to her brother, a violent and powerful king who had murdered his brothers to take the throne. He had tried many times to persuade Gorwst to join his raiding parties, but Grandfather had forbidden it. Gorwst suspected Marchell had married under instruction from Coroticus – ambition certainly ran in her family. He had struck lucky though; she was beautiful and clever, and her tendency to push him hard was a character trait that could only benefit him.

They arrived at Luguvalium just before dark and sought shelter at the large mansio near to an impressive Roman fountain which had frozen in the cold conditions.

Ninian left to stay with his deacon at the local church but promised to be ready to depart at dawn. The troop of six soldiers took the horses to the stables behind the mansio.

The innkeeper and his wife braved the cold to help the visitors with their luggage but brought the worst possible news.

'Have you heard?' asked the man as he struggled with the heavy saddlebags. 'The king is dead, just this morning.'

Gorwst heard the words, but he couldn't let them reach his heart in front of strangers, in front of anyone. They entered the building and were shown to a plain room with no fire, a pile of sheepskins in one corner their only means of keeping warm.

When the innkeeper left them alone, Marchell looked at Gorwst with that faint, wry smile he knew so well.

'I told you so. Now are you grateful we are with you?'

The grief he had been holding back came tumbling forward, and he turned toward the pile of sheepskins to hide the tears that rolled down his cheeks.

'We will all be ready to leave at first light, husband, so we will make good time and arrive at Banna just after midday.'

Gorwst nodded, not trusting himself to speak, careful to keep his back to the two women. He started to arrange the sheepskins for everyone's comfort.

Cara whispered to her mistress, shaping her words with the Scotti accent she had never lost. 'News of a bairn, unnatural weather and now the king passes – the gods are all mixter-maxter. What will the morn bring?'

Marchell replied purposefully, 'News of a king and queen.'

Gorwst chose not to comment. Instead, he slipped out of the room and stepped outside the mansio. He looked up at the clear, starry sky dominated by the nearly full moon.

'What now, Grandfather. What do I do now?'

He stood silently for some time, but no answer came.

*

The dawn brought the promise of bright sunshine to warm Gorwst and his party as they mounted their horses. By mid-morning the snow was melting quickly, and the sound of droplets falling from trees accompanied the final part of their morning's journey. Soldiers standing watch on the western gate turret loudly announced their arrival, though the gates were already open to allow for all the activity between the village and the fort. Curls of smoke from many hearths rose from within the walls, giving Gorwst a warm sense of homecoming swiftly tinged with a sadness that nothing would ever be the same again.

The party of riders dismounted at the hall, and the guards walked the horses on to the stables. Gorwst looked around at his beloved Banna; he knew every inhabitant and every corner of the fort.

'Mother!' he shouted as he walked into the great hall. Brianna was stood in the centre holding out her arms. He ran to embrace her, not caring that he must look like a little boy in his eagerness to reach his mother. When they broke their embrace, he saw that her eyes were brimming with tears just like his were.

'I'm so glad you are here, Gorwst.'

He stood aside and made room for Marchell to embrace his mother.

'Marchell, welcome, and I see you have brought Bishop Ninian.' The bishop bowed. 'Was the journey difficult?'

'Slow and cold,' Gorwst reported, still peeved at their delays.

'It was so unexpected,' his mother suddenly blurted. 'The king had a fever, but he seemed to be improving, then without warning, his old body just gave up... Taly and I were with him at the end. Myrddin must have sensed it was time for he arrived yesterday morning.'

'Is he still here?' Marchell asked, looking across to Ninian.

'No, he has left for now. Taly was the last to speak with him.'

'Does Mor know?' Gorwst asked, gaining some comfort from stroking Grandfather's dogs who had all gathered around him.

'We sent word several days ago that the king was sick and suggested he made his way back. Did my messenger reach you yesterday?'

'He did not,' Marchell replied sharply. 'We heard the news from travellers and decided to set off.'

'Where is the king? We must pay our respects before we settle in,' Gorwst said.

'I will take you to him,' said his mother, reaching for her cloak.

*

Taly was sat by his fire composing the king's elegy. Honouring Cymry heroes was a most sacred duty, and this would be the most important gorchan he would ever compose. A gorchan had to emphasise the attributes of the fallen hero, describing their stature, abilities and martial achievements, but honouring a king was a far mightier challenge than any ordinary gorchan. Most others required little more than a few lines of repetitive rhymes, but Coel's would have to be special. Singing a gorchan gave it a mystical quality, calling to the dead hero in a last tender display of grief and loss. Taly had heard many sad gorchans, beautifully sung accompanied by the lyre, but his strength was his ability to instil the words themselves with otherworldly power through their message, their sound, their rhythm. He would make the mourners experience the battles, hear the cries, fear the foes and picture the slaughter.

Having recently recounted Coel's history to Cian, he was reminded of the king's long career, and he was daunted at the challenge he faced to do justice to his achievements. It would take time to memorise each line, but Taly had developed an innovative technique. Taught to write in Latin, he had used this knowledge to develop a method for using the Roman letters and sounds to record Cymry words in the written form, seeing his language come to life for the first time in ink. He had recently taught Cian his method so the lad would carry on chronicling the Cymry language in writing, rather than relying on the oral tradition of previous generations. This was the skill Taly was using to compose the elegy, but it was hard to see what he was writing in his dark hut. Writing strained his eyes, and after three hours, his head was aching. Suddenly, Bryn appeared through the door.

'Gorwst, Marchell and Bishop Ninian have arrived.'

'Thank you, Bryn. I must have been too immersed in my work to notice all the commotion. Writing takes a great deal of concentration these days; my old eyes find it hard to see what I'm doing without squinting. Wait just a moment, and I will walk to the hall with you.'

He put his work aside and stepped outside. After the darkness of his hut, the sudden contrast of sunlight reflecting off the snow initially blinded him, and he blinked like a mole, much to his embarrassment. When his vision cleared, he saw the visiting party returning from the bath house, and he walked across to join them.

'Welcome, Gorwst, Marchell and to you too, Ninian – it has been a while since our paths crossed.'

Brianna walked at Taly's side as they filed into the hall. Gorwst turned to Taly.

'Mother tells me you have everything in hand?'

'Not everything. There are plenty of ways your help will be welcome.' Taly smiled, feeling some of the weight lift from his shoulders now that Gorwst was here.

'Who is to be king? Did Coel nominate his successor?' Marchell loudly interrupted.

The atmosphere suddenly changed, the sudden tension returning the weight to Taly's shoulders. He could give no reply though. How could he when he had not come to a decision?

'Marchell, he is not yet cold. Our first task, as his family, is to honour his life,' Gorwst interceded sharply.

'But what did he say, Talhaearn?' she persisted.

Brianna looked shocked, Gorwst was visibly furious, and Ninian looked at the floor.

'Marchell,' Gorwst said curtly, 'enough questions. Mother, Taly, it has been a long, cold journey, and we have brought some happier news – my wife is with child.'

Taly sensed everyone relax, and the weight lifted from his shoulders once again.

'Congratulations to you both,' he said.

He looked at Brianna. His heart lifted to see her eyes, which had been so sad for many days, now sparkling with excitement.

'Taly and I spoke of our hopes for this only yesterday. Come, everyone. Sit down, and I will call for some food and drink. Lyn! Bryn!' she shouted. 'Come hear the news.'

Gorwst turned to Taly and spoke in a lowered voice away from Marchell's ears.

'Bishop Ninian is our guest. My wife persuaded him to come. He shares an interest in this succession.'

'Many do, Gorwst, but it is not so straightforward. Ninian will not take sides, he never does. Let Mor arrive, so we can honour your grandfather, *then* we will confer and plan. There are pressing issues at every frontier, as well as within our own militia. The treasury is empty; we guard nothing more than grain. Your grandfather fought relentlessly to create this kingdom, and it is his leadership that has held it together all these years, but times have changed, and there are many new challenges alien to the land the Romans left behind.'

'I too am worried about the future,' said Gorwst.

'We can nominate kings and protectors, but titles are meaningless without control. We may all yet need to take an oar in this boat of state. I am, of course, genuinely pleased Ninian is with you; his counsel will prove useful.'

Gorwst listened intently, as had always been his way. 'I'm sorry for the subject being raised so abruptly, Uncle Taly; my wife is ambitious for me.'

'Your wife is lovely and will make a fine queen, but for now, heed my caution.'

'Will you ride out to hunt with me tomorrow? I will bring the king's hounds, and you can bring Plato – I've missed that old hound of yours. We can make the most of having some time to talk in private.'

'Yes, that is a splendid idea, but can it wait until after midday? I shall be busy until then. I will probably bring my aide, Cian, since he will be helping me all day. With luck, Mor will arrive tomorrow, and there we will no need to change our plans to bury Coel in three days' time.'

Lyn tapped Gorwst on his shoulder.

'Hello, Lynn.'

'Do you wish to sleep in the hall, or would you prefer the privacy of the rooms in the commander's house?'

Marchell overheard the question and jumped in to answer.

'In the hall, and Cara will remain with us.'

'Very well, ma'am, but most of the fort will be in here tomorrow night to hear Taly sing his gorchan for the king.'

Gorwst grimaced and gently corrected his wife's intervention.

'Lyn, we will take a room in the commander's house whilst we all honour the king, but it will be nice to return to the hall after the mourning is over. Please take Cara into your service to help with all the extra work, unless Marchell has a pressing need of her. Do not be fooled by her Scotti way of speaking, she is an escaped slave and Cymry born.'

Taly took the time to look at his nephew and his pregnant wife. Gorwst looked relaxed in his family's company, but Marchell was clearly agitated, eyeing everyone with suspicion.

'On his deathbed, the king appointed Taly to be the Bear of the tribes,' announced Brianna.

Marchell first turned her glare on Taly – she really was fiercer than most warriors he had faced – then Gorwst.

'Does that mean you have to fight him to be king?' she asked her husband.

Once again, the atmosphere changed.

Taly looked across at Gorwst and laughed. His nephew had grown into a powerfully built warrior, way out of Taly's league these days.

'Marchell, we do not fight each other in *this* family, which is just as well, because my nephew could dispatch me to Heaven with his first blow.'

Gorwst laughed too. 'Aye but if my first blow missed, Marchell would be a widow, and my unborn child would be without a father.'

Marchell looked like thunder but asked no further questions.

XI

Corstopitum

Winter 427

Dawn was not far off as Mor and his six companions crossed the bridge over the River Tinea in darkness. They encouraged their exhausted horses up the hill toward Corstopitum. The pace they had kept up since leaving Isurium had been nothing less than brutal. They had set off with spare horses and had switched steeds at Vinovia after travelling for twelve hours without a break. Leaving their worn-out rides in the fort stables for Padell and his troop to collect, they had set of again straightaway. Now they needed to find more fresh horses and continue west, taking the road along the Great Wall. Fortunately, they had not been greatly impeded by the snow, having chosen to follow the road that avoided the Pennines. In normal conditions, this alternative route would have added an unnecessary day to the journey, but the route was relatively free of snow and benefited from towns with stables and inns. It would afford them a breakfast stop to accompany this further change of horses, allowing them to fuel their strength and resolve before continuing their sleepless journey. The excitement of the previous day's fighting had helped maintain high spirits through the night, and the full moon reflecting on the snow had lit their way, but weariness was now beginning to weigh heavy.

Mor had not spoken much on the journey; he had too much on his mind to care for idle conversation. The miles had passed quickly whilst he reflected upon Vortigern and Sevira, Gundad and the plight of Crannog's southern Brigantes. Fear for Grandfather's health also gnawed at him – Taly's message had clearly been an urgent recall.

He looked around at his small party. The horses had worked hard. Their saddlebags were stuffed with coins and silver, considerably increasing the noble beasts' burdens. Mor had tethered Freuleaf's horse to one of the guards. If the boy attempted to escape, the guard would kill him, but the lad was far from any part of the country that he knew so was unlikely to be foolish enough to flee.

At last, they reached the village at the top of the hill and found stables for the horses. It was here that a blacksmith broke the news of the king's death. After all he had been through over the last few days, coupled with the depth of his exhaustion, Mor's grief hit him like a punch to the gut. Without pausing, he walked outside to be on his own.

So many memories. The king, Grandfather, had encouraged him to study, recognising his grandson's aptitude for learning. They would read together until the candle flickered and went out. He could accept that Grandfather was old, that death was to be expected at such a great age, inevitable most would say, but God could have granted him just two more days to let Mor tell him about the meeting and the ambush, to say his farewells. He leant against a wood partition and quietly wept for Grandfather.

After several days of high excitement, Mor felt the stark contrast of sudden depression and uncertainty brought on by the news. He was going to need Taly's support more than ever if he was going to persuade Gorwst to the seriousness of the developing Saxon threat.

After a short while, he gathered himself enough to rejoin his men who he found sharing fresh bread which had been delivered to the stables by a local girl clearly enjoying the diversion provided by a group of visiting warriors. Her company had lifted their spirits, and they were having fun with the flirtatious teasing she provided. Mor sat next to Freuleaf to share his loaf with the young captive. They had not spoken since the start of the journey, and he now addressed the boy in Latin.

'We are half a day's ride from Banna, and shortly, you will see the Great Wall that the Romans built to defend us from marauding Picts. We are a long way from Eboracum.'

The boy nodded, acknowledging his gratitude for the food and his understanding of how far he was from anything and anyone familiar.

The men had set about switching the tack and saddlebags onto the fresh horses, and one hour after daylight, they were once again riding along the military road that led directly to the Wall. Mor now had Freuleaf's horse tethered to his own. There were only a few wispy clouds in the sky, glorious sunshine pouring down on the landscape, as the Wall came into view. Always an impressive sight, the imposing fortification stood out in the bright light against the snow. Mor watched his captive's face, satisfied to see the lad's look of amazement and awe.

They turned at the base of the structure, following another road west. They had travelled a further four hours when the road veered away from the Wall to avoid a hilly section. It was boggy in places, and the horses had to step carefully to avoid slipping in the snow and sludge.

'Not far now,' Mor said in Latin to his captive.

Once again, the road veered, returning to the Wall, and the ground firmed. In the distance, three riders with a group of hounds looked to be hunting. They were distant dark dots against the white landscape, growing ever larger as Mor's group drew closer. Mor recognised Jet, Taly's black stallion, whilst they were still some distance away, but he resisted the temptation to shout or break into a gallop. The dogs reached him first, barking and running around Mor and his exhausted companions. By now, he had recognised Gorwst and Cian as Taly's companions, all looking rather serious. Taly was first to hail him.

'Greetings, Mor. Well met. You look as if you have had an eventful journey?'

'Greetings we are exhausted after riding for two days without sleep. If you don't mind, we will not yet dismount – I fear that neither us men nor our horses would have the will to complete the journey if we do. Are you hunting?'

'Not with any conviction; we have been more interested in discussion. I very much regret to advise you that the king is dead.' Taly said.

'You are not the first to give us the sad news,' Mor replied. 'It has travelled along the Wall, and I was told earlier today.'

'It's a hard way to hear such news, brother,' said Gorwst. 'Let us all ride back to the fort together.' He looked at Freuleaf and frowned. 'Have you been capturing stray boys? For that matter, where is the rest of your troop?'

'I have much to tell you both.'

*

Marchell, Brianna and Lyn had come to the decision that the hall would not be large enough for the many people attending the evening's event. It had been decided that the old drill hall should be opened up, cleaned out and a fire lit at the far end where the roof was now missing. The many families and soldiers attending were all bringing a contribution of food, but there was plenty of mead, and three hogs had been slaughtered and were already roasting. The bakery had been in constant production since before dawn, and Bryn, Lyn and Cara were rushed off their feet. There had not been a wake on this scale at Banna since the death of Ceneu, but that had been a sad and tragic event, whereas this was more a celebration of a long life, lived to the full.

Marchell had seen the return of Taly, Gorwst and Mor and watched as they entered the main hall already deep in conversation. The door remained closed for some time.

Two hours passed before Taly and Gorwst emerged, each heading for their lodgings. Marchell found Gorwst sat on their bed, deep in thought. Much to her frustration, he did not volunteer any news from the meeting.

'Well, husband, did you speak with Taly?'

'About what?' he replied.

Marchell felt her temper rising at his numb answer, but she had promised herself she would remain calm.

'About who will be king?'

'We are meeting tomorrow to discuss everything; Taly wants Ninian to be present.'

'So, what took up all that time?'

'Mor brought news of unwelcome alliances between Vortigern and the Saxons, then he told us that, on his journey back, he was ambushed by Saxons, sent by Gundad, at a river called the Nidd.'

'How did he survive?'

'He anticipated their plan and contacted the southern Brigantes. The reinforcements outflanked the enemy, and jointly, they destroyed a large force of Saxons. They captured five keels and have brought north a hostage, a chieftain's son. Mor's men are still two days behind him because he came ahead when he received a message urging him to return two days earlier than we did. The militia is already praising him as a hero.'

Vindication flooded through Marchell, her suspicions confirmed.

'Now do you see the threat, husband. Taly and Mor are plotting against you.'

'No, Marchell, they are not, but my hopes to succeed Coel could be threatened by this turn in events.'

'How so?'

'The southern Brigantes had great respect for Coel; after all, he recovered their lands. But the northern armies are remote to them. In their minds, we are merely token leaders. Now that Saxons threaten their borders, they will either turn to their own leaders or expect us to rally to them, but we have no resource to do so.'

'Why should this worry you?'

'They are confederate allies who helped us fight the Picts. Coel would consider it a terrible betrayal to abandon them. Worse still, if we ignore the threat, and they are defeated, our own land and property will be threatened in turn.'

'Coel is dead, husband. The Romans have left. The army of the North is perhaps nothing more than a memory, so we must protect ourselves and consolidate our position. My brother will help you.'

'Taly and Mor have some ideas which we are to discuss tomorrow.'

Marchell feigned a laugh. 'I'm sure they do.'

XII

Banna

Winter 427

Cian had been given the duty of looking after Freuleaf. It was a great honour to be trusted with such a task, a sign that he had skills and attributes that most others did not, and he would make use of his Latin, but he was not relishing the extra responsibility. Mor had explained that the hostage was to be treated with respect, but he was not a guest – he would sleep chained-up in the slaves' quarters. The prince had also told Cian to put the young captive to work wherever he thought it appropriate. He found the boy asleep in the stables, where he had been ever since dismounting his horse. Cian had to shake him violently to wake him.

'Freuleaf, you must come with me.'

The startled boy was surprisingly compliant. Pleased, Cian led him across to the kitchens to find Bryn. He spotted her in the bakery and shouted through the door.

'Bryn, can we speak?'

She looked up and walked out under the disapproving glare of her mother.

'Cian, of all the times!' she said.

'I need your help, Bryn. This is Freuleaf; he is a Saxon. Prince Mor has asked me to put him to work, but his Latin is slow which is going to make explaining things to him difficult. I was wondering if he might speak the language of your father?'

Bryn looked the young Saxon up and down then spoke in a Germanic language that sounded strange to Cian's ears. Freuleaf smiled and replied.

Bryn listened, shook her head with a gentle eye-roll and turned to Cian.

'I told him to follow me, if he is strong enough to lift and carry. He replied with, "I will do whatever you ask of me, sweet lady." He's quite a charmer! Leave him with me.'

Cian wasn't sure he was so keen on leaving the Saxon with Bryn after all, but his other duties called, so he reluctantly left them to their work.

Outside, the fort was full of people who had arrived from all over the region. Children were making snowmen, and sparks from the many bonfires drifted upward into the evening sky. There was a delicious smell of roasting hog in the air, darkness was falling, and the old drill hall was filling up with a large audience for Coel Hen's gorchan. Cian knew the sentries had been reduced to a minimum to allow as many as possible to attend the wake.

There was a sudden hush as the senior captain of the guard, Primus, along with five comrades, bore the body of King Coel from the old bath house toward the drill hall. The body had been strapped to staithes. Following the king's body were two more men carrying his sword, helmet and shield, the polished metal glinting in the firelight as they passed the bonfire. The arrival of the small procession was Cian's cue to get ready.

He hurried to Taly's door and heard his master talking to himself through the solid wood. He pushed the door open and found Taly practising a recital of his poem.

'Ah, Cian, just in time. Do you play the lyre?'

'Hardly at all.'

'Good, hardly at all is all I need. Now, help me into this coat of mail and listen to this poem.'

*

Leaving Taly to make the final preparations, Cian hurried across to the drill hall carrying the lyre. He went to his position between the audience and the dead king. The large building was full to capacity; many families had braved the weather to come and pay their respects. There was a reverent hush as Brianna, Gorwst, Marchell and Mor, accompanied by Bishop Ninian, took their seats behind where Cian was stood. In the absence of Taly, all eyes fell on Cian. His role was not important, but it was hard not to feel the weight of all those expectant eyes. He caught the eye of his father who waved at him from the crowd. In keeping with the gravity of the occasion, Cian gave a simple nod in acknowledgement. Myrddin had reappeared and had seated himself close enough to the royal family to indicate the importance of his role in the spiritual governance of the tribe but on the other side from both Bishop Ninian and the local priest, presumably to indicate his separate beliefs. Myrddin both fascinated and frightened Cian. The bishop stepped forward, bringing the large crowd of five hundred or so to silence.

'Dear Lord,' cried Ninian, 'we are here to honour King Coel. We beseech you to receive his worthy soul into the Kingdom of Heaven.' Only the crackling of the fire intruded on the silence. 'Say with me the prayer of St Ambrose.'

Cian bowed his head and recited the words along with the compliant crowd.

> *'O Lord, who hast mercy upon all, take away from*
> *me my sins,*
> *and mercifully kindle in me the fire of thy Holy Spirit.*
> *Take away from me the heart of stone,*
> *and give me a heart of flesh,*
> *a heart to love and adore thee,*
> *a heart to delight in thee,*
> *to follow and to enjoy thee,*
> *for Christ's sake,*
> *Amen.'*

When the murmuring voices accompanying his own had quietened, Ninian then recited a prayer which Cian had never heard before, presumably one of the bishop's own composition.

> *'Deep peace of the running wave to you,*
> *Deep peace of the flowing air to you,*
> *Deep peace of the quiet earth to you,*
> *Deep peace of the shining stars to you,*
> *Deep peace of the Son of Peace to you, forever.*
> *Amen.'*

Cian looked across in the direction of Myrddin who was reverently standing with everyone else, his gaze lowered. A baby cried. Some small children were chattering. Then suddenly, a clash of weapons sounded from behind the crowd. Everyone turned to see the cause of the commotion.

It was Taly in full mail, helmet and bearskin, striking the flat of his sword against his shield. He walked through the audience with his characteristic limp, like a warrior returned from battle. The atmosphere in the drill hall was suddenly tense, feeling like that moment when the lightning had flashed but the thunder had not yet crashed.

*

Taly had taken up his position. He stood silhouetted against the roaring fire and signalled to the audience to sit. Cian had heard recitals by Taly before, and they had mostly been humorous, but Taly intended this one to be theatrical – his entrance was a good start. He stood adjacent to Cian, sheathed his great sword and cried out:

> *'Coel the Protector.'*

Cian strummed the lyre once, and Taly began the gorchan.

> *'He climbed the nemeton at the secret grove,*
> *Though God did guide him forth,*
> *They told him of the talisman,*
> *Dark days fell upon the North,'*

The silence betrayed how Taly already had the audience rapt.

> *'Coel's hands were tied, he fought for Rome,*

> *and then great Maxen made his claim,*
> *With Cymry spears he was not alone,*
> *But the mongrel host did come again,'*

Taly pointed north, drawing an imaginary line across the room.

> *'A painted army swarmed the Wall,*
> *Brave Cymry died at Rome's frontiers,*
> *Scotti serpents slithered onto western shores,*
> *But far away emperors shed no tears,'*

Taly shook his head to emphasise his disdain.

> *'The bear threw off the yoke of Rome,*
> *To protect his den from enemy spears,*
> *The eagle spied but did not swoop,*
> *And has not returned in all these years.'*

Taly paused, silhouetted by the fire. Cian waited for his prompt.

> *'Coel the Brave,'*

He strummed the lyre, and Taly unsheathed his sword.

> *'His soldiers courageous on spirited steeds,*
> *Splintering alder with their mighty blows,'*

Taly raised his sword with two hands making a slow downward arc.

> *'Heroes charging a thousand foes,*
> *Leaving their corpses as food for the crows,'*

He rested his sword whilst honouring the heroes.

> *'Ceneu, brave cub with hacking red blade,*
> *Painting heathens with their gore,*
> *Aguluf, warhound, palisade with his spear,*
> *Pierced five hundred Picts or more,*

Now he picked up his shield as if astride a horse.

> *'Terrible bear in the van of the battle,*
> *Fur running red from the blood of his prey,*
> *Steaming mailed stallion trampling the fallen,*
> *Flashing blue steel cleaving the way,'*

He lowered his shield as if the battle was over.

'Fiercely, we followed this Bear into Hell,
With a canopy of cawing black ravens
Expecting to gorge on the dead of the day,
We all earnt our mead in Coel's haven,'

He lifted the pommel of his sword as if drinking, and the tension broke. His audience laughed and cheered. He smiled, placed his sword back in its sheath and his shield on the floor then shouted:

'Coel the Great,'

Cian took his cue and strummed the lyre once more as Taly pointed at Brianna and her sons.

'The kingdom safe and Coelings will prosper,
Fearful Scotti point their prows away,
We vanquished Talorc and his many sons,
Their severed heads still on display,'

Taly sliced his finger across his neck. The audience laughed again, and he paused, completely still, waiting for silence, the next line too solemn to risk disruption. He bowed in the direction of Coel's corpse.

'The king is dead, great Coel is gone,
His long reign complete with merit,'

But now he turned to the royal family.

'No longer the Wall that faces the North,
But a land of kings known as Reged,'

Again, the audience cheered, but Taly remained solemn, waiting for silence before quickening his delivery.

'Grief and loss, unbearable companions,
Unnaturally, I have lived too long,
But at last, I see my purpose full,
Three sides to Coel, his gorchan, this song,'

He hung his head in respectful duty.

The audience began to applaud, but he cut them short by raising a hand and turned his solemnity into controlled aggression.

'Bring me twenty foes, for ten will not do,

> *And I will charge the last rampart*
> *That stands before the hall of souls,*
> *Where my journey to Heaven must start,'*

Cian could feel the anticipation in the audience; they sensed Taly was reaching the climax of his performance.

> *'The Bear waits there, the warhound too,*
> *Brother cub will be joyous I come,*
> *The court of Coel will convene in the stars,*
> *Great king, your work here is done.'*

Taly raised his arms to Heaven.

There was loud cheering and applause. Everyone was on their feet. Taly bowed, first to Brianna and her sons, then to the rapturous crowd.

Somewhere at the back, a male voice shouted, 'Taly the Bear.'

It was echoed from several positions in the hall and then, 'Taly for king,' also echoed around the room.

He patted Cian on his shoulder, waved at the crowd and limped toward Brianna who was on her feet and in tears.

'Was that fit for a king?' Cian heard Taly ask.

She held out her arms and pulled him into a hug. 'It was – fit for one and by one.'

Mor and his brother were still clapping, but Marchell was hissing something in Gorwst's ear. Cian joined Taly and they walked over to Ninian.

The bishop smiled. 'I enjoyed your performance,' he said, 'although I sense you are weary of slaughter?'

'I listened to your prayer, Ninian. Sadly, peace has never proved to be a close friend to me.'

The bishop gave him a searching look.

'There is still time for peace to become a friend to you. Perhaps we can work on this together?'

'I have concluded that a warrior's goal should be peace, but we have been fighting for so long it is hard to rationalise that objective. At the heart of all this, there is always the simple will to survive. That instinct, combined with the bravery necessary to confront those who attack our lands and our people, always washes away any hopes of peace.'

'Join me on Christ's battle-lines; you would be a welcome warrior for that cause.'

'Ah yes,' replied Taly looking at Cian and winking, 'convert our enemies rather than kill them.' He laughed. 'Although, we may yet be able to marry the two causes. Ninian, we are meeting in the hall tomorrow to discuss who should lead us, but perhaps we should examine first where we wish to be led! Will you please attend? Your wisdom would be most welcome and, I think, much needed.'

The bishop's brow furrowed. Surely, he would not decline such an important invitation?

'I believe that is the purpose for which I was summoned. Will Myrddin be contributing?'

'Not tomorrow. Myrddin has entrusted me with his contribution to the discussion. Now, if you will excuse me, it is high time I remove this bearskin and coat of mail – they are heavy and stifling and serve as a reminder of the past when it is the future that we should be looking to. Follow me, Cian.'

'Quite so,' replied Ninian.

Taly walked through the dispersing crowd, and seeing Cian's father, patted his arm rather than pass him.

'Greetings, Sennius.'

'Talhaearn, what a remarkable gorchan. Of course, without my son's tuneful lyre, it would have been quite ordinary.'

They roared with laughter, much to Cian's embarrassment.

Taly composed himself, seeming to suddenly remember that it was a solemn occasion. 'It is good to see you. I am pleased you were able to attend. Are your family well?'

'Yes, but I must return straightaway, because of the weather, tempting as it is to linger.'

'Cian now works closely with me. He has a promising career ahead, which I fear will keep him away from your villa for some time.'

'His mother and I are delighted with his progress, though we miss him greatly. He tells me you may be posting him elsewhere in the Patria?'

Cian glanced at Taly and widened his eyes, trying to signal a message through the force of his gaze. Fortunately, it only took a second for Taly to understand.

'Yes, not confirmed but very likely… He may be away for years.' Cian relaxed his shoulders. He had written to his father saying that his betrothal was not conducive to his career, citing a likely absence as justification. His father had not yet agreed to release him from his obligation.

'It is a different path to the one we originally chose for him, but we wish him well.' Sennius turned and smiled at Cian who held his breath. 'We have spoken to the parents of Fabia. They are, of course, disappointed, but you are free of the obligation.'

Cian bowed disguising his relief. 'Thank you, Father.'

Taly tapped Cian on his shoulder.

'If you will excuse us, Sennius, I need to borrow your son to loosen the laces on this coat of mail. There is food and mead in the kitchen; he will meet you there.'

Cian dutifully followed Taly to his hut and helped him ease off his armour. Taly waited until the awkward job of removing the mail was completed before he spoke.

'I presume you have requested to abandon your betrothal?'

'Yes, prefect, please forgive my exaggerating the importance of my responsibilities. I apologise for any embarrassment I caused you, but thanks to your words, I feel like a great weight has lifted from me.'

Taly laughed. 'You know, this armour has never felt so heavy as it did tonight, so let's just say, one good turn deserves another, and leave it at that.'

'Will you come back to the hall with me to enjoy a cup of mead?' Cian asked.

'Thank you, but no. I intend to help return the king's body to the bath house and to pray for his soul and our safe deliverance from our many challenges.'

*

Cian bid Taly goodnight and set off in the direction of the kitchen. He spoke with his father for a short while before wishing him well on his journey home in the dark of the night. Cian looked around but could see no sign of Bryn and Freuleaf. After asking around, it transpired that Lyn had sent them to the drill hall to tidy up. Cian made his way across the yard and found the large building almost deserted and the two people he was looking for chatting together by the fire.

'Cian,' Bryn called out, 'I thought you had abandoned us to become a travelling musician.' She had that mischievous glint in her eyes that he liked so much.

'I can see that my lack of musical skill is going to require much defending – the barracks will be merciless.'

Bryn gave him a playful nudge with her shoulder, before turning and waving her hand toward Freuleaf. 'This boy has been telling me about his home and family. He believes his father will raise an army to find him, but he is frightened for his life – there is no honour to ransom in Angle culture, so they will not pay for his return.'

I will speak with Mor, but I suspect he will be too busy with other matters to make any decisions about the future of a minor hostage just now. Although Freuleaf is to sleep chained-up in the slave quarters, tell him his life and safety are not at risk, and I give him my pledge to that. I've been instructed to treat him with respect, not hardship nor cruelty.'

Bryn turned to Freuleaf and spoke to him in his language. He seemed to relax a little, but only nodded glumly in response. 'He is a good worker,' she said. 'Will he be helping me in the kitchen again tomorrow?'

'No, Padell and his troop are expected, so the stables will require Freuleaf to help with the extra workload. But... I would like to speak with you... about future plans.'

'For Freuleaf?' The boy was picking up their language quickly; his ears had visibly pricked up at the mention of his name.

'No, for us,' answered Cian, pointing at himself then Bryn, watching her closely for her reaction.

Bryn flushed red, but she kept her voice level, giving him little to go on. 'Where shall we meet?'

'Taly's hut. I will ask his permission – he'll be attending a meeting in the hall.' Freuleaf was looking between them, clearly trying to follow their conversation. He was clever, quick to learn; they should remember that. Cian jerked his thumb over his shoulder and followed up with, 'Follow me,' in clumsy Latin.

They headed for the slave quarters.

XIII

Banna

Winter 427

The weather was turning again, a frost overnight had given way to increasingly dense cloud cover and snow had begun to fall heavily. Taly had asked Cian to breakfast with him, and the lad had agreed to keep an eye on Plato and the fire whilst Taly attended the family meeting in the hall.

It had been an early start for Taly. Worries about how the decisions he had finally made would be received had quickly filled his mind. His determination to speak his mind far outweighed the nerves though. He had no doubt that he had found the best path to harmony. Whilst it was his duty to honour Coel's wishes, the unity of the tribes was paramount. Without it, the family could easily lose itself amongst the many tyrants vying for control of the void left by the Romans.

He ate in silence, going over his decisions, searching out any weaknesses to what he was going to propose, all the time vaguely aware his distraction could be interpreted as rudeness, hoping Cian knew him well enough to know that was not his intention. When Bryn had brought them their breakfast, she had mentioned that the family and Bishop Ninian were all breakfasting together. That was good; Taly would wait for an hour or so before joining them, give them a little time to consolidate their viewpoints.

A sound drew him from his reverie. Cian cleared his throat, again – the lad looked nervous. 'Prefect, may I invite Bryn to talk with me by your fire in your absence? I have some matters I wish to discuss with her.'

'Yes, of course, Cian. Plato will keep his eye on your behaviour and report anything untoward to me on my return.'

His apprentice coloured at the inference.

Taly smiled. 'I have a question for you.'

Cian looked apprehensive; he would have known that Taly had been deep in thought about the succession, rumours had been rife about what changes were to come.

'If I decide to go with Mor to support and assist him in the southern reaches of our kingdom, would you accompany us? It may mean a long stay in Elfed.'

Cian's eyes widened in surprise. 'Of course, master, but you are the Bear, surely you are needed here, in the heart of the kingdom?'

'Elfed *was* the heart of the kingdom before the Romans pushed us north. We must prepare ourselves to face an enemy of such strength once more. The Bear goes where the threat is the greatest, and right now, that threat lies in the south.'

'Does this have anything to do with Myrddin's counsel?'

It was pleasing to see that lad was taking notice, thinking through the implications of what he saw and heard. 'He has spoken of a mighty serpent from the east that seeks to swallow up our way of life. We should not ignore such dire predictions, especially when they are confirmed by our own eyes! But we will talk more on this after my meeting.'

*

When Taly walked into the hall, it was clear a debate had been underway for some time, words said that were not popular with everyone there. Marchell and Gorwst looked particularly put-out.

'Good morning,' said Taly, taking the place that had been left for him next to Brianna whilst they all responded to his greeting.

'Your gorchan for Coel was a triumph,' said Mor.

'It was wonderful,' said Brianna. She followed that up without even taking a breath. 'So we have all decided that you are the one best placed to succeed Coel as king, for the stability and continuity of the tribes.'

Such a definitive decision was unexpected; Taly was completely disarmed for a moment. He gathered his thoughts in the short silence that followed the announcement, wanting to give a considered response.

'I do not wish to appear ungrateful, but I have no desire to be king – it would neither respect Coel's wishes nor solve our most pressing issues.'

There was a murmur of disquiet, though Marchell visibly brightened.

Brianna frowned and shook her head, confusion playing across her lovely face. 'But Coel appointed you the Bear, and out of everyone here, you clearly command the most loyalty.'

'Coel always intended his grandsons to succeed him, not me. The Bear's authority was given to me for the purpose it was intended – to bring unity. This is a time for change and consolidation. True, the older captains are loyal to me because they remember our shared victories, but those times have passed. There is no sense in perpetuating the past. We need to plan for a future where the Church and this kingdom co-operate to achieve a lasting peace. Our people have had enough of war – they seek prosperity. Remember, we hold the role of protectors, not aggressors.' Taly looked pointedly at Gorwst and Marchell.

'Up until now, we have been protected by Coel's reputation, but that will now fade with his death. Our enemies are evolving. The Pict and the Scotti threats have mellowed whilst their leaders consolidate their positions closer to home, whereas the Saxons grow braver, driven on by an envy for the richness of our lands. But they all have one thing in common – they are heathens. Heathens who only understand the way of the warrior, who have not yet embraced the peace of our Lord. Those who attack us do so for the basest reasons: to please their gods, furnish their tables, pay for their warriors—'

Gorwst interrupted. 'This is all true, but our army is reduced to just a collection of regional militias made up of farmers. We have no resources to pay a standing army, so our soldiers are reluctant to serve. However, if we were to raid our enemies, like Coroticus does, we would win the riches to pay our men, and the rewards would attract new warriors.'

'Marchell's brother plays cat-and-mouse with his fierce neighbours, but his kingdom is a secure island fortress, easily defensible, whereas ours stretches from sea to sea and north to south for more than a hundred miles. If we raid our enemies, they will raid us. Did Coel not show us that the only way to end the threat to our people is to defeat our enemies?'

Mor spoke up. 'Surely, Reged's prosperity will always attract raiders? War with our poorer neighbours is an inevitable, continuous part of life.'

'To some extent, I agree with you both, but it is important that any action we take comes from a position of strength. We want our territory to be a prosperous and God-fearing land that is defended by a formidable army. Last night, I used Coel's preferred name for our kingdom – Reged. A land of kings, where tribes and cives live side by side in peace.'

'So, what is the solution, Taly?' asked Brianna.

'I will come to that, but first, I wish to draw on Ninian's expertise.'

The bishop had been sat silently, avoiding eye contact so as not to be drawn into anything too controversial. Reluctantly, he lifted his head and looked at Taly, awaiting the question.

'Your Grace, I firmly believe that the future of this realm and our enemies beyond its boundaries rests with your Christian mission. Not just me, but all of us here should join you on Christ's battle-lines.'

Surprised looks passed between his family and the bishop. Good – his switch in tack had them all hanging on his every word.

'You are all welcome to join the Lord's fight, brave Taly, but what weapons will you all be taking up?'

'For seventeen years now, we have been holding our breath, not daring to move forward in case the Romans return. We have all kept to our stations, continuing the roles given to us by our invaders wherever it is still possible. Thanks to our continued discipline, the army of the North maintains a feared reputation, but Gorwst is correct, it is becoming little more than a collection of farmers whose resentment for their military duties grows by the day. If this decline in our defensive capabilities continues, we will be swept away by the heathen hordes who are beginning to grasp the opportunities presented by the weakened Empire.'

He paused, allowing an opportunity for any contrary opinions to be expressed, but no one spoke, all eyes remaining fixed on him.

'Coel and I discussed this many times. He stood as a giant, representing both the Empire and the Brigantes, but now, the new political landscape requires something different. Education, army discipline, public works and yes, even the Church are no longer what they once were, but the threats along our boundaries have not diminished at the same rate, indeed some are growing. Noble Ceneu might have addressed this imbalance sooner; the Lord knows I have not been strong enough these past years, wallowing in my self-pity. Only now can I see what we should do. The seafaring tribes that surround us steal our trade then rob us of what is left. The Church has become isolated from Rome. Mor tells me there is no longer even a bishop at Eboracum and the church there has burnt to the ground, but we should not look to Rome for the answers – we should look to God.'

Ninian shifted uncomfortably in his seat. 'This is a depressing summary, Talhaearn, but I fear it is the truth. Many churchmen have chosen to become ascetics rather than face the heathen spears. The mission has stumbled in the void they have left behind.'

Taly looked around the room. He was painting a grim picture, but it had everyone listening intently, even Lyn and Cara had moved their duties to within hearing distance.

'If this decline continues, we will degenerate into regional war bands, relying on local farmers for food and fighting for survival with ancient weapons. There will be no hope, no future for our people.' Taly looked at Ninian. 'And your mission will fail.' Ninian nodded his head, and Taly turned his attention on Mor and Gorwst. 'An effective and disciplined army needs payment, a failing we must resolve, but it also needs purpose. A safe and peaceful existence which creates prosperity and enables everyone to seek their salvation is not just worth fighting for – it is worth paying for. Brianna and Ninian will remember the Publicani, Roman tax collectors loathed by the cives, who were ejected along with the other officials. We saw the wealth the Romans took in taxation as their spoils of war, but the burden was paid Empire-wide, and the proceeds financed the protection and prosperity of everyone within the Empire. We must look on Reged as a small empire, and that leads me to my proposal for Ninian – something that will not only accelerate his mission but also bring our kingdom closer to the Church, hopefully extending the influence of both.'

'Are you suggesting I become a tax collector?' Ninian's bemusement looked almost comical.

'The word of the Lord entitles you to collect tithes, but you are not able to do so, not consistently over such a wide area. However, if you had representatives in every community helping to shepherd each flock, this would become easier. These agents should not be soldiers nor should they require ordaining, but they should represent both the Church and this kingdom by fulfilling religious duties at the same time as having the authority to call for protection when necessary and to help resolve disputes. They would be trained by the Church to hold prayer meetings and give religious instruction, even going into areas beyond our region's influence. Half of the proceeds collected will be paid to our treasury, and we will help you organise this. I think we should call these agents: culdeis – partners of God.'

'This is progressive thinking indeed,' said Ninian. 'Though we should not underestimate the difficulties posed in implementing such a proposal... That said, Matthew, the disciple, was a tax collector, and I see the advantage of combining administrative and religious power. It is precisely for that purpose that I agreed to join this meeting.'

Taly finally allowed himself to smile. 'Does everyone here understand this proposal?'

His small audience looked to each other, but again, there was silence. He took a moment to gather his thoughts. The words he must speak next had come easily to him when he explained it to Coel's still form in the cold bath house the night before. Pray God, that clarity would not desert him now.

'The king always said that he wanted his grandsons to rule this kingdom. We came up with the name "Reged" to convey that idea of joint kingship – the land of kings. But Myrddin has warned that joint rule would be disastrous, that the tribal leaders will never accept it—'

'So? What business is it of his?' Marchell – diplomatic as ever.

'It is very much his business,' replied Taly. 'As Ninian knows well, Christianity has not yet thoroughly penetrated the Pennines, and Myrddin speaks for the majority of the Southern Brigantes. It would be unwise to underestimate his influence and power. He has no interest in opposing Christianity. Rather, he moves through the dreamworld where omens are shared and the dead speak. We all know that evil exists, that given a chance, it will disrupt fate, causing pain and suffering. Myrddin walks dangerously close to evil's margins, listening carefully for any hint of its plans, seeking to counter and obstruct its diabolical designs. He takes all that he sees, all that he learns, and uses his knowledge to advise the Bear in private counsel. I have received my first briefing in my new role from him, the detail of which was... terrifying. He has seen a threat rising from the east. If we do not prepare to meet it head-on, it will swallow up our territories and enslave all our people.'

'Do you believe him?' Marchell asked, her interest surprisingly genuine.

'I do. Especially now we know that Mor has already witnessed the first signs of this rising threat. The eastern estuaries, in particular the Humber, make us vulnerable. If these easterners find their way through the Aire-to-Ribble passage and make it to this side of the Pennines, we will be cut off from the rest of the Patria and fighting on every front, squeezed like fruit in a press.'

Mor nodded and looked across at Gorwst. 'They are not small bands of raiders, brother; they are more like how Grandfather used to describe the Goths – an infestation.'

'A good comparison.' Taly said. But would it be enough to convince Gorwst and Marchell of the significance of the threat? 'Coel suggested we split the kingdom down the centre from north to south, Gorwst in the west and Mor in the east. But with recent events, I think we should split it from west to east. The northern part of the kingdom centred on Banna in Reged and the southern part at Isurium in Elfed would provide us with our best hope of protecting our territories. I have long thought that you, Gorwst, are the man to succeed Coel as the scourge of the Picts and Scotti. You are admired as a warrior, you work well with our allies, your work ethic is outstanding, and your beautiful queen watches out for you. You must temper your temptation to raid though, and Ninian will be there to help you with difficult decisions. The threat from the east, however, is new, and we do not yet have the measure of it. I am encouraged by Mor's recent alliance with Crannog, but there is still dissent in the Pennine tribes which will cause Mor difficulties if he were to try and rally the tribes, unless he has the Bear by his side. Myrddin believes unity in the tribes is more important than retaining the kingdoms of Reged and Elfed. But I disagree and see it the other way around. These kingdoms, the lands where we make our homes, are our future. The Bear, although still important to the people, is a relic of the past, associated with the old ways… and old gods.' Taly looked directly at Ninian.

'I am relieved you see it this way, Talhaearn.'

'I have thought about this for some time. If we fight for the Bear, we will be going down the wrong path. Coel knew well its power as a rallying cry and used it to its full effect, but we no longer need to raise the standards of the past. Rome is gone and finished, and we are free of those obligations. It is crystal clear to me now that we should fight for our Lord, that He should be our rallying cry. Our tactics, techniques and discipline will not change, but we will have a clear purpose that we know will lead us to Heaven whether we fall on the battlefield or die in our beds.'

A new vigour buzzed through his listeners, his plan meeting with the accord he had hoped for. Maybe it was as masterful as he had secretly told Coel it was during the long vigil in the bath house the night before. Gorwst and Marchell were beaming for the first time since their arrival, but Mor was not looking so convinced.

'Where on earth do we even begin, Taly?' he asked.

'You already have begun, Mor. You began when you brought that Angle prince here as a hostage. It will provoke them, and you and I must go to Elfed as soon as the snow melts, there to make plans to counter these threats. Tomorrow, we bury Coel and say goodbye to the great defender of the Patria. But we should do it knowing that we no longer have need to be afraid, for through both of you, Mor and Gorwst, we have the strength and resolve to vanquish our foes, no matter from which direction they arrive.'

His gaze fell on Brianna. She was smiling, though her eyes were sad. 'And who will tend my garden?' she asked softly.

Taly smiled and reached for her hand. 'There will be children's voices in the hall once more, my sweet, and your hands and heart will be full. Mor needs my help, for he faces great danger from new and unknown threats, the outcome of which will define all our futures, and…' He paused. 'And I'm not much of a gardener.'

'We need drinks to toast our new kingdoms,' called Gorwst. 'Cara, Lynn, Bryn, where are you? Bring some mead.' He clapped Mor on the shoulder then ruffled his younger brother's hair. Mor grinned.

It was good to see the brothers at ease with each other again.

*

Across the yard in Taly's hut, Bryn jumped up when she heard the shouting from the hall.

'I must leave, my love. My mother will be looking for me.'

'You promise you will come to Elfed?'

'If you keep your promise to marry me.'

Cian held her for one last long kiss.

'I regret it must remain a secret until we get there, Bryn, but we mustn't offend my parents.'

'I'm so happy, Cian,' she said. Her cheeks were flushed as she adjusted her hair and chemise. Giving him a bold smile, she grabbed her cloak and ran out of the door.

Cian sat back and gave a quiet whistle. Excitement and happiness sang through his whole body. Taly's hound heard the whistle and lifted his head.

'Plato, you saw and heard nothing.'

The hound put his head back on his paws, looking more than happy to forget all about what he had witnessed.

XIV

Clausentum

Martius 427

Ambrosius reined back his horse as he descended the steep hill toward the little port of Clausentum. The day was clear but cold, and he could see as far as the island of Vectis. There had been a little snow on the high ground around Venta, and patches stood out here and there on the distant island's hills, but by the coast, the snow had not settled, leaving a slippery slush to make the ground treacherous for his horse. His slave, Protus, and his secretary, Briginus, were both encountering similar difficulties with their ponies.

'These conditions are terrible for travelling anywhere, but I must speak with the captain of that boat moored in the harbour before he sets sail.'

His gaze swept over the same coastal inlet where he had first landed as a twelve-year-old boy, some eleven years previous, his fate entrusted to a handful of loyal retainers. Protus had been amongst that trusted group, one of those who had delivered him to his safe haven on Britannia. Every week, he rode to Clausentum to collect mail and hear news of the Empire, and each time, he reflected on how he might avenge the slaughter of his noble family. As a high-born Roman, it was his duty to recover his family's reputation even, perhaps, their property, but conditions had worsened in Gaul and the opportunity for retribution slipped further away with each boat that left the harbour. Emperor Honorius, the architect of his family's destruction, was at last dead, but the remnants of the Theodosian dynasty clung to power even though their influence was a pale shadow of what it had been in his parents' days.

Ambrosius could barely contain his thirst for news as he arrived at the harbour. He had been told that the captain of the boat moored alongside the stone quay had sailed from Bononia, bringing wine in exchange for grain. Some of his information was confirmed as accurate when he saw the deckhands busily offloading amphorae into wooden frames for transportation. Ambrosius waved at the local factor.

'Good morning, Bruccius. My good friend, Nataline, informs me this trustworthy captain is sailing for Bononia?'

'That he is, Ambrosius. If you wish, he will deliver your letters to our trusted factor at the port.'

'Does he have any news of the Empire?'

'He knows only that grain is in short supply, so the cost is rising, but he brought some passengers who have been delayed here in the harbour by this morning's weather – Christian men on their way to the west.'

'I have several letters which Briginus will entrust you to give the captain. Where are these Christian men?'

'They are sat by the fire in my storehouse. Come, follow me.'

Bruccius led Ambrosius' horse to a rail next to the door of the building adjacent to the quay. Dismounting, Ambrosius went inside where three men, all with tonsures, sat in conversation.

'Gentlemen, good morning.' The three monks lifted their heads. 'I am Ambrosius Aurelianus. How was your journey?'

'Stormy, Ambrosius, but God kept us on course. I am Palladius, deacon to Bishop Germanus of Auxerre. These are my companions, Sylvester and Solinus.'

Ambrosius nodded to the monk's companions, but he had recognised the speaker's name.

'Palladius? Son of Exuperantius? My father, Sebastianus, was acquainted with your family.'

Palladius stood and grasped Ambrosius by the arms.

'It is God's miracle you are alive; I see your likeness now. We live in terrible times. My own father was killed three years ago, an army rebellion... There is no longer any order, but perhaps that is God's plan.'

'I am hungry for news, Palladius; will you break from your mission and join me at my home for cena. I will make arrangements for your onward journey tomorrow, or stay longer if you wish?'

'That is a kind offer which we gladly accept,' the deacon replied, looking across at his tired companions.

'Good. Probus, arrange transport for our guests. We shall meet later at my house in Venta Belgarum.'

*

Ambrosius' townhouse was central to the small city of Venta Belgarum which bustled with cives and shopkeepers. Palladius had witnessed urban decay across the Empire, accelerated by barbarian attack, sweeping plagues and neglect of public works as Rome struggled to survive, but Venta Belgarum seemed in reasonable order and relatively secure. The walls were intact and manned by militia, a credit to those in control. If only the rest of the Empire had maintained the old standards, perhaps things would be different.

On their arrival, Probus had met them at the entrance and shown them to their quarters, and now they were sat by a roaring fire with Ambrosius and his young wife Helena. Servants brought food and drink, and lit candles and torches against the encroaching darkness of a winter's evening. Palladius admired the dolphins on the mosaic floor.

'This is fine work, Ambrosius,' he said.

'It is old work but, as you say, remarkable craftmanship. Alas, there are few left here capable of this type of work these days.' He looked at Palladius with a quizzical expression. 'Tell me, is your mission for the Church a secret, or are you at liberty to speak of it?'

'It is sensitive, Ambrosius. We are here at the request of some clerics who fear the spread of the doctrine of a certain Pelagius, a native of this island who is rumoured to have returned from Egypt and now attempts to influence the course of our religion. We are to report back to Bishop Germanus if we find any evidence of his teachings taking hold amongst the population.'

'I see. Fastidius, the former Bishop of Londinium, held some strong opinions, particularly about Roman aristocrats like myself, but I cannot say if his teachings were tainted by Pelagian thought. I have yet to meet his successor, Vodinus. The Britons are always inclined to take their own view on matters!' They all laughed, and Ambrosius continued. 'Is the doctrine of Pelagius heresy, Palladius?'

'It is considered such. The purity of Christian thought must be maintained to ensure that we may all enter the Kingdom of Heaven.'

'Quite so,' replied Ambrosius.

'What of the tragic news we have heard about your father? Can it be true?'

'He was murdered by army mutineers in Arelate, a tragic and treacherous conclusion to a noble life. He was Praetorian Prefect of Gaul and supported the usurper, Joannes, but Empress Galla Placidia sent the forces of the East against him, and his troops changed sides. The Theodosian regime will stop at nothing to maintain what they consider is their God-given birthright.'

'An arrogance I have witnessed to my own personal cost. They treat the Empire and its people like their toys, and they manipulate our religion for their own advantage.' Ambrosius sounded as vexed as Palladius felt with the state of the Empire's leadership. His host gave Palladius a searching look and seemed to come to a decision. Ambrosius continued. 'I sense we are kindred spirits, and you are a man I can trust. I am a wanted man. When still just a child, I was sent here to escape the assassins of Honorius. There is a bounty offered for my head on a spear.'

'You are safe here, young lord. The Empire lurches from crisis to crisis, and it no longer offers anything we in the Church care for. All we require is our freedom to worship the true God. We can save our souls, but we will not save this sad imitation of the glorious Empire we were born into.'

'That is how my family view the situation, but still, we remain unwelcome overlords here in Britannia. Vitalinus or, as he prefers to be known, King Vortigern particularly resents my presence and unfairly attributes any Roman influences to me. As if someone in my position would support any such thing. He fails to grasp my disaffection with the old regime which leaves me no option but to plan for my defence.'

'We were told Britannia is guided by a council?'

'That is true, but the soldiery is under the control of tyrants who we believe purposefully neglect the security needs of their neighbours. Picti and Saxon attacks are becoming too frequent, and there is a suspicion they are being launched from the east of the island. They do not penetrate this far south, but on the far side of the road from Londinium to Deva they are unrelenting. Vortigern has arranged for us all to meet soon to discuss a plan he has devised.'

'I was told there were Christian armies to the north that played a pivotal role in the rebellion against the Empire?' Palladius enquired.

'Ah, yes. Cymry warriors led by King Coel. They defeated the Picti around about the time I arrived here. Their horsemanship is renowned, but their numbers have dwindled, and they struggle to maintain the frontier. Coel is unable to stop the raids that come ashore south of the Pennine region. They are an old confederation of tribes and respond to necessary calls to arms, but they are not a standing force of mercenaries, more a collection of fighting farmers. Coel is now very old, and his only son died in one of his many battles. I know nothing of the next generation.'

This young, educated Roman was providing excellent hospitality. Palladius saw no reason to be in any rush to bring the conversation to a close. 'At least the frontier is intact, despite this island's many vulnerabilities, but I can assure you that conditions on the Continent are far worse. Bishop Germanus attempts to mediate between the Empire's powerful general, Aetius, with his army of Huns, and the needs of his Grace's flock which the general readily neglects and abuses. Aetius quells the enemies of Rome by giving them the lands of

Gallic nobles. The barbarians gratefully receive this property, turning the true owners into slaves and stealing their gold and silver. Many families have been subjected to this sequestration and have given up hope.' He paused to drink. 'Young lord, there is nothing to return for, and nothing that can be done. Make your future here.'

Palladius felt the weight of the awkward silence that followed his pronouncement. He had no doubt that it would have come as a bitter blow to a Roman exile like Ambrosius. From boyhood, the nobleman had probably harboured thoughts of a triumphant return to claim his birthright, taking restitution, even revenge, from those who had stolen so much from him. He studied the man before him and was gladdened to see disappointment turn to gradual acceptance in the set of his shoulders. Ambrosius stole a glance at his wife Helena, heavy with her first child, and sat even straighter.

'Thank you for your advice, Palladius. Both our families have suffered much in these terrible times, but our futures are set. Piety, but with protection, will be my future course, and I will pray to God to relieve me of my bitter resentment for this exile, so that I may come to forgive those who have inflicted it upon me.'

'You must do this, Ambrosius. Otherwise, it will eat away your soul and erode your character, robbing you of your role in this theatre of life.'

Ambrosius nodded in agreement. 'Wise words indeed, Palladius. It is strange to think that I have always thought that I had been made to leave the Empire, when in truth, it was rather the Empire that had left me. That Rome might fall was unthinkable to our parents' generation. When it began to look inevitable, it even led to speculation that Alaric of the Goths was the Antichrist made flesh, but he died. Then his brother, Ataulf, was murdered, I'm told whilst bathing, which is quite an irony for he boasted about how he bathed in the blood of my father and uncles. Now it is Theodoric who faces Aetius... another Goth barbarian.'

'We live in a time when the Empire is more barbarian than Roman, Ambrosius. But look not to the Empire, rather look to the Kingdom of Heaven, for that is how we Christians will inherit the Earth.'

XV

Isurium Brigantum

Spring 427

The sun glinted off the river in the bright spring sunshine as the wagon train approached the walls of Isurium Brigantum. The pink limestone walls of the city seemed to blend with the pungent spring blossoms that decorated the surrounding landscape. Taly was relieved to arrive, after an arduous four-day journey, with the young king's troop and household intact.

Their journey had followed an intense period of planning and preparation. Padell had sought volunteers for the posting, young men mostly, those without commitments, but a long train of artisans and servants had also thrown in their lot with Mor. Taly had meticulously ensured that the younger king had received his fair share of Coel's property – horses and weapons in particular. This even-handedness had created a great deal of friction, particularly with Queen Marchell, but agreements had eventually been reached, and their departure had ultimately proved to be a sad parting. His own goodbyes to Brianna had felt particularly final.

Messengers had been sent to Alwin and Crannog, officially declaring Mor as their king, but neither Taly nor Mor were naïve enough to believe the reaction to such a pronouncement would be free of tension. Cian had been promoted to king's secretary, and Taly had persuaded Lyn to allow Bryn to accompany the new king as his chief housekeeper – though the fierce widow had extracted a solemn oath from Taly that he would personally protect her daughter.

Taly had spent an hour in reflection by Coel's grave on his last evening. His tranquil farewell had been rudely disturbed by the bellow of a bear stood on the cliff above the river. It was a rare sight in those parts, and Taly had watched as it turned and left, heading back toward the uplands. Perhaps it was looking for a mate or a lost cub, but he preferred to think it was Coel saying farewell and good luck. For years, Taly's life had been without purpose; he had often wished for death to speed his way, but now fate had thrust the future of the Patria into his care, giving him no choice but to shake off his dark thoughts and hermit ways. At first, he had given much thought to wondering if this was what Coel had planned all along, but then he had turned away from his suspicions. The how and the why did not matter – his sense of purpose had returned, and life had meaning again.

Both he and Mor shared an apprehensive look as they approached the city gates. They had avoided any expectations of a big welcome at Isurium but were relieved to see that a cheering crowd had gathered, lining the road to the forum where two old comrades who Taly had not seen in ten years waited.

'Greetings, King Mor,' said Alwin, taking hold of the king's reins whilst he dismounted.

'My God, you've aged, prefect… or should I call you Bear, Taly?' said Crannog, delight beaming from his face from the moment he caught sight of his old commanding officer.

'It's good to see you, Crannog, but I note your impudence has not dulled.'

'And I note you're still falling off your horse,' Crannog replied as Taly limped toward him.

Taly looked his old captain up and down. 'I suspect I am still quicker than you, for I see you have fed well all these years.' He slapped Crannog's portly waist. The shared laughter with his old comrade felt good. 'This is Plato. He will show your hounds how to hunt boar.'

The old dog had watched his master's encounter with interest, exercising restraint until his name was mentioned. Now, he bounded over for his introduction.

Taly's old friend, Alwin, was looking characteristically nervous at the prospect of so much imminent change. 'We have repaired one of the better townhouses for the comfort of Your Majesty and… the Bear,' Alwin said, managing to avoid eye contact with Taly, 'but there is much work still to do to accommodate everyone. It has been the planting season, and labour has been short.'

'We shall set everyone to work tomorrow, but first, we must stable and stow our horses and possessions.'

Taly grimaced when he thought of what a tough job that was going to be. Every soldier had brought a spare horse and the wagons each had two horses pulling with two tethered at the rear.

'We have abundant safe pasture between the city wall and the river,' Alwin said, indicating the lush green fields.

'That is excellent. Now, all of these people have useful skills, Alwin, so they will help you with all the extra work, and we have brought plenty of everything. Today, we meet and plan, tomorrow we organise. Where is this townhouse?'

'I will show you,' said Crannog. 'Follow me.'

He led Taly and Mor through some streets that had seen better days and pushed open a gate to a yard which led into some airy, spacious rooms with patterned mosaic floors. Plato followed with his nose to the ground, enjoying the new scents.

'This will make an excellent meeting room,' said Taly, looking round a particularly large and light room.

Mor pointed at the floor. 'What is this supposed to be, Taly?'

Taly and Crannog began to laugh. 'Well, I think it's meant to be Romulus and Remus being suckled by a wolf,' said Taly.

'A wolf!' Crannog chortled. 'With the face of a cat and the arse of a horse!' He gave an apologetic shrug through his mirth. 'It'll be one of Alwin's repairs.'

They howled with more laughter. It felt like no years had passed at all as Crannog's company took Taly back to more carefree times.

Freuleaf seemed to recognise exactly where he was. Cian and Bryn were still charged with setting his daily work detail, and he had accompanied Bryn on the long journey from Banna. Bryn watched him carefully as he looked around the forum, his expression grim.

'You know where you are?' she asked, but he did not reply. 'Help me unload this wagon then.'

The Angle prince dutifully complied but suddenly spoke in the midst of picking up a large, wooden crate. 'Bryn, this place holds bad memories for me.'

'Well, don't be making things worse by shirking your work,' she said, urging him to focus on the job at hand.

His reaction had worried her, and later, she asked Cian to chain him up for the evening, so she could concentrate on her chores.

'He's scared. I'm sure he's going to make a run for it. You need to warn, Taly,' she said to Cian.

*

Alwin laid on food and drink for the arrivals. As darkness fell, it began to rain so they withdrew indoors. Mor, Taly, Crannog, Alwin and Padell sat around the mosaic that had caused so much amusement earlier.

'Tell me, Crannog,' asked Mor, 'are you happy with this outcome to the succession?'

'May I speak openly, my lord?'

'Yes, of course.'

'Your reputation as a warrior king following our battle has spread far, but it has caused as many problems as it has won hearts.'

'How so?'

'Our people are afraid of retaliation. The Angles have been looking for their prince, and some of our homesteads were attacked and burnt before they accepted that he had been taken far to the north, but now you have brought him back, they will surely come again. Do you intend to ransom him?'

'I've not yet decided *what* to do with him,' Mor replied.

'It will not be long before news reaches Eboracum that your army is such a short distance away, and that too will have consequences. Do you have a plan?'

Taly took his cue to answer the question from the look Mor gave him. 'We believe the easterners are planning to unite against the Cymry, so we are here to help defend the western passages and build a militia to secure our boundaries. Removing Gundad from Eboracum will be our first objective.'

'Well, my scouts tell me he has already returned to Guinnon,' Crannog replied. 'We suspect he knew Mor would come, and he has abandoned the city for now, although some of his men are still there.'

Mor had been listening carefully. 'I suspected he might flee. Were it not for the death of my grandfather, we would have dealt with him already.'

'You should be aware that he is still in league with Vortigern,' said Crannog. 'Saxons have been building their homesteads on the land that Vortigern said he would put aside for them, and we have seen many keels on the Humber.'

'That is no surprise to me, but I doubt the Council have any idea that Vortigern has pre-empted an agreement to his proposal. What say you, Taly?'

'We must be prepared for attacks but avoid confrontation where possible. Most importantly, we must establish a forward defensive line, but Isurium is not the right location for it.'

'I agree,' said Crannog. 'At the edge of the Pennines, in the Forest of Elfed, there are high hills from which the whole Humber estuary and Aire Valley may be viewed – that is where we should build our defences. The Romans called it Cambodunum, and our ancestors built a great fort there. My people of Loidis will feel safer with your presence, and I'm sure it will attract new recruits to us.'

Mor nodded then turned to Padell. 'Go and fetch Cian; I wish to speak with him.'

Padell did not take long to find Cian. When the lad joined the meeting, he sat down alongside Taly.

'How are your fighting skills?' asked Mor.

'I am fully trained, my lord, but my experience extends no further than a single skirmish.'

'Is the Angle boy a trained fighter?'

'I'm not sure, my lord, but I suspect not. I think sailing and navigation are more his areas of expertise.'

'I want you to train him. Be harsh, push him hard. I want him black and blue by tomorrow night.'

'I am chaining him up tonight, my lord. We suspect he may consider escape now that he knows he is close to his home.'

'That's good thinking. Now, carry on, Cian.'

The young man left the room.

'What are you up to, Mor?' asked Taly.

'I have a plan for our hostage.'

*

Cian returned to the kitchen where Bryn and Freuleaf were finishing their labours.

'I have some bread and cheese for you both.' Bryn directed them to sit.

Cian spoke Latin to the boy.

'The king has instructed me to teach you to fight with a sword.'

Freuleaf looked surprised and repeated Cian's statement in his Germanic language to Bryn. She too looked surprised.

'What's going on, Cian?' she asked.

'I really don't know, but those are my orders, and I am to be harsh with him. Now, tell him to eat up, so I can chain him up for the night.'

Bryn gave him one of her stern looks that she had inherited from her mother. 'The king gave his word no harm would come to him.'

'Then give him that comfort for now, but by tomorrow night, he will be bruised and sore from the blows I have been ordered to inflict.'

*

Cian was awake long before dawn and set off to the barracks to locate practice swords, staves and shields. When he shook Freuleaf to wake him, the Angle prince looked startled then apprehensive. Cian released him from his manacles and indicated that he should help with carrying the equipment.

The wispy clouds reflecting the approaching dawn light suggested a fine day, so Cian had decided to train on the meadow grass outside the city walls. The meadow was a sea of daisies and dandelions still damp from the rain the night before – it would be slippery underfoot, but at least the landing would be soft.

First, they sat together on the practice shields whilst Cian explained the theories of warfare in stilted Latin, the same theories he had been taught at a similar age. Padell had been his teacher, and the seasoned warrior was notoriously meticulous about detail and discipline. Cian could still hear him now. *The Romans conquered the world through discipline*, he would say, followed by, *Practice, practice and more practice, and when you think you've mastered the skills, practice again and again and then some more*. Padell had gained his considerable experience whilst serving alongside Coel and Taly; he knew what he was talking about.

After the tuition came the practice. Cian started the lad off with staves, repeating attack and parry over and over again, until he indicated it was time to fight properly. At first, he knocked Freuleaf to the ground every time, but the lad got back up again and again, and Cian had to admire the youth's courage. Freuleaf's drive and determination soon began to pay off, and he managed to get a few blows past Cian's defence. The bright sun rose in the sky. All around them, Mor's newly arrived warriors and household got on with their work, but the two young men barely noticed any of it. Soaked in sweat, they fought on relentlessly. The boy's resolve was truly impressive. It was around midday when Taly's voice cut through Cian's concentration.

'How's he getting on?' his mentor shouted across the meadow.

'Very well – he has many bruises already!'

'I would say he's beginning to dislike you.'

Bryn joined Taly and indicated the water and bread she carried. 'Food for the gladiators,' she announced. Her expression turned to one of shock when she noticed Freuleaf's condition. 'What have you done to him? He's a complete mess!'

'He's been rolling around on the ground a lot,' Cian said, not sure why he felt he needed to defend himself.

He was sure he saw Taly smother a smile before he turned to Bryn. 'The king wishes to speak with you, Bryn; he has some special duties for you.'

'What? More than I have already.'

Taly did not bother to hide his smile this time. 'Do you know how much you sounded like your mother just then?'

Bryn thumped him playfully on the arm then set off back to the gate.

'Taly,' Cian shouted, 'will you help me show the boy a thrust and parry exercise with these shields?'

Taly obliged, and they demonstrated the exercise, first at half-speed, pulling their blows, then building up to battle tempo with full-weight blows. Taly handed the sword and shield to Freuleaf, saying in Latin, 'Good luck, he is a skilled warrior.'

Once more, Cian followed up the tuition with intense combat training. As exhaustion set in, the boy began to take a battering, unable to hold his shield up high enough, so Cian called a break, and they rested for a while under a tree to get out of the strong sun.

'Why is your king teaching me to fight? Am I not his enemy?' asked Freuleaf.

'I don't know his reasoning. Perhaps he will tell you when we have finished.'

'How much longer till we finish?' said Freuleaf. 'I have never been so blistered and bruised.'

'A turn with the staves and another with the sword should take us to sundown,' Cian said.

They only stopped raining blows on each other to take an occasional water break, and it was late afternoon before they finally put their practice weapons down. Cian held in a groan when he saw the king and Taly walking toward them with steel swords and alder shields. The combatants stood to attention as the king reached them. Mor spoke in Latin so the boy could understand.

'Well done, men. Now, I wish you to fight with real weapons until one of you yields.'

Cian was sure that his expression reflected the same surprise and anxiety that was all over Freuleaf's face. But he felt an odd pride when the lad obeyed the king and reached for his sword and shield with the same certainty as Cian. Without warning, Freuleaf charged at Cian like a galloping horse, perhaps thinking attack was superior to defence. The sound of clashing steel brought spectators to the wall and out of the gate. Freuleaf fought hard with his newly acquired skills and showed great courage. It took Cian longer than he had expected to overcome the Angle prince, eventually forcing the boy to the ground with a series of blows so powerful that they shattered Freuleaf's shield and wounded his forearm.

'Well fought. Impressive defence,' the king shouted as Taly rushed between them, wisely removing their swords before the mounting intensity of the encounter turned any more bloody. Relieved that the wound was only slight, Cian swiftly ripped off a piece of his sweat-sodden shirt and wrapped it around the youth's arm, tying it tight to stop the bleeding. The crowd finished their cheering then went about their duties. Cian indicated to Freuleaf that he should take a moment to catch his breath, then he handed him one of the wooden ladles, filled to the brim with water. In unison, they swallowed large draughts of cool, sweet water.

'Cian, you have trained him well. Join me for cena later; tomorrow, we scout Eboracum in advance of the main recovery operation, and we must make plans.'

Cian nodded, trying not to frown. Why was Mor speaking so loudly in Latin and in such a theatrical manner?

The king continued. 'Prince Freuleaf, I want you to know that you may return as a friend or fellow soldier whenever you so choose. But wherever you have a choice of what direction to take, consider taking the path to our God because His way is truth and honour.'

Taly picked up a pot that he had brought from the fort and coated one of the retrieved swords with what looked like blood. He then proceeded to smear and splatter the boy with what was left in the pot.

*

Freuleaf flinched away, bemused and a little frightened, until the king explained in Latin.

'It's pig's blood, do not fear, lad. You have escaped. You overcame three guards, killing one of them, and you have stolen a coracle from the quayside. The river flows quickly south, but beware, we will fall upon Eboracum in a matter of days, and I will not want to find you there. Now...' The old warrior they called Taly handed him the gore-covered sword. 'Run for your life!'

Freuleaf turned his aching body and ran with all the strength he could muster toward the quay. Waiting by the river, next to a coracle, was beautiful Bryn. She thrust a muslin cloth containing food into his free hand.

'Farewell, my friend.' She kissed his cheek and held the coracle as he climbed aboard. He used the moment to will away the rising colour in his cheeks then turned toward her.

'Farewell, Bryn, you are what we call "good people". If Cian doesn't marry you, I certainly will!'

He was pleased to see that it was her turn to colour, her cheeks flushing red as she blew him a kiss and pushed him off from the bank. Within a few seconds, he was paddling downstream to freedom.

*

Mor helped Taly and Cian carry the training weapons back to the fort.

'There is no honour in ransom,' he said, feeling the weight of his companions' curiosity in their silence. 'The boy will deliver our message, gaining the respect of his tribe at the same time as he alerts them to our intentions.'

Taly smiled. 'Coel used to say, *A good general wins his battles, but a clever general achieves his objectives without ever having to fight.*'

Cian looked comically at them both. 'I've been fighting all day long!'

They were all still laughing when they reached the forum, but the look on Crannog's face brought their mirth to an abrupt stop. He looked toward them, stepping away from the messenger on horseback he had been talking to.

'This is one of my men, Mor. He brings news that more of our people's homesteads have been attacked and burnt. They murdered the adults, stole their cattle and took their children as slaves.'

'Who are "they"? Do we know?'

'A trader returning to Loidis found a severely injured survivor on the Ryknild road. He told of a savage attack at a place called Caintley, but he could not identify the assailants.'

'Is Caintley east of here?' asked Taly.

'Apologies, I forget your unfamiliarity with this region. Caintley is to the east of Danum, in a clearing in the Great Forest.'

This was concerning news. Mor looked to Taly, guessing they were having the same thoughts.

'If Myrddin's prophecy is true, we will not always be able to protect such settlements, but we must offer the survivors sanctuary,' said Taly, affirming Mor's direction of thought. 'Where is the Ryknild road, Crannog?'

'It runs south-west to Derventio and skirts the Great Forest. Nobody uses the roads through the Great Forest anymore out of fear for their lives – Ryknild follows higher ground but can itself be a dangerous journey.'

Mor could find no fault with Crannog's anger and frustration; he had the same feelings himself, and *he* had not spent his whole life on these lands, with these people.

'I had intended to scout Eboracum first, but this changes our priorities. Instruct your messenger to go to Cambodunum and tell them that I will be bringing a troop there in two days. We will start work on our fortress so that we have a strong forward defence as soon as possible, somewhere secure to send our patrols out from. Where is Padell?'

'He's training the boat crews for our assault on Eboracum,' said Taly.

'Inform him of this change of plan. I suspect our ruse will have already taken effect. Eboracum is likely deserted by now, and that is why the threat has moved further south.'

Winning the hearts of the people was more important than recovering an empty derelict city. Mor had no plan to garrison Eboracum; he had intended its recovery as nothing more than a show of dominance. Clearing the Ouse of Saxons and protecting his subjects was a much more important objective.

'Lord Crannog, tomorrow we will set out to find these children and avenge their parents' murders. I swear upon God's name, to you and your people, that Saxons will learn to fear Elfed; every outrage they commit will be met with five-fold retribution.'

*

Taly set off to find Padell. As he walked down the path to the quay, he met Bryn walking slowly back to the fort, picking flowers from the hedgerow.

'These are for the king's chamber,' she said a little defensively.

He is certainly becoming a king, he thought. *Now he is out of his brother's shadow, he is showing that he has Coel's wisdom and confidence.*

'He will appreciate the flowers, Bryn.'

Taly walked on. The horrors of war were closing in around him once again. 'Dear Lord, will it ever end?'

A summer breeze tugged at the trees, and blossom fell on the path before him.

'Probably never!' he said, answering the question for himself.

XVI

A large villa to the north of Corinium

Julius 427

Viracus watched as the tonsured bishop paced up and down waiting to be admitted for an audience with King Vortigern. It had been a hot day, and the intensity of the sun must have made Agricola's three-hour ride from Corinium uncomfortable. He certainly looked flushed and agitated, but at least it was cool in the corridor. One of the many servants carrying platters and amphorae to the king and his guests stopped on his way back to the kitchens and whispered to Viracus.

'We may enter now,' Viracus said.

He escorted Agricola into the large room and watched with amusement when the bishop's look of relief that his audience was about to begin became one of apprehension when confronted with such an illustrious gathering of military leaders.

'Come and sit with us, Agricola.'

'Thank you, my lord.'

The bishop sat in front of the men whilst Viracus took up his place, standing adjacent.

'How is Corinium?'

'Busy as ever. It is pleasant to be in the countryside although a little too warm for long rides.'

'Yes, I can imagine. Here, won't you partake of the wine, water and food we have prepared for you?'

A servant responded to Vortigern's invitation and placed food and drink before the bishop.

'Let me formally introduce you to my companions,' said the king. 'This is Conomor of Dumnonia. He passed through Corinium only yesterday.' The oldest man of the group raised his right hand in wordless greeting. 'This is my brother-in-law and general, Viktor Caninus.' He gestured at the middle-aged man to his left and then turned to his right. 'And this is Cunevindus, a prince from Viroconium.' The last to be introduced was the youngest man in the room but the largest. Muscular with the neck of a bull, he was wearing the clothing of a hunter.

Both men raised their right hand in acknowledgement. These were the four most powerful men in the west of Britannia – Viracus did not envy Agricola the task of navigating the discussion to come.

'My lords, the king knows I am an adherent of the Briton, Pelagius, and preach both his and my father's enlightened views to an expanding flock. I have no wish to separate from the Church of Rome, but it seeks to isolate and discredit me.'

'I see you are not a native Briton,' said Conomor, looking pointedly at Agricola's dark complexion. 'What brought you here?'

'I am from Carthage; my father, Bishop Severianus, was a friend of Pelagius. I came to Britannia to seek out and study under Bishop Fastidius. Only recently, he sadly died, but I hold the see of Corinium with his and'—he looked toward the king and bowed his head—'King Vortigern's approval.'

'You are a fine bishop, Agricola,' Vortigern added, as he continued to eat.

Conomor looked intrigued. 'What does the Roman Church find so distasteful about Pelagian thought? Is it because he was a Briton?' They all laughed apart from Agricola.

'The Roman Church is run mostly by retired soldiers and civil servants. They worship conformity and control. Pelagius and my father dared to interpret the scriptures in a manner which recognises our free will and individual right to redemption. In other words, we can all reach God without the Church and its prelates.'

Conomor smiled. 'This is a liberal interpretation that our continental friends will loath. Is Pelagius correct, do you think?'

'I believe so, my lord.'

'So, Agricola, tell my comrades of your experience.' Vortigern made a gesture to hurry him along.

'In Martius, a certain Palladius with two companions came to Corinium via Venta Belgarum. After a brief stay with the local leader, Ambrosius Aurelianus, they sought me out, questioning my faith and casting doubts upon my training, credentials and conduct. Palladius is a deacon to Germanus, Bishop of Auxerre, the Roman noble and ex-military commander.'

All three men looked at Vortigern, their expressions sharp and knowing.

'They accused me not just of heresy but also acquiescence to the annexation of Church property by tyrants. They then left the way they came, returning to Auxerre.'

Viracus had been present when Vortigern had initially been advised of both the visit by Palladius and its purpose, but he sensed that the reason for Agricola's journey this day was more immediate, for something more pressing than updating Vortigern's allies on religious squabbles from the Continent.

'Yesterday, I received a letter from Bishop Germanus.' Agricola pulled a scroll from his satchel. 'I am to desist preaching the doctrine of Pelagius upon threat of excommunication, and I am to advise the tyrants who have stolen the land and estates of Melania to return them to the Church.'

There was a stunned silence.

A look passed between the four Briton leaders, and Viktor Caninus turned to the bishop. 'Please, enjoy the food and drink whilst we discuss this between ourselves.'

They switched from Latin to Cymry. Viracus noted that, though Agricola would not be able understand what was being said, he could not miss the aggression in their tone.

'Germanus? Who is this arrogant bastard?' exclaimed Conomor.

'According to my sources, he is a man of influence. He has the ear of the great and the powerful, in particular Aetius,' said Vortigern.

'Does this indicate a change of policy toward their former territories here; should we be worried?' asked Viktor Caninus.

Vortigern looked calm.

'Worried, no, but mindful, yes. When our parents finally ejected the Roman officials, they waited to see if Rome might return. It has now been seventeen years, and our generation has become bold in the long absence. We have taken over the property of landlords who either deserted it or will never fulfil their promise to return. Their slaves ran away leaving estates to fall into ruin. Look around you – this great estate is one that belonged to Melania, but where are the people who ran it? This is now our property and no longer belongs to absentee landlords masquerading as prelates. The only Roman landlord still on this island is Aurelianus who, like our friend Agricola here, ran away to Britannia to escape the Empire.'

Conomor had been listening with a look of concentration furrowing his brow. 'Our mutual neighbour, Ambrosius Aurelianus, is popular. He maintains Roman law and religion. His militia are trained like Roman soldiers. We would do well to befriend him, particularly since I have heard that Londinium wish for him to represent them on the Council now that Fastidius has died.'

'Surely he has benefited as much as we have from not having to pay taxes? We are all wealthy men now. Why bring back the Romans? He must understand the advantages of our independence from the Empire?' exclaimed Viktor Caninus.

'It is the eastern cives, barricaded in their towns to defend against relentless raids, who scream for a return of the Romans. Men like Aurelianus are born to wealth, and now he fools himself into believing that he is no longer pursued for his dead father's follies and that he has more in common with Aetius and Germanus than he does with us.'

Cunevindus spoke for the first time. 'Why don't we just kill him?'

The big man looked around, beaming in self-congratulation as if he had just made a clever comment.

'Perhaps it will come to that but be advised – it would not be the Roman legions who get sent to our shores but their pet barbarians – Alans, Huns, even Goths – and they are brutal.' Vortigern shook his head. 'These men of the Church are naïve to think we will do what they ask out of subservient Christian piety.'

Vortigern now switched back to Latin.

'Have no fear, Agricola. We wholeheartedly support you and your special branch of Christianity. In our opinion, it is not necessary to reply to this letter. Go about your duties and shepherd your flock for now, but I have an offer for you. Our magnificent newly built church in Viroconium is presently without a bishop. I would like you to take up that position and worship the Lord without the fear of interference and threats from Roman bishops. We are holding a Council there in September and would be honoured if you would agree to travel with us then and take up your see thereafter?'

Agricola looked delighted to be relieved of the responsibility of recovering Church lands from the Briton warlords. 'Thank you, my lords. That is an offer I would be honoured to accept.'

'So, gentlemen,' Vortigern said, reverting to his native tongue, 'it looks as if we will be facing Aurelianus at the next Council meeting. It will be a stormy encounter. King Mor and King Gorwst are unlikely to support my proposal of foederati-paid Saxon mercenaries. The northern tribes present no threat to us since they are occupied defending their northern frontier, but we should never underestimate their strengths. The Pennines harbour a different world to our civilised lands, one which even the Romans could not master. The Brigantes, out of necessity, can be as savage as the Picts, Scotti and the Saxons. I predict they will not oppose our plan, but they will not participate either. If we can convince them to reluctantly agree, that will suffice. They, like us, do not want the Romans to return, but we must keep their forces pointing north. The Saxon Shore from the Humber round to Rutupiae will be our defence from Pictish raids and a deterrent against the return of the Romans, but we must stay alert – these Saxons play a double game, robbing us with one hand whilst waving a sword pretending to defend us with the other. Mor is no fool, and his encounter with Saxons north of the Humber following my visit was an unfortunate affair, especially for Gundad. He will be wary at Council.'

'Has he replied to your request for a meeting, Vitalinus?' Conomor enquired.

'Not yet, but a journey to Viroconium will suit him better than one to Londinium, and perhaps it will be too far for Aurelianus to travel, enabling us to appoint the Saxon federates without interference from the south.'

'Was that your reason for calling the meeting so far to the north-west?' asked Cunevindus, grinning in undisguised admiration for the guile of his leader.

Vortigern smiled. 'Magnus Maximus visited Viroconium many times. It is a fitting location for our guests, and it is midway.'

Vortigern turned to the bishop who had been waiting patiently, unable to follow the discussion. The king spoke again in Latin.

'Agricola, will you stay? I have some special entertainment laid on for these men.'

'Thank you, but no, King Vortigern; I will enjoy the ride back in the cool of the evening but many thanks again. May the Lord be with you.'

The bishop's hurry to leave was likely a consequence of him being aware of Vortigern's reputation. Viracus smothered a smirk. The man of God would not want to get caught up in an evening likely to rival Sodom or Gomorrah, but he was clearly so pleased to have the warlords' support and his new appointment that he would not voice his disapproval. As Viracus escorted the bishop from the room, he saw Agricola's attention drawn to a line of young, scantily dressed slave-girls who stood outside laden with fruit, food and drink, waiting to gain access. He turned to Viracus.

'Where is the queen?'

A captain of the Cornovii guard, Viracus' loyalty lay firmly with Queen Sevira. Most men enjoyed the company of young, compliant slave-girls, but Vortigern was obsessed with them, his behaviour overt and outrageous.

'She will be at prayer,' Viracus replied blandly.

The bishop nodded and left.

Yes, she is at prayer, thought Viracus – *one hundred miles from here*. That beautiful woman's honour abused by these Dobunni oafs! Viracus liked to think his queen was in love with him, and he enjoyed their secret letters and briefings. Perhaps, one day, she might consider him... No matter. He would spare her the detail of this orgy as he did all the others, though she was too intelligent not to know all about her husband's constant infidelity.

Viracus resumed his post by the door.

XVII

On the Road to Viroconium

Early September 427

They could ill afford the time, but Mor had been summoned to Council. Taly had already agreed with Marchell that on this occasion he and Mor would jointly represent Reged and Elfed, as a show of unity, but thereafter, Reged would send its own representative. In truth, he wondered if Vortigern's long-term plan was to disband the Council because he was certainly doing a very good job of undermining its authority. With so much still to do, they could barely justify the ten-day trip, but Mor had received a letter from Queen Sevira. She had already invited him to stay at her villa to meet her cousin when they had met at Eboracum, but this letter was insistent that he take up the invite whilst indicating she had reason to fear for the future. Mor had shown the letter to Taly, and they had both agreed it was too intriguing to ignore.

Elfed was safe enough for them to leave it in Crannog's hands. The old veteran's choice of the Brigantes' earthworks of Cambodunum for their forward defence had been inspired, and they had successfully completed the perimeter stockade before departing. It would serve as sufficient defence against the occasional skirmishes with marauding brigands from the Great Forest. The Angles and Saxons on the Humber had yet to test them and were unlikely to do so now, not this late into the season. Rather than taking a full troop that would attract attention and deplete Elfed's defences, Mor and Taly had decided to travel incognito with only two riders, chosen by Crannog, to act as escort. One was Crannog's son, Winnog, who had travelled the route many times, and the other was Spurcio, a powerfully built German veteran. Riding by his side, Taly was keen to hear about Spurcio's adventures.

'Crannog tells me you were an officer with the German foederati?'

'Yes, that is so, prefect,' he replied in his heavy accent. 'My unit defended Ratae until a Saxon raid destroyed it. That's when I threw in my lot vis Crannog – I like him; he is funny.'

'Indeed,' replied Taly. 'I find him so too. I am told you know the Great Forest?'

The German's laugh was deep and guttural. 'I vos chased through it by Saxon scum; it is full of zem!'

'No Picts then?'

'No.' The answer was emphatic.

'What about you, Winnog?' asked Taly. 'Have you heard of Picts raiding along this road?'

'Never. The forest is a hundred miles long and thirty miles wide. There are deer, wolves, bears, brigands and Saxons, but no Picts!'

*

It took them two days to reach Derventio, making good progress past the lead-mining district where activity seemed to have completely ceased. The fort and town were abandoned and derelict but provided temporary shelter for a night. Mor thought it looked like a ghost town with no one left to tell of the fate of the people who had lived and worked there. Lead mining had suffered in the same way further north, but Spurcio looked particularly uneasy and checked every building still standing just in case the rumours of Picts raiding in this region had some truth to them. Mor had only ever seen raiding as a burden for the North to bear; he had not appreciated that the problem had become so widespread.

'So, Spurcio, would you say the raiders land on the Humber and then either sail up the Trent or use this forest to hide their keels and cover their movements?' Mor asked.

'That is how it vorks in this territory, my lord.'

'That's what I thought,' Mor said, unrolling his cloak. 'I'll take first watch.' He turned to Taly. 'You remember that tribute we got from Gundad which appeared to be made up of looted property? Do you think he is in league with these forest brigands?'

Taly reflected before replying. 'Raiding is abhorrent. It is unchristian. "Thou must not steal" is one of the commandments we are sworn to live by, but raiding has become a plague amongst the tribes. These thieves have settlements in the forest right under our noses, but the Cymry are no better. Gorwst and Coroticus miraculously acquire Scotti gold and slaves whilst Ninian looks the other way. Their argument seems to be that it is morally acceptable to steal from heathens but not vice versa.'

Mor was amused. 'Property is a concept evolved by those who first stole it.'

Taly laughed. 'Our king is a philosopher!'

'Hardly. But I am a pragmatist. If so much loot is changing hands in this region, perhaps it is time we disrupted their routines and took advantage of their complacency. It seems they have had it easy for too long. We might even save some poor souls from slavery. What say you, Spurcio?'

'Stealing from thieves is dangerous. The enemy vill not relent; vee can expect that our new fort will become their target, and if we are to do this, we must expect to have to kill them all.'

Winnog joined the discussion. 'My father, much to his frustration, has never been able to take such a step. He has only ever retained a handful of warriors, whereas these Saxons rove the countryside in large bands and do not hesitate to murder and steal. Most of our people are farmers, not soldiers.'

Mor looked at Taly. 'We must become both. Isn't that so, Taly?'

'It is, my lord. Coel believed the best defence lies in attack, and we know this canker is prophesied to grow to terrifying proportions. As Spurcio said, we will have to kill all who come at us, if we are to secure our territories and protect our people.'

'Fear not, Winnog,' said Mor, 'we will ensure our people are ready before we take the fight to our enemy; we will not run until we can first walk. I am four months amongst your people and our plans are yet to formulate beyond ideas, but I see irreversible change wherever I look. The time of the Romans is over, and only strong kingdoms will survive these times. Our worst enemy might yet prove to be hesitation.'

'It will be interesting to hear how all the other provinces are faring; it is hard to picture what threats to the comfort of their everyday lives they face?' Taly reflected

'Vortigern gave an impression of great prosperity when we last met.'

'Yes, perhaps it is only the North that has suffered such change,' Taly added.

'Tomorrow, we follow the mighty River Trent,' said Winnog. 'The Saxons cannot get their keels beyond the point where we meet the river, and the countryside will be less threatening from there.'

'Good, I vill feel more at ease after tomorrow,' said Spurcio.

*

The evening and night passed without incident, although Spurcio said that he thought he heard voices at one point. A mist had formed in the night and was swirling around Derventio in the dawn light, lending an eerie appearance to the deserted buildings. They were all relieved to mount their horses and follow the road out of the town. After an hour or so, the route ran parallel to the River Trent which coiled like a snake, flowing sometimes near and sometimes in the distance, but always following the same direction.

Mor drew alongside Taly.

'I've always admired your stallion,' he said, watching the horse's movement with a practised eye.

'I've trained this one well. One of his predecessors, also called Jet, broke his leg on the battlefield, and I was badly injured in the fall.'

'I think I remember that from when I was a small boy. Fighting from horseback is the strength of our northern army; a well-trained horse is worth three men on the ground.'

Taly nodded in agreement. 'We will need to focus on our skills and strengths, because we cannot afford the huge armies of the Romans. Raiders know they have superior numbers. The Saxon keels carry forty men or more – that's a lot of warriors to counter, particularly in a surprise attack. We are more familiar with repelling the Scotti raids, with their smaller boats which carry less men, and their access is restricted to a limited stretch of coastline.'

'That is true. The Saxon raids are large, and this river allows their keels to easily penetrate to the centre of the Patria.'

The day's journey was a pleasant one; the road was easy to follow, and since the summer had been dry, it was firm going for the horses, but once again, there were no other travellers and very little evidence of people.

'Is this route usually so deserted?' Mor asked Winnog.

'No, my lord, it has always been bustling with travellers when I have travelled along it on previous occasions.'

As they drew close to Letocetum, they could see a fortified barricade built across the road and the spears of guards on the walls and gate towers.

'Well, at least *this* town is not deserted, so there may be food and drink here,' said Spurcio.

As they reached the gate, the soldier in command shouted, 'Identify yourselves!'

Taly replied, 'We are soldiers of the northern army travelling to Viroconium on official business.'

A spear was waved, and they passed through the entrance between the towers. Mor spotted some men sat drinking outside what looked like an old Roman mansio. He nodded toward them, and the others followed his lead, dismounting and leading their horses over to the drinkers.

'Is there stabling nearby we can hire?' Mor asked politely.

'The smith has left, but the stables are over there next to the wall. Have you seen any Picts on your journey?'

'Picts?' replied Mor. 'We haven't seen any for months... unless you count all the Pictish heads mounted on our militia's spears.'

The man's companions grinned. Mor caught sight of an officer of the local militia heading in their direction. Reaching them quickly, the man addressed the group in an urgent manner.

'May I ask about your journey?'

'Of course,' Mor replied.

'We have reports of a marauding band of Picts who were last seen in the hills to the east.'

'We have travelled from the north, soldier, and have seen none. If they are Picts, they are surely lost?'

'You might think so, but that is our information. Raids in the countryside have increased around here, farms and villages are deserted. You are the first travellers for several days.'

'Who is your commanding officer?' asked Taly.

'We are a unit of the cohort of the Cornovii, our commander is Cunevindus. You are representatives of our Protectors in the North? My father often spoke warmly of his time serving at Pons Aelius with the northern army.'

'Thank you, soldier. I remember the cohort and am honoured to have fought alongside them.'

'The road from here to Viroconium is safe,' said the soldier, before returning to the tower by the gate.

They stabled and watered their horses then secured lodgings for the night. Spurcio looked pleased to be able to eat in comfort, and the group enjoyed a relaxing meal in the security of the fort. Mor couldn't stop pondering the idea that Picts could have travelled so far south.

'They have not come by land, so how are they here and what are their intentions?'

Taly was also intrigued. 'We defeated and killed Talorc, but Drest, the new king, Talorc's former rival, consolidates his power and has ceased raids on the Great Wall region. Talorc had many brothers, so I'm wondering if this is a rogue adventurer in league with the Saxons?'

'We will need to be careful on the return journey for, whoever they are, they are surely camped in the Great Forest,' Mor cautioned.

Taly looked at Mor. 'I am beginning to wonder if these events are all connected to Myrddin's prophecy. I sense fear in these people. We have lived on frontiers all our lives, and we are accustomed to such stresses, but these have always been the safe, protected mid-lands of the Patria – how is it that this sanctuary now finds itself on the edge of Hell?'

'The Council will surely be able to explain it when we see them.' Mor paused, considering their next move. 'We are two days early, so I propose to first call on Queen Sevira – her family's estate is not five miles from the city, and I am keen to meet her cousin.' Mor winked at Taly.

'Then we shall find out if the stories are true even sooner than I had feared,' Taly replied, his expression serious.

'Which stories are those?' Mor asked cautiously.

'That Cornovian women are ugly and beat their husbands.'

The group roared with laughter.

XVIII

Lactodurum

Early September 427

'My God, this journey is without end!' exclaimed Nataline.

Ambrosius agreed. 'Yes, my friend, but it is pointless to hurry; our horses will stay fresh at this pace, and we have three further days travel before we reach Viroconium.'

'I think Vitalinus is purposefully inconveniencing us all, and this old Roman armour isn't helping – the chafing gets worse with every mile.'

'He's testing our resolve. He sees us as Roman rivals to his political ambitions, perhaps he even sees us as his enemies. It seems only fair that we look and act the part.' Ambrosius had ensured that his troop's uniform and equipment were in keeping with Roman tradition, and so far, the response had proved enlightening. 'Have you not noted how warm our reception has been along our route? The cives think we are representatives from Rome, and their relief that order and security will be restored is palpable.'

'Thirty recruited cavalry men hardly constitutes the return of Rome's protection, Ambrosius.'

'It is a start, a signal. They will see that our intention is clear. Look! I see our meeting place.'

'Ah, yes. It looks deserted. Call the captain to send scouts ahead.'

They watched as two cavalry men galloped toward the town and cautiously inspected the gateway. A waving sword glinted in the sunlight, and the troop continued their slow journey.

Ambrosius turned to his fellow estate owner.

'This is the furthest north I have travelled in Britannia. We are close to the first frontier beyond Lactodurum, where I am told the landscape changes – forests then mountains.'

'Apparently so, who would have thought that such a small province would be subject to such a pronounced north–south divide?'

'Indeed. The cives beyond this point have endured the brunt of the raiding over the years. I am curious to see how they respond to our apparel.'

'Are you sure you are not taking yourself too seriously? I will just be relieved to make it to our destination without being attacked! I suspect the northern peasants have little love for Roman rule.'

'That sentiment will only last until they realise how defenceless they are without us.'

The troop filed through the unguarded gate and proceeded to the central forum where their meeting was arranged. Sat in the evening sunshine outside the mansio that was now an inn were Didius and Elafius, the magistrates of Londinium and Verulanium. Ambrosius and Nataline dismounted as their troop filed past toward the town stables.

'Greetings, gentlemen,' Ambrosius said, walking toward them.

'Greetings, Ambrosius, Nataline. That is an impressive troop, a rare sight these days,' said Didius, the elder of the two.

The new arrivals sat down, joining their companions in the evening sunshine. Elafius signalled to the innkeeper to bring four more beers.

'Viroconium is still three days from here. This is a significant inconvenience that Vitalinus puts us all to! Six hard days on the road. I hope his solution to stop the raiders is worth this trip,' grunted Didius to his companions.

'It is a blatant show of power,' said Elafius, 'but we do need his help.'

'I think he wants us to understand how sheltered we have been from the frontier, until now, what an expanse of territory we must protect, and whilst Viroconium is far away to us, it is the closest city to the centre of the Patria,' said Ambrosius. 'Representatives of the northern army will be there. Brigantes from the Great Wall.'

'Prepare to be shocked gentlemen; they are quite savage,' said Didius.

'Who will represent the eastern colonae?' Ambrosius asked.

'Apparently some local tribal leaders who have remained – most cives have fled, unable to withstand the repeated attacks. Lindum has neither a magistrate nor a bishop,' said Elafius. 'The cornfields by the Trent have not been planted for some years, and the entire province is facing famine. This could be why the Saxons and Picts have started to attack further afield, reaching closer to our own lands.'

'There must be vast tracts of the eastern region where agriculture has become nigh on impossible,' said Didius. 'Vortigern's lands may not have been subject to *these* attacks, yet, but let us not forget that Scotti have been raiding western shores for hundreds of years.'

'Yes,' replied Nataline. 'But the west is a rugged coastline which the Cymry know well, and whilst the Scotti raids are troublesome, they are more easily repelled.'

'Vitalinus is arrogant, but he is no fool,' said Ambrosius, keeping his voice hushed, 'and he calls this Council meeting as a means of endorsing his decisions. He fears a return of Rome which would be a disaster for his ambitions, given that he has assumed that absent landlords will not return and has illegally acquired their properties. Some of these properties border our own, and the Church is alert to these outrageous practices. Palladius has informed me of the Roman Church's concerns. Bishop Germanus has written to our bishops asking that they seek the restitution of Melania's properties to the Church, but without Roman soldiers to enforce the command, nothing will be done about it. It is unlikely that the Western Empire will reunite, so perhaps, we should all just try to salvage what we can.'

'I hope you are not suggesting we all behave like Vortigern?' said Elafius.

'Of course not, but we must be realistic and protect what is ours.'

Everyone nodded in agreement, and Ambrosius continued.

'It will be interesting to hear the North's opinion, but I doubt it will differ from that of Vitalinus. All these men we are travelling to meet believe in the authority of the Emperor-sanctioned military appointments they hold, Magnus Maximus' so-called "Protectors", so let's hold them to their commissions.'

'Vortigern considers you a threat, Ambrosius,' said Elafius.

'That is why I look forward to meeting him. My father faced the Goths; I am not afraid to face this King Vortigern, but in truth, he is wrong to think that I seek to undermine him. He controls a greater portion of the Patria than anyone else and is keen to let us all know that he is most senior on the Council, so it is his responsibility to find a way to help the eastern people and prevent raiders reaching further into the Patria.'

'That's true,' said Elafius; 'he must, but any military solution requires funds, and none of us have any. There are only a few cives remaining who have any experience of military service, and they are old, like Didius here.' They all laughed, but he continued, his tone serious. 'We only have small militias with few weapons, little enthusiasm and no confidence. The incentive required to keep a professional army is pay, but we do not have the coinage to sustain such an undertaking. We will hear from the remnants of the northern army, but I suspect their plight will mirror ours. The constant war in the North has cost the Empire more than the entire Patria's worth. That is why Rome has no interest in mounting a return.'

Didius had served in the army as a young man, Ambrosius had been told, which made the old warrior one of the few remaining cives with any military expertise. The structure and discipline of the legions were gone. The militias fought to maintain their local king's power and their tribal lands and, like those they fought, had become prone to raiding to recoup their losses and earn recompense – dog eat dog. Gold and silver were scarce, but slaves were plentiful, becoming the preferred currency amongst the barbarians.

The beers arrived, interrupting the debate.

'Good health, gentlemen. We have three further days on the road to discuss these dilemmas,' said Ambrosius, before taking a long draught from his cup. He imagined his expression was much like the expression he saw on the faces of his companions. 'This tastes how I would imagine horse piss tastes. Let us hope that Vitalinus' hospitality is of better quality.'

'Or his horses' piss is sweeter,' said Nataline.

XIX

The Villa Octavius

Early September 427

They followed the long road leading west to Viroconium. It was bustling with people going about their usual business and taking in the harvest. Mor looked across the fields and was heartened to see the year's crops were almost in.

'This is much more like the Patria of my youth,' said Taly.

'Yes, such a contrast to what we saw in the east, like a different country,' agreed Mor. He saw a pronounced and isolated hill loom into view. 'See that hill,' he said, pointing, 'that's the Wrikon. When we pass beyond it, we take a turning that will have us ride due south until we meet a great ridge – it's there we will find the Villa Octavius.'

'Octavius, you say?' said Taly.

'Yes. Do you recognise the name?'

'We are in the Cornovii heartlands; Octavius was their king back when Coel was summoned by Magnus Maximus. I believe the Emperor even married Octavius' daughter… Elen, I think.'

'That's right,' said Mor. 'Queen Sevira is the daughter of Magnus Maximus, although sadly, she never met him.'

'I am looking forward to meeting her, but we should be apprehensive, she is clearly a powerful queen.'

'I just hope she'll be at the villa. I'm following the instructions she sent for the meeting with her cousin that is planned for two days' time. It may be rude to turn up early, but it seems pointless to linger in strange countryside when we are so close to friendly hospitality.'

*

It had proved a long day's ride, so when the villa loomed into view, it was a welcome sight. The complex was much larger than Mor had expected. As they approached, he could see a compound of wooden stakes had recently been added giving it the appearance of a fort. They followed the path around to the entrance. Through the gate, he could see the main residential building surrounded by a stone wall. It was an impressive two-storey house with an extended wing on either side. The walls were white-washed, and the roof was pitched and made from grey shingles. In the surrounding compound, there were several wooden huts, stables and barns. He could see many hands at work, including some armed guards. Taly called a halt at the outer gate, and they dismounted. Two guards ran forward, startled by the sight of strangers at their gate. Mor exchanged a look with Taly. Discipline and security were poor.

'What is your business?' asked the taller one gruffly.

'My name is Mor. I am invited by Queen Sevira.'

'Wait here,' he said, and he walked briskly into the inner walled area.

Some minutes passed before Sevira herself emerged from the front door, walking serenely toward them.

'Prince Mor! You are two days early, but welcome. My cousin, Igerna, is away in Viroconium with my two children for their schooling, but they return tomorrow evening.'

'Queen Sevira, thank you for your welcome. Forgive our early intrusion, but we felt safer moving quickly along our route – the roads are dangerous in the east. I was not certain you would be here yet. Is the king with you?'

'He is not. Vitalinus travels directly from Corinium to Viroconium and is due there in three days. I see you have left your soldiers behind?'

'Yes, it is easier to travel long distances in a small group of trusted companions, makes it much easier to remain incognito.'

'Well, your men may join mine, for there is space in the guard room and stables.'

Mor glanced at Taly who gave a discreet nod of his head.

'Once you have stabled your horse, please come to the house for refreshments. I will send my servants to attend to your men.' Sevira turned and walked back to the main building.

'You don't want me to ask Sevira to accommodate you in the villa?' Mor asked Taly as they walked toward the stables.

'No need for that, I am much happier with the men. There is no need to disclose who I am. I must say she looked pleased to see you, and she is a beautiful woman. Do you intend to take this proposed engagement to her cousin seriously?'

'I'm not yet sure, but I can see many advantages to linking our families.'

'Take care, Mor. High-born women are easily offended and hold little respect for those they consider beneath them. She is the daughter of an emperor, and queen of both the Dobunni and the Cornovii.'

'I will be on my best behaviour, Taly.'

*

Mor left the stables and walked through the compound to the wall that surrounded the villa complex. Up close, it was easily larger than many villages he had seen. He walked through a garden and entered the hallway where he was met by an older gentleman wearing a Roman militia belt.

'King Mor, may I take your sword? It will be safe here in this alcove.'

Mor handed over his weapon. He was then led through the villa, his eyes taking in the Roman décor – murals on every wall were complemented by high-quality mosaic floors. They found Queen Sevira sat on the floor in a day-room with a maidservant and a little boy.

'Ah! Mor, here you are. May I introduce Pascent? He is the one you haven't yet met.'

Mor waved at the boy who waved back enthusiastically.

'How old is he?'

'He is two, and quite a handful, but Vicana is a wonderful help.'

The young maid smiled, before scooping Pascent from the floor and leaving the room with the compliant, but still waving, little boy.

'Come and sit over here by the window. I have wine and cool water.'

It was late afternoon, and the sun was just above the trees. The day had been warm, and beyond the garden, the farmworkers were still busy bringing cartloads of corn to the barn.

'This is a wonderful setting, Sevira.'

'This villa has been in my family for as long as anyone can remember. I am told it was my grandfather who commissioned much of the recent work, in particular the lovely murals and mosaics. Come, let me show you around.'

They returned to the main entrance where the old soldier was sat.

'Do you remember Viracus?' the queen asked.

'Of course, your captain of the guard who accompanied you to Eboracum.'

'Well, this is his father.' She turned to the soldier. 'Gavius, this is King Mor, grandson of King Coel.'

Gavius nodded. 'I met Coel when my unit manned the Wall.'

'Do you remember Prefect Talhaearn?'

'I do. And Ceneu, the king's son. Was he your father?'

'Yes, Ceneu was my father, though he has been departed many years now. Talhaearn, on the other hand, can be found sleeping in your stable tonight.'

'No! A man of his station? You must bring him to the house, Mor!' the queen exclaimed.

'He does not want that, Sevira, but I know he always enjoys a good catch-up with an old comrade.'

'I will seek him out later,' said Gavius, clearly pleased at the prospect.

Mor was shown the entire house, from the kitchen in the east wing to the bath house in the west.

'It is some time since I have seen a functioning bath house.'

'We try to maintain standards, but it is difficult. I fear there are some skills that have left these shores forever.'

Whilst returning to the day-room, Mor noticed an apse with an altar and statue. Painted on the wall by an unskilled but competent hand was a depiction of the face of Jesus superimposed on the labarum. A large crack now scarred the plaster, but the image was still striking. At the risk of being considered irreverent, Mor ran his finger down the crack.

'I've never seen the like,' he said.

Sevira was standing close, the scent of her perfume delicate and beguiling. *Vortigern is a lucky man*, he thought as he turned to look into her eyes.

'My mother was devout; she painted this and spent many hours in here. She is with Him now.' Sevira now ran her finger down the same crack. 'I should get this repaired. I pray every day for the Lord to give me my mother's strength.'

'Are you here at the villa often?' asked Mor.

'Most of the time,' she replied, but she did not offer any further explanation.

They returned to the day-room and sat once more by the window.

'Are you looking forward to meeting Igerna?' she asked, watching him intently.

'Very much,' said Mor. 'Is she as beautiful as you?'

Sevira's cheeks flushed slightly. 'She is beautiful, bright and precious.'

'Might I enquire her age?' asked Mor.

'She is still young, twenty-three years old.'

'And yet no suitors?'

'To the contrary, there are far too many.'

'I hope I am not pressing you to answer questions you do not wish to?'

'Of course not, your curiosity is understandable. Igerna's parents died, so she became my mother's ward, and I promised I would find a suitable husband for her.'

'There must be a great many to choose from?'

'There are specific exclusions which I will outline once I know your intentions. Igerna's father was Conan, only son of Octavius, my grandfather and King of the Cornovii. Her life has been beset by tragedy. Her mother died giving birth, and Conan died fighting for Constantine, so we all returned here from Armorica. I never met my grandmother, for she had already passed on, and Octavius was old and sick. The news of Conan's death devastated him, and his health deteriorated further. He knew change was imminent, and he was concerned for our future security, so in an agreement with his long-standing ally, Vitalinus, my husband's grandfather, I was betrothed, as an eighteen-year-old, to his grandson who was eight at the time. We married eight years later. The Dobunni and the Cornovii were thus fused together, avoiding dynastic challenges. Igerna was only three when we returned, so I brought her up as if she was mine.'

'I cannot say I noticed any age difference between you and your husband.' Mor's observation was genuine – he had actually thought Vortigern the elder of the two. 'Some beauty is ageless,' he added.

Sevira showed no reaction to his comment. 'Tell me of your plans, Mor?'

'With the death of my grandfather, we have split the kingdom in two to better protect our borders. I have recovered Eboracum from the Saxons, so that it now forms an uneasy border with the east, but I am building a more defensible fortress in the Forest of Elfed at Cambodunum.'

'We heard of your encounter with Saxons after our previous meeting. Gundad took liberties which, I am told, he regrets.'

'He has fled to the safety of his own tribe, the Gaini. A wise decision, for if he sets foot north of the Humber, I will put a permanent end to his ambitions.'

'Were you aware that he is to address the Council?'

'I was not, but it comes as no surprise, because I expect your husband is pursuing his plan to hire mercenaries?'

'He is. Will you support him?'

'He knows my position. I will not pay for them, and should they cross into our territory, we will treat them as we would any invaders and show them no mercy. The treaty arrangements will need to be robust indeed, if we are to avoid a full-scale incursion from within.'

'If you marry Igerna, a Cornovii princess, will you ally with our kingdom?'

Mor had anticipated this question.

'Does she come with a dowry?'

'A modest one, from my own fortune.'

'And what would you expect from me, your ally, in return?'

'That you come to my aid should I require it.' She paused and looked directly into his eyes. 'Not to my husband's or his generals' aid, my aid and the aid of your Cornovii family – Vortimer, Catigern and Pascent.'

Mor answered carefully. 'If I marry this Cornovii princess, I will come to the aid of you and your family should it be required.'

'Will you give me a solemn oath of your loyalty?'

'I will. But do not make war without first making your case to me!' Mor smiled. 'I take it you anticipate a schism between your interests and your husband's? Is there perhaps some dynastic friction after all?'

'The Dobunni and the Cornovii have remained allies for decades, but my husband becomes too bold and heavy-handed. He encourages a distant relation of ours to enforce his policies – a man called Cunevindus who is a poorly disguised assassin for Vitalinus. He is recently widowed – by his own hand, I hear – so now he pursues Igerna, hoping to consolidate his claims to Cornovii lands.'

'What do my cousins, the sons of Cunedda think of this man?'

'I'm not sure. He is pompous, a bully, and untested as a warrior, but they drink with him. He is careful not to incite their anger.'

Mor laughed. 'He is wise to take that approach; the Gododdin are as fearsome as they are volatile.'

'And what are you, Mor?'

'Carvetti,' he replied, choosing to avoid the real question.

The sun had dipped below the trees but was flooding the sky with a beautiful sunset. Sevira clapped her hands, and a servant appeared.

'Please ask the groundsman to light a fire to warm the bath suite.'

The servant bowed and left.

'Three days on the road have left you covered in dust, so will you join me to bathe? We have attire that will fit you whilst my servants launder your clothes. We will eat cena afterward.'

'I sense that we still have much to discuss, Sevira. There is a fear which you are yet to disclose?'

'Igerna will be here with the boys by mid-afternoon tomorrow. Between now and then, I will explain myself fully, and we shall make plans. Trust me, once she arrives, you will only have eyes for her.'

A woman beautiful enough to distract him from Sevira? If that was true, Mor had even more to contend with than what was already laid before him. Events were moving too quickly; he needed Taly's counsel.

'Sevira, will you please excuse me whilst I check on my men. There was mention of taking a hunting party out tomorrow, and there are arrangements to be made.'

'Of course. Meet me in the bath house in one hour.'

Mor nodded at Gavius as he left the villa, indicating that he did not require his sword returned to him just yet. As he had suspected, his three companions were enjoying a drink in the evening sunshine. Taly looked up as he approached them.

'Ah, Mor, are you married yet?'

They laughed but stopped when they saw his concerned look.

'Taly, walk with me.'

They strolled out the gate into the lush countryside, and once out of earshot, they stopped to speak.

'Sevira is direct. She wishes me to marry Igerna to counter Cornovii and Dobunni dynastic claims. I get the impression that she fears for her family's safety and wishes to secure an alliance that is loyal only to her. If I accept the marriage proposal, there is a modest dowry, but the marriage will likely inflame one of the Cornovii warlords, a man called Cunevindus.'

'What is Vortigern's position?'

'She seems to be acting independently of him, in effect offering me a place as part of her family. Igerna is the daughter of Conan, son of Octavius.'

Taly whistled. 'What does she want from you?'

'That I swear loyalty to her, that I will come to her and her children's aid should she require it.'

Taly was quiet for a short while, thoughts flickering behind his wise eyes.

'It seems reasonable. You would make a powerful ally for her, and we will have eyes and ears at the heart of the Patria. Vortigern's ambitions will be less of a mystery, less likely to catch us off-guard.'

Mor considered Taly's words and nodded. The old warrior had a way of revealing the simplicity at the heart of any dilemma. It's why Mor had not hesitated to seek out his counsel. 'I have told Sevira we plan to go hunting in the morning. I will discuss any further developments with you then.' He was about to turn for the gates when he remembered what else he had to tell Taly. 'Oh! Sevira's captain of the guard here at the villa is a man named Gavius. He claims to know you?'

Taly's face lit up in recognition. 'I remember Gavius. His unit fought with the northern army along the Wall. The Cornovii are a proud people like us and protective of their territories and their own royal family, suspicious of threats even from their closest allies. If Sevira has one from her own tribe protecting the villa, it may be a sign that she feels threatened by someone close to her, maybe even Vortigern?'

'I have been considering the same possibility; I aim to learn the truth of it this evening. It is to be a very Roman evening – I am invited to bathe!'

Taly laughed. 'Good luck! I will have your horse waiting in the morning, one hour after daybreak. We will hunt and talk some more.'

Mor walked slowly back to the villa. There was so much to think about, if he could just put it all together. His attraction to Sevira was clouding his judgement, and he had no doubt she was wise to the consternation she caused him. He had little experience of women, and none at all of one who wielded such political power, but Taly had made it all sound so simple. Too much thinking was likely to lead to indecision and opportunities missed. The dowry would be most welcome for Elfed's depleted coffers, but he still wished for more time to make such a far-reaching decision.

He stood in the garden admiring how the Romans lived – the palatial villa a far cry from his timber hall. Igerna would find her new home sparse and crude in comparison. How would she feel about such a change in her living conditions? So many questions. Sevira had been pushed into marriage herself, so surely, she had considered the risks involved in such plans? *Fate is a fast-flowing river*, his grandfather used to say; *it will take you wherever it is going*. He looked at the villa entrance with some apprehension. The decisions he made tonight would change the course of his life forever.

Woodsmoke in the air brought him back to the moment, reminding him of the fire it came from, the one lit to warm the bath house. Mor steeled himself and stepped into the hallway where a female servant stood waiting for him.

'My lord, you are to follow me.'

The bath house was in poorer condition than the rest of the villa.

He had seen many on his travels as a young soldier, but these days there were few to be found in the Patria. Their maintenance required skills and knowledge no longer held within the territory which led to their general decay which led to a decline in their usage and the eventual repurposing of the buildings. Only bath suites belonging to the rich still functioned. This one was fed by a fast-flowing spring from the hillside so promised a refreshing experience.

Inside the tepidarium, he removed his belt, tunic and trousers. They had travelled in hunting clothes for comfort and also to avoid drawing attention. Made of leather, the clothes offered resistance to weather and chafing. Mor was a taller than the average man, but his boyish looks and fair hair had a softening effect on his powerful frame. Like his older brother, he had trained with the army from the age of twelve, and he already bore several scars from both the training ground and the battlefield. Taly often said he looked more like Coel than Ceneu had. He remembered Sevira had offered to launder his clothes, so he removed his purse from the chest pocket and placed it in a recess provided for that purpose. The corner of his mouth quirked at the thought that his purse still contained the lock of Sevira's hair. The maidservant took his clothes, and another appeared holding a pot and a strigel. He removed his sandals and put on the wooden clogs provided then entered the caldarium. He lay on a towel on a bench whilst the girl covered him in oil.

'Are you a slave?' he asked. She did not reply, so he asked again, this time in Latin. 'Are you a slave?'

'Yes,' she replied, with a Scotti accent. 'The plunge pool disnae fill, but there's water through there.'

He sat up to make it easier for her to strigel his body and noticed the crumbling brickwork in the empty pool. The strigeling was a pleasant experience, both relaxing and bracing. He could hear the roar of the hypocaust fire, and the floor and walls were heating up quickly. In the background, he could also hear trickling water. There was no sign of Sevira. Thinking she might have changed her mind, and with the dirt and oil removed, he decided to enter the frigidarium and take the plunge. With constant spring-water available, the large pool was going to be very cold. Mor loved to swim in rivers and lakes, so he knew this would be his favourite part of the experience. He walked straight into its depths, and with his head underwater, splashed and rolled. It was incredibly refreshing, the icy spring-water washing away the turmoil that had engulfed his mind. He surfaced to find a naked Sevira stood watching him from the doorway. Absently shaking the water off his face, he stared.

'King Mor! I thought someone had released a seal into my pool!'

Mor was lost for words as she descended the steps into the water. She took her time, toying with him. The gasp from her lips as her body slowly immersed to her neck was possibly the most erotic sound he had ever heard. Her hair was piled on top of her head revealing the elegant line of her neck, still framed by the jet necklace she had worn when he first met her. Mor composed himself.

'That was quite a treat for a boy from the North.'

She laughed with a freedom she had not displayed before. His sense that they had unfinished business from their first meeting heightened dramatically, but she was a queen, and he knew better than to act upon such thoughts. He resorted to humour, pressing the backs of his hands together in a clapping motion whilst barking like a seal. He then submerged and rolled, splashing wildly. Sevira stood up to avoid getting her hair wet and laughed again.

'A very naughty northern seal,' she said and climbed the steps. Mor was relieved the moment had passed, but had she wanted him to respond to her flirtation, had he offended her by playing the fool instead? No matter. If she wanted him, she would say so.

'Join me in the tepidarium,' Sevira said, whilst towelling herself.

Mor watched from the pool. She was in good shape for a mother of three, and the most elegant woman he had ever met. It was now dusk, and servants appeared lighting candles and oil lanterns which threw enticing shadows across her body as she moved into the tepidarium.

Mor got out of the pool and towelled himself dry before joining Sevira who was reclining in a thin chemise. A servant was pouring wine for them both. Mor tied his towel around his waist and sat down next to Sevira. The room was pleasantly warm, the atmosphere charged with anticipation. It was a heady mix.

'What shall we discuss first?' said Sevira.

She passed him a cup filled to the brim with wine. He sipped a little and replied. 'Will it offend you if I ask some questions?'

'Only if I am bound to answer,' she said with a smile.

Direct questions weren't going to work. She was too clever to give anything away by that method, so Mor switched tack.

'How about this,' he said; 'let's share secrets. I will tell you one, then you can tell me one of yours. Let us start with our worst fears.'

She nodded.

'The Brigantes have a seer called Myrddin. He has dreamt that a vile serpent will come from the east and lay waste to the Patria. We believe the serpent refers to the Saxons whose numbers and boldness are growing rapidly.'

'Is this why you have repositioned to Elfed?'

'Yes, but not just on the strength of the prophecy. There is overwhelming evidence of incursions becoming more frequent and more savage. We have fought too many Saxons to ever consider them as allies.'

'So, you think my husband misplaces his trust?'

'I do. He is inviting the wolf into the sheep pen. These people are thieves and murderers who can do nothing other than exploit any trust we show them; it is their nature.'

'What would you do differently to protect the eastern cives from the raiders?'

'Develop a national militia.'

'My husband will never do that. He is not a military man, and he fears handing any power to generals who command the loyalty of armed men. He wants to be High King of the Patria, but he doesn't plan on achieving it by slashing with a sword from the back of a horse. Gratian, his father's friend, was murdered by the military, and he fears both you and Ambrosius Aurelianus.'

'So is it Vitalinus who wants me to marry Igerna, or is it you? Who will I be giving my oath to?'

'It is me, Mor. He would rather see her marry Cunevindus, but then the lands of the Cornovii might pass to a family unworthy of the privilege. Whereas I know I could trust you to hold them in trust for Vortimer, Catigern and Pascent.'

'Surely Vitalinus will ensure that is so?'

'He does not love me. I do not trust him, and he has other consorts. He has no self-control; his reputation is an embarrassment.'

Mor could not find the words to respond to so frank a disclosure, but Sevira wasn't finished.

'I am trapped – surrounded by men of poor quality and terrified for the future of my children. Our world is crumbling around us whilst my husband and his allies drink and fornicate.'

'The Roman Empire itself is in its death throes,' Mor replied. 'They will not return to our troublesome islands. It is up to us make the best of what we are left with, believing in our God and finding our own ways to security and prosperity.'

Sevira was quiet for a moment.

'It is hard to believe that Magnus Maximus wooed my mother in this very room. He was no saint, but he was not afraid to fight.'

Her shift in focus was taking their conversation to a dark and hopeless place; they would achieve nothing in that frame of mind.

'Do you think he wore this towel and these sandals, Sevira?' said Mor, giving her a smile and waving his hand down from his torso to his feet. 'I'm not sure I fit them too well.'

There was a tear in her eye, but she managed a smile. She swung around to face him, and placing her hand on his cheek, she kissed him gently.

'They look a perfect fit to me.' Good. She had returned to teasing him. 'Now it is my turn. What do you hope for most?'

'Peace, prosperity, the love of a woman, and children I can watch grow to adulthood.' Sevira was listening intently, watching him as he spoke. 'Your father died, my father died, Igerna's parents died, Talhaearn's parents died. All of them before we knew them. Why should God be so cruel? It is no wonder you fear for your children, and it is no wonder your mother prayed every day. No one is coming to save us, not Him, not Rome and certainly not mercenary armies made up of those already responsible for the murders of our fellow cives.'

'So, what is your plan?'

'My brother and I will defend the North to as far south as the Humber and the Merse. These are Coel's territories. We have strong allies to the north, but to the south, we only have Cunedda's sons who defend the north-western plains and coastline to Seguntium.'

Sevira frowned. 'If only Conan had survived or Vortimer was older. My husband corrupts those around him with a false sense of security. He calls it diplomacy.'

'It is the Roman way these days to pay others to fight for them, but your husband's ambitions are too transparent, and by manipulating the Council, he is buying time only for himself.'

'That is the only person he cares about.' Sevira shook her head, her expression one of disgust.

Mor laughed. 'When Vortimer reaches his fourteenth summer, entrust him to me, and we will teach him to be a Cymry warrior with the education of a Roman.'

'So, will you marry Igerna?'

'In principle, yes, and you may call upon my support until Vortimer is old enough to fight your battles for you.'

'My husband must never discover or even suspect this agreement between us. He would have us all murdered.'

'Vortigern will congratulate you on your diplomacy – a Cornovii princess removed from where she could become a rallying point for dissent and his northern rival brought into line as part of his wider family.'

'He will worry about claims upon his domain from the North, and Cunevindus will take it as a personal insult.'

'Then I will elope with Igerna after the Council meeting, and I shall marry her in Reged – that way no one can blame you.'

Sevira's eyes lit up, and she smiled. Even so, she looked around as if checking that their conversation had not been overheard.

'That, King Mor, is an excellent plan. I am suddenly hungry; we should change for cena. My servants have laid out some clothes that belonged to Conan for you – you have a similar build.'

'Thank you, Sevira. The towel of Maximus and now the toga of Conan – my grandfather will be watching with great pride.'

Sevira laughed, her eyes sparkling. 'You know, King Mor, I do believe we are kindred spirits, you and me. It is good to entrust my fears to someone who can allay them so decisively.'

*

Darkness had fallen when Mor stepped out of the villa for a breath of cool air. The toga that had been laid out for him was a comfortable fit. He could hear voices and laughter in the outer compound and wondered if it was Taly and Gavius catching up on old times. His thoughts turned to his own evening's discussions. Sevira's intoxicating presence made it difficult for him to remain focused at times, but he was confident that their agreement was reasonable. He would need to ensure the dowry matched his expectations, and she would require him to swear his oath before God. She was an exciting woman, caged in a man's world, driven, yet her maternal instincts were not diminished by that drive. He found that he trusted her already, even knowing she had purposefully drawn him into her web of intrigue. Regardless of how she had got him there, it felt like the right place to be. He had avoided taking much wine so far; it was still early and the details had not yet been agreed. Heading back inside, he walked toward the east wing.

The dining room was adjacent to the kitchen where the food was being prepared. It was to be traditional Roman dining, and from the settings, it appeared they would recline facing each other. He sat and waited for some time, helping himself to a glass of wine from a jug. Servants kept appearing, placing all manner of food on the table. When Sevira arrived with her maidservant, she looked ravishing. Her hair had been restyled around a tiara, and she wore a beautiful light blue gown thrown back over one shoulder. Her familiar perfume reminded him of their first meeting.

'My apologies for the delay; I wanted to be sure Pascent was asleep before joining you.'

'Do Vortimer and Catigern miss you when they attend school?'

'Of course, but Igerna is like their big sister. We shall all miss her terribly.'

'I will regret bringing sadness to you. You look beautiful, Sevira, and that perfume – I would recognise it in an instant.'

'How so?'

'It still clings to that lock of your hair you gave me. I carry it with me everywhere.' He tapped the purse now secured on his belt.

'You must return that to me, now you are to be married.'

'Perhaps I should trade it for one last kiss?' he said, making light though longing for her to take his words seriously.

Sevira dismissed her maidservant and took a seat opposite Mor.

'I have been reflecting on our conversation. I am convinced it is the right path, and I believe Igerna will approve – she loathes Cunevindus, saying he is ugly and arrogant and would surely mistreat her.'

'Sevira, you must ensure that Igerna understands that we don't live like this, like the Romans, in the North. She will be loved and cherished, but our lifestyle is simpler, more utilitarian.'

'Conan and my father were much the same, soldiers like you. She will find her way with it.'

'Before we continue down this path, is Gavius your senior captain of the guard?'

'He is. Why do you ask?'

'Did he build the stockade? It looks unfinished.'

'Vitalinus said it was not necessary to finish it, that we had no need for such defence.'

'Will Gavius take advice from me or perhaps Taly?'

'I'm sure he would, but why?'

'Your security is inadequate, not just the number and alertness of your guards but also the strength of your defences. He needs to train the men up to repulse a minimum of thirty attackers. A ditch needs to be dug all the way round, and you would do well to have a drawbridge. Four scaffold towers would greatly improve the killing zone—'

'Speak freely to him tomorrow,' she said, cutting him short. 'Will you come to the little chapel with me before we retire? I wish you to swear your oath of allegiance before God.'

'Of course. May I ask about the arrangements for the dowry?'

'I propose that you collect Igerna the morning after the Council. She will be accompanied by a trusted maidservant – they are both competent riders. In their saddlebags will be one thousand solidi. No one must know of this – Vitalinus does not know I maintain reserves. I will claim that I introduced you but was completely unaware of your infatuation with one another.'

'She will be safe with us.'

'I would not entrust her to your care if I did not believe so.' Sevira raised her glass. 'I propose a toast, King Mor. To those we trust.'

As they drank, Sevira's eyes betrayed her excitement. Mor was impressed with what she had achieved – a powerful husband for her ward, a protector for her family and a foil to her husband's attempts to claim her tribal lands.

The business complete, they both relaxed, and the rest of the meal passed with entertaining conversation and easy laughter. It heartened Mor when she confessed that she could not remember enjoying herself quite so much for some considerable time, especially because he could not either. They had much more in common than was initially apparent, and as the evening progressed, their laughter filled the room. Finally, it was time to proceed to the apse. Mor collected his sword from the alcove, the front door now closed and locked. In the flickering candlelight, the cracked image of Jesus looked on as Mor, on one knee, holding his sword by its blade, swore an oath to love and cherish Igerna and also to protect Sevira and her children should they be threatened or require help. It was a solemn moment. Mor rose to his feet, and Sevira kissed him gently on the lips.

'I'm already jealous of my cousin.'

They walked quietly to the bedrooms and bid each other goodnight, shutting their doors. Mor placed his sword by his bed on the floor, his mind full of the day's events. He blew out the candle and closed his eyes.

Just as he was drifting into the dreamworld, he heard the door open then steps in the dark. He reached for his sword, but a soft hand stayed his arm. In the faint moonlight, he saw Sevira, naked once more. She lay down on the bed next to him.

'I've come to reclaim my lock of hair,' she said softly.

XX

The Edge

Early September 427

Mor woke at dawn. There was a seasonal coolness to the room, and the morning chorus was more tranquil than it had been in recent days. He looked out the small upstairs window and inhaled the cool air. A low-lying mist had formed in the vale between The Edge and the Wrikon. If his mother was here, she would call the mist dragon's breath, and wonder at the impending change it heralded. He saw that his hunting clothes had been returned and laid out for him whilst he slept. He dressed quickly, girding his sword, and tip-toed out of the villa.

The servants were already moving about, fulfilling their morning tasks, but Mor did not linger. He left the inner compound and headed for the stream. He knelt and dipped his head into the water, rinsing his face and hair, and after a few sips of cold water, he sat back on a stone. Only now did he dare to think about the previous day's events – had it all been a dream? His memories certainly had a dreamlike quality to them. Excitement welled inside him as he relived every detail, but there followed a strange feeling of remorse. Sevira had shown none, but they had parted in the dark… It had been an encounter to surpass all others. Never before had he experienced such tenderness and passion culminating in an uncontrollable climax that had challenged his belief in his own existence, so otherworldly, heavenly had it been… but now, his remorse was profound. Another man's wife, witnessed by such mighty ghosts, just hours before meeting his wife-to-be, his enthusiasm for her surely jaded by so recent a passionate, wanton encounter. God's fury would be something to behold – only hours after swearing a holy oath to protect the woman, he had molested her with no thought for his promise to the Almighty. Not only was he consumed with carnal longing for the Cornovii queen, but to make his transgression even worse, his feelings for her were growing. And he would have to face everyone later this day, not just Sevira and her children, but Igerna. The great tower of pride, ambition and self-esteem he had built for himself as he had grown into his kingship came crashing down around him. Vortigern was a fool for torturing such a beautiful, rare creature with his careless infidelity, but could Mor claim to be his moral superior?

'Good morning.' Taly's voice penetrated Mor's brooding, bringing him back to the impending hunt.

'Ah, Taly. Good morning.'

'You seem preoccupied. What troubles a man so young on the day he will be meeting his bride-to-be?'

'A great many things. Tell me, Uncle, have you ever been gutted by love?'

Taly gave him a quizzical look. 'I have, Mor. It feels like a deep wound that never properly heals.'

'Did it affect your judgement?'

'It still does, but what marks a man out is how he carries his wounds and what he learns from their infliction.'

Mor wanted to tell Taly everything but could not bear to see the disappointment in his old teacher's eyes.

'A good day for hunting?' he said, instead.

'Yes, but we have no dogs. Gavius tells me the ridge leading south-west is thick with red deer, so we should follow its course.'

'Countryside this lush should provide rich fare for the queen's table.'

They wandered over to the stables where their comrades were readying their horses.

'Good morning, my lord. Have you breakfasted?' Spurcio's constant hunger ever informed his choice of subject matter.

'Not yet, Spurcio.'

'Then I shall go see if the bread I can smell baking is ready.' He left for the kitchen.

Mor turned to Taly.

'I think it would be wise to leave our shields and saddlebags under the protection of Gavius, what say you?'

'He will not object to that responsibility. He's a fine old soldier. He tells me the Cornovii cohort has been disbanded, and that the queen's defence is now in the hands of young men keen to show prowess but lacking the proper training for such a responsible role.'

'I spoke of my concerns about the security here with Sevira last night, and she has given her consent for us to speak with Gavius on the subject.' He lowered his voice. 'Taly, there is more. For reasons I shall explain later, I have agreed to elope with Igerna the day after the Council.' Taly did not try to disguise his look of surprise. 'We should make plans to travel directly north so that we reach the safety of our own territory as quickly as possible.'

'Are you expecting pursuit from an army of rivals?' Taly's laugh was cut short by Mor's serious expression.

'We will be carrying a considerable dowry, and yes, there are complications. Remember how Igerna is the granddaughter of Octavius? Well, Vortigern does not want any rivals for her Cornovii inheritance.'

'There is a viable route via Mamucium which gets us to our territory quickly, but with women, we will be adding an extra two days to a three-day journey.'

'Then, so be it,' said Mor.

*

Spurcio had returned with fresh bread, a more than adequate meal to start their day. They then left the compound, following Gavius' advice and riding up the hill to the ridge and entering the forest that ran along The Edge, as Winnog informed them this area was called. After two hours or so following a hunter's path, they heard a great bellowing from far to the east. Taly was relieved to see that Mor was beginning to enjoy himself.

'Stags rutting,' said Winnog. 'A sight to behold, and there's bound to be a herd nearby.'

They left the forest track, heading toward higher ground, following the bellowing sounds whilst taking care not to break cover from the forest margin. Winnog signalled them and pointed to his right. Taly turned with the others and saw a large herd of red deer in the foreground of a steep hill. The herd was grazing, overlooked by a mighty stag which stood alert like a sentry, its gaze intent, switching from one direction to another.

The hunting party tied their horses to a tree. Arming themselves with their bows and quivers, they stalked through the undergrowth to a safe distance from which to observe the herd. There were many does, and the old stag clearly had several rivals. He thrust out his impressive, branched head and roared. Two, or perhaps three, other stags roared in reply. One was close by. They watched as a young contender trotted into view. The rival stag advanced then paused.

Spurcio, crouching behind a tree trunk, offered up a challenge. 'The young one looks vigorous; I'll wager a beer he defeats the old boy.'

Taly took up the challenge. 'I'll take that – experience counts for a lot.'

They all watched, awed by the display of strength and fury. Another roar from the senior stag, and they rushed at one another, full of aggression, clashing in a furious clatter of antlers. Both staggered, stunned for a moment, but then, with legs splayed, they struck again and again. The other stags now made their appearance, taking advantage of the distraction to try and mate with the herd. The one that had bellowed close by broke cover. Winnog, who was nearest, loosed off an arrow that went clean through the stag's neck. It stumbled, and another arrow rapidly followed, entering its belly as the animal crashed to the ground. The battling stags and the rest of the herd were unaware of the hunters. Antlers clashed again, but this time, the older stag had the superior footing, giving it the leverage to force its young rival to its knees. The youngster was quickly back on its feet, but now it retreated, roaring defiance as it abandoned the encounter.

Spurcio laughed. 'He's telling him he'll be back tomorrow.'

Taly watched Winnog crawl toward the felled, panting stag. He slit its throat with his knife and its pain ended. In that moment, the whole herd became aware of the presence of men amongst them, tensing, the victorious stag looking in their direction. In an instant, they answered to a silent signal and bounded off as one, not stopping until they reached the slopes of a distant hill.

'That was a remarkable shot, Winnog,' exclaimed Mor.

'Thank you, my lord. We are at the butts every day, but this stag was easy prey; his mind was on the ladies.'

'Ah, yes,' said Taly. 'A mistake easily made – may that be a lesson to us all.' He looked at Mor who refused to meet his eye. 'And you owe me a beer, Spurcio!'

They tied the stag over the back of Winnog's horse, its great body dwarfing the horse, heavy antlers dangling limply on one side. Low cloud clung to the hills and dreichy rain had begun to fall.

'Now we have our offering, let's head for that road,' said Mor, pointing. Taly peered through the grey veil of rain and saw what looked like an old military road following the valley floor. 'It probably leads to Viroconium and will bring us around the hills at the very least.'

Picking their way carefully down the steep valley, they approached the road at the point where it led into the forested area. A group of around twenty riders suddenly emerged from the treeline.

'Turn back or continue on?' asked Mor, his voice steady, his posture calm.

'They've seen us,' said Taly, proud of his nephew's composure. 'We won't outrun them. Only choice is to carry on and find out if they are friend or foe.' The mounted troop was waiting on the road, their attention very much on the approaching hunters.

'Onward it is,' said Mor.

They continued their descent.

As they reached the road, the lead rider, a well-built man of about thirty years of age looked angry.

'Who are you?' he enquired curtly.

Mor raised his eyebrows at the rude tone and looked to Taly. 'We are visitors to these lands,' said Taly.

'And how do *visitors* take it upon themselves to poach our deer?'

'We have been hunting with the queen's permission,' said Taly.

'Which queen is that?' said the man.

Mor looked puzzled. 'We understood there was only one hereabouts. Queen Sevira.'

'You need *my* permission to hunt deer on these lands!'

'We were not aware that anyone had that kind of authority over the queen's lands. Who are you?' enquired Taly.

'I am Cunevindus, leader of the Cornovii. Poaching my deer is a crime punishable by death. Arrest them!'

'Wait!' said Mor. 'Why risk losing any of your men in a fight against trained soldiers? We will just give you the stag and be on our way'

'Trained soldiers!' howled Cunevindus as he looked around at his audience of followers. 'How about I fight you, young upstart, and we will see how well you are trained? If you win, you keep the stag; if you lose, I take your head.'

This was getting out of hand. 'Let me fight him!' said Taly, under his breath. 'You are too important to the future of the North.'

'No, Taly. Remember I said there were complications? This man is one of them.'

There was nothing more that Taly could do without shaming the young king. He watched Mor and Cunevindus dismount. The persistent drizzle had made it damp underfoot. Mor was the taller of the two, but Cunevindus was built like an ox, and he wore a heavy coat of mail. 'Do you want to fight with shields, young upstart, my captain will lend you his?' he said, placing his helmet on his head.

'Your choice,' said Mor, loosening up by throwing his sword from hand to hand and stretching his neck to either side.

'No shields then. I will dispatch you quicker without.'

Taly took in the situation, considering the options. He could ride over Cunevindus and strike him down. If his king got into difficulty, Taly would not hesitate. He had watched Mor's father die, but he would not watch the son do the same; he would give his own life before he allowed that to happen. His hand was already on his sword hilt, the move mirrored by Spurcio. Cunevindus' men looked young, inexperienced and boisterous – many would die if it came to a fight.

Cunevindus suddenly charged like a bull, but Mor parried the first mighty blow, deflecting its force by spinning out of the way. He charged a second time, and this time Mor spun to the other side. Cunevindus flailed in the wrong direction and stumbled past Mor who delivered a quick playful slap to his opponent's arse with the flat of his sword.

'That's a bigger target than I am used to in training,' quipped Mor.

Cunevindus turned puce with rage and struck out with a combination of mighty blows, forcing Mor back toward the edge of the road. Once again, Mor's agility left the big man facing the wrong way. The young northern king was now positioned behind the ox, in the perfect position to strike him down but making the choice not to. Cunevindus wheeled around and ran at Mor with his sword raised high. This time, Mor dropped to the ground and rolled under him, knocking the heavy man over like a skittle. He went down hard, smashing his face on the cobbles. Mor jumped to his feet, kicked away his opponent's weapon and pushed the point of his sword under the helmet of the prostrate Cunevindus.

'Now, shall I take *your* head?' Mor asked.

Before Cunevindus could answer, there was a clatter of hooves, and more riders arrived. Taly recognised Vortigern.

'King Mor, stay your weapon immediately. What on earth is happening here?'

'Ah, King Vortigern. So good of you to join us,' said Mor, not taking his eyes off Cunevindus. 'We have been enjoying Cornovii hospitality. This is no more than an amicable wager though.'

Cunevindus sat up, blood streaming from his nose and mouth.

'The stag is yours,' he muttered.

'We are guesting at the Villa Octavius,' Mor said to Vortigern, paying no attention to Cunevindus.

'Yes, I was told of the invitation.'

'We were out hunting to restock provisions at the villa and repay the queen's excellent hospitality when we encountered this gentleman.' Now he deigned to look at his vanquished foe. Mor held his hand out to help Cunevindus to his feet. 'He insisted on a wager for the stag.'

'You are *King* Mor,' spluttered Cunevindus. 'Why the bloody hell didn't you say so?'

Without sparing the ox so much as a glance, Mor addressed Vortigern. 'You will understand that we did not wish to disclose our true identities, for we number only four. Please let me introduce you. This is Prefect Talhaearn who trains the northern army. This is Tribune Spurcio, responsible for eastern defence, and this is Optio Winnog, Commander of the Forest Archers.'

'Well, Mor, we shall look forward to seeing you at Council tomorrow. Please convey my best wishes to Sevira and let her know that I will see her at the banquet. Do you come to Viroconium tonight?'

'No. We will arrive in the morning. My lords, please forgive our urgency, but we are due back mid-afternoon. The mist has lifted, and we can now see the path that brought us here. We will return by that route.'

Mor climbed back on his horse and turned. Taly took the cue and led the group back in the direction of the hills, retracing the path to The Edge.

*

Mor and companions followed the route back between the hills but then turned to mount the southernmost rise, gaining a view of the surrounding countryside. At the top, they could see that Vortigern's column was long. It included several carriages that were making slow progress – almost walking pace.

Winnog broke the silence. 'We are all pleased with our new appointments and promotions, my lord, but Spurcio wants to know where the eastern front actually is?'

They roared with laughter and, for an entire hour, recounted the confrontation whilst following a path along The Edge.

*

Vortigern rode next to Cunevindus.

'It is unwise to pick fights with hardened warriors, my friend.'

'How was I supposed to know who I was up against? I will kill that bastard,' Cunevindus replied.

'Not if he sees you first. Did you even ask for his name? The Brigantes are ruthless. Our friend Gundad will attest to that. He is petrified about having to face Mor at Council. After our last meeting in Eboracum, that man defeated eighty Saxon infantry with only thirty cavalry. Only two of Gundad's men and a boy survived. Mor is ruthless and capable – don't be taken in by his princely manners.'

Cunevindus remained silent, but unfettered violent revenge simmered just below the surface.

XXI

Villa Octavius

September 427

Taly turned to Mor, and the young king knew what was coming. 'That was impetuous and dangerous. Your mother will roast me alive if she discovers that I allowed such foolishness.'

'There was good reason, Taly. Sevira has told me Cunevindus is Vortigern's assassin. He has murdered his own wife and now pursues a union with Igerna. She has not fully disclosed her fears, but I suspect Sevira believes that both Vortigern and Cunevindus might prefer her dead, and that they will make a prisoner of Igerna whilst they control her inheritance. These warlords are trying to exorcise the ghost of Octavius and absorb Cornovii lands into a larger territory. Sevira believes my marriage to Igerna will put a stop to all of this.'

'That would explain why Gavius became less and less complimentary about Vortigern the more we drank last night. The Cornovii will protect their queen long before they will take orders from a Dobunni, even if he is a king! Well, you can be sure that Vortigern and his cronies see you as a threat already although they just won't be expecting the attack to come from the marital bed!' Taly laughed.

Mor suddenly turned in his saddle, various clues suddenly slotting into place.

'It was Mother, wasn't it?'

'What was?' replied Taly, guarded.

'My mother. She is the wound that never healed.'

'It is them all. Your mother, your father… but of them all, I hope you never experience the grief of burying a wife and child. Bewyn, my boy, should be riding with us now.'

'Forgive me, Talhaearn,' Mor bowed his head. 'Sevira has cast an inexplicable spell over me that clouds my thinking. I forget my place.'

'Powerful women excel at that, particularly those ambitious enough to expect there to be a need for you to go to war on their behalf!'

They rode the last hour to the villa in silence. Mor wondered at the situation he found himself in. Had he been drawn into a web of intrigue best avoided? His resounding victory in his fight with Cunevindus would strengthen their hand at the Council meeting in the morning though. And maybe it was time for the North to secure its position with a bit of political manoeuvring rather than relying solely on their military prowess.

The villa looked just as busy as it had the day before, but there were more curls of smoke. Perhaps because the weather was cooler, and the children had likely returned with it now being beyond mid-afternoon. Up until that moment, Mor had forgotten about his impending meeting with his bride-to-be. He was late, and his personal appearance was far from well-groomed. In the end, it was his tardy arrival that took precedence over his fears about his appearance, so he left his horse with his companions, hurried into the inner compound and walked through the front door. Gavius was there to relieve him of his sword. Taking a deep breath, Mor strode into the day-room. All nerves were dispelled when Vortimer, Sevira's nine-year-old, leapt to his feet and saluted.

'King Mor, how is your army, and have you fought any battles today?'

'We have confronted some adventure but no battles, young scamp.'

'Hush, Vortimer,' said Sevira. 'Let the man catch his breath.'

'Greetings, with apologies for my late arrival,' said Mor, not yet daring to look around the room. 'We encountered some delays whilst we were out hunting which I will tell you more about later.'

Sevira looked him up and down. 'You look as if you have been rolling in mud, but come, sit with us.'

It was only then that Mor allowed his gaze to drift toward the young woman sitting on the mosaic floor playing with the children with her back to him. She had long, raven-black hair brushed into a ponytail. At Sevira's words, she stood and turned, first smiling at Sevira and then directly at Mor.

'Mor, meet my cousin Igerna.'

She was taller than Sevira, lithe, almost muscular with a beautiful, characterful face and piercing blue eyes that seemed to see into his soul. She was a Cymry princess from head to toe and looked as if she was perfectly capable of jumping on a horse and racing him.

'My lady.' Mor bowed awkwardly. 'I've heard so much about you but… but I had no idea that you would be so… well, beautiful and athletic.'

'Prince Mor,' she replied. 'It would seem that I have you at a disadvantage – my family have not stopped talking about you since the spring, providing me with a detailed description of your physical attributes on several occasions!' She laughed and glanced briefly at Sevira before turning her piercing blue gaze back to Mor.

Vortimer picked up his wooden sword and charged at Mor who parried with his arm, lifting the boy and spinning him around in the air.

'This is the second time I've been attacked today, Vortimer.'

'Is it true you are going to be my uncle?' the boy asked, disarming everyone.

Mor looked directly at Igerna, replying, 'I do hope so, but is it not tradition that a Cymry princess chooses her own consorts?'

They all laughed. 'She is not Cartimundua!' exclaimed Sevira.

But Mor had meant what he said. He held Igerna's gaze, letting her know he was sincere. 'The Brigantes revere their queens. Should you choose to make your life with me, you will be much respected in my world.'

Sevira smiled. 'I have planned an open-house roast to which everyone is invited later, but first, we three must speak privately.' She clapped her hands, and three servants appeared. The children were ushered to a different room, and yet another servant brought wine and water.

Mor watched Sevira in admiration. This was not the soft seductress of the night before; this was the queen – commanding and in control of all around her. Igerna seemed apprehensive, probably just as nervous as he was, but Mor could see she was devoted to her cousin, the trust between them deep and unquestioned.

With little time to spare, the meeting that followed was full and frank. Igerna was taken aback at first by the proposed elopement but accepted its necessity with little need for persuasion. Both women looked shocked when Mor described his encounter with Vortigern and Cunevindus. Sevira seemed a little distant, but Mor understood why. Powerful women didn't stay powerful without astute minds and great personal control, whereas men behaved much more like the stags he had witnessed earlier – hot-blooded and mindless when they had the scent. He was not immune to such feelings, and he could not help comparing the two women. Sevira was fair and elegant, carrying more weight but in a soft, sensual way, her every move was poised and controlled, her maturity just giving greater strength to her sex appeal. Igerna, by contrast, was whip-slim, sparkling and full of innocence. Her reactions were quick but precise, and her hopes and enthusiasm for the future bubbled from her lips like a mountain waterfall, cleansing and sure in direction. He held no doubts about going through with the plan and no regrets, other than knowing he would have to exercise control as masterful as Sevira's to put his attraction for the queen aside and never allude to the previous evening again.

With the serious business of agreeing the plan out of the way, Igerna relaxed a little, taking the time to look into his eyes, not in a lovelorn way, more searching for the man who was destined to be the father of her children. She was on the cusp of womanhood, a future full of hope. Naturally, she was somewhat emotional at the prospect of leaving Sevira and her children so much sooner that she had expected, but the queen was insistent that there was no time to waste if Igerna was to escape Vortigern's ambitions.

The evening was a great success. Taly was able to advise Gavius about the queen's security. Winnog recounted a humorous rendition of Mor's encounter with Cunevindus, and Spurcio spent the evening amusing the maidservants who kept him supplied with more and more food and drink. Mor and Igerna played happily with the queen's children, but later, after Sevira had retired, Mor took the opportunity to walk with his princess. They spoke earnestly about their future and sealed their engagement with a passionate stolen kiss behind the bath house.

What a day!

*

Sevira lay awake. She was sad to be losing her surrogate sister and couldn't help feeling jealous. If only her father had arranged someone like this young king for her. Her attraction to Mor still lingered, and she knew it would only take the slightest encouragement from her to get him back in her bed. Part of her longed to throw caution to the wind… but it was a selfish fancy. Instead, she comforted herself by reviewing her achievements. She now held this handsome hound on a long leash; he had already snarled a warning at those who threatened her. Mor might not be in her bed, but he was certainly in her corner

XXII

Viroconium

September 427

'How did you sleep, Ambrosius?' asked Nataline.

'I slept well, eventually. These campaign tents have seen better days, but they are adequate for summer.'

'There was some sort of celebration until late into the night. The noise of it kept me awake.'

'Ah. That. Yes, our scouts reported that Vortigern and a long column of troops and travellers arrived in the town yesterday afternoon,' said Didius, catching up with them.

'Bit of a difference from the night before when all we heard was a blacksmith's hammer and the church bell. Perhaps tonight will prove more tranquil,' added Elafius who had joined his comrades.

Ambrosius and his troop had reached Viroconium a day early. Between Lactodurum and Letocetum they had detected a great deal of tension amongst villagers along the route. Rumours of raiding Picts were rife, so they had decided to keep moving, riding cautiously through the night and arriving a full day early. It was a sensible decision, and although tired, the Council members had enjoyed having the opportunity to walk around the city and appreciate the recent building work. They were camped one mile from the town, a decision taken by Ambrosius to flag their peaceful intentions and avoid confrontation.

The dawn had been glorious, and it was now a beautiful bright day. The Wrikon hill was pronounced in the morning sunshine, towering over the landscape as the four men representing the south walked to the Council meeting. They had dressed formally in Roman-style togas, since they were expecting to debate until mid-afternoon and thereafter enjoy a traditional Ides of September banquet in the large mansio adjacent to the church where the meeting was to be held. Ambrosius had taken great care not to display any military rank or presence. His troops were instructed to keep a low profile during the visit. He was aware Vortigern had been reluctant to allow his presence. Their peaceful stroll was interrupted by the sudden clatter of iron-clad hooves on the cobbles.

They turned to see two barbarian horsemen advancing toward them at speed. Ambrosius managed to curb his alarm and avoid making a fool of himself thanks to his eye falling on the warriors' shields just before he called out in fear. It was true that the riders' attire was typical of the barbarian style, but their shields were emblazoned with the Chi Rho, and now they were closer, he could see they were wearing military belts and buckles.

'They are Cymry militia,' said Ambrosius, pleased at how level and matter-of-fact his voice was.

'Good God, they dress like Picts,' exclaimed Didius.

'More like Goths,' replied Ambrosius, drawing on his vivid memories of his father's enemy.

The men's horses were sweating and frothing from the gallop, though the magnificent beasts didn't seem particularly amenable to being reined back to a more sedate walking pace. The black stallion was particularly frisky and difficult to restrain.

'Those are lively beasts!' shouted Didius. 'Are you cavalry officers?'

The younger of the two replied in perfect Latin. 'Good morning, gentlemen. We are the representatives for the North. I am King Mor, and this is Prefect Talhaearn of the northern army. I presume that detachment of cavalry camped back there is your personal guard?'

'Indeed, it is. I am Ambrosius Aurelianus, and this is Nataline, Elafius and Didius – city tribunes and Council members. We represent the south. We have all travelled far for this meeting with Vitalinus, or do you call him King Vortigern?'

The northern king laughed. 'We call him trouble. I have been very much looking forward to meeting you, Ambrosius. We have much in common with our lands bordering this unsettled mid-land.'

An unexpected ally perhaps? Ambrosius quirked an eyebrow at his companions. 'Indeed, King Mor. We should consult later today.'

The king nodded, his horse spinning. 'Please excuse us for now. These horses are fractious after being given their heads for the fast ride across open country. There will be no chance at polite conversation until they have been shown their stables.'

The two men loosened their reins, and the horses leapt forward, ears pricked, as they continued on their way.

'Not at all what I expected,' commented Nataline, watching them go.

'The senior commanders of the northern army were always held in high esteem. If only we had men like that to defend our eastern shores,' said Didius.

'I am told there are many factions and tribes to the north, not all of them so civilised or disciplined,' said Elafius, not seeming as impressed as his companions.

'No doubt we will have the measure of him by this evening, but it sounds as if he is no friend to King Vortigern.'

*

Mor was impressed by Viroconium.

'This is how I remember Eboracum,' said Taly. 'Shopkeepers, taverns, public buildings, a church and a forum still in use.'

They stabled their horses and arranged accommodation at a nearby tavern. They then walked to the church where they were welcomed by a prelate with a dark complexion. Once inside, after leaving their weapons at the back, they joined those delegates who were already there, all chatting to each other. A quick scan of the gathering let Mor know that King Vortigern had yet to arrive. Ambrosius and his companions were amongst those already waiting, and Mor recognised Gundad who was speaking with both Viracus and a facially bruised Cunevindus. Before Mor could approach Gundad, Vortigern walked into the church. He wore a splendid outfit that marked him as someone of great wealth. He was accompanied by the prelate as he made his way through the delegates, greeting them with nods of his head.

Mor caught Gundad darting several glances in his direction, but the nervous-looking merchant never allowed his eye to linger long enough for them to acknowledge one another. No matter. There was plenty of time left for that confrontation. Vortigern sat himself in a grand wooden chair placed in front of the apse containing the altar. There was no other seating, and Viracus invited the delegates to stand either side. It was an airy building with eight carved wooden columns supporting the roof, and Taly gave a nod toward one of them. Mor shrugged and followed Taly, taking up a leaning position alongside him – it would likely be a long debate. The prelate addressed the gathering.

'I am Agricola, bishop of this see. King Vortigern has asked me to offer a prayer to bless this Council meeting.

> *'Beneath your compassion*
> *we take refuge O Holy Mother;*
> *do not despise our petitions in times of trouble*
> *but rescue us from dangers,*
> *only pure, only blessed one.*
> *Amen.'*

There was a moment's silence before Vortigern began his address.

'Welcome all. There has not been a meeting so important to our future since the Romans departed, and with God's help, I hope we can achieve a consensus here today.'

Mor's gaze moved over the gathering, noting where the delegates were positioned. Vortigern was flanked by his allies and advisors. Mor and Taly were positioned to Vortigern's left, further back than the Dobunni king's tightly gathered supporters. Over on the other side, to the right of Vortigern, but facing Mor, was Ambrosius and his companions. It seemed the lines had already been drawn.

Vortigern continued. 'It is now seventeen years since we broke with Rome. Since then, the five principal regions have arranged their own defence. Many hoped this state of affairs would be temporary and that Rome would return, but their barbarian enemies on the Continent have proved too strong a foe even for the mighty Roman Empire, especially as they now face constant challenges from within their own ranks.' Vortigern looked directly at Ambrosius, as if the man needed reminding that his own father had been one such challenger. 'Our fathers fought bravely against any enemies who challenged our own territories, and for a time, we enjoyed peace and prosperity, but now there is no denying that a change is upon us. Our enemies grow bolder, raiding has intensified, reaching ever deeper into our lands. We do not have the resources to counter this threat. Here in the west, we continue to match our old adversaries – the Gaels and the Scotti. Their tactics do not greatly vary, and the west coast has many natural barriers to restrict their attacks. However, the east, from the Humber to the Thames is wide open to incursion from all manner of people. There is talk that they do not simply raid anymore, that they have set up secret ports and settlements along our eastern coastline, that our enemies now live within our own boundaries.

'Prince Mor.' Vortigern turned, and his supporters cleared a path through their tightly packed ranks so that he might see Mor whilst speaking. 'Please accept the Council's condolences for the death of your grandfather. He maintained a fearsome military force to defend our northern frontier right up until the last. As a leader of this force, the only significant militia left in the Patria, how do you see these new threats?'

'Much as you do, King Vortigern. The western attacks are unwelcome but predictable. My brother Gorwst is allied with Coroticus to the north. The Scotti and the Picts fear this combined defence, no longer daring to invade overland. Our forces are well prepared to counter the occasional random raid from that quarter. Christian missionaries now move freely through those barbarian kingdoms, keeping us informed of troop movements and signs of unrest.'

'So, do they know why the Picts are raiding south of the Humber now? Do Christ's missionaries have any insight on this?' asked Vortigern.

'There has been no word, nothing to indicate that Picts are raiding to the south of the Patria. All we know is that they are not coming overland, and the Picts are not renowned as mariners. If they are indeed raiding south of the Humber, we can only assume they are receiving assistance from Saxons or have established a base somewhere within the Patria.'

'How can we be sure it isn't you sponsoring these raids, *King* Mor? After all, you look like a Pict,' barked Cunevindus, his snarling features made angrier by the purple bruising.

Mor tensed, his response not far from his lips, barely registering Vortigern's look of alarm, but Taly gripped his wrist, staying the furious words, and stepped forward.

'My king is a member of the Council, a Protector. His father was killed by Picts and his grandmother murdered by Scotti alongside my wife and child. All our lives, we have fought a relentless war defending the Patria. If we are to be accused of falsehoods and insulted, we will immediately withdraw from the Council.'

There was a stunned silence. Mor gathered his calm and spoke before anyone else got the chance.

'My speculation is likely no better than anyone else's, but it is my duty to protect the North and that I will do. We have repositioned some of our forces to the south of our territories, in Elfed, so that we are better placed to protect our interests. Having suffered at the hands of raiders for so long, we would not bring such suffering on anyone. We will only cross our boundaries if it is necessary to protect our territory and our people. To answer your question, Lord Cunevindus, let me make it perfectly clear: we will never raid, but if provoked, we will surely invade.' He stared resolutely at the big man.

Vortigern shifted uncomfortably on his wooden throne. Mor knew the self-styled high king would be fretting. For all that he needed to keep his attack dog on-side, he needed his plans to be ratified by the Council more. Surely, he would not allow Cunevindus to undermine all he wanted to achieve just to satisfy some damaged pride?

'Cunevindus,' Vortigern said, his tone sharp, 'if I wish you to speak, I will ask it.' He turned to Mor. 'King Mor, we know the North is in safe hands, and we do not doubt your word.' His gaze then abruptly shifted to the other side of the room, a clear indication he considered the matter dealt with. 'Didius and Elafius, it is good to see you here. I was sad to hear of the death of Fastidius; he was an exceptional bishop and will be much missed. Has his position been filled?'

'It has, King Vortigern. By the most pious Vodinus, his deacon,' answered Didius.

'And how fares Londinium?'

'All cities in the east struggle to function as they once did. We live in only half of the area and close to the fort for protection. Our militia has dwindled, and we are vulnerable to attack. Saxon raids are frequent, making both agriculture and trade difficult to sustain.'

'It is the same in Verulanium. The city is in turmoil,' added Elafius.

Vortigern nodded, his expression grave. Then he seemed to notice Ambrosius for the first time. 'Ambrosius Aurelianus!' he exclaimed. 'Welcome. How fares the far south?'

'It is a pleasure to meet you as last, Vitalinus, although I did not expect to have to come so far north to meet my neighbour. The south suffers sporadic raiding from Gaels, but our cities are secure and protected, and go about their usual business much like this one. This is mostly thanks to our militia which we have maintained and expanded over the last few years.'

'How many men at arms do you maintain?'

'A thousand or so, half of which are funded from my personal coffers, whilst the other half are funded by the cities.'

Vortigern nodded toward an older man in his party. 'My friend, Conomor of Dumnonia, tells me you are popular.'

Ambrosius laughed. 'That depends on who you speak to.'

'And what is your business with this Council?'

'I am here to support my friends from Maxima Caesariensis in finding a solution to their security issues but also to raise a significant property dispute with you.'

'Well, shall we deal with security first?'

'That seems appropriate.'

'In the depths of winter, I met with King Mor to discuss a proposal to employ a tribe of Jutes as foederati. He approved, provided the Council is in accord and there is an acceptable treaty in place to defend against insurrection. The proposed settlement is on the Humber, facing across to Mor's territory, so his prior agreement was crucial. Since that meeting, I have appointed Cunevindus to draw up a treaty and to co-ordinate and control all foederati in my domains. We have already settled one tribe of warriors under a leader called Gewis on land along the upper Thames, and they are ready to deploy in support of Londinium if you require it.'

'We are aware of their settlement in the wetlands of the upper Thames. This borders our territory, and we were hoping you might advise us of their purpose,' said Nataline.

Vortigern passed over the landowner's comment and continued. 'The Jutes we propose to settle on the Humber are proven fighters. Their leader is a fearless warrior called Whitgils who is supported by his sons, Hengist and Horsa. They will use their maritime skills to defend against the Picts and any others, including their own countrymen, who threaten our eastern coastline. They have a mighty fleet of at least twenty keels, three of which we plan to deploy to Rutupiae. The successful general, Aetius, has used mercenaries to

Rome's advantage on many occasions, and I see no reason why we should not adopt similar tactics. I know that I already have the support of many of you here, but for those of you who are hearing about this proposal for the first time, what say you?' Vortigern looked toward Ambrosius and his companions.

'You have given us much to consider, King Vortigern,' said Didius. 'We beg your patience whilst we discuss this amongst ourselves.' The southern cives crowded around one another, speaking animatedly in tones too hushed for anyone else to hear.

Mor was not surprised when Taly turned to him with a querying expression. 'Did you agree to this?'

'Not as amicably or as easily as he has presented it, but no matter. It still surprises me that Vortigern is so keen to take responsibility for settling Saxons within the Colonae. He thinks he is buying an army and a navy that he can use to control the Council and justify his pre-eminence, but if they turn against the Cymry, he will have no way to defend against them.'

Taly grimaced. 'This is not the place to mention it, but that is Myrddin's prophecy made real. If all the Saxon tribes of the Colonae combine, they will become a mighty army with no one but the North capable of opposing them.' He nodded across the church. 'We have movement.'

It seemed that Ambrosius had been elected as spokesman for the southern cives, for it was he who approached Vortigern. The Dobunni king was now flanked by Gundad and Cunevindus, the three of them cutting short a whispered discussion when Ambrosius cleared his throat.

'The landholdings, are they to be agreed as permanent settlements?'

'Yes,' said Vortigern.

'And do these warriors require us to fulfil further obligations in addition to providing them with new lands?'

'Yes. Supplies of a general nature which Gundad will co-ordinate.'

'Who pays for these supplies?'

'We will split the cost equally between Britannia Prima and Maxima Caesariensis. The North has understandably already refused to bear any costs, so they will have no further say in any agreement.'

'Will you arrange Christian tuition for these barbarians?'

'Agricola will send missionaries to their settlements,' said Cunevindus.

Ambrosius gave a short nod and returned to the huddle. The group's discussion continued for at least an hour. Mor spent the time observing the interaction between Vortigern and his supporters, watching the Dobunni king become increasingly impatient with the lack of resolution coming from the southern huddle. With all the headshaking and gesticulating, there was no hiding that the group had many misgivings about the proposal – would it be enough to put a stop to the ill-conceived plan though? Eventually, Ambrosius returned to Vortigern, and Mor stood up straight, paying close attention.

'Do we have an agreement between our provinces?' asked Vortigern.

Ambrosius spoke up. 'It is a bold step, Vitalinus. My father and his brother made pacts with barbarians, and it did not go well for them. You are making foreigners, cousins to those who raid our land and people, responsible for the Patria's defence which is no small undertaking and a heavy burden for you to carry. But yes, in the absence of any other viable solution, you have the agreement of the southern provinces. You should know that my friends would prefer a return of the Romans though, and they will continue to canvass for that. I too long for the Empire of our forefathers but want nothing from it whilst under the current Theodosian regime. We must make the best of things as they are. However, much like King Mor, I will make my own arrangements for the defence of my own domain.'

Vortigern nodded, visibly relaxing. 'Your agreement is most welcome. Now, you wish to speak with me about property, Ambrosius?'

'Yes. Germanus of Auxerre has written to both Nataline and myself requesting that we recover the former properties of Melania and farm them on behalf of the Church of Rome. I am led to believe that you currently have control of these properties and that your Saxons are camped there, so what is your response to the Church's claims?'

'I say no, Ambrosius. We will continue to farm the properties and remit an income to Bishop Agricola and Bishop Vodinus. The land was abandoned and should be used for the benefit of the people who did not abandon our shores. Germanus reaches beyond his borders, even accusing our bishops of preaching something called Pelagianism. He sits in the middle of Gaul and thinks he can still tax our people. Frankly, it is insulting. No, definitely no.'

Ambrosius seemed to have expected this response. 'I will write back to Germanus with your answer. It is likely that it is Pope Celestine who is seeking this restitution. The Church does not recognise borders or empires; it only recognises the Kingdom of Heaven. Germanus wants nothing for himself, caring only that the word of the Lord is promulgated.'

'Quite so, Ambrosius. Yet, we are fighting against the incursion of heathen barbarians and need all the funds we can raise to defend our Christian cives. I'm sure Germanus would not argue against that taking precedence in these dark days.'

With this final comment, Vortigern stood. 'You must excuse me, gentlemen. I wish to speak with my family before the feast. I believe our discussion is concluded, but Agricola, Cunevindus and Caninus will stay to answer any further questions you may have.'

Vortigern turned and spoke quietly to Cunevindus and Gundad. Mor couldn't hear what was said, but judging from the looks in his direction and the murderous frustration in Cunevindus' expression, he guessed Vortigern was telling them to steer clear of the northern delegation and avoid rocking the political boat.

The sun was streaming through the church windows, making the outdoors seem so much more enticing than the dark shadows of the nave. Mor gave Taly a nudge and nodded toward the door. They collected their weapons and left the church. Finding a tavern further down the street, they settled on a bench.

'So that is *High King Vortigern*,' said Taly thoughtfully. 'He's doing a good job of spreading the Saxons around the countryside.'

'Aye. It would seem to be more than just that settlement on the Humber. He clearly has a much grander plan that he is not being entirely open about. It will be interesting to see if the attacks on the cives cease now. Heads up – here come our fellow councillors from the south.'

Ambrosius and his colleagues had just left the church. Taly turned and waved to the approaching group of men, beckoning them over.

'I think Vortigern is playing with fire, but let's see if our new friends agree,' murmured Taly.

'It is good of you to invite us to join you, Prefect Talhaearn, King Mor,' said Ambrosius.

'Not at all. We are enjoying this late summer sun, and it will be all the better with company,' said Taly.

'Will you be attending Vortigern's feast?'

'A brief appearance,' replied Mor. 'Unfortunately, we must return to Elfed with some haste.'

'That is a shame; your company will be missed,' said Ambrosius. 'Do you believe that Vortigern holds enough sway over these Saxons to keep them under control?'

'He seems to think he does, but the Colonae is a complex region made up of many tribes. Most of the raiders who attack your cities are likely launching their keels from just north of your own coastal borders, others, we now think, are using the southernmost region of the Great Forest to cover their movements.'

214

'So what would be your advice, Mor?' asked Ambrosius.

'Rely on your own militia for your defence; they are the only fighting force you can truly trust. This audacious plan of Vortigern's is flawed, but it buys you precious time to prepare your men and your defences.'

'So where does the North stand in his scheme?' asked Elafius.

'On the outside. The North now considers itself a separate Christian kingdom which we will defend against any and all incursions. We do not have the resources to help defend other territories, and for us, it is only a matter of time before the Picts come overland once more. We must ever keep one eye to our enemies in the far north.'

'We are impressed by your valour and strategic thinking, King Mor. Such leadership is sadly lacking in the south,' said Didius, who looked the most worried of the group by far.

'Leaders will come in time,' said Taly, 'but first, you need an army for them to lead. It would be wise to double or even treble the size of your militia, Ambrosius.'

'That would be my response too, but I am concerned that Vortigern might consider such a step provocative?'

'Don't be taken in by King Vortigern's show of pre-eminence,' said Mor. 'It is a façade, and he remains just one king amongst many. This treaty with the Saxons falsely represents both his authority and his intentions. We are fortunate in the North, isolated as we are by physical barriers that also complement our defence, but the lowlands to the south are easy prey for raiders. I cannot say if these Saxons will remain loyal or that their objectives are entirely honourable, but it is not my intention to undermine this treaty. We believe Vortigern's plans are well meant but misguided; he wants to be seen as the leader who protected the people, but he also seeks to isolate you from Rome, that is clear from the planned deployment of Jutes to Rutupiae.' Mor noticed Taly signalling it was time to make a move. 'So, my friends, let's stroll to the mansio and toast the decisions of this day whilst remaining mindful of the future.'

As the party walked down the busy street, Taly took hold of Mor's elbow, slowing him down so that they hung back a bit.

'I believe our business here is complete. It might be wise to take our leave today.'

'I agree, Taly. We will bid them farewell before the feast begins. I'm sure the tension our presence causes will not be missed.'

'Your marriage plans will hardly improve that!'

Mor gave Taly a grim look. 'There will be trouble from that, and I truly hope the queen does not suffer rebuke for it. But we depart this evening and cast the die, for good or ill.'

XXIII

Banna

Late September 427

Marchell cast a glance to Gorwst surrounded by his dogs. She sat sewing by the fire, heavy with child, just two or three weeks more to wait. She was not in her best mood, frustrated with herself for the tears that had been rising unbidden all day. It wasn't like her to be so emotional.

'You keep too many dogs,' she said, without lifting her head. 'Why you insist on having a pack following you everywhere is beyond me. You only need Hercules.'

'My boy will love these dogs.'

'Yes, if they don't eat him first, and who says it's a boy?'

'Mother says it is.'

'Oh, she still has *some* interest in her king's wife then?'

'Of course she does, Marchell. Why say such a thing?'

'Well, since your brother and Taly arrived with their princess, she's been all a-flutter and hardly seems to notice me.'

'Come, come, Marchell, that is to be expected with their visit being so brief.'

'How can you be so sure?'

'Mor told me himself, and we've had word that Ninian will be here by tomorrow.'

'Gorwst!' she said, raising her voice. 'You've been sat there gawping at me in silence all this time! Why didn't you mention that?'

Did this mean they planned to marry straight away? Nobody had mentioned any such plans to her or Cara.

Gorwst put his head down and stroked Hercules.

'I didn't want to disturb your concentration whilst I was quietly admiring you,' he said softly.

'Mor's Roman girl is the true beauty; go and watch her – everyone else does. I'm only the queen carrying the king's heir. How dare you keep me in the dark so long!'

Gorwst did not reply. He had made no attempt to hide how pleased he was for his brother. Banna was buzzing with people saying how special Igerna was, how unlike the usual Cymry princess she was. What did they mean by that? Apparently, she rode as well as any man and could even use a bow from horseback. She was as tall as Gorwst, which was slightly intimidating, and Marchell had heard she was incredibly engaging, quick to smile and ready to laugh. Marchell already felt as swollen as an overfed sow, she didn't need Igerna's lithe, statuesque body gliding about the place, making her feel even worse. The whole fort thought she was a fine bride and Mor a lucky devil. Marchell did not have the slightest intention of congratulating Gorwst's smug upstart of a brother. Suddenly, the dogs stirred, barking toward the door. It opened, and a voice called, 'May I come in?'

Much to Marchell's consternation, Igerna entered, and the pack bounded over to welcome her. She greeted them enthusiastically before spotting Hercules standing-off properly, awaiting his personal invitation.

'Now you're a handsome brute!' said Igerna, stroking the hound. Gorwst stood to greet her. 'I didn't mean you, Gorwst!' She laughed, eyes sparkling.

Marchell forced a smile. How she hated her already.

'Your brother requests your company at the tavern, and I need some advice from Marchell,' Igerna said.

Gorwst needed no encouragement to spend time at the tavern with his brother. Marchell narrowed her eyes as she watched him leave immediately with all his dogs following. No sooner had he closed the door, she dropped her head and continued to concentrate on her sewing.

'So Ninian comes to marry you to Mor?'

'He does. We sent him a messenger from Luguvalium when we passed through. He comes tomorrow.'

'I imagine he will wonder why there is such urgency for this wedding. I imagine that we all wonder the same thing.'

Igerna looked quizzically at Marchell. 'Well, we eloped in sudden and difficult circumstances and planned to ride for Elfed. But due to the... circumstances we revised our plan and took the western road north so that I could meet you all. It was a hard six-day ride mind, through challenging terrain, but I am so glad we took the opportunity, for who knows when we might be free to travel up here next? I hope we are not imposing on you, but I am so pleased to be here.'

'Your future husband can be impetuous,' said Marchell, with a sniff. 'They all are – it runs in the family.'

She lifted her head and looked Igerna up and down. *I'll wager that Mor has warned her to be wary of me*, she thought.

'You will know by now there are no Roman comforts this far north; and your sort find it very cold.'

Igerna laughed. 'Yes, you are right; my maidservant, Felicia, is from Armorica – she hates the cold and thought Viroconium chilly. So far, she has loathed the journey and is yet to warm through, whereas I am enjoying the experience. The air here is so fresh.'

Marchell's attempt to suggest unsuitability had not gone as planned. She shifted uncomfortably on her stool and held her side, taking a sharp intake of breath when she felt a kick from her unborn child.

Igerna sat down next to her. 'Is the baby moving?'

Marchell nodded, and a tear ran down her cheek. 'The baby will be here soon.' In her oddly emotional state, female company felt comforting.

'I was present at the birth of my cousin's children. It was lovely, but scary. Do you have someone skilled to attend the birth?' Marchell shook her head, not trusting herself to speak. 'Felicia is a skilled midwife,' continued Igerna. 'I could leave her with you should you wish it? I know how difficult the first months are.'

Against her initial instinct, Marchell was warming to the girl. By contrast, she would never offer Cara's services to anyone else and was always furious with Gorwst whenever he did so.

'That is a kind offer which I will consider. My maidservant, Cara, is loyal but has no birth experience. Gorwst's mother will help, though she is easily distracted. I wish my own mother were here, but I was the youngest and she is now quite old.'

'Really?' Igerna smiled. 'I know so little about this family. Mor has told me you are the daughter of a great warrior and sister to a king. He also told me of your beauty and watchful eye, saying his brother is in safe hands. I have been yearning to speak with you ever since I arrived.'

Marchell was pleasantly surprised but doubted that Mor had been quite so complimentary. She was certain he loathed her influence over Gorwst.

'Och well, this is hard country alright. Family is very important. The boys' grandfather, King Coel, was a towering influence, and they were both raised as disciplined warriors. Talhaearn is the same, and has ever been a father figure to them both. They are God-fearing, but beware, they relish war, thrive on confrontation and can be reckless. I fear for this child's future.'

'How so?'

'We will all be widows, mark my words, I sense it. There are more widows than soldiers in the North these days. So tell me about yourself, Igerna. I have so far only heard about your beauty,' she said, wincing slightly at the faint sarcasm she had failed to keep from her tone.

'Well, my grandfather was Octavius, chieftain of the Cornovii, and I am daughter of Conan, his only son. His sister, my aunt, was Empress Elen who was so cruelly widowed and harshly treated by the Romans. She fled to Armorica to be with her brother whilst heavily pregnant with Sevira. My father later married Ursula, but my mother died giving birth to me. Elen and Sevira brought me up whilst Conan waged war after war until he sadly died on the battlefield. We returned to Viroconium to seek the protection of Octavius, but he was very old and distraught by Conan's death. He forced Sevira into an unhappy marriage to King Vortigern. She now spends as much time as possible living apart from him to lessen the impact of his mistreatment of her.'

Marchell couldn't quite believe what she had just heard. 'So, you are an emperor's niece?'

'Yes. Not that it counts for anything. I rarely bother disclosing it. I tell you now, in confidence, because I want your trust.'

'What a sad story, and here I am feeling sorry for no one but myself. Who arranged this marriage to Mor? Was it Vortigern?'

'Goodness, no. It was Queen Sevira. The king will be furious if he finds out she had anything to do with handing an heir to Cornovii territory to the North. Vortigern is not to be trusted; he consorts with other women and is particularly close to a rival family. I was under pressure to marry a vile man who now styles himself as leader of the Cornovii. But Mor rescued me from that fate, on Sevira's suggestion.'

There he is again – Mor the hero. 'Will this man come after you?'

'Unlikely. The North is too strong. I am not sure if I am supposed to tell you this because Brianna mustn't hear of it, but Mor fought him in single combat and won.'

This really was too much. Mor's recent heroism was insufferable.

'How reckless, but romantic. Was this over you?'

'No, over a stag!'

They both started to laugh, and Marchell felt another kick, but she couldn't stop laughing, holding her side whilst she rocked back and forth in mirth. She could not find it in her heart to admire Mor, but she was enjoying Igerna's company.

'I will say it again. Reckless!'

Marchell realised that she now felt at ease in her future sister-in-law's company.

'I am so excited the bishop is coming tomorrow,' said Igerna. 'It actually brings me to the reason why I have come to speak with you. May I ask you if you will kindly be my maid of honour, Marchell? It feels so strange to be getting married in a place where I have no family or friends. I barely even know *where* I am!'

'I know exactly how that feels! Yes, of course I will do it. These men of ours need strong women to keep them on course!'

They chatted for a further hour, and Igerna sent Cara to collect Felicia so that she could be introduced to Marchell. When Gorwst returned from the tavern, Marchell's mood had completely changed. She did not scold him for drinking, but instead, she recounted all that Igerna had told her, finishing with, 'And I should tell you, your brother is nowhere near good enough for that fine woman!' Gorwst's look of surprise was so comical.

*

Taly sat on the bunk and looked around his old hut. It was damp and smelt of decay. In the corner was the pile of sacks that had been Plato's bed. How he missed his faithful hound who had made the journey to Isurium and then to Elfed, only to die of a sudden sickness in the first winter. He was old for a dog, fifteen years, but there should have been more time. Taly had nursed him for two days, though they had both known the old boy was dying. Tears pricked at Taly's eyes as he remembered pressing his face to Plato's snout to say goodbye, and Plato had tried to lick him, but even his tongue was too weak by then, and he died there and then in Taly's arms. He was with Bewyn now, hunting in Heaven.

His eyes roamed around his old hut once more. Brianna had promised him she would keep it just as it was for his return, but it just served to remind him how much had changed, that nothing could ever be the same again. Brianna...

Taly stood, leaving his memories in the damp and decay. He walked toward the southern gate, drawn to the view over the valley. As he passed through the gate, the warmth of the sunset was a welcome contrast to the shade within the walls. And there was Brianna, on her knees, digging and tugging at vegetables. He watched her – still so beautiful – until she noticed him. He waved and smiled then limped to the cliff edge. The familiar view over the river valley was comforting, the lush land as colourful as always – there were some things that hadn't changed. He sighed as Brianna stepped up beside him and linked her arm in his.

'I miss this view,' he said wistfully.

Brianna did not reply, just squeezed his arm with hers, pulling him closer.

'How is the garden?' asked Taly.

'I'm coping without you.' She paused. 'When are you coming home?'

'I cannot say. Someday, I hope.'

'When the leaves fall, you can see the bridge from here.' Brianna looked up at him and added softly, 'The bridge where you saved me.'

They had never spoken of it nor what had followed...

Taly squeezed her arm.

'In truth, my love, it was you who saved me – something to live for, someone to cherish.' He stopped short and turned to face her. Her hair was just as grey as his; her beauty was undiminished. Their eyes met. Taly uncoupled her arm and held her hand. Drawing it to his lips, he kissed it, saying, 'I will think of you every day.'

He returned her hand and saw tears welling in her eyes. Her lips shaped to speak, but all she could say was, 'Oh, Taly.'

He closed his eyes. He knew he should leave, but he could not. Not yet.

'Oh, what the hell,' he whispered. He pulled her to him, holding her body tight to his. One last kiss, that's all. It was just as he remembered, and what they had both wanted ever since, though they had denied themselves out of respect for their ghosts. A voice broke the spell.

'Mother!'

They jumped apart. Taly certain they had been caught, concerned for any scandal his impetuous kiss might bring on Brianna.

'Mother!' the voice called again, and Mor walked through the gate, Igerna at his side.

They had not been seen. Their farewell kiss would remain a precious secret.

'We've been looking everywhere for you. There are wedding plans to finalise.'

Brianna looked as flustered as a young maiden, her pink cheeks pretty against her sparkling eyes. 'Of course, coming, dear.'

Taly tilted his head and smiled, watching as she skipped across the garden to join them.

He looked to the sky.

'That's the last time, I promise,' he said quietly to his gallery of ghosts.

*

Ninian arrived the following day and was delighted at the prospect of marrying Mor and Igerna. He was especially pleased to spend time with Taly, and many hours passed as they discussed the progress with the Christianisation of the Picts. There had been some success but not without the odd martyr, and although the culdeis were a new idea, they had been well received in Reged.

'There are no bishops in the east, Ninian. The church at Eboracum burnt to the ground, and the Lindum see is also vacant. I intend to build a small church in Elfed, and we will need a priest. Can you arrange one?'

'There is one man I have in mind. Much like you, he is a warrior turned to God. I will send him to Elfed before Saturnalia. He is called Martin.'

*

The marriage ceremony was held in the little church in the valley below Banna. It was a windy day showing the first signs of autumn in the leaves that danced around the meadow. Many well-wishers had come from around and about. When the church doors opened, they cheered and applauded the newly married couple.

Coel's grave, only yards away, had become a massive cairn of rocks. There were no monumental masons left in the area, and Gorwst had started the pile, bringing more rocks every week. As the couple greeted the well-wishers, Taly's eyes alighted on the ridge above the valley, and there, fur glinting in the autumn sunshine, stood the brown bear he had seen in early spring. He tapped Gorwst's shoulder, pointing at the rare sight.

'I've seen him,' he remarked. 'He's appeared a few times this year, usually when I'm stood by Coel's grave; he seems to like the view from there. Marchell chides my superstition, but I believe it's Grandfather.'

Taly squeezed Gorwst's arm.

'So do I, and I'm very glad he's here.'

XXIV

Isca Dumnoniorum

Sextilis 429

King Conomor had already heard that four Roman monks had landed on the coast after the storm. The Plym was a popular haven for passing ships to shelter from the turbulent Oceanus Britannicus, but the estuary was also a favourite entry point for raiding Gaels, and with late summer their favourite time of year to attack, his sentries were alert to every potential threat. Unseasonal storms at sea were usually accompanied by tragedy. The coast around Dumnonia was treacherous and boats and bodies regularly washed up on the shoreline sometimes with their cargoes. The sea protected his realm, and he always prayed that the bodies discovered on the beaches should be raiding Gaels and not his subjects. Tales of survival at sea were sung in court as shanties, but the waylaid monks now stood in front of him did not present him with a song but with a request for assistance so that they might continue their onward mission. He was not yet sure why he should help four marooned Romans, but he did not want to tarnish his renown for being a man of deep religious beliefs and his coastal domains already hosted a collection of ascetics who sought solitude by the wild seas.

He looked at their hopeful faces and sighed. 'What has brought you fine Christian men to my domain?'

The monk who had taken on the role of spokesman for the group answered, 'We embarked at Coriallum in Gaul, intending to sail to one of the ports sheltered by the island of Vectis, but last week's storm blew us two hundred miles west, and we eventually made landfall at the mouth of the Plym. It is thanks only to God's mercy that we are alive. It has taken us two days to walk to Isca.'

'Surely your captain could have sailed you back to Vectis once the storm had passed?'

'There were other passengers, in particular my companion, Palladius, who goes to become Bishop of Hibernia. It seemed unnecessary to further delay his journey when the storm had taken him in the direction he wanted to go, and we were just pleased to be on dry land after such an experience. The storm tossed the boat about like a toy, most unexpected in late summer.'

'Indeed. I have had word that several of our fishermen were lost at sea.'

'May they rest in peace.' The monks briefly bowed their heads. 'It is a mystery why God chose to spare us and bring us to this place, though we are certain that He will reveal His plan in His own good time.'

'And what are the names of the men God has chosen to deposit on my shore?'

The tonsured monks looked at each other, nodding ascent to their spokesman.

'I am Bishop Germanus of Auxerre, this is Bishop Lupus of Troyes and these two are deacons, Julius and Philus.'

Conomor eyed the four, recognising the bishops' titles. 'A high-powered delegation indeed. Tell me, why does the Patria warrant such a visit?'

'We have been sent by Pope Celestine to ensure that our Church continues to teach the Grace of God, in the absence of the Empire's influence and protection.'

'Germanus, were you not one of the Empire's most senior ducs? I have relatives in Armorica who, I am certain, used to speak of you.'

'That was once my chosen path, King Conomor, but whilst I retain interests in that most beautiful province, I am now dedicated to Christ and the Church.'

'Well, I see you carry few possessions and no weapons, but does an army follow behind you?'

'Only an army of saints, good king, there are no longer imperial ambitions for Britannia.'

Conomor smiled at Germanus. 'And what is your intended destination?'

'Bishop Vodinus awaits us in Londinium.'

'Well, who am I to stand in the way of God's plan? I will give you horses for your journey, and you are welcome guests until you are ready to depart. Do you visit Ambrosius? I note your ship's route would have taken you into his estuary?'

'We do. He retains an interest in Gaul much like you do in Armorica. Palladius tells me he is refreshing company.'

'Indeed, he is. Please, join me for cena. I have much to discuss regarding Armorica, and I believe I know why God has brought you to us.'

That got their attention. Bishop Germanus looked particularly intrigued.

'Please, King Conomor, do not keep us in suspense.'

'I have recently been blessed with a son rather late in life. He is named Constantine after the greatest of the Christian emperors. He needs baptising.'

Conomor was pleased when the men of God laughed at his little jest.

'That would be a pleasure, but you should give thanks to God for the storm that sent us your way.'

'In Dumnonia, if we were to give thanks for every storm, we would never be off our knees!'

The clerics laughed again.

'Until cena.'

'Thank you, King Conomor.'

The delegation left to return to their lodgings. The king stood and called to a servant.

'Find my secretary and prepare a messenger. King Vortigern should hear of this visitation with all speed.'

XXV

Ypwines Fleot

September 429

Despite the dank fret that rolled in from the sea making navigation out of the Humber impossible, Hengist and his men were stripped naked carrying cauldrons of steaming pitch to their keels. This was a task everyone loathed. The sticky tar got everywhere, and even with the greatest care, they would be finding it in their hair for days to come. No matter, it was a vital task that had to be done before the onset of winter. In Jutland, they would have used the tar of the sweet pine, but Hengist had learnt from the fen people how to burn peat and extract tar. It had a stronger smell but was just as effective. It was one of the few advantages to the tanet that the Britons had awarded to his father. Yes, there was plenty of fish and fowl, but it was otherwise a barren landscape poorly suited to agriculture. Even the wolves avoided it. He heard his name being shouted and looked up to see Horsa running toward him along the shoreline.

'Hengist, come quickly. Whitgils summoned us; there are important visitors – Britons.'

There was not a hope that he could clean all of the tar off before meeting the visitors, but he dived into the water anyway and swam toward Horsa.

'Brother, find me clothes. I do not wish to shame our guests through physical comparison!'

Horsa laughed. 'I don't think it would be our guests feeling the shame, and that,' he said, pointing, 'will not require much hiding!'

Suitably attired but still black from the pitch, Hengist arrived at Whitgils' hut to find the elders sat outside with a splendidly attired

Gundad, who Hengist had met before, and a proud-looking military officer accompanied by four guards.

*

Gundad made the introductions. 'Hengist, Horsa, this is Cunevindus; he is a king of the Britons.'

The brothers nodded at the Briton who acknowledged them both. Gundad continued.

'Neither he nor his guards understand our language so speak freely but behave respectfully. We have travelled only a short distance from Guinnon from where we will be distributing the supplies that he has brought in accordance with your treaty. He wishes to know your plans for countering the Picts so that he can report back to King Vortigern.'

Hengist looked at his brother before replying.

'Gundad, in the year since we arrived, the Picts have not raided south. We sailed to Pictland to warn them of our commission. We met with their king, Drest, who assured us that he does not seek confrontation.'

Gundad turned to Cunevindus and spoke in Latin.

'There have been many confrontations at sea with Drest – all victories for our loyal friends.'

Cunevindus replied, 'These savages certainly look fierce. Is that war paint?' He pointed at Hengist. 'Ask them why there are still Picts raiding the mid-land.'

Gundad turned to Whitgils.

'You remember our agreement not to attack my friends in the caves to the south of the Great Forest?'

'Yes,' said Whitgils. 'Balorc and his renegade party of Picts and thieves!'

'Well, it's time to murder them all. You may keep any booty you recover.'

'They are well-protected in a deep labyrinth of caves the Britons call *Tigguo Cobauc*,' said Hengist.

Gundad looked at the young Jute.

'Murder them all and either fire or keep their vessels.'

Gundad turned to Cunevindus, once more speaking in Latin.

'It is good news. Hengist has discovered renegade Picts in caves the locals call *Tigguo Cobauc* and plans to attack them. They are keeping watch awaiting their opportunity and will fall upon them soon.'

'This is good news indeed. I knew that bastard Mor had let some through – I'll wager he's in league with them.'

'That is indeed a possibility, but we must remember our instructions not to provoke him.'

Cunevindus scowled as Gundad turned to Whitgils.

'Remember: do not provoke the northern Britons, never sail beyond the hook. Bring me Balorc's head, and I will reward you well. Mention nothing to the Angles.' He paused. 'King Cunevindus gives you his thanks and authorises the distribution of your supplies.'

'Thank you, Gundad; the Gaini are always helpful.'

Gundad stood to leave.

Cunevindus spoke as they walked toward their mounts. 'A good report, Gundad. I presume you are retaining a portion of these supplies?'

'Of course, and you will return to Viroconium with my gratitude heavy in your purse.'

*

Horsa walked back to the shore with his brother. They could see steam rising from the boats, a sure sign the pitch was still being applied.

'You look pensive, brother?'

'The Angles have an interpreter, but without one of our own, we are no better than blind. We must find one or learn their language, brother.'

'Gundad is ruthless and untrustworthy. He now sends us to murder his associates.'

'Balorc is no longer useful to Gundad but we are retained to fight Picts because the Wealas are weak so that is what we shall do.'

'The Wealas king seemed unaware of Balorc.'

'That brother is why we need an interpreter. Now strip off, Horsa, for I have dirty work for you to do. These keels must be waterproof if we are to see winter with our families in Jutland.'

'One day, we will bring them here – when our children are men.'

'That is my hope and my ambition.'

XXVI

Isurium Brigantum

October 429

Igerna sat in the day-room of their villa suckling Arthwys whilst Morgaine crawled across the mosaic floor under the watchful eye of Felicia.

'It feels cooler today, Igerna. I have asked Alwin to arrange for the heating to be lit.'

'Then we shall soon all be choking on smoke. Last year, it took an age to find all the leaks in the walls!'

Felicia ignored the complaint; the girl would rather be warm and choke to death than cold and breathe freely. 'Does the king return from Cambodunum today?' she asked.

'He does. They have been working so hard on the fort and hall. It is so exciting to think we will soon be living in the beautiful Forest of Elfed.'

Bryn walked in, as if summoned by talk of Igerna's husband.

'The king has returned; he is at the stables. A messenger arrived from Queen Sevira too. I have the missive here.'

'How exciting. Tell the messenger he must rest and stay overnight; I will reply by return.'

Bryn handed the scroll to Igerna who passed a now sleeping Arthwys to Felicia and eagerly broke the seal.

'My cousin is always full of news.'

Out of the corner of her eye, she noticed her husband appear in the doorway. She waved in his direction but did not take her eyes off the letter. Mor waited for a greeting, but none came.

Felicia explained. 'It's a letter, just received.'

Morgaine crawled toward her father who swept her off the floor. 'Perhaps my princess is pleased to see me?' He threw her in the air making her giggle. 'You have you mother's hair and eyes, but hopefully not her terrible manners.'

'Tush, husband. It is a letter from Sevira with much news. Tell me yours later when I will give you my undivided attention.'

Mor gently placed Morgaine on the floor with her wooden toys.

'Where is this smoke coming from?' He looked around the room. 'I thought the hypocaust was fixed. I'll go and check before we all choke to death.'

*

When Mor returned, he was pleased to see the smoke had cleared and Igerna had a cup of mead waiting for him. She gently kissed his lips and smiled.

'Sevira is taking her family to Londinium to meet Bishop Germanus who has travelled from Gaul. There is to be a theology debate between the bishops. Vortigern has instructed her to attend with him. They have hardly spoken since he forced himself on her after the Council.'

Mor looked at the floor. 'That was our fault, Igerna.'

'She's a survivor, and she has beautiful Britu as compensation. She says that Vortigern plans a show of strength – the whole court has departed for Verulamium.'

'I have never heard of this Bishop Germanus, who is he?'

'Apparently my father knew him. He was Duc of Armorica.'

'And now he's a bishop?'

'According to Sevira.'

'I will wager he's a Roman spy come to assess their chances of launching a successful invasion. No wonder Vortigern is taking everyone to Verulamium. At least Sevira will have a safe journey though.'

'How so, husband?'

'Two days since, a renegade Pict surrendered at Cambodunum. He was part of a group exiled by Drest five years ago – apparently a rival. They had been living in the caves of the Great Forest. He claimed to be in league with Gundad, yet it was Gundad's ally, the Jute, Hengist, who stormed the caves and killed all his comrades.'

'Well, that clears up the Pict mystery.'

'I suspected Gundad from the outset – Vortigern is a fool to trust him. But this Hengist is becoming a renowned warrior, though the Jutes have yet to make any attempt at testing our defences.'

'Perhaps you have misjudged them, husband?'

'Myrddin is adamant the threat is real. His dreams of imminent invasion are intensifying. It can only benefit us to remain alert.'

XXVII

South of Lindum

Februarius 430

'That was without doubt the most depressing aspect of my visit to Britannia so far. To see a city like Lindum deserted, save for a handful of Christians…' said Germanus, shaking his head. 'Although, I was pleased to have the opportunity to pray at the shrines of Aaron and Julius, martyrs equally as important as St Alban.'

'The Colonae is almost a Saxon realm now, your Grace,' said Elafius who had advised against the visit. 'Raiders, the plague and fear have turned Lindum into a city of ghosts. It has no need for a bishop anymore, because there is no flock to tend!'

'I hear Eboracum is the same?'

'Worse, your Grace. The church has burnt down, and the bridges have collapsed.'

Elafius was relieved that they were finally on their way back to more civilised territories. The Britons no longer patrolled north of Corieltauvorum for fear of attack. The easterners were now mostly Saxons and had all but annexed the Colonae. It was no place for a Roman bishop, and Elafius had tried his best to avoid the responsibility. He had considered accompanying the prelate with a handful of disguised companions, warriors dressed as monks. It may well have allowed them to pass without drawing attention, but it also might have attracted brigands hoping to relieve the monks of Roman Church silver. So in the end, he had opted to bring thirty cavalry led by a seasoned captain with them from Durobrivae, the frontier fort manned by the only militia of Britons left in the east. The return journey would be more dangerous than their untroubled trip into Lindum – word would be out that a large force of Britons was moving through the territory, and the locals would have had plenty of time to set up an ambush along the route. The captain had informed Elafius that an ambush was a very real possibility since some of his patrols had been attacked . Elafius chatted to the bishop and tried to appear relaxed whilst being alert to danger.

'I hear your quarters burnt to the ground in Londinium, your Grace.'

'That is so. I was lucky to escape. This trip has been remarkable for the number of near misses.'

'The common people consider them miracles.'

Germanus laughed. 'It it helpful they see it that way.'

Elafius fervently hoped there would be no more.

'But a worthwhile trip, nonetheless. Your eloquence seems to have reversed the influence of Agricola?'

'We shall see. King Vortigern protects him, but Queen Sevira told me she will try to have him banished! There seems little harmony in that relationship.'

'The rumours suggest there is no relationship. It is well known Vortigern maintains other consorts, but the stories are too indelicate for your Grace's ears!'

'I have not always been a bishop, Elafius, so tell me what you know. This tussle with Pelagianism may not be over, and I may yet need to return if His Holiness so directs. The more I know, the more leverage I can bring to bear on the enemies of the Church.'

'Incest, your Grace – a dreadful sin. Vortigern maintains a home in the western mountains where he consorts with a woman and their own daughter. If the rumours are true, the daughter has borne him a son.'

'If that is so, Elafius, he is beyond redemption. He seems a desperate man hiding behind theological arguments whilst knowing in his heart that no amount of reinterpretation of God's laws will save his soul.'

Germanus became thoughtful for a moment.

'Poor, Sevira. I knew the family in better days. She sought a private audience with me, and I blessed every one of her children at Verulamium, but she did not mention any of this. She is noble and proud.'

A forward scout galloped toward their column. He reported to the captain who then brought his horse alongside Germanus and Elafius.

'There is a very large group of Saxons converging ahead of us on the Salt Road.'

'Do they have horses?' asked Germanus.

'No, your Grace, but the scout has seen carts and oxen and spears.'

'What is this valley? Could they simply be coming to cross the river?'

'This place is called Causennis. It is where several routes meet at a crossroads. The east–west route leads to the Saxon settlements. They may well be raiders returning home. Do you wish to make a run for it, your Grace; we are no more than fifteen miles from safety?'

'I've never run in my life, captain. Hide half your men in the forest on the far side of this ford. Elafius and I will hide with the other half in this steep wood. When the Saxons begin to make the crossing, I will shout "Alleluia" three times, and your men must reply in unison as loud as possible.'

Germanus turned in his saddle to speak to the soldiers.

'Trust me, God is with us. If the Saxons choose to fight, then we shall fight.'

Elafius did not know what to make of what was happening, but he could not show doubt in the bishop, especially not when God was with them. He fell in with the bishop and followed his lead.

They hid in trees alongside the men, and there was not long to wait. The Saxons arrived. They were many but did not look as threatening as first thought since it was now clear the train included women and children. Germanus cried out his Alleluias, the three successive calls echoing across the valley before being swiftly followed by the same in a chorus of gruff soldiers' voices. Elafius watched, dumbstruck, as the Saxons, surprised by the noise, threw down their possessions in terror and ran for their lives, going west as fast as they could, children screaming. Their warriors held on to their spears, walking backward so they could face the enemy, but when they realised there was no enemy to be seen, they too ran for their lives, likely fearing supernatural ghosts from their heathen imaginations. The Britons waited a good while, watching the Saxons' terrified flight until they had all disappeared over the horizon. Germanus stepped out of his hiding place, Elafius following him in awe, and the soldiers joined them with a loud cheer.

'Leave their possessions,' commanded Germanus. 'God has given us a bloodless victory, and we will not repay his merciful love by plundering these poor people. Now, let us return to our course.'

Elafius couldn't believe what he had seen. Germanus was truly a saint. When they finally reached the fort, Elafius wasted no time in telling everyone there the news of the miracle.

The following morning, he watched as many soldiers and residents of Durobrivae were baptised by Germanus in the river despite the cold. The Alleluia victory had made Elafius realise something important. The Romans used money and citizenship as incentives to fight for them, but in the end, the slaves always rebelled and toppled their masters. Bishop Germanus had galvanised soldier, master, slave and cives alike to fight for one unifying cause, to fight for God. It didn't matter what tribe you were or how rich you were, the only battle that mattered was Christians against heathens. King Vortigern was not the man to lead them, and employing heathens was not the way to save them.

XXVIII

Elfed Forest

Martius 437

Martin swept the floor of the little wooden church that Talhaearn had helped him build on the hillside deep in the Forest of Elfed. To help settle the dust he opened the door. It was early Martius, and the sun rose from behind the hill, breaking through the trees still bare from the ravages of winter. The dawn chorus was sounding more tuneful with each day and the elms were beginning to bud. It would soon be his favourite time of year when the warm rays of searching sunlight filtered through the forest canopy, bluebells adorned the hillside and his church filled with the scent of wild garlic. It had been nearly ten years since Ninian had sent him south to find Talhaearn. Along with the gruff old warrior, he had built two churches – one at Cambodunum where he fulfilled his pastoral duties and this one as a retreat for solitude and reflection. It was a blessing to have found such purpose and tranquillity, though he was yet to find the peace of mind that he craved.

The advantage of the strong physique that he retained from his former life was it prevented people having the courage to ask too many questions about the scars on his body that he did his best to conceal. Martin's far-north origins and illustrious lineage were known only to Talhaearn. Priest he might be now and a man in his prime, but even his name wasn't his, his true identity best kept from all who might talk of it. His past was a place he tried not to dwell, wished he could leave behind. He prayed constantly to God asking that He grant him the mercy to forgive his brother's sins, ashamed that his faith wasn't strong enough to find it in himself. Martin had reached for it so many times, thinking it in reach, only for it to be snatched away the moment he remembered that dreadful night. Time and again, he failed to follow his Lord's path to forgiveness, stumbling at every attempt.

Cynwyb was the name he had been given at birth. It felt strange to hear it, even in his own mind. One of three brothers, all sons to Cinhill, King of Alt Clut. A sister too. He and his brothers were Christian warriors, fighting Pict and Scotti alongside one another from an early age. Their father died in battle, and his elder brother Cynloyp became king. Brothers all. Until the youngest, Coroticus, had become consumed by jealousy and a greed for power. One day, whilst his older brothers knelt at prayer, Coroticus and his accomplices had attempted to hack them both to death. Badly wounded in his arm, neck and side, Martin had fought his way out of the church and run for his life. Unarmed and in agony, his younger brother chasing him down like an animal, they had finally cornered him on the edge of the cliffs to the west. With a choice between death at the hands of his brother or death in the cold, clean waters of the Clyde, he had thrown himself into the river.

How he had survived, he did not know. He was told by the monks that they had found him clinging to a floating tree branch and had fished him out of the river. His wounds had been terrible, and it had taken a week under Bishop Ninian's care before he regained consciousness. That he had survived was nothing less than a miracle. His body had repaired but his mind had not. It was God's will, he knew that; what other explanation could there be? But Martin's nights were now plagued with strange dreams, not all of them connected to the experience he had survived.

He thanked God for the mercy that he had never married, because travellers had told the monks how Coroticus, in his orgy of murder, had subsequently killed his brother's wife and children. The same travellers had confirmed that the brother who had fallen from the cliff was given up for dead.

Honourable Talhaearn had been shocked by Martin's story of regicide, though the old warrior was well aware of the brutality that came with family power struggles. It seemed, by Talhaearn's account, that Martin's sister, Marchell, had never disclosed her version of events and remained close to Coroticus, ensuring him as a strong ally to Gorwst. What had driven Coroticus to such a bloody betrayal? Martin had come close to madness on more than one occasion trying to answer that question.

His mother had died young, and Coroticus and Marchell had been born to his father's second wife. His elder brother was arrogant and had been known to mistreat the second family, but Martin had been fond of both Coroticus and Marchell, thinking them close. The betrayal had cut him deep, the bitterness an unresolved canker on his soul. Did he want revenge? Was he a coward for not seeking it? If God had saved him for a purpose, what was it? Why did he constantly fail to achieve perfection in adherence with God's teachings? He was a priest. He wanted to be a good priest. He could not share his inner turmoil, burden anyone else with his uncertain faith, with his lapses in Christian forgiveness, not without losing all credibility.

His gaze fell on where he had concealed his sword, one here and one in his other church. One day he might be discovered. One day they might come to finish what they had started. Occasionally, he practised his sword-work in secret, hoping God would forgive him for how good it felt to hold a sword in his hand again. He filled his days with as much work as possible to distract him from the past. With Taly's help, he was educating Morgaine and Arthwys. He was humbled that the king and queen placed such great confidence in him, entrusting him with their children's education. They considered him a good balance to Myrddin who distracted but fascinated the children with tricks and fabulous stories. Taly's relationship with the seer was rather odd, and it was strange how a Christian court took the old pagan's prophecies so seriously, but there was something intriguing about the concept of second sight. Since his near death, Martin had experienced strange coincidences – things he couldn't explain. At least in his role as tutor, he could forget about being an imperfect priest. He had the certainty that Igerna held him in high regard, that he was devoted to the children, and that he would hold true to his oath to protect them.

Each morning was an exercise in blocking out the past, so he could embrace the day. He would take solace that his bitterness was not growing; it was just ever present. His turmoil put away, it was time to set off. He put his satchel over his head, reached for his stave and shut the door behind him. His heart lightened at the prospect of the seven-mile walk to the fort. He looked forward to taking in the views over the Gar cliff, glorying in God's creation laid out in the form of a beautiful green forest all the way across the valley to the Pennines.

*

Igerna had set about tidying the large wooden hall with Felicia's help. It had been a long winter and the whole building needed airing and dusting, particularly since Mor was hosting his annual Ides of Martius feast the next day. She hoped the weather would be fine and dry so they could hold the feast outdoors, but who could say what the changeable weather would bring. There would be many guests, mostly the barus, Mor's appointed retainers who managed the regions. They would be riding in from all across the vast dales and plains of Elfed and Crafen. Igerna shuddered at the thought of all those muddy feet. What a mess they would make if there were any of the downpours so common at this time of year. Some of the visitors would bring their families, and they all needed temporary accommodation and food. At least now they had the five round wooden huts which Mor insisted on referring to as the mansios. *Rather too grand a description for such simple accommodation*, she thought. Even so, the huts would all need cleaning before the guests arrived – just another thing on her extensive to-do list. She caught the scent from the kitchens where Bryn was already preparing for the feast, and she felt her mood lighten. The men of the fort may be finding the cooking and baking smells a torment, but Igerna took comfort in their promise of reward for all the hard work.

She had three of those men of the fort right here, getting under her feet. Mor, Cian and Taly were deep in discussion sat around a wooden table.

'Can you three go somewhere else?' Igerna asked as she swept around them.

Mor looked at her through the dust hanging in the shafts of light that stole into the dark hall.

'Gladly, wife, for we are choking from this fog you have stirred up!'

'Thank you,' she said. Then added, 'Have you discussed Sevira's letter with Taly?'

Taly looked quizzically at Mor.

'Not yet, it only came yesterday,' Mor said.

Only yesterday? That was a whole day and a night ago! Igerna turned to face the old bard. 'I am worried; it is very bleak and most unlike her.'

She saw Mor wink at Taly. 'There are some concerning matters we should discuss.'

Winking, indeed. The letter merited serious consideration and had she not been so busy she would have spoken with Taly herself.

The three men stood and walked out into the spring sunlight, leaving her in peace to get ready for the celebrations.

*

Even after ten years, there were still carpenters hard at work around the fort.

'This is now a remarkable stronghold,' said Taly over the sound of hammering.

Mor grimaced. 'I fear its strength may be tested soon. Sevira's letter is concerning, but this report from our scouts about the arrival of some forty Saxon vessels on the Humber is more concerning. I do not know if they are summoned by Vortigern or by Hengist, but the raids ceased long ago so why the sudden need for reinforcements?'

'I can see no reason for Vortigern to request such a force,' said Cian.

'Do you think Hengist plans to invade?' asked Taly.

'It looks that way. The new arrivals are warriors not farmers. They will need feeding and paying, and there is only one way for them to get the resources they need for that... They know we are well prepared for them, so we won't be their first target, but we must be ready.'

'Are you sure that this isn't some ploy of Vortigern's? He and Cunevindus haven't exactly been subtle about trying to grab as much power as they can in the past,' Cian said.

It was a good question from the young warrior. 'That is possible,' said Mor. 'But to what purpose? The Council did not agree to pay for so many warriors, but now they have arrived, what is the Council to do? It has become a problem that cannot be solved. It reminds me of an event my grandfather recounted about the Goths and how they massed on the borders until Rome succumbed and resettled their enemy within. Now they are sometimes allies, and sometimes enemies. Whatever the Saxons plan, they appear to outnumber us three to one.'

Taly looked at his companions. 'I think we all know this is Myrddin's serpent, gathering its strength before it strikes at our heart.'

The sun was warm on their faces, a welcome promise of spring, but the news chilled their souls. They watched Igerna come out of the hall, leading Arthwys and Morgaine out of the gate heading toward the wooden church in the village where Martin would soon be starting their lessons.

'What does Queen Sevira's letter say?' enquired Taly.

Mor turned his gaze to his old friend. 'They write to one another regularly with family news. Aliotus, the merchant, brought this most recent letter. Queen Sevira says Cornovii confidence in Vortigern is at a low ebb. The king does not visit his wife anymore, and Cunevindus is throwing his considerable weight around ignoring the tribe's traditions. Vortimer, her eldest son, had already come to hate his father, but now he refuses to have anything to do with Cunevindus as well – apparently a spell in the military under the man's command went badly. Now Vortimer has left home intending to fight with Ambrosius Aurelianus and his militia. Of course, Vortigern is affronted and has disowned his son and heir, whereas Sevira still plans for the lad to be the future leader of the Cornovii. She is terrified for his safety and has attempted in vain to secure his return. A long time ago, I suggested that he might join our military, but his father forbade it. As my wife says, the letter is indeed bleak because it so clearly indicates that the old order and alliances instilled by the Romans are crumbling as surely as their masonry. The Council is toothless which means the likes of Vortigern and Cunevindus do whatever they want without anyone to hold them to account, other than perhaps the Church.'

Taly nodded. 'Which is itself still divided in the Patria thanks to Pelagianism. Bishop Agricola is shielded by Vortigern.'

'Queen Sevira wrote there was hope in Germanus, but for all his famous showmanship at Verulamium, he has not been heard of for six years,' said Mor. 'and I hear Palladius was banished to Hibernia and has disappeared into the far north where he attempts to convert the Picts.'

'Drest was baptised but he will need God's protection for that mission,' added Taly ruefully.

'Will Rome support the cives if the Saxons attack?' asked Cian.

'Highly unlikely. Rome has not shown any interest in the Patria since they left. We no longer receive any news from Rome, but there are rumours that Aetius has his hands full, and some say North Africa has fallen to Vandals who are refusing to supply Rome with corn. Sevira's letter is full of despair, yearning for the past, but we must trust in God's plan for the future. It is through Him we have won our freedoms and, by His grace, we must protect them. I fear a severe test is coming for us all.'

Taly stroked his grey beard and stifled a yawn. 'Will you excuse me, my lords? I must pray before the middle of the day. I have much to consider before tomorrow.'

'Of course, Taly.'

The old bard got up stiffly and limped toward his wooden hut.

Mor noticed Cian watching his mentor. 'Soon there will be so few who even remember the Romans. How old is Taly now, my lord, mid-sixties?'

'Yes, thereabouts, but there is no one with better intellect and experience, and although he struggles with his eyesight, his mind is as sharp as a knife. He is still the Bear of the North, and everyone who comes tomorrow knows and respects that. He just hibernates more these days.'

Cian laughed. 'Yes. I will be sure to rouse him from his horizontal prayers later.'

*

It was close to sunset, and Igerna, Felicia and Bryn along with an assortment of maids and slaves had just finished the preparations for the next day. Looking across the main courtyard, Igerna could see a stream of guests already arriving through the gate. She and her small team couldn't have timed it better. Her gaze lifted to the clear sky which had saved her the worry of muddy footprints traipsing through her clean huts but would bring a chill to the night. She must ensure there was enough firewood to warm the guest quarters.

This annual feast was such a lovely way to meet their more important subjects, involving them in the plans for the year ahead. Igerna had always loved the occasion, so full of the optimism that comes with spring. But this year's event would not be such a light-hearted affair, and she felt for the families who were yet to learn of the difficult times ahead. Mor, Taly and Cian had spent most of the day planning. Even when Crannog had joined them later on, the concern on their faces had not lifted. Something told her that there would be no boisterous drinking affair on the night before this feast.

*

It had been a great relief when Igerna had opened the shutters on their bedchamber to see that the dawn had broken with glorious sunshine. Now she sat at breakfast quietly running through all the tasks that still had to be done. Taly and Cian had joined Mor for breakfast so that they might continue planning their strategy, their conversation providing background for her own planning. The conversational rhythm ceased, and she looked up to see that Padell had entered the hall.

'They are all here, my lord, apart from Catavignus who I'm sure will arrive soon.'

'Very good, Padell. Alert Martin that he is to take prayers an hour earlier than scheduled.'

Her husband was wearing full uniform – yet another reminder of the seriousness of this year's proceedings. Normally, such formal attire was dispensed with, and military matters were far from everyone's thoughts.

'Myrddin is here,' she said, feeling the sudden need to distract her thoughts. 'Arthwys, Morgaine and their friends are already following him around. He will get no peace today.'

Taly laughed. 'He does not expect it and loves nothing better than answering their questions. But be ready for all the tales of strange creatures that will be circulating before evening.'

'As long as he does not give them nightmares!' said Igerna sternly.

'My queen, he gives us all nightmares.'

*

His congregation was gathered outside the hall facing three empty chairs. Martin waited before the silent crowd as the king, the queen and the Bear arrived, each taking their place standing behind one of the chairs. Satisfied that all were settled, Martin positioned his hands to pray, and everyone lowered their heads. He had chosen his favourite morning prayer 'the Lorica'. The full version was rather long, but he would lead his flock through the two verses he always favoured.

> *Dear Lord*
> *I arise today*
> *Through the strength of Heaven*
> *Light of Sun*
> *Brilliance of moon*
> *Splendour of fire*
> *Speed of lightning*
> *Swiftness of wind*
> *Depth of sea*
> *Stability of earth*
> *Firmness of rock*

He paused. Though he meant every word he spoke, none of the warmth of his prayer reached his soul. Why did he feel so forsaken?

> *I arise today*
> *Through God's strength to pilot me*
> *God's might to uphold me*
> *God's wisdom to guide me*
> *God's eye to look before me*
> *God's ear to hear me*
> *God's word to speak to me*
> *God's hand to guard me*
> *God's way to lie before me*
> *God's hosts to secure me*
> *Against snares of devils*
> *Against temptations of vices*
> *Against inclinations of nature*
> *Against everyone who shall wish me ill*
> *Afar and anear*

Alone and in a crowd
Salvation is of the Lord
Salvation is of Christ
May thy salvation O Lord be ever with us
Amen.

Martin stepped away, taking up a position to the side, whilst the king and queen sat. Taly remained standing.

'Welcome to you all on this beautiful morning. I hope you all enjoyed a restful evening.' There was a murmur of good-humoured assent. Martin saw the old warrior square his shoulder, preparing himself for his address. 'Ten years ago, we pooled our resources and began a campaign to make Elfed a safe and prosperous region. Everyone here has benefited. Great herds of cattle populate our dales protected by you, the king's barus. During this time, there has been no conflict to deflect us from our purpose. But some of you will remember why we came from the North, that we came to protect the Pennine passes from the Saxon threat with a show of strength. Until now, the simple presence of a well-armed, well-trained militia has been sufficient to protect your homes from that threat. But our reason for taking this threat so seriously was not simply a mistrust in these tribes from across the sea. Ten years ago, Myrddin told me he had dreamt that a great serpent would grow in the east and devour the Patria. We always believed this prophecy to be a warning that the Saxons will rise against us, and we have prepared and waited for them to reveal their treacherous intent. Now we have learnt that a great army of Saxons, more than a thousand men, has landed on the Humber. Though there has been no show of aggression yet, we must assume that it will come, and soon. What other intent could there be for so many armed men?'

The gathering erupted in a commotion, cries of alarm rising above the general hubbub. Taly sat down, and the king stood to speak, his calm authority enough to bring the crowd to silence.

'Taly is right. These are worrying times. We have not seen an army of this size in the Patria for over thirty years. Taly, Alwin and Crannog remember the invasions in the North, and we expect these Saxons to follow a similar pattern. If they do not attack in force, they will scavenge and raid – taking your supplies, eating your livestock and destroying your homesteads.'

The commotion rose once more with even greater intensity.

'What are we to do, my lord?' shouted a member of the audience.

'We must counter their tactics, because we can be sure they will not sail away without plundering the richness of our lands first. Though we are scouting their movements to keep ahead of any attacks, there is no doubt they are scouting our movements too. Our strength is our abundance of resources; their weakness is their lack of the same. They must take ours if they are to survive. So, I propose we remove all encouragement from our enemy, leave them with nothing for their efforts. We must drive all our stock inland to the dales behind our strongholds. This year, we will not plant crops beyond where the River Aire meets the Ouse. Homesteads must be abandoned, and the barus will be responsible for giving shelter to all those who require it. All spare feed and seed should similarly be brought inland. Anything that cannot be moved must be fired or destroyed. We will lay a wasteland before us, and our necklace of forts adorning the Pennines will protect our resources and our people in the rich valleys beyond.'

The gathering was quiet, though the looks that Martin saw pass between the people were those of great worry.

Catavignus from the Swale was the last to arrive but first to break the silence. 'Do we prepare to attack this army, my lord?'

'We will hold our defensive position until we are sure of their malicious intent. Each barus already maintains a turma of thirty cavalry which I am entitled to call upon. I now ask that you double this commitment so that you will have the same again in reserve to maintain your own home security when I undoubtedly call upon my entitlement in the very near future. But the onus is not all on you, my good people.

Rest assured that I take my obligation as your Protector very seriously. Here in Cambodunum, we maintain three trained turmae with revolving duties. We will advance our current recruits' training to make a fourth. Altogether, this will give us two hundred and ten cavalry we can field with one hundred and fifty in reserve, protecting our homes.'

Taly stood, and the king gave him a nod.

'Those of you who can count will realise we are still heavily outnumbered by as much as three to one, but that was always how it was with the Picts, and we successfully defended the Wall year on year with those odds. However, as the king outlined, we expect they will attempt to scavenge in our direction, though they may not risk marching north in strength. We Brigantes have a fearsome reputation, and the Saxons know that we will ensure their losses are greater than their gains. The south and west are softer targets, which makes the very people who paid the Saxons for their protection the most likely targets for an all-out assault. May God help and protect them, for we cannot.'

Taly sat down, returning the floor to Mor.

'From here on, we all maintain contact with each other, sharing all intelligence as swiftly as possible. If Saxons are observed in your region, send alerts to the nearest two forts. Instruct your fighting men that there must be no mercy and no fraternisation. If they see Saxons, kill them, even their women and children, so that they fear to set foot in Elfed. Believe me when I tell you that they will reap a terrible slaughter from us if we give them any reason to believe we are weak.

'Now, our next step must be to send messages to Council members and to Vortigern. He may be blind to these developments.'

'He already knows, King Mor.' The shout came from a soldier stood with three companions at the back of the crowd. Martin did not think anyone in the gathering had seen the men arrive.

'Viracus!' the king called out, clearly recognising the newcomer. 'Step forward. Come tell us what you know!'

'Forgive our intrusion, my lord, my companions and I have only just arrived. I come from Queen Sevira with a message for you and Queen Igerna which I can only disclose in private.'

'I will hear Queen Sevira's missive directly, but first, tell us what you know about this Saxon army.'

'The Saxon kings, Hengist and Horsa, say they had to send for more men to fight off the Pictish threat. The leaders of these new arrivals are Octha and Ebissa. They are the kings' sons. It is claimed by Gundad that they have won great victories against the Picts in the Orkney Islands and have come to the Patria to claim their reward for protecting our shores.'

'That claim is preposterous! The Orkneys are deserted save for a handful of farmers. I'll wager they have not been anywhere near those islands, and these Saxons are just making these claims to give them excuse to fleece the cives.'

'I agree,' said Viracus. 'And so does the Council. They have lost patience and refuse to provide the Saxons with any more supplies.'

'Is that so?' asked Mor. 'Have they all refused? Even Ambrosius Aurelianus?'

'Ambrosius is the most powerful voice on the Council. It is he who leads their objections.'

'Thank you, Viracus,' said the king, before turning to the crowd. 'Let us not dwell on troubles that are not yet our problem. We shall all reconvene one hour after midday for the feast. In the meantime, Crannog and Padell will lay out our plans in more detail and answer your questions on my behalf.'

Mor nodded at the trusted aides he had just named then turned to Viracus. 'It is good to see you, old friend. Come into the hall where we may speak in private.' He looked around. 'Taly, I need you to listen in on this, and bring Cian. Martin, can you keep an eye on the children whilst we hear Sevira's message. Do you know where they are?'

Martin stepped forward. 'Before the meeting began, they were playing with the visitors' children over by the spring. Myrddin was sat with them, but I will go and join them.'

*

Mor entered the hall accompanied by those he wished present for Sevira's message. Preparations for the feast were in full swing, the long central table was piled high with food waiting to be distributed amongst the visitors. He dismissed the servants whilst Cian helped Igerna move some chairs to a corner of the hall where they could listen to Viracus in private.

'First of all, you should know I have retired as captain of the guard to King Vortigern, and I have taken my father's old post so that I am better placed to protect the queen.'

'It is a relief to know that her security is in safe hands during such troubling times,' said Mor, knowing that this would also go some way to easing Igerna's fears for her cousin.

Viracus continued. 'I will come directly to her message. You may already know that Vortimer is opposed to both his father and the general, Cunevindus. He has left the kingdom to join Ambrosius Aurelianus, and his father has disowned him. Vortigern is furious at the mounting opposition to his authority and is planning a surprise attack upon Venta Belgarum at the spring equinox, six days from today.'

Igerna gasped, and reached for Mor's hand, seeking reassurance through his touch. He saw his own alarm mirrored in Cian and Taly's expressions.

'He intends to use the Saxon mercenaries from the upper Thames along with a detachment of the Dobunni and Cunevindus' war band. The queen and I have informants who are loyal, but she does not dare to openly oppose Vortigern. There's no telling how he might react. Vortigern is already convinced it is Sevira who has poisoned Vortimer against him.'

'Has she sent a messenger to Ambrosius?'

'No, she would be charged with treason if such a thing were intercepted. She is terrified for Vortimer. Ambrosius' militia is untested, so there is a good chance he will be defeated, and Cunevindus will murder Vortimer at his first opportunity.'

'What sort of man puts his son in such danger?' asked Mor.

'I do not think he has ordered his son killed, but he should know it is a likely consequence with Cunevindus in command. There is more. Vortigern did not invite this Saxon fleet – that was Hengist so that he can use them to apply pressure to gain more favourable terms – but now we hear Vortigern intends to solve this dilemma with a decisive campaign. After sacking Venta Belgarum, Cunevindus is to march north-east to Londinium, Verulamium and then Durobrivae, crushing the last garrisons of the cives with the help of this Saxon fleet. Vortigern claims it will solve all his problems.'

'Good God, the man has gone mad.'

'Yes, but I can respect his strategy,' said Taly, to everyone's surprise. 'He's all out of options – diplomacy has failed, so he must resort to force. A civil war is his best chance of maintaining pre-eminence now that the other members of the Council are becoming bold enough to oppose him. He has the strongest militia in the southern territories, and he believes he has the Saxons on his side. If he can sweep away all opposition in the south and east in one decisive stroke, he will stand poised to come for the North next.'

There was silence as the audacity of Vortigern's plan sunk in. The right response to the news of Cunevindus' impending attack on Venta Belgarum had just become crucial to their own survival. Mor turned to Viracus.

'Did Sevira say what form our assistance should take?' he asked. 'The only sure way out of this is for Ambrosius to win a decisive victory. If we allow an all-out civil war to take hold, Vortigern will send his Saxons against us, and we will become embroiled in a way we are ill-prepared for. Does Vortigern intend to lead the force?'

Viracus laughed. 'No, he is not a soldier; he considers himself a statesman still. And he won't want to be present at the murder of his son.'

Igerna interrupted. 'That leaves Cunevindus with a free hand. He will kill Vortimer for sure. We must stop him!'

Mor's mind was racing. 'Do you know if Ambrosius has cavalry?'

'I believe his militia is mostly infantry.'

'May I offer an opinion?' asked Taly. Mor nodded, always eager to hear the old warrior's advice. 'The greatest threat to the North comes from the Saxons moored on the Humber. If Vortigern defeats Ambrosius, and the Saxons receive their supplies, then Vortigern's position is strong, and he may well choose to direct his mercenaries to attack us. However, if Ambrosius defeats Vortigern, then Vortigern's position is weak, and he will fail to supply the Saxons who will likely turn on him first. All hangs on Ambrosius defeating an army that he has no idea is coming for him!'

'What are you suggesting, Taly?' asked Mor.

'We have no choice but to send a turma to notify and support Ambrosius and Vortimer. And we must win. If we kill Cunevindus so much the better. Vortigern's power base will crumble, and the Cornovii will ally with us. What say you, Viracus?'

'Queen Sevira has faith that you will come to her aid and has risked much by sending me here. If your answer is no, I am still bound to ride immediately to Ambrosius to alert him.'

Igerna spoke before Mor could form his response. 'Viracus, I know you and your father were loyal retainers of Octavius; you know well the mood of the people. Who will the tribe support after this confrontation?'

'Cunevindus is a murdering upstart. It is only Vortigern's support that gives legitimacy to his leadership of the Cornovii. He thinks of himself as leader of the Saxons too, but all know that he is blinded by his vanity, unaware that the Saxons manipulate and exploit him at every chance. He does not command the respect of the Cornovii or the Saxons. If he is defeated, the Cornovii will look to Queen Sevira and then Vortimer if he still lives at the end of the battle.'

Igerna turned to Mor. 'So husband, what do you say?'

'I am solemnly sworn to protect Sevira and her children. She anticipated such troubles many years past and wisely secured our loyalty. There is no question – I will ride with you, Viracus.'

Igerna nodded her approval.

'I wish to accompany you, my lord,' said Taly.

'And I,' said Cian.

Mor looked at Taly. 'No, my friend, you will remain to protect my family, but you, Cian, must come, for we shall need a bard to record the fate of your reckless king! I will not deplete our defences any more than necessary, so I will ask only for volunteers, but we must leave at first light. So come, let us enjoy this feast, for a gruelling journey awaits us on the morrow.'

Mor slapped both Viracus and Cian on the back and winked at Taly. He hoped he had not offended his faithful secretary, but several days hard riding and then a desperate battle would be too great a test for Taly's physical strength now. These days, as he had just shown, it was the strength of his mind and his experience where he excelled.

*

Martin sat by the spring listening to Myrddin keep the children enthralled. He easily put aside his discomfort with the seer's pagan beliefs where the entertainment of children was concerned.

'Are there giants, Myrddin?' asked one.

'There were. I have seen their handiwork. Great stones which no man could lift arranged into patterns. There was one that lived not far from here called Simon. He would sit on the top of the hills to watch all the goings on below, and he raised a great pile of rocks to make his seat. The rocks are still there, all worn flat by his big bottom.'

The children laughed. Morgaine put her hand in the air.

'Tell us about the Draco, Myrddin.'

'Ah yes, Draco sits in the northern sky alongside Artio the bear. You can see their shape in the stars.'

'Are they alive?' another child asked.

'In their own way. After the sun sets, they are always there, night after night.'

'Were they here in our world first?' asked Morgaine.

'Yes, the stars reflect our past and our future. Some men can read the stars.'

'Do you, Myrddin?' Martin suddenly asked the seer. All eyes turned in his direction, and he found himself wondering what had possessed him to ask such a question.

'I try to interpret their meaning. I am fascinated by the constancy of some over others – there is meaning in the way they relate to one another.'

Mothers began calling to their children that the feast was about to start. As one, they all jumped up and ran in the direction of the hall.

'Tell me, Martin,' said Myrddin, turning his otherworldly gaze on the priest, 'when you touched death; what did you see?'

Martin waited for the last child to disappear from earshot before replying. 'How could you know such a thing? I have told no one here.'

'I saw it. You jumped to your death but came back. Now you refuse to accept the gift you were given. The future is yours to see, but you hide from it.'

This was sacrilege. But the seer's words rang with a truth that Martin longed to hear.

'God is my future,' he replied defensively.

'You have made Him so, Martin, but have you found Him yet? Did you see Him in the dreamworld before you came back?'

'No, Myrddin. All I remember is pain and many incomplete nightmares, none of which made any sense.'

'And what do you see in your dreams now?'

'I relive the night I was betrayed, but I also see flashes of... of what I sense is the future, though it cannot be. I try to block them, but they just come again. When I arrived at Elfed, I was shocked to realise that I had seen it all before, knew what would be where before I was shown.'

'I do not share your religious beliefs, Martin, neither do I object to them, but I will say this. Your future seeks you out. You may serve your God if it is a passive future you desire, but it is man's nature, when he is offered a life of engagement and purpose, to grasp that fate rather than resign himself to nothingness in solitude. I have seen your future, Martin, and I believe you have seen it too. Soon, you will be called upon to protect the Bear. You will not falter. After that, we will speak again. For now, be comforted that your father and brother are watching over you.'

'How do you know about my father and brother? What do they say... no, that cannot be... I...' Martin was lost for words. Nothing the seer had said made sense, and yet, all of it did.

Myrddin stood to leave, turning toward the gate.

'Are you not coming to the feast?' asked Martin.

'No. I only came here to see you.'

Martin shook his head, trying to clear his thoughts. Myrddin's words had struck a chord that continued to resonate through him. How could the seer know these things? The secrets that Martin kept so close for fear of swords in the darkness, somehow, this old man plucked them out of the air like they were there for all to see. His privacy felt violated, yet he could not deny it was comforting to know that his father and poor brother might be watching over him, perhaps trying to reach him through Myrddin? The priest dropped to his knees and wept. Relief flooded his body, though he knew not exactly what he was relieved about. Through his strange reverie, a voice called to him. It was Morgaine, sent to find him. Of course! Prayers before the meal! He quickly wiped his tears.

'Are you unhappy, Martin?' asked Morgaine, holding out her hand to him.

He took her small hand in his as he got to his feet. 'No, but I am unburdened,' he replied, realising it was true. 'Now, let's race to the feast!'

They ran, laughing all the way to the hall.

XXIX

Ypwines Fleot

Late Martius 437

It was a grey, bitter morning. The weather had changed, and the sky reflected in the great river that flowed past the mooring posts driven deep into the muddy banks. The estuary had only just shrunk back from the winter levels still leaving vast areas of the plain under water. As Hengist looked east, to where grey sky merged with grey river, it seemed as if a veil had been cast, shrouding them in a world with no horizon. Early signs of spring lined his path, bringing splashes of colour to his walk. Green shoots amidst the fresh yellow of newly blossomed buttercups signalled that winter had lost its grip on the stark landscape. By the end of summer, the reeds would be taller than a man, as dense as a forest, shielding their keels from view, but in barren, early spring, there was no concealing the forty or so vessels moored to the posts or the copious curls of smoke rising from the campfires and huts. No, there was no hiding that at least a thousand people sheltered here. He filled with pride. It was his leadership that had brought them here. His gaze drifted to the opposite bank, and he wondered what the scouts who camped there made of it all. Periodically, he would send over a keel to chase them away, but the spying eyes always returned. Let them watch. Let them count his superior numbers. Let them fear his attack. The northern Britons would be left wanting; Hengist had other plans.

From where he stood, the great river coiled upstream like a serpent meandering around two sweeping hooks, thereafter, splitting in two, one branch heading for the deserted city of legions, the other heading for Elfed – both King Mor's territory. In the opposite direction, the great estuary was joined by the largest of all the tributaries, a river the Britons called the Trent. The territory on the Trent's eastern bank belonged to his allies, the Angles, and further south, the Gaini. His own land, the land granted to the Jutes, had appeared generous at first. True, the area was large, but they had soon discovered the grazing was poor and the soil difficult to work. For ten years, they had tried to farm their new land, but every winter brought the floods, and his people were forced to begin all over again the following spring. Hengist felt he had honoured his obligations, attacking Picts and pirates, but with each spring, his sense of injustice had deepened. They never received the full value of supplies promised for his warriors, and the Britons were always suspicious and ungrateful. Vortigern and his general, Cunevindus, arrogantly flaunted their wealth whilst his tribe starved on this unworkable, waterlogged island.

Now was the time though. Along with his brother, Horsa, they had put the call out across the sea, and their sons had answered. Hengist's son Octha and his nephew Ebissa had brought many seasoned warriors, the numbers bolstered by a few refugee families escaping the brutal raids by the Huns. He cared little that his fellow Saxons in the Colonae, the Angles and the Gaini, were uncomfortable that his warriors now outnumbered theirs. He cared even less for the difficult position Gundad now found himself in. At first, the Gaini merchant had seemed to be a friend, but Hengist knew the reason for their supplies coming up short was that Gundad skimmed a portion off the top, which he shared with that oaf, Cunevindus. Over the years, Hengist had learnt to speak some Latin but the Britons refused to speak directly to him and Gundad's trickery remained unfettered. Now he had sent a message directly to Vortigern demanding a larger land area and a five-fold increase in supplies. He knew the king would refuse. *He wanted Vortigern to refuse*. Three months had passed with no answer, and his warriors were becoming restless and difficult to control, primed to cause havoc and mayhem in whatever direction he pointed them. Today, he had summoned duplicitous Gundad and Freuleaf, King of the Angles, to a meeting of warriors to discuss his planned invasion of the lowlands.

*

The meeting finally convened at noon. Hengist was not impressed with the reluctant tardiness of his guests. Gundad was particularly jumpy. The sly merchant had no backbone when it came to bringing the fight into the open. War would undermine the prosperous status of both the Gaini and the Angles, risking their trading partnerships and political alliances with the Britons, so it was crucial that he found a way to cement their agreement. He could not be worrying about his fellow Saxons at his rear. Not surprisingly, Gundad was emphatic that Vortigern was not disrespecting the Jutes. He had not yet replied for the simple reason the southern Britons had yet to agree to the cost. It didn't take a scholar to realise that Gundad's interests were best served by maintaining stability; the fickle merchant would want to keep trading routes open and wealth flowing – preferably in the direction of his coffers.

'You must give Vortigern more time, Hengist. He has a plan to bring pressure on the southern cives which involves your warriors and is to everyone's benefit.'

'I cannot restrain my warriors much longer,' said Hengist, nodding toward where his senior commanders sat listening in stony silence. 'They know the Britons are weak and that there is easy plunder just waiting to be plucked.' This elicited a general rumble of assent.

Freuleaf cleared his throat. The young man had only recently become king of his people, though he wore the role with confidence. Hengist liked the Angle, thinking him a leader more akin to himself. The young king's contributions were always measured and thoughtful.

'The southern Britons are weak, but the northern Britons are not. There are now two armies in the North, both of which are made up of highly trained cavalry. Is that not so, Gundad?'

'Yes. Their forces are well prepared to defend their territory. They are ever watchful, facing you over this stretch of water,' added Gundad, far too enthusiastically.

'We have no argument with the North. There is no love-lost between Mor and Vortigern; the northern army are sleeping dogs and will remain so provided we do not disturb them,' Hengist replied.

Freuleaf nodded. 'Vortigern probably chose this stretch of land for your homelands so that you would provide a buffer to any threat the North may pose to him. I suspect the sudden arrival of so many Jute warriors has worried them. You may well have already poked them a bit too hard. Tread carefully, Hengist, for you wake those sleeping dogs at your peril.'

Horsa stood up, and Hengist gladly gave the floor to his brother. 'They watch us, but we watch them too. Two days ago, a large cavalry force left their stronghold, following the road at the edge of the forest, heading south.'

'Yes. Something has given them enough cause for concern to send troops over their border,' added Hengist.

'Then their defences are weak!' shouted Ebissa, Horsa's son. 'We should attack!'

He stood and waved his seax in the air, encouraging a cheer from some of his fellow warriors.

Hengist frowned at his brother. 'Horsa, your son has been here less than one month, and he is shouting out orders,' he growled. 'Tell him to shut up, or I will cut out his tongue.'

Horsa's fury at his son's lack of discipline was evident in his reddening face. 'I will do it myself,' he said, brandishing his own seax at his son.

Ebissa had the sense to look chastened and sat back down.

Hengist allowed a moment's silence for everyone to settle after the disturbance. 'We know King Mor's army is strong, consisting of hundreds of men posted at different locations. We have studied their routines, and they are disciplined and vigilant. I cannot say why the cavalry force has deployed or where they are headed, but we do not yet seek to pick a fight with the Brigantes, not when there are softer, more profitable targets available.' Hengist paused and turned to Gundad. 'Tell Vortigern he has until midsummer to provide us with our supplies. If they have not arrived by then, we will recover payment for our services by other means. Can we count on support from the Angles, should the need arise, Freuleaf?'

'I will speak with our elders. We do not benefit from your supplies, but if the Britons believe they can get away with cheating one Saxon tribe, they will likely try it with us all. Your grievances are justified, in my opinion, but we will see if our elders agree.'

'And you, Gundad, what of the Gaini?'

Gundad's eyes darted about, taking in the Jute warriors, their mighty keels, the smoke from hundreds of cookfires. His expression settled, and he turned to face Hengist, his gaze direct. 'We are only a small tribe of merchants, King Hengist, but I also agree that your grievances are fair.'

*

Hengist sat by the shore waiting for Octha. His son was young and enthusiastic, but recklessness would not be tolerated and maintaining discipline was crucial to the success of their mission. Octha clambered down the slope and sat at his father's side.

'Keep your men under control for they will be seeing action soon enough. Vortigern is certain to refuse our demands, at which point we will immediately reposition our keels. Half will sail up the Trent and half to Wippeds Fleot in preparation for our attack. From what I have seen of you, my son, I trust you to keep a level head, but Ebissa is a fool. Can you keep him under control until it is time to let him off the leash?'

'I believe so. His impetuous spirit is just bored from the lack of fighting, but he is a fearless warrior.'

'Well, he needs to understand that being a great warrior is about more than just boyish bravado; discipline and strategy are what win wars and kingdoms. Even a raw recruit should know that raiding is best left until after harvest when the corn has been collected, the animals are brought down from the hills onto the meadows, and the calves and lambs are grown sufficient to herd. Stirring up the North just now would yield only bloodshed.'

'I understand, Father. I will explain it to him.'

'Whilst you're at it, explain that I will flog him in public if he speaks out in my presence again.'

XXX

Calleva

Two days before the spring equinox 437

They could see the two sentries hiding across the river, no doubt terrified by the sudden appearance of a large, heavily armed cavalry troop on the opposite bank. Did they think the horsemen were a Pict or Scotti raiding party? Surely not. Their attire and weapons were clearly Cymry militia, but the sentries remained frozen in their hiding place, perhaps hoping they had not been spotted.

'Oi, you over there, we can see you,' Mor shouted in Latin. 'Stand up and show yourselves.'

There was a moment's pause whilst the sentries had a frantic discussion. Eventually, one stood up, reluctantly followed by the other. They lay down their spears in silence.

'I am King Mor. I am travelling to meet Ambrosius Aurelianus. We have come from the North, but we cannot find a way across this river. Is there a bridge nearby?'

'No, my lord,' replied one sentry.

'Is there a ford?'

'Not for fifteen miles.'

'What happened to the bridge?'

'Are you friend or foe?' asked the older of the two.

'For God's sake! Friend, of course!' shouted Mor.

There was another frantic discussion, at the end of which the younger sentry climbed into a coracle whilst the other began to remove branches from what appeared to be a line of boats. Two ropes were tied to the stern of the little craft that the young sentry was rowing across the river. As it arrived on the opposite bank, the sentry passed the ropes into the hands of bemused cavalrymen. Looking across to the other sentry, Mor saw that he had finished removing branches and was signalling to the men holding the ropes.

'Pull the ropes,' said the sentry in the coracle.

Mor's men started to pull, and it immediately became clear what the sentries were guarding. A pontoon swung perfectly into place where it was lashed to sited posts. To the great relief of all, it seemed in reasonable condition.

'Thank you, gentlemen,' said Mor. 'Please forgive our initial frustration; we are on a mission of great urgency.'

Viracus caught the attention of the sentry who had crossed the river.

'Do you belong to Ambrosius' militia?'

Mor noted they wore only simple clothing with no belts – poorly equipped if they were militia.

'We take turns to guard the bridge,' the sentry replied, 'but we are only simple Belgae farmers.'

'Have you seen any Saxons or western militia hereabouts?'

'No, my lord, no one 'as crossed 'ere, but further west, this river turns north, so there is no need to cross at all for travellers from the west.'

Mor nodded at Viracus, acknowledging that he had correctly guessed the route that Cunevindus would follow south through the Savernake Forest.

'When we are across, warn your town leaders that armed men, enemies of Ambrosius, could be coming through this way. Man your town walls and let no one else cross this bridge until the equinox has passed. The expected force will mostly be made up of Saxons, but since they approach from the west, you may be fortunate enough to see no sign of them at all.'

'Thank you, my lord. We will relay your message to the town elders!'

The sentry's gaze then passed across the mail-clad men and horses, and his expression clouded with concern.

'Now, gentlemen, walk these 'orses across slowly and keep two boats apart. It should 'old if you do that. Mind, cause it's very slipp'ry.'

'How far is Venta Belgarum?' asked Mor.

'If you push on, you'll be there by nightfall.'

'Hear that, Cian?' said Mor, turning to the young bard. 'Nightfall – not far to go now.'

The journey had been relentless and gruelling. Cian had been brave to volunteer for such a mission when he was relatively untested on the battlefield. The lad would be anxious, worrying not just for himself but for the young family he had left at home. It was a source of great joy for Taly that one of Martin's first tasks when he had arrived at Elfed had been to marry Cian to Bryn, and they now had a little boy of five called Agiluf. Taly was his godfather. There was no doubt in Mor's mind that Taly would protect Cian's family along with his own. The old warrior had always protected them. In turn, Mor would do his best to protect Cian on Taly's behalf, so that they could all be together again when this was all over.

'We will return safely, Cian,' he said. 'We just have to kill a few enemy first.' The lad's face was pale; he had probably not made his first kill yet. Mor's eye dropped to the sword at Cian's hip, Taly's sword. 'That sword has killed more men than all the other swords we carry added together.'

Cian put his hand on the hilt. 'Yes, just touching it gives me a confidence beyond my own experience. Taly will not tell me how many kills though.'

'I don't suppose he's counted.'

'Perhaps not, but he said he's counting on me to add to the tally!'

Mor smiled. They may have left Taly behind in Elfed, but his humour still found a way of keeping up with them.

*

They made good progress, and Mor was pleased when, in the late afternoon, they got their first sighting of Venta Belgarum. He rode at the head of the column with Spurcio and Viracus alongside him.

'I see no sentries,' said Spurcio. 'There are spears on the battlements, but the gates are wide open.'

'We don't want to cause any alarm,' said Mor. 'Slow the troop, make sure their weapons are lowered.'

They approached the gates and entered without challenge. There were no sentries in sight. Mor looked up at the battlements, only to find them unmanned too, the spears Spurcio had seen simply mounted against a turret wall. Their column continued toward a large forum which was still busy even at the late hour. The cives of the city showed only a passing interest at the sudden arrival of fifty armed cavalry and continued to go about their business.

'Good God!' exclaimed Mor, shaking his head. 'Cunevindus will be inside their defences before they even know he is their enemy!'

He dismounted and approached a man stood watching their arrival. 'Can you tell me where I might find Ambrosius Aurelianus?'

'I will take you there,' the man replied. 'Are you here for the spring festivities?'

Mor laughed. 'No, we are here on official business,' He turned to his men. 'Padell, you're in command. Dismount the men and water the horses. Cian, Viracus, come with me.'

They followed the man to a large mansio, where their guide left them at the entrance. A guard stood inside the open wooden gate.

'We are here to see Ambrosius,' said Mor.

The guard led the visitors into a large, cool hallway lined with statues, its walls painted with murals, the floor a patterned mosaic.

'May I ask who calls on my master?' asked a servant.

'I am Mor of Elfed; these are my companions.'

They could hear laughter and many voices from behind the door that the servant went through, then sudden quiet, presumably when the servant interrupted proceedings. On returning to the hall, the servant bid them to follow him.

They entered the dining room – more ornate than the hall – and encountered a truly Roman scene. There were both men and women reclined in traditional dress around a table lavishly adorned with drinks, meats, bread and fruit. Mor immediately recognised Ambrosius, Nataline and, to his great relief, Vortimer.

'King Mor, it *is* you! Welcome. Have you lost your way? The North is that way.' Ambrosius pointed in the approximate direction as his guests laughed at his jest. He stood to welcome them.

Mor laughed politely. 'We have been lost once or twice in the four days it has taken us to ride here. But our visit is not social; we bring a warning. I am here with fifty cavalry and Queen Sevira's representative.'

There was an abrupt pause in the merry buzz of conversation. No one could fail to realise that such a journey indicated a serious matter.

'Please sit, gentlemen. My servants will bring you refreshments.'

Three chairs were brought, and Mor sat in the one closest to Ambrosius.

'Does the news you bring affect us all? If it does, speak freely, King Mor.'

'I am afraid it does. Vortigern has ordered a heavily armed force of Dobunni and Saxons led by Cunevindus to sack Venta Belgarum. They are on their way here now, intent on murdering both you and Vortimer.'

There was a communal gasp, all eating and drinking ceased. Vortimer and several other men in military attire moved into sitting positions, all semblance of relaxation dismissed.

'My companion, Viracus, this man here,' Mor said, clapping Viracus on the shoulder, 'is captain of Queen Sevira's guard. He brought this information to us with a request that I provide any assistance necessary to protect Vortimer.'

Ambrosius acknowledged Viracus who got up from his seat, nodding toward Vortimer who he had known since the lad was a young boy.

'My lords,' said Viracus, 'what King Mor tells you is true. There is little time to prepare. Cunevindus' army plans to launch their surprise attack in two days' time at the spring equinox. We presume the plan is to catch you off-guard during your spring festivities.'

'From which direction do you expect them to come?' asked Ambrosius.

'They are most likely to cover their approach by coming through the Savernake Forest.'

'Ambrosius,' Mor interrupted, 'I have brought fifty experienced cavalry to fight alongside you, but we estimate their force to be anywhere between five hundred and a thousand men. We must begin preparations immediately. Where is your city guard?'

'They are at their homes or in their barracks. We never expected an attack from our fellow countrymen! Our focus is on preventing raids from the sea, so we garrison the coast much like you garrison the Wall.' Ambrosius gestured toward Nataline and a man sat next to him. 'I am not a soldier, but Nataline here is an old military commander, and his son, Natalinus, is our general.'

Mor hoped he kept his dismay from his expression. He had been hoping for a more professional structure and greater leadership experience.

'General Natalinus, how many men can you muster in a day?'

The young man looked at his father and then at Mor. 'There are two hundred here in the city. Thirty of which make up a cavalry turma. If I send out messengers now and withdraw coastal garrisons, perhaps another two hundred that can be with us by tomorrow night. We can withdraw some of the garrison from Sorviodunum, perhaps one hundred men. There are also many hunters round and about who we can pay to fight.'

'Do any of these men have any battle experience?'

'Not much. The northern raids have never penetrated this far south, and the Gaels' raids amount to no more than coastal skirmishes.'

With it now clear that the gathering had turned into a council of war, the ladies began to quietly withdraw from the dining room. Ambrosius and Nataline were speaking quietly to each other, discussing the threat.

'Ambrosius,' Mor said curtly, 'what will you pay the recruits we need to save your city?'

Ambrosius looked at Nataline. 'Shall we say three siliqua per man?'

Mor shook his head. 'Say five, and we have a chance that some will show up.'

Ambrosius and Nataline again put their heads together, though this time their debate was more animated. Mor was getting restless by the time they finally turned to him after five minutes or so.

'We agree, King Mor, on condition that you are our battle leader. We have no one with your level of experience.'

'I remember discussing that very problem when we last met!' Mor said, trying to contain his frustration at the complacency of these southerners. 'I accept, but there is no time to lose. As a precaution have your cives prepare your city for a siege. We will meet this army in the open – away from forest cover. I believe there are chalk downs to the west?'

Nataline cleared a space on the table in front of him. 'The River Test runs in an arc eight miles west of the city like so.' He drew an imaginary line on the table. 'The roads cross here and here, so whichever route Cunevindus chooses, he will need to come through this vale here to cross the river.' He placed a piece of bread on the table. 'Here stands an old, deserted Belgae fort. It is in a commanding position surrounded by open countryside. Anyone in that fort would see an army approaching from miles away.'

'Excellent!' exclaimed Mor. 'That shall be our rallying point. Send out your messengers, muster as many men as possible to that location by tomorrow night. I am particularly interested in employing your hunters, Natalinus. Men who can use a bow will be most useful.'

'Yes, my lord,' said Natalinus.

Mor looked around the room.

'One last thing, gentlemen, before you all go about your duties. Battle is terrifying and brutal, some of us will die, but no matter the cost, we must not let this army reach your city. The Saxons are vicious murderers, and once over your city wall, they will do their worst. Your women and children will be at their mercy, so we must not fail.'

The silence that followed was heavy with grim determination.

'Why isn't my father leading this army?' asked Vortimer, his voice quivering with emotion. 'Why does he not come to face me himself?'

'Your father, Prince Vortimer, pulls the strings of his puppets. That way he may later wash his hands of any dark deeds that may be done – he is a politician not a general. May I speak with you in private?'

Vortimer visibly composed himself before answering. 'Of course.'

Mor stood and indicated that they should leave the room. Nothing was said until they reached the hallway.

'It is good to see you, Vortimer. I wish we had more time for pleasantries. Tell me, will you fight with us or your new comrades?'

'I am commander of their turma, King Mor. I must fight with my men.'

Mor placed his right hand on Vortimer's shoulder. 'Well said. Bring your men to meet mine. We will fight side by side and turn the tables on this Cunevindus.'

'His men are a rabble, chosen for their flattery of him and their drinking skills. His war band is an insult to the proud tradition of the

Cornovii.'

Sevira's letter about how Vortimer's time under Cunevindus' command had not gone well came to mind. 'Is there anything you can tell me about the Dobunni militia?' asked Mor.

'They are better soldiers but mostly infantry. Their leader is Viktor Caninus, an old retainer of my father's family.'

'And what about our own forces? Do you have confidence in this young General Natalinus?'

'I do. He will deliver the soldiers you need.'

'That is good to know. Now, you must go and prepare, Vortimer, as I must too.'

Mor watched the lad walk away. He had not seen Vortimer since he was a boy, but he appeared to have become a fine young man. It was high time Mor took the young prince aside to discuss his future, but that would wait until after the battle – there was no need to tempt fate.

Mor rejoined Ambrosius in the dining room. Nataline and his son had already departed, so too had all the remaining guests.

'King Mor, thank the Lord that you have come to our aid. But what prompted you to risk so much so far from home?'

'If you were to lose this battle, Ambrosius, the Patria would be wide open for the Saxons to conquer. It would seem Vortigern has lost authority over them already. Like the Goths, the Vandals and the Alans that so dominate the Continent, the Saxons, unless defeated, will come to dominate our lands, destroying our culture, denying us our religion and enslaving our children. There is an ever-increasing concentration of Saxon warriors in the Colonae which will burst forth and spread across the Patria. They must, because there are too many of them for their lands to sustain; they are brutal killers with nothing to lose. Vortigern created division amongst us to enhance his personal power, but the outcome is a weakened Patria. He behaves like a wounded and cornered wild animal, lashing out with little regard for the consequences. This is a desperate act, by someone who senses his time is nearly over. After all, what sort of king sends an army to murder his own son?'

Concern was etched on Ambrosius' face. 'Yes, poor Vortimer. I can't imagine… I have a nine-year-old called Ames, and you, Mor?'

'I have two, a son and daughter, Arthwys and Morgaine. The fate of all our children depends on the outcome of this battle. May God be with us all.'

He shook hands with Ambrosius, and the Roman gave a heavy sigh. 'My men will ensure yours are fed and comfortable.'

'Thank you, Ambrosius. Tomorrow we will set up camp on Nataline's hill and send out scouts to track the approaching army. I will know better what tactics to adopt once I see the terrain.'

'Will you be my guest this evening, Mor?'

'That is kind, but no. There is much planning still to do, and it is better done in the company of my men.'

'I trust you sleep well then. Until tomorrow, Mor.'

*

Ambrosius sat back at his table. He was still marshalling his thoughts when his wife, Helena, interrupted his reflections.

'Everyone is scared, Ambrosius. The women are crying and asking what we should do. What should I tell them?'

'Tell them to pray to God and thank Him for sending us a mighty guardian angel. I have heard many tales about the northern Cymry, their heroics and their brutality. King Mor is a man of remarkable honour. He has travelled the length of this country at the request of another tribe's queen to save the life of his enemy's heir, and now he finds himself pledged to lead men he has yet to meet into a civil war. We must not stand by and watch. I want every man who can hold a spear or swing an axe stood by him on that hill! Please spread the word to everyone, servants and friends alike. We must defend our freedoms and destroy this enemy.'

XXXI

North of Corinium

Late Martius 437

Aircol and his young son, Cunorius, were not looking forward to their audience with King Vortigern. The long journey from the western tip of the island to Glevum had taken five days, but the king had not been there when they arrived. They had been informed he had moved his headquarters to a villa north of Corinium, so their miserable journey had been prolonged for another day. Every three years, they were expected to pay their taxes to Vortigern, but it had never been so difficult to raise gold and silver as now, and they were carrying less than half of what was due. Aircol's last offering had been similarly lacking, but this time he would be receiving his royal humiliation in front of his son. He prepared Cunorius for what was to come as he saw the villa come into view in the distance.

'Now say nothing and let me do all the talking.'

'But what *are* you going to say?'

'The man is arrogant; he thinks himself high king of the whole island, so we just have to crawl a little and make up a few stories that he cannot check.'

'Like what?'

'Well, our cousins, the Connachta, hate the Deisi. As such, they have raided our coastline, stolen our gold and made our children slaves.'

'But we don't fight them, we trade with them!'

'He doesn't know that, and he always believes what I tell him. Listen to me, we survive by whatever means. There have been a dozen raids in three years, nearly one each summer month. We have beaten these invaders back to the sea, protecting the rest of the Patria in the process.'

'Will he believe you?'

'He will think I am exaggerating but not to the extent that I really am.'

'It doesn't seem right that proud warriors like us should be made to suffer such subjugation.'

'It is a few hours of fawning, son, that is all, and it is important for you to see what needs to be done and said.'

The villa was impressive, the largest Aircol had ever seen. It was guarded by soldiers, but there was no stockade.

'Well, what have we here?' said a young officer. 'Savages from the hills.'

'I am Aircol, Chief of the Deisi, and this is Cunorius, my son.'

'You sound like Gaels,' said the officer.

'Well, that's because we are Gaels. Now if you will advise King Vortigern of our arrival, you will discover that he is keen to see us.'

'Stay there.' The officer proceeded through the entrance, leaving the two visitors under the watchful eye of a sentry.

The officer returned.

'I am to arrange water and feed for your horses to supply your return journey, and King Vortigern will see you now.'

They were led into a grand room painted with murals and adorned with statues. Vortigern stood behind a table with several other men, some in military dress.

'Aircol, my old friend, and who is this?'

'This is Cunorius, Lord King, my son and heir.'

'Come and sit over here.' He signalled to a slave. 'Bring some refreshment for these fine men. Marcus,' he called to a soldier in uniform, 'join us and listen to what our western warriors have to say.'

The soldier pulled up a chair.

'These men are Gaels but also protectors of our shores. They are here to report.' Vortigern turned to Aircol. 'Well, what do you have to tell us?'

'Gael raiding has intensified, my lord. There has been more than a dozen over the past three years. My people have had their possessions and produce stolen, and our children have been taken as slaves.'

'So I imagine your tribe has not raised the required level of tribute, again?'

'Exactly, my lord.'

There was silence, and Vortigern scowled.

'How much have you brought?'

'Eighty solidi, my lord.'

'It should be three hundred.'

'I know, my lord, we will make it up next time.'

'Have you considered raiding across the sea to ensure you meet your obligations?'

'Yes, I have thought about it, but we are just a small band of warriors. If we left our posts to raid elsewhere, King Niall of the Connachta would invade and march on Glevum.'

Vortigern looked at Aircol's son.

'What say you, Cunorius?'

The boy stuttered his reply. 'Everything my father said is true'— then remembering his manners—'Lord King.'

'Ah, a faithful son, Aircol, I only wish that mine were so.'

The old warrior saw how this statement distracted the king and seized his opportunity to change the subject.

'Why is that, my lord?'

'A mighty war lies ahead of us. The Patria is no longer united, and my son has chosen to fight for my enemy.'

Aircol looked at Cunorius; they had heard nothing about this war in the west.

'Our loyalty is with you, Lord King, but our warriors are already stretched guarding the coast.'

'I wish everyone were so faithful. King Conomar of Dumnonia has declined to support me – much like yourselves, he cites raids on his own coastline as the reason, but as you have said, your warriors are best placed defending our shores.'

'What has brought us to war, my lord? Have the Romans returned?'

'Not yet, but some of our cives would welcome it. Can you believe, Aircol, that some of my subjects refuse to pay their agreed taxes!'

The old warrior grimaced; he wanted to steer clear of that subject.

'So, who *are* you fighting?'

'Well,' Vortigern said, looking at Marcus, 'My generals, Cunevindus and Viktor Caninus, will attack Venta Belgarum the day after tomorrow. Thereafter, they will march on Londinium, Verulamium, and they will trap the last of the cives' militia at Durobrivae. Once we hear Venta Belgarum is taken, Marcus here will ride to our Saxon friends and command them to meet my southern army. There will be no more resistance to my plans, after that.'

'So, it is a civil war, but to what purpose?'

'Control of the Patria.'

'But what of the North and the sons of Cunedda?'

'They have turned their backs on us for now, but we shall see what they say once I am Emperor of the South. We will also see what the Romans have to say. The Empress and her generals – perhaps our threats will at last equal theirs.' Vortigern looked sternly at Aircol. 'I am busy and have said enough. Your loyalty is noted. Now, return to protect our coast, but your missing taxes will be added to your tally and must be paid – I will keep you to that. Be warned: next time, I will hold your son as hostage if your tribute is light.'

Aircol was as relieved as his son looked as they left the villa.

'A powerful man with powerful ambition,' said Cunorius.

'Yes, but your mother always says ambition either makes a man or finishes him quickly. He is picking a fight with mighty enemies.'

'Yes, Father, it is much safer to make up stories like you do.'
'You cheeky whelp, I'll leave you as a hostage next time.'

XXXII

Savernake Forest

One day before the spring equinox 437

The dawn broke with a biting wind carrying squally showers into the faces of the marching soldiers. Vortigern's army had camped in the forest overnight but now broke cover following the River Avon.

'Day after tomorrow, we will be at Venta Belgarum's gates,' Cunevindus said to the man riding next to him.

'You seem keen for this war to begin,' replied Viktor Caninus.

'We are warriors, Viktor. These men need war like ordinary cives need air.'

The large column of nearly five hundred men behind them consisted of two cohorts of Cornovii, two cohorts of Dobunni, one hundred Saxon mercenaries and a turma of cavalry consisting of chosen warriors from the king's personal guard.

Cunevindus was battle leader despite the greater experience of his fellow general. Viktor clearly resented the command being given to a younger man, but Vortigern had been insistent that Cunevindus should lead, and as the supreme general of this fighting force, Cunevindus was not going to argue with the wisdom of a king.

'Did the king say why King Conomar declined to join this campaign?' asked Viktor.

'There are Gaels raiding his coastline so Ambrosius will likely have his militia deployed along the coast for much the same reason. He will be ill-prepared and easily overcome.'

Viktor was the head of a Dobunni land-owning family and a retainer of the king. Along with many other established families, he had become wealthy under Roman rule and wealthier still after their departure by annexing properties left behind by Roman landlords. It was a bold but controversial practice, their rights to these lands disputed by many tenants, particularly in the territory of the Belgae. Cunevindus didn't see the problem. The more powerful you were, the more fighting men you could command, the more disputes you could crush. Who cared if the cives didn't like it? What were they going to do about it?

'Yes, well, news will reach Ambrosius soon that our forces have crossed into his territory,' replied Viktor, his fearful expression betraying his reluctance. The man clearly had no heart for the brutality of war. Cunevindus understood why Vortigern had given command to him – he may be young, but he would not hesitate to do what was necessary.

Vortigern had suspected all along that Viktor's interest lay not so much in the fight but in the lands he could grab for himself, and Cunevindus was suspicious of his motives.

'Maybe. But he doesn't know what we plan to do, and he won't expect us to come by the route we will take. Any scouts will report that we are heading toward Sorviodunum. By the time we reach the Downs and turn for Venta Belgarum, it will be too late for Ambrosius to prepare.'

Even though Vortigern was the closest friend the young warlord had, Cunevindus still loathed the Roman entitlement that prevailed throughout the Patria's leaders. Ambrosius, Viktor, Vortimer... all had their privilege handed to them the moment they took their first breath. Cunevindus had fought his way to his exalted position, and he would continue to fight to secure that position for his future.

'Why are you and Vortigern so intent on war? What if Ambrosius sues for peace?'

'Our orders are to sack the city. It is our duty to carry out our king's orders without question.'

Vortigern was the only man alive who could command such absolute loyalty from the ambitious warlord. Cunevindus' grandfather had been a distant and poor relation to the leaders of the Cornovii, a warrior, earning a small family a stronghold in the hills. But when his father and mother had both died tragically young of disease, Cunevindus and his sister had been left to fend for themselves. He had only been twelve and his sister fifteen. That first winter, they had nearly starved to death. They *would* have starved to death if the young Cunevindus hadn't taught himself to hunt. Then all the gods of fortune had smiled upon them in one chance encounter. During a fierce autumn storm, a young nobleman had sought shelter in their humble abode after becoming separated from his travelling companions by a bolting horse. Cunevindus' sister had taken the stranger into her bed, and he had given her silver for her considerable efforts. The young noble became infatuated, returning again and again over many years, swearing them to secrecy, each time bringing silver.

Their standing altered dramatically after his sister bore the young man a daughter. They had known all along that the man was a prince, and when his father, King Vitalis, finally died, Vortigern became less secretive, turning their small stronghold into a fortified hunting lodge to make his regular visits more comfortable and secure. Cunevindus then became his trusted enforcer and made responsible for tax collection. His band of men became so notorious for their success that he was given increasing levels of responsibility. Eventually, Vortigern had granted him a portion of Cornovii territory. much to Queen Sevira's strong objection. Well, her objections had been fruitless, and it was well known that Sevira's marriage was an arrangement from which Vortigern had acquired all her family's territory. The king's insatiable appetite for women was a weakness that Cunevindus encouraged and indulged, and now, his sister and young niece both slept with the king.

News that the king had begot a child by his own daughter, a boy, spread in whispers through the territory. They might point at Cunevindus and name him facilitator, but he didn't care. He was not a Christian. The old gods protected him, and incest was just a word to them. The old nobles with their old blood could look down on him all they wanted, but they feared him more than they dared oppose him, and that suited Cunevindus just fine.

'It seems strange that King Vortigern chose not to lead his own army,' said Viktor.

Cunevindus' orders were to defeat and execute Ambrosius, and if Prince Vortimer got in the way, it wouldn't be so bad if he suffered the same fate. Vortigern's hands could not be bloodied by what must be done at Venta Belgarum, but none of that was any of Viktor's business.

'He has his reasons. But he will be there at the head of our column when we march into Londinium.'

XXXIII

Nataline's Hill beyond the Test

The Spring Equinox 437

Mor gazed out across the Downs from the hill fort on Nataline's hill. Not for the first time, he thanked God that he had more than his own experience of battle to aid them in the campaign ahead. There weren't many men who could say they had learnt everything that the mighty King Coel had to teach about warfare. Mor's grandfather had held nothing back from his grandsons. Even outside of their formal training, he would use every anecdotal war story to teach them about why one side lost whilst the other prevailed. Whether it was a siege on campaign with Rome or a skirmish with the Picts along the Wall, Coel had imparted all of his vast experience, and Mor had taken it all in. He knew how to read the battleground, when to engage the enemy for maximum effect, how to take advantage of the high ground, plan the killing zone, build in an element of surprise... With the disadvantage of inferior numbers, discipline was going to be crucial to the success of this particular battle. His primary task would be to pull this inexperienced rabble together and keep them focused on their orders. If they lost their heads and charged about trying to kill the closest enemy soldier, their small fighting force would be easily overwhelmed by Cunevindus' superior numbers. Numbers that were so tight Mor had only been able to spare forty militia to defend the city, but his concern for the safety of the cives was alleviated somewhat by the news that that the old and the young of the city had volunteered to swell the numbers manning the walls.

At dawn the previous day, Vortimer's turma had joined Mor's northern cavalry, and together with one hundred and thirty militia, they had marched to the hill fort described by Nataline. The young prince had looked comfortable in command of his men, his orders being obeyed readily and without question. It was good to see and meant that Mor had one less thing to worry about.

On arrival, he had discovered that the old hill fort's position was as commanding as Nataline had described. This had made for a swift and decisive meeting with his more experienced commanders where they had planned their tactics and allocated out their expertise to prepare their newly acquired fighting force for their specific roles. Tension had mounted throughout the day as scouts and messengers began riding in. The first report to arrive had come from Nataline's own estates and described an army of 'well over a thousand'. Not what any of them wanted to hear! But later, as the invaders marched through the Avon valley, scouts there had trimmed the number to 'about six hundred'. Having heard what direction the enemy soldiers were taking, the garrison commander at Sorviodunum had refused to release any militia, fearing an imminent attack on his position. But the enemy had set up camp for the night on the edge of the Downs, and according to Mor's scouts, had turned for Venta Belgarum that morning. It would not be long now before the enemy's own forward scouts spotted Ambrosius' militia waiting at the hill fort. At least, that was what Mor was counting on.

Natalinus had managed to muster the two hundred men back from the coast. These were all properly equipped with short swords, spears and shields. What no one had expected though was for the woodsmen, hunters and farmers to turn out in such numbers, eighty in total, no less appreciated for their pitchforks, axes and bows. They had trekked in throughout the course of the previous day, each new group welcomed with cheers from their comrades.

Mor had spoken with Natalinus, and they had assigned the most experienced captains to the command positions. The frontline infantry would be commanded by Viracus and Spurcio with Natalinus to the rear with the reserves. Winnog would command the archers and other non-militia. The cavalry had been split into two groups, one on the right flank and one on the left. Vortimer and Padell would lead the right flank, whilst Mor and Cian would lead the other. The plan's success depended entirely on persuading the approaching army to commit to attacking their position. Cunevindus was heading for the city, so they needed to first get his attention and then goad him into engaging with them rather than make for Venta Belgarum. To be sure to catch Cunevindus' scouts' attention, Mor's men had lashed together several long poles to ensure their flying pennants would be visible from a great distance. At the top of the hill fort, with these rain-lashed but colourful pennants fluttering in the brisk wind overhead, Mor outlined his final plan to Ambrosius and Nataline.

'The infantry will deploy with shields and spears at the base of the hill in three ranks. The first rank commanded by Spurcio, the second by Viracus and the third by Natalinus. They will face the initial advance whilst positioned in front of the first ditch. On each flank, further up the slope above this ditch, the archers and axemen will be stationed. From their position, the archers will loose their arrows over the front rank of infantry targeting the enemy in their cross-fire. If any enemy soldiers break through, they will be caught out by the ditch and find themselves at the mercy of the axemen.

'The cavalry will be concealed in the woodland on the left and right flank. This will tempt the enemy to overcommit and gives our cavalry charge the element of surprise. The flanking cavalry charge will force the enemy infantry to squeeze together and narrow their front rank making it easier for our infantry to deal with them. In the meantime, the cavalry will engage with Cunevindus' mounted troops on two fronts. If the pressure from the enemy infantry becomes too great, our men are to retreat up the hill one ditch at a time, but it is essential they keep formation to hold the enemy and control the pace of advance. Our troops will become overwhelmed in no time if they break rank, so it is crucial that the infantry captains maintain that discipline in their lines. Winnog will command the archers and axemen and ensure they retreat in line with the infantry. He has been training his men since before dawn and says they have enough arrows for a good number of volleys.'

A shout went up, and the message that the enemy had been sighted was repeated across the hill.

'To your positions,' Spurcio called out below them.

Mor continued his briefing.

'Ambrosius, Nataline, fear is our greatest enemy whilst we wait for the battle to begin. I need you to ride along the ranks, looking the men in the eye and rallying their courage. Words they can shout back will keep them focused, along the lines of 'Victory will be ours', 'No mercy, kill them all', 'God is with us', that kind of thing. Keep talking to them right up until engagement is imminent, but do not become embroiled yourselves. Extract yourselves before the enemy lines engage with ours and gallop your horses back up the hill to the top. I will be in the thick of the fighting, so if I fall and we become overwhelmed, you must be in place to take command of an orderly retreat up the hill. One way or another, we will carry this day. Where is that priest you brought? Get him amongst the men to bless them!'

Nataline went in search of the priest, and Mor mounted up, galloping to join his cavalry unit where they were concealed in the woodland on the left flank.

*

The scouts had told him about the pennants fluttering high on a nearby hill, and as Cunevindus' troops marched closer, he was able to make out three ranks of lone infantry drawn up at the base of the hill.

'It seems that the fools are in a hurry to lose this fight, Viktor,' said Cunevindus.

'Yes, but they're not as foolish as you might think; this way they get to choose the battleground. Look – they have the high ground at their backs,' Viktor replied.

'No matter to us. We outnumber them at least two to one, and not all of them are properly armed. They don't even have any cavalry.'

Viktor Caninus surveyed the scene, and Cunevindus took some pleasure from the grudging nature of the older man's nod. 'You're right,' said Viktor.

'This could turn out to be even easier than I imagined.'

'Yes. Swift victory here, then we stroll into their city unopposed. Look! That is Ambrosius himself riding up and down like a frightened chicken.'

'Deploy our Dobunni cohorts on the left, Saxons in the centre and our Cornovii cohorts on the right. The Saxons will break through first, clearing a corridor for our cavalry to charge up the hill to finish them all off. I will locate Ambrosius and Vortimer and ensure they don't leave this battlefield.'

The south-westerly wind was blowing rain squalls in their faces, but nothing could discourage Cunevindus, not now that he had the scent of his quarry. At about two hundred and fifty yards, he watched his troops deploy to their battle positions. They marched toward the cowering southerners in loose formation, shouting insults and growling like wild animals.

*

'Here they come,' shouted Winnog. 'Ready your bows.'

He had piled stone cairns at two hundred yards and at one hundred yards to help his archers get their range. The wind was at their backs which would send their arrows further and extend their kill zone. The sea of men swarming toward them loomed larger with each step. As they approached the first marker, Winnog shouted, 'Nock!' There was a clatter of arrows against bows. 'Draw!' The enemy infantry reached the marker. 'Loose!' The first volley left the bows, and the next arrows were already being drawn. Winnog put his hand on the shoulder of the archer at his end of the line. 'Loose on your left man.' Winnog let his arrow fly, the archer on his right did the same, and every man to his right followed suit. The second volley was swiftly followed by the third and fourth. There were screams as silent death rained from above. Shields held above heads thunked, knocking men to their knees with the force of the impact, others, not so lucky, stumbled, fell, did not get up. Another two volleys and the remaining soldiers reached the next marker. His archers had done a good job of funnelling the attackers, narrowing the width of the rank their own infantry would have to engage on. The enemy charged at thirty paces to impact. The archers now loosed their arrows at will. Winnog got off another six before he cast aside his bow and drew his sword.

The crunch of clashing shields reverberated across the Downs. Screams and shouts mixed with the ring of steel. Men were crushed, impaled, stabbed, gouged, trampled, punched, bitten… There was no glory in war, only blood, terror and death. At the front line, the crush was so tight that men could hardly swing a sword let alone stab with a spear. Blood flew as men fought with tooth, nail, fist and knife whilst slipping and stumbling on the dead and wounded underfoot.

Winnog watched the enemy's rear ranks fan out and begin to overrun the foresters bravely defending the flanks with their axes. The cavalry were now spread out behind the enemy infantry, pushing them forward.

*

Mor had waited with his cavalry out of sight beneath the trees. It had been tough to watch the infantry engage, to hear the screams and know that men died whilst he waited. Waited for Cunevindus' full force to commit to the battle, so that none would get away. The impatient enemy commander sent his cavalry forward to support their own infantry. And the waiting was over. Mor's cavalry charged, wind rushing, hooves thundering, shields on their arms, swords in their hands.

Mor glanced across at Cian. The lad was pale as fog in the moonlight, gripping Taly's sword as he galloped toward his first target. His sword cut down on the neck and shoulder of a flanking soldier, and

Mor was past and swinging his own sword, taking down enemy soldiers who would never know where death had come from. His men pushed forward, using their horses to press the attackers against Ambrosius' spears. All the time, Mor struck out left and right, taking down any attacker within reach. Time lost all meaning, his body inexhaustible.

A continuous scream cut through his bloodlust, and he looked to its source. There was Cian, seemingly oblivious to the terrifying sound coming from his throat whilst he hacked at man after man, bodies piled in his wake. Taly's sword would not be retiring anytime soon. Mor's attention was drawn back to the battle. Their attackers were starting to get orders from their commanders to turn and fight the flanking cavalry, but they were now so jammed in that they had little room to manoeuvre. The crush was so tight that the enemy's own cavalry had got caught up in it when their infantry on the flanks had folded in. Horsemen trampled over footmen in a bid to join the fight.

It was finally dawning on the enemy cavalry commanders that they had been lured into a trap. Orders were screamed across the churning mass of struggling men, and horsemen began to find their lines and turn to face their mounted adversaries. Mor could see Vortimer and Padell hacking their way in from the right flank. His own troops were caught in a vicious scrap with the fierce Saxon tail. But no matter the opposition, bit by bit, his troops progressed ever closer to the enemy leader, a man so purple from screaming with apoplectic rage that Mor hardly recognised him as Cunevindus.

*

Mor had reined back a bit to get a better view of how the battle was progressing. The Saxons had been close to breaking through the front rank when he saw Spurcio go down, wounded. But Viracus had been vigilant, quickly stepping forward to take command, ordering the men to shore the gap, and the line had held. Cian, still making that terrifying noise, had taken a small section of cavalry and was pushing forward, going deep into the enemy ranks with the axemen falling in behind.

Terror gripped the Cornovii soldiers, and they tried to make a break for it, running away from the battle only to be hacked to the ground by the waiting axemen.

Over on the right flank, Mor saw Vortimer's horse suddenly fall, throwing the young prince to the ground. But the Dobunni cohorts were in disarray, and Padell dismounted without hesitation. Vortimer picked up a discarded shield, hefted his sword, gave Padell a quick nod, and the two of them fought alongside each other, battling any enemy soldiers who fled in their direction.

A corridor suddenly opened up between Mor and Cunevindus' position, the milling maelstrom's ebb and flow providing him with a clear path. He kicked his horse and galloped through the battle. Cunevindus looked up from bravely holding off the closing cavalry with only a handful of surviving retainers in support. Mor charged straight at him, losing none of his warhorse's momentum. He locked eyes with his enemy and swung his sword. Was that a flicker of recognition in the general's eyes? The mighty blow landed, partially severing Cunevindus' head from his shoulders. His body slid from his horse, hitting the ground like a slab of meat. Mor would never know for sure if Cunevindus had recognised his executioner, but it made no difference either way – dead was dead.

In the ensuing panic and confusion amongst the enemy ranks, Mor could hear Natalinus encouraging his own infantry ranks to push forward. The enemy soldiers stumbled over their dead as they tried to retreat and were easily cut down. Many of what was left of the attacking force fled in all directions, and Mor joined the rest of his cavalry in chasing them, hacking down as many as he could catch. When there were no more to chase, he turned his horse back toward the hill fort and was greeted with a triumphant roar. Ambrosius and Nataline had made their way down the hill to join the men who had won them such a decisive victory. Mor raised a fist and his cavalry formed up to face the remaining enemy soldiers, the ones who had not run.

Corpses littered the battlefield, and the deadly effectiveness of the archers was macabrely illustrated by the crop of fletched feathers planted in so many lifeless bodies. The scent of butchery carried on the wind, the intermittent rain showers washing the blood down the warriors' faces. The elements were not going to allow them to escape the enormity of what they had done that day. Mor accepted the taste in his mouth, even whilst the squalling rain forced the smell of slaughter up his nose. This was their penance, and they would all suffer it regardless of rank or tribe.

With nowhere to go, trapped between the infantry's spears and Mor's cavalry, the surviving enemy soldiers threw down their weapons. Mor suddenly realised that he hadn't seen Vortimer since the battle's end. He looked frantically around the field and was relieved to see Vortimer and Padell together. They were holding a man at sword-point but seemed to be having trouble getting him to move toward the other prisoners. Curious, Mor rode across to join them.

'King Mor, a fierce battle; I saw you strike down Cunevindus. This is my Uncle Viktor,' said Vortimer, spitting on his prisoner.

The man on his knees was begging for mercy. Mor dismounted, still holding his sword running red with gore. He pointed the sword at Viktor and looked at Vortimer. 'Has he been bleating like that for long?'

'He tells us he did not want this strife and that it was my father and Cunevindus who wished me dead,' said Vortimer, barely able to look at his uncle.

Mor waited for Ambrosius and Nataline to join them. They had just handed their mounts to a couple of soldiers and were picking a route through the dead and mortally wounded.

'The victory is yours, Ambrosius. Unpleasant as it is, we must dispatch the wounded. Warriors should not be left to die in slow agony. Where is that priest?'

One of his cavalry men pointed to where the priest was already making his way through the strewn bodies providing religious succour for the dying as he went.

'Shall we execute the prisoners for you?' Mor asked.

'No,' said Ambrosius.

'What about this snivelling wreck? He is one of their commanders, a Council member no less. Do you want me to execute him?'

'No. But I am interested to know what you would do with them, if it were your decision to make?'

'If they were Picts or Saxon raiders on our lands, we would execute every last man. But this is a civil war, so a merciful approach might be the best way to prevent it turning into a drawn-out, bitter conflict that reaches far into future generations.'

'Let us thank God before coming to any decisions,' said Ambrosius.

Every man who heard him dropped to one knee, and all those who saw them kneel for prayer followed suit, until there was not a man left standing anywhere on the battlefield.

'Dear God, we thank You for this great victory. Forgive our sins and forgive the sins of our enemy. Amen.'

When Mor got to his feet, he kicked Caninus so hard that the defeated commander groaned and convulsed. 'God may forgive you, but I don't. We are surrounded by the dead cives of our Patria. For all of these unnecessary deaths, you and your king will suffer. Ambrosius offers clemency, but I would execute you here and now.'

He took his horse's reins and turned to Padell. 'Count our men. I would know our losses. And look to the wounded. This is the part of warfare I dread the most.' He mounted up. 'Cian, ride with me,' he called.

'Where are we headed?' asked Cian, as he mounted his own horse.

'To the river to wash off this blood.'

*

They sat exhausted by the River Test, a narrow tranquil river flowing over a chalk bed. An immediate and welcome contrast to the cacophony of war.

'I am shaking like a leaf,' said Cian, his voice breaking from the sudden exhaustion and emotion that would be new to him. Not so for the veterans of warfare – it was just the price you paid for the bloodlust that had seen you through the battle.

The lad removed his helmet revealing a macabre mask of blood, stark in its pale frame unsullied by the day's slaughter. He bathed his bloody hands, inspecting two swollen fingers that were probably broken – fingers didn't usually bend in that direction. He was nursing them more out of curiosity than with any semblance of concern. That would come soon enough, when his body remembered how to feel pain. Mor also removed his helmet, wondering if Cian would be likening Mor's bloodstained face to a macabre mask. He stripped to the waist, washing his face and body vigorously. He could sense Cian's troubled thoughts and his naïve relief. The thoughts would fade to a background crowd noise, and the relief... well, war was never done. Let the lad learn the harder lessons in his own good time. There were no victories, just a series of pauses, moments to breathe before the next battle began.

'Come, Cian, we should not delay,' said Mor, putting on his shirt. 'Now that we have done our duty, we have our own families to protect. I'll ask Ambrosius to deal with the aftermath so that we can leave as soon as possible. He is an honourable man who can be trusted to do the right thing. And there is the matter of returning Vortimer to Sevira, as I am sworn to do.'

'Of course, my lord. Just point me where I must go. I can barely think straight. All of that slaughter... the horror. I feel numb. Aren't we commanded by God not to kill? I am truly damned.' He winced and looked at his broken fingers in surprise, suddenly going pale.

'Philosophers make poor warriors. Taly once said that to me. Vortigern is the one who should be damned,' said Mor. 'Get those fingers set by one of the older cavalrymen. They'll have fixed their own enough times to do it right and save you what pain they can. Come, Cian, our misery is yet to worsen, for we must now discover which of our courageous brothers will never see their homes again.'

XXXIV

Guoloph

Spring 437

The relentless wind and rain barely registered as factors in the worst experience of Cian's life. Nobody had warned him that the fighting was the easy part. The aftermath of the battle was a strange, terrible concoction of tasks, information, emotions and cold death. Not the hot death that passed you by so easily when your sword was swinging, but cold death, unmoving, inescapable and stinking. He felt enormous relief to have survived, followed by guilt for that relief when sorrow flooded in with the dreadful sight spread before him. The gore of the dead soaked into the earth so that the mud ran even redder as the rain cleansed the twisted and mutilated bodies. There would be bravado and drinking later, tales of bravery and heroism would be told. What else could they do? There were no words to describe this scene of horror, no way to undo what was done. He imagined Hell looked like this. It was grotesque but strangely fascinating. Only now could he fully appreciate the tragic edge that Taly wove into his elegies. Bravery and heroism inseparable partners to death and despair, each a companion to the others. The soldiers could not find the words, but a skilled bard could, Taly could. Maybe that was all that prevented a warrior from drinking himself to death. The right words. Cian resolved to pay even closer attention to the craft Taly wove through his verses.

The bloody work continued. Cian picked his way across the treacherous battlefield, joining the other survivors in stripping the corpses of their enemies, relieving them of weapons that had not saved them and possessions they would not use again. He watched his comrades bear their own dead to the mass grave hurriedly dug at the bottom of the hill, trying to make the drop into the pit as respectful and honourable as possible.

'Cian!' shouted Winnog. 'The king needs you, come straight away.'

Cian hurried from the cold death, trying not to look too eager to get away. He went straight to the largest campaign tent. The enemy had thought to pitch the colourful shelters outside the walls of each of the Patria's most important cities as their wave of brutal destruction swept across the land. Instead, the unconquered had put the tents to good use providing dry spaces for their commanders to plan and strategize.

When Cian entered, Mor was sat with Ambrosius, Nataline, Natalinus and Vortimer. On the ground were two prisoners in chains.

'Ah, Cian,' said Mor. 'How is your Saxon tongue?'

'Not as good as Spurcio's, my lord, but between us there's not much we couldn't cover.'

Mor waved one of his sentries toward the exit, and the man hurried off to find Spurcio. Those in the tent waited patiently for the wounded warrior to arrive. He made a surprisingly quick appearance for a man with his thigh so heavily bandaged.

'Welcome, Spurcio,' said Mor. 'Take a seat, rest your leg. So, this one is Viktor Caninus!' Mor pointed at one of the prisoners. 'We have agreed to spare his life provided he withdraws his membership of the Council and remains within his own territory from here on. He must also persuade Vortigern to command all the Saxons to return to their continental homelands. Prince Vortimer, with the queen's permission, will become King of the Cornovii. Ambrosius and Vortimer will share the mid-lands, and there will be a new border between the Cornovii and the Belgae. The Melania estate will once more become the property of the Church. Nataline will oversee the proper disposition of the lands. If Vortigern crosses the Severn without the express permission of either Ambrosius or Vortimer, he will be arrested and executed. Can you remember all of that, Caninus?'

'I can, my lord.'

'We will escort you and any of your soldiers who remain loyal to you to Corinium, but do not harbour hopes of revenge. Ambrosius will be making your men a very generous offer in return for them joining his militia. I suspect that many will gladly take that offer. King Vortimer.'

'Yes, King Mor.'

'We will accompany you and Viracus back to your own lands along our return journey north. There is much to be done to get your Cornovii rabble prepared, for I fear it won't be long before you face a mighty Saxon force. Hengist has no intention of going home and every intention of putting his fighting force to good use. We know that his army already outnumbers the combined forces of the whole Patria. It will take a strong alliance between us all if we are to stand any chance of containing them within the Colonae.'

Cian nodded along with everyone else, and Mor moved over to the other prisoner. 'Now, we know this Saxon's name is King Esla, but he speaks no Latin. Spurcio, Cian, tell him that we will spare his life and the lives of his men if he swears loyalty to Ambrosius and remains within Ambrosius' settlement, only deploying on the orders of General Natalinus.'

Together Spurcio and Cian were able to make the Saxon leader understand the terms. The man nodded furiously, as if afraid that his captives may doubt the sincerity of his agreement.

'Ambrosius, I will accompany Vortimer and the Cornovii prisoners back to Viroconium. I think you should deliver Caninus, with those Dobunni who wish to continue in his service, back to Corinium. Leave them chained in the forum so that their cives will know of their defeat and the depth of their shame. Will you write to the other cities on the intended campaign trial to let them know what has happened here today and warn them of the Saxon threat?'

'I shall, King Mor. I will also ensure that Germanus and, through him, Aetius hear of this. They should be left in no doubt that the cives of Britannia defend themselves valorously.'

Cian watched the kings of Britannia shake each other's hands with great solemnity. There was an undeniable sense of optimism arising from this new accord, but it did not prevent the foreboding he felt at the Saxon threat looming ever darker. All Cian wanted to do was get home to Bryn, Agiluf and Elfed.

XXXV

Viroconium

Aprilis 437

Six days after the battle at Guoloph – someone had finally asked for the name of the hill upon which they had defeated Cunevindus – the large group of cavalry and prisoners arrived at Viroconium.

It had been an eventful few days. Mor had chosen not to return to Venta Belgarum and had set off the day after the dead were buried. Spurcio had lost a lot of blood from his thigh wound but still clung to life. Ambrosius had invited him to stay and be treated by the Roman lord's physicians, but Spurcio had chosen to ride home with his king, and so far, there was no sign of poison in his wound.

Altogether, Mor had only lost ten of his volunteers, but the slaughter on both sides had been terrible. The Saxons had lost three-quarters of their men, and both the Dobunni and the Cornovii had lost over half of theirs. Ambrosius' militia, which had withstood the brunt of the attack had lost a quarter of their men. Spurcio and Viracus had both described the fighting on the front line as brutal. The battle would live long in their memory.

The Cornovii prisoners had been marched north under Vortimer's supervision, but he had released them from their bonds when each swore loyalty to him as leader of their tribe. The head of Cunevindus was also brought north and had been placed on a stake in the forum. There seemed little interest in his fate or sadness at his passing, and even less in the disgrace of Vortigern whose whereabouts were not known. Rebuilding the Cornovii militia would be a tough job, but Viracus was committed to the task and had already proved himself capable of inspiring men in the most difficult of circumstances. He was a fine and trustworthy commander who was devoted to both Queen Sevira and Vortimer. It was therefore fitting that he accompany Vortimer and Mor to the Villa Octavius.

Mor left his troop camped at the crossroads by the Wrikon and led his companions along the path he had first taken ten years earlier. As they approached the villa, Mor was relieved to see that the compound's defences had been improved and now looked capable of resisting attack.

*

Queen Sevira had been informed by a servant that a large group of soldiers had arrived in Viroconium, and she feared the worst. Cunevindus had insisted that she supply a number of soldiers for his treacherous campaign from her own household, but she had remained stoic, refusing to send men to fight against her own son. She feared that the return of a victorious Cunevindus would yield dire consequences for her, and also for Viracus whose absence had been noted. She was digging in her front garden when the group rode into the outer compound, but she did not dare look up. Her stomach churned with fear as she heard the horses approach her.

'Mother!' shouted a familiar voice.

She raised her head to see what she had most hoped for but least expected. The relief was so great that she dropped to her knees sobbing with joy. Her son dismounted and ran to her, lifting her from the ground to embrace her. Mor and Viracus tactfully took the three horses to the stables whilst Sevira composed herself.

'Cunevindus is dead, Mother. Mor killed him.'

*

They received a joyful reception from everyone in the compound, even the dogs in the kennels picked up on the excitement, their barking incessant. Mor and Viracus walked toward the villa.

'You have a lot of work ahead of you, Viracus. Vortigern may yet challenge Vortimer, so a strong militia is important.'

Gavius joined them. 'My son, I've just heard the news.' He clapped both men on the back.

They walked into the villa whilst Viracus gave his father a potted version of events.

Queen Sevira had gone to change, asking everyone to wait in the day-room. It was an animated scene with servants, retainers and family all wanting to hear the news. Mor stood back, giving Igerna's family space to enjoy the relief that came from the favourable outcome. Seeking a private moment to reflect, he wandered down the corridor to the little apse with the altar. It was adorned with yellow narcissi, and a candle was burning. Sevira had clearly been at prayer earlier that day. He remembered the night he had given his vow and the cracked face of Jesus, but more of the plaster had sheared from the wall now leaving only half the face of Jesus. He ran his hand along the edge. It would not be long before it all fell away. The damp Briton climate did not suit Roman plasterwork, and he had no doubt that, by the end of his lifetime, many such monuments would have crumbled into obscurity. Mor was overcome by the realisation of what a big impact this little apse had had on his life, and he knelt in reverent prayer. He was not superstitious, but a sense that the damaged portrait of Jesus held a message for him sent a chill up his spine. What was it that had drawn him here, to this altar, yet again? His thoughts were interrupted by a boy's voice.

'Hello, I've been sent to find you.' Mor turned and for an instant thought it was Arthwys. Shaking off the notion, he stood and ruffled the boy's hair.

'Are you Britu?'

The boy nodded.

The pair stood staring at one another, the spell breaking when Sevira arrived. 'There you are, Mor. I don't know how I will ever thank you for what you have done.'

'You don't need to thank me, Sevira. After all, it was you and this apse that changed my life forever for the better all those years ago; so much joy has come to me from our agreement that night.' He smiled.

Looking at her more intently, he noticed that she had aged more than he had expected, but she was still beautiful.

'I see you couldn't save Him?'

'Who?' asked Sevira, her brow crinkling in puzzlement.

He gestured at the wall. 'Jesus!'

'Ah, no.' She laughed. 'We tried, but to no avail. Plastering is a skill lost to the Patria.'

'Well, let's hope He saves us,' Mor said. 'You have a fine young boy here.' He ruffled Britu's hair again. There was no need to say it. He had known instantly that the boy was his.

'Igerna knows,' she murmured, looking at the boy with fierce love. 'We are far too close to keep such matters from each other. She understands...'

Britu ran down the corridor to join the family, oblivious to the deep currents flowing through the adult conversation.

They both watched him go. Sevira turned to Mor. 'I will never tell him, but you may choose to one day?'

It was not a decision he would take without having Igerna's opinion on the matter. He was suddenly eager to be home.

'We shall see what my queen has to say... But I am here to advise you that Vortigern lives on, and none can say what he will do next. Vortimer must consolidate his position and will need all the support you can provide for him if he is to succeed. Like all cowards, I expect your husband to take a conciliatory approach until he finds a way to rebuild his strength, *if* he finds a way, but it is his Saxons who now pose the greatest threat.'

Queen Sevira looked at him, her gaze probing.

'*Prince* Mor was never so serious,' she said with a twinkle in her eyes.

Mor laughed. 'And look at the trouble that got him into!'

XXXVI

Elfed

Aprilis 437

New lands, they'd said. New lands and Roman treasure with plenty of fighting and killing the soft people of this island – the Wealas. That's what they'd said. But since his arrival, Ebissa had spent more time fishing than raiding, more time counting his rations than counting treasure. Hengist had lost his fighting spirit, and Horsa, Ebissa's own father, was no better – always deferring to Hengist like he was the fount of all wisdom and not just his elder brother. Even Octha, Ebissa's cousin and brother in arms who had been lured to these shores with the same promises, was too in awe of his father to speak up. Their fathers were no longer warriors; they had been sat on their arses for too long and had turned into time-wasting talkers.

The Briton king's army had travelled south. The Jutes' toughest opponents had been left undefended, vulnerable for once. Why wait for their return? Why waste this opportunity? Now was the perfect time to raid, to weaken the enemy. Ebissa had not sailed across the sea to clash heads with Hengist; he had come here to kill the Wealas and take their rich lands, and that's what he intended to do. Once he lit the spark that began the war, Hengist wouldn't be able to sit around talking anymore, not with the Wealas banging on his door. He knew Hengist would be furious, but it was his keel and his men. They had slipped away in the night to avoid confrontation. No doubt there would be plenty awaiting him upon his return, but with victory under his belt, who would care about a bit of insubordination? Ebissa looked through the dense, long grass toward the fortress gates and couldn't help grinning. His plan would give his men some action, win them some riches and start the war he so desperately wanted. The weakened Wealas fortress would fall easily, and Ebissa's people would no longer be relegated to cowering in the marshes.

It had not been difficult to find the fortress. The scouts had told him the way there and also where to hide their keel in the marshes. With eighteen of his own trusted warriors, he had rowed upstream in the night. Around the forbidden hook, the river had narrowed but was still deep, and they had followed the fork that headed toward the distant hills. They had hidden their keel in the marshes and followed the route that the scouts had described, travelling at night in the forest to avoid detection. Now they lay in the long grass at the edge of a large clearing silently watching their enemy.

The village lay ahead, the large gate and palisade of the timber fortress rising beyond. Just after dawn on the first morning they had thought themselves discovered when thirty men on horses with dogs baying at their heels came galloping out the gate. But they had turned east, showing no interest in the long grass at the other side of the clearing where Ebissa's men watched from a safe distance. Even so, if the dogs had come much closer, the Jutes' presence would have been detected. Thereafter, the gate had remained open as the people of the village went about their daily routines, and apart from the sentries at the gate, no other warriors were to be seen. The cavalry had returned after midday, and the gates had only been closed toward evening.

'There are more Wealas warriors than we expected,' said a companion lying next to Ebissa.

'True, but if their morning hunt is a daily event, the fort is poorly defended for those hours. It is an opportunity too good to pass up. We watch for one more day. If the pattern repeats, we attack.'

*

Bryn had not slept well. She had been awake for hours before dawn worrying about Cian. It had been over two weeks since he had left with the king, and every day she had prayed for his safe return. Her husband had been riding into terrible danger, and her fear that he might never return was well-founded. As each day had passed her worry had intensified.

Perhaps he was already lying dead in some distant field. Bereft and widowed – what would become of her and her children? She had been a similar age to her son when she lost her own father, a devastating experience for a child, and now as a mother, she mourned his loss more than ever. Bryn had kept herself busy each day as a distraction from the worry, but her grim thoughts would be there, without fail, each morning when she first woke in the darkness. Then the dawn could not arrive soon enough to bring little Agiluf to fill her heart and her duties to fill her thoughts.

Today, as she opened the shutters, she noticed the bird song was more muted than on recent days, although she could hear the clamour of rooks high in the forest canopy. Perhaps there was a sleepless owl lingering in the morning light hoping to catch the wary songbirds unaware. Bryn shook her five-year-old who had taken to sharing her bed in the absence of his father. Outside, the fort was coming to life, and the hunt was gathering in front of the hall. Dogs were howling in anticipation of their morning sport. The forest was full of red deer, and the hunt could be counted on to return around noon with plenty of game to supplement the king's larder. The extra food was needed now that there were going to be so many more bellies to fill around the fort. New recruits would be arriving in a few days, needing fed as well as accommodating, equipping, training, managing… As the king's chief housekeeper, Bryn's responsibilities were similar to those of her mother's at Banna. With her extensive duties and Cian's absence, she had worried that Agiluf would feel neglected, but he played well with the king's children, and Taly had proved helpful, sometimes watching or playing, and other times tutoring, if Martin had other duties.

'Is it time for lessons, Mummy?' Agiluf asked.

'After breakfast, Agy. Let's go see Arthwys and Morgaine first.'

Bryn closed her door, and they walked hand in hand toward the king's large timber hall. They watched the horsemen and baying hounds stream out through the gate. Taly was also on his way to the hall. When he saw them, he caught up and scooped her son onto his shoulders.

'Hello, you two. Lessons with Martin then riding this afternoon.'

Agiluf's face lit up with excitement. There was no doubting that Taly was his favourite grown-up. They entered the hall, and Taly lowered her son to the floor. Agiluf ran to join Arthwys.

Igerna greeted them, her face showing the weight of concern she shared with Bryn.

'Fifteen days now, Taly. When do you think we might expect the king's return?'

'Well, overall there is at least ten days' journey time, my lady, and who can say what other time is necessary? I should try not to worry until twenty days are passed.'

'I hope it will be soon. Bryn and I have much we need to ask about the arrangements for the recruits who will arrive shortly. Crannog has kept them busy working on his estates whilst the king is away, but we are still short of a great many things they will need.'

'After I have walked the children to Martin, I shall come and see if there are any aspects to your planning I can help with.'

'That would be a great help,' said Igerna, though Bryn knew that the queen was more interested in her husband's return than planning for the recruits' arrival. She knew it because she felt exactly the same.

Igerna began looking over her lists whilst Taly watched over the children as they ate breakfast.

Bryn turned to Igerna. 'I can hardly sleep with worry for our men.'

'I feel much the same, but I'm sure they're safe – I feel it,' replied Igerna.

The children finished their breakfast, and Taly herded them out the door as they raced each other.

'Mor thinks it's so simple to say we should bring in more recruits, but he isn't the one who has to source everything for these men. We are running short of everything from clothing to weapons. Even pots are in short supply. We will ask Taly to check our lists and let us know if we are missing anything important or if there are existing supplies of some items stored somewhere we don't know about. That should keep us all busy.'

*

Across the clearing, Ebissa and his men crouched in wait. The hunt had only left half an hour since. The Wealas soldiers were likely still close enough to hear the tell-tale sounds of an attack. They would wait a further half an hour but could not risk leaving it any longer.

*

Bryn looked up from her work to see Taly returning to the hall.

'Children safely delivered; Martin has a full house today.'

'Bryn and I would like you to check our lists for us,' said Igerna. 'Will you take a look, Taly?'

A hoarse cry penetrated the hall. 'Saxons!'

Bryn looked at Igerna, seeing her horror mirrored in the queen's expression. Taly tore out the door grabbing a spare sword and shield from the wall. Igerna followed with her bow and quiver, and Bryn grabbed a spear before chasing after them.

'Where are they?' shouted Taly at the sentry above the gate.

'Coming across the clearing.'

'How many?'

'Twenty or so.'

Bryn only had one thing on her mind. 'The Children!' she screamed at Taly.

He ran through the gate shouting orders to the sentries in the tower.

'Sound the alarm and shut the gates!'

'But the children!' screamed Bryn again as she followed Igerna up onto the battlements.

She saw Martin's response to the commotion when he appeared at the church door holding a sword. He turned and spoke quickly to the children inside and slammed the door shut before running to stand by Taly.

Igerna turned to Bryn. 'I didn't know he had one of those, did you?'

Bryn shook her head, unable to take her eyes off the church door. Four shrill blasts of a loud horn echoed from their battlements and out across the forest. Its wail was repeated over and over. Bryn's gaze was finally drawn away from the church by movement along the treeline. She watched in horror as the Saxons ran up over the perimeter ditch. One Saxon was felled by a woodsman's arrow shot from behind a hut in the village to the left of the charging raiders. The Saxon leader sent two warriors in the direction the arrow had come from whilst the main force continued its advance along the main thoroughfare. Standing in their path were Taly and Martin, weapons raised, prepared to defend all they held dear.

A distant horn replied. Three blasts signalling that help was on its way. But would it be soon enough? Taly and Martin looked so alone, so vulnerable.

The Saxons stepped into range of the fort's only archers – the two sentries and Igerna. Their arrows flew true, but the Saxons' advance continued undeterred, their shields catching most of the arrows. The clash of steel told her that Taly and Martin had engaged with the enemy. Terror filled Bryn as she watched the Saxons fan out and enter the villagers' huts. Screams from within filled the air making her want to cover her ears. The attackers had almost reached the church, but they had not reckoned on the strength of the resistance from the old man and the priest. With skill and experience, Taly and Martin had butchered each Saxon who came against them. The Saxon leader finally took the threat seriously and directed his warriors to converge upon the two defenders making it impossible for the archers to get a clear shot.

Igerna shouted to Bryn. 'Quickly, follow me. They need help.'

Bryn didn't hesitate. She grabbed her spear and threw one of the sentries' spears to Igerna as they ran down the steps. Igerna shouted instructions to the gateman to let them pass. As they squeezed through the gate, Bryn saw the Saxon leader throw his spear at Martin. It glanced off the priest's arm making him flinch. In the same instant, the Saxon drew his sword and charged. Martin parried, spun and slashed knocking the young warrior to the ground where the priest skewered his sword into the Saxon's gut.

Bryn ran with Igerna to place themselves in front of the church door. Taly was nearly overwhelmed by two Saxons with spears, but Martin saw the danger. One swing of his hefty sword sheared through a spear and struck down the attacker who had been wielding it. No longer having to defend on two fronts, Taly quickly dispatched the remaining Saxon.

Even Bryn could see that the Saxon attack was faltering. Their leader lay dead, and the thunder of approaching horses at the gallop put fear into those who remained. They turned and ran. Bryn felt her heart soar when she saw Crannog and his cavalry recruits charge through the village eagerly swinging their swords as their steeds pursued the raiders down the main thoroughfare.

Taly's 'whoop' as he watched them go drew Bryn's attention, making her smile. He turned to wave at her, but her relief turned to fear when she saw a Saxon appear from a hut behind Taly and throw his spear. The old bard reacted to her terrified expression and turned toward the danger, but the spear took him in the side, and he fell to the ground. Even as her heart broke, Bryn heard the shouts from the children as they ran from the church to their mothers. Clasping Agiluf to her, she looked at Igerna, unable to reconcile her relief with the great sorrow that engulfed her.

'Please take Agiluf. I must help Taly.'

She ran to the old warrior, getting there at the same time as Martin. Taly had propped himself up, his clothes turning crimson.

'Pull it out, Martin,' he said through gritted teeth.

'This is going to—' And the priest yanked the spear out in one swift movement.

Taly yelled agonised profanities before glaring at Martin. Bryn wrapped her shawl around the wound – for all the good it did.

'What?' said Martin. 'It's better when you're not expecting it.'

'Says who?'

Martin shrugged unapologetically, and Bryn helped him to get the wounded warrior to his feet and back to the fort. She tried not to think about how much blood had already pumped through the shawl.

Taly turned his glassy gaze on Martin. 'Impressive!' was all he said.

Igerna caught up with them, pressing linen pads against the wound as they stumbled to Taly's hut. Once they got him on his bed, Bryn carefully removed his tunic. Then with Martin holding him up, Igerna wound more linen around his torso to keep the pads in place, but nothing they did would stop the bleeding. The wound was a gaping hole. Taly was horribly pale, but he propped himself against the side of his bunk.

'Igerna, I need to speak to Arthwys... family business.'

Arthwys had been hovering just outside and stumbled, ashen-faced, into the room as soon as he heard his name mentioned.

'Don't be afraid, lad. Come close. Please, leave us in private for a moment,' Taly said, holding tightly to Bryn's hand. She stayed whilst Igerna and Martin stepped outside.

'You were very brave, Uncle Taly. I watched you fight through a gap in the timbers.' Arthwys stared in horrified fascination at the blossoming crimson flower on the white linen.

'I have a secret to tell you. Myrddin is the only other person who knows it, and he will be able to explain more and answer your questions, but you must not speak of it to anyone else. Now, listen carefully and repeat each line after me. You must memorise this rhyme.

> *'The temple of Myrddin stands proud in the vale*
> *but high on the mountain old spirits prevail*
> *A high cliff doth Venutius' cave protect*
> *Below a black pool in which stars reflect*
> *The dragon's long back is the only safe path*
> *Obscured by his breath that blows hard in his wrath*
> *Fear not this dragon, he is not the Bear's quarry*
> *For he guides you forth from the deep gloomy corrie*
> *To the top of the cliffs where the rooks stand sentry*
> *On the steep facing rocks guarding the entry.*
> *The risks are many and the Bear must beware*
> *But the prize is great with Caledfwich there*
> *It is said that the sword holds powers beyond ken*
> *And in the Bear's hand proves him leader of men.'*

Arthwys had repeated every line and then repeated the whole riddle before nervously asking, 'What does it mean, Uncle Taly?'

'Well, the Bear is the leader of the Brigantes tribe, which *was* me! Now you have memorised the rhyme, it is *you*!'

'What must I do?'

'Your duty, young cub. As the Bear, it is your duty to protect the tribe.'

Arthwys' eyes grew wide with wonder. Bryn was impressed. He was handling this much better than she would have! Taly continued. 'The sword belonged to Venutius, hero of the North, but it has never been recovered. The cave is where our people hid their weapons from the Romans. Only seek the sword if you have need of it.'

Taly groaned. Pain was etched in every line on his old brow.

'Arthwys, always be brave and honourable. Myrddin will explain what you don't understand. You must not be afraid of him. I have always thought the cave is on a high mountain called Blencathra. That is all I can tell you. Now run along.'

Arthwys looked reluctant to leave his uncle, but he stood with great solemnity and walked away, glancing back briefly with tears in his eyes and a brave smile on his lips. Then he stepped out, and Igerna and Martin immediately returned.

'Fearless Igerna, Mor will return – Martin has dreamt that the descendants of Coel will rule for a hundred years. The path will not be easy, but Mor has the strength and wisdom of his grandfather, and he will not fail whilst you are his queen.'

Igerna looked at Martin who did not avert his gaze from Taly.

'There is much about Martin I have yet to discover.'

'Much more…' The old bard smiled through his pain. 'Ah, Bryn, lovely girl,' Taly whispered, 'tell Cian to keep my sword, stallion and other possessions.'

Bryn couldn't control the sobs that shook her body. 'You have been a father to me, Taly,' she said, her quivering voice thick with tears.

She held his blood-encrusted hands, feeling them shake from the loss of blood.

Martin was murmuring a prayer.

'Martin,' Taly interrupted.

'Yes, my friend.'

'Do not be afraid of Myrddin; he is part of your journey to finding yourself. God sent you here for greater purpose than you yet know. Now, please leave me with Bryn.'

*

Igerna and Martin stepped outside just as Crannog galloped back into the fort. He jumped off his horse and hurried across to them. 'Taly?' he asked.

Igerna shook her head.

'Did you kill them all?' Martin asked.

'I think so. I've sent men down to the river to search for their keel. When the captain of the guard returns from his morning sport, we shall be having words. Why didn't he heed the horns? Why didn't the hounds detect the presence of so many Saxons? Too busy hunting instead of patrolling – though the Saxon scum do smell like dogs. Shall we burn the bodies, Martin?'

'No, I have an idea. One where we can take advantage of the Saxons' fear of spirits. We will need their keel though, so let me know when your recruits find it. In the meantime, pile the bodies in a cart.'

*

Bryn sat by Taly. He was fading quickly, his breathing laboured.

'Please message Brianna and let her know I thought of her every day,' he whispered.

Tears rolled down Bryn's cheeks and then she realised the room was silent, no more laboured breathing. He was gone. She lay him down as best she could and closed his eyes.

He was with them all now. His wife and son, Coel, Ceneu, Peithien and Bryn's father... Despite the gore, she thought he had never looked more at peace.

*

When the recruits found the Saxon keel, Crannog informed Martin. Together, they took a group of the returned soldiers and decapitated all the Saxon corpses, before placing their heads on stakes by the river and throwing their torsos into the keel which they cast adrift to float downstream.

'We are ready for the bastards now,' said Crannog as they watched the dead drift east.

*

Mor arrived back with his troop two days later. There was great sorrow at the fort for the loss of ten heroes in the southern conflict, but Mor was inconsolable at Taly's death blaming himself for not being there. Cian was instructed to write a gorchan for the fallen heroes, but it was decided that the old warrior should be buried first, laid to rest by

Martin's little church in the forest. He had spent many happy afternoons there discussing history, philosophy and religion with the priest.

Martin conducted the service. Myrddin attended and so did hundreds of mourners. Mor had hewn a coffin from oak for the man who had been a father to him, and Taly made his final journey in its sturdy confines. Followed by the long retinue of mourners, he made his slow way over the Gar cliff to his final resting place.

These were sad days for Elfed. Even the air was heavy with sorrow, and none doubted that the storm Myrddin had prophesised a decade earlier was about to break.

XXXVII

Ypwines Fleot

Aprilis 437

One thing. Hengist had asked Octha to do one thing, and his son had failed catastrophically. All he had had to do was keep an eye on Ebissa, the lad's own cousin. How hard could it be? But when Hengist had been notified of the missing keel and the missing warriors, he had instantly guessed there would be trouble. He had turned his wrath on his hapless son, brutally battering Octha whilst threatening to do the same to Ebissa when he returned.

Three days passed with Hengist's fury mounting every hour and then the missing keel had floated into the Humber with its crew of headless, fly-bloated corpses. It had been an unbearable sight. In particular, the elders were devastated to see their youth had been slaughtered in this manner. Some cried out to the gods in fear that they had angered the deities, others swore bloody revenge. Horsa, distraught with grief and the disgrace Ebissa had brought upon him, wanted swift retaliation to mend his reputation and avenge his son's death.

From the wounds on the corpses, the Jutes could see that their sons had died in battle, but Hengist knew this was not the time or place to retaliate. Now he was having to navigate an intense meeting of the elders. Emotions were running high, but Hengist was determined to hold firm to his original plan. Once Gundad returned with an answer from Vortigern he would have his premise for rebellion. A rebellion supported by all the Saxon tribes. He did not seek Mor's territory or war with the northern kings. Ebissa's foolish actions had set back his plans. Now he would have to find ways to appease both the northern army and his own men, who were baying for revenge, before he could turn in the direction he wanted to go.

'The Brigantes watch us like hawks. Ever since our fleet arrived, they have been expecting our attack, preparing for it, waiting. They do not trust us, but they do not trust Vortigern either. Ebissa's foolishness has all but ruined my carefully laid plans. The ghost keel should be taken seriously as a warning from King Mor. His tribe are strong, disciplined, alert; there is more to lose than gain from turning our forces in that direction. Attack him now, and we will be seen as nothing more than raiders, no different to the Picts and Scotti they fight on their northern borders. It's true that we are better sailors than these northern Wealas, but they are better trained for fighting on land, and we have no equivalent to their cavalry. They would crush us in a land battle. But our goals are grander and to achieve all that we hope for, we must carry our neighbours with us – the Gaini, the Angles and Wippeds tribe by the Wash. Hengist looked around at his captains and their men now calmly listening.

'We need a homeland, a kingdom of our own, more than we need revenge. Though have no fear, we *will* have our revenge when the time is right. Where is the sense in fighting the warriors of the North when all the wealth is in the soft south? Their tribes are divided which is to our advantage. For now, I say we leave King Mor well alone. Let us strengthen and consolidate our position, take the fertile land and plunder the wealth in the south. The North can wait. Let them fester, become complacent, then when we are ready, we will wreak our terrible revenge.

'I have ordered Octha to take command of the bulk of our keels and sail them down the coast to the havens of the Wash at Wippeds Fleot where they will be hidden from view. It is yet too early to send them up the Trent, but they will be poised, ready for when our time comes. Patience and cunning will win us our kingdom, my friends. Are you with me!' he said, raising his voice to a shout.

A rumbling roar of assent accompanied the clatter of weapons on shields.

Hengist put his hand on Horsa's shoulder.

'We shall avenge Ebissa, brother. We shall avenge him by drenching our new lands in Wealas blood.'

XXXVIII

The Fort of Cambodunum in Elfed

Maius 437

The fort was packed full of visitors. The barus were all present with their retainers. Even old Alwin had come, helped by Spurcio whose wound had not festered and was mending well. As comrades of the fallen, the turmae were all in attendance, and they had brought their wives, children and some of their elders. The sadness that had gripped Cambodunum following the death of Taly would end this day. Mor had invited everyone to Elfed for this festival of memory on the Kalends of Maius. It was time to let their heroes go and look to the future.

Bryn, as chief housekeeper, had been cooking and baking for a whole week. When Cian had reminded her that it was the tradition for the visitors to bring food and drink, she had huffed at him and told him to hang his tradition – the reality was most would turn up empty-handed. The king's reserves of mead and wine were going to receive a battering too. Everyone knew the story of Taly's death, reports had spread like wildfire, becoming more embellished with each telling. Martin's martial skills had come as a surprise to everyone, earning him frequent pats on the back whilst he circulated amongst the visitors. Queen Igerna's skill with the bow had earned equal acclaim, though her title as Diana, goddess of Elfed, was only ever whispered where she would not hear, for it was well known that she wanted no reminder of the traumatic events of that day.

All this flowed through Cian's mind, barely registering in conscious thought, his nerves in tatters as the flickering flames cast eerie glows and shadows over the faces gathered around him. He had opted to sing his gorchan for the fallen heroes after dark with everyone sat around the campfire. It would add to the drama, but with the food and drink having come first, he was worried he would struggle to hold the attention of his audience. Myrddin was out there in the shimmering darkness, though the ancient seer had been more interested in deep discussions with Martin than calming the nerves of Taly's successor. The friendship between the seer and the priest had come as a surprise to everyone. As planned, the two of them sat close to the royal party, the children of Elfed, who doted on their company, sat at their feet.

The mood of the occasion had lifted considerably with the news that the Saxon fleet had sailed away and not returned. This was a celebration of life rather than the mourning of death.

Cian had considered accompanying his singing with his lyre, but in the open air, he had decided it would be better for his loud, clear tones to be all that filled the silence.

Martin stood, and Cian raised his eyes to the canopy of stars above taking a deep breath to steady himself.

'Let us pray,' said Martin.

Everyone bowed their heads.

> *'Be to me bright flame before me*
> *Be to me a guiding star above me*
> *Be to me a smooth path below me*
> *Be to me a kind shepherd behind me*
> *Today, tonight and forever.'*

'Amen,' said the crowd.

The fire crackled in the silence that followed, and sparks leapt into the evening sky. Cian paused. He was the king's bard now; he must do Taly proud. He swallowed hard and stepped into the light. In his loudest voice he began.

> *'The sun that bathed Rome has finally set*
> *But fear not – this darkness will end*
> *We shall light Cymry torches to guide us forth*
> *The Patria is ours to defend.'*

He was surrounded by faces bathed in firelight, their expressions rapt.

> *'We must fight for our future, we know that is so,*
> *The Cymry must never be chained*
> *Our tribes and our kings do battle hard*
> *To secure the freedoms we've gained.'*

He paused, schooling his expression into one of deep solemnity.

> *'Fifty mounted men with their king went to Guoloph*
> *There to meet an enemy swarm*
> *Brave heroes all faced a forest of spears*
> *Only forty survived the morn.*
> *All the ten who fell on that violent day*
> *Were to us a brother or friend*
> *With honour we buried their broken bones*
> *Now their souls wait here to ascend.'*

He held out his arm as if the heroes were standing with him.

> *Cynla, Dinda, Nython and Troth*
> *Struck down five-fold their number of foes*
> *Belli, Brigin, Dythy and Frac*
> *Heroes all as they rained down their blows.*
> *Senyart and Arla were at my side*
> *As we cleaved our gore-sodden swathe*
> *Both wounded by spears they fought till they fell*
> *I carried them both to their grave.*

Cian hesitated, head bowed out of respect for the fallen, then swept his still-strapped hand across the assembled militia in the audience.

> *'The forty stand ready to say their farewells*
> *But one more leaves before the morrow*
> *Great Talhaearn, brave soldier, is here at their side*
> *Our homecoming met even more sorrow.'*

The crowd looked around, searching for his spectral image.

> *'Talhaearn the Bear leaves us also this night*
> *Honour guard of ten at his side*
> *The best of us all fell fighting for Elfed*
> *Defending his queen and our tribe.*
> *Was there ever a man so selfless and strong*
> *Fearless warrior, wise, and so clever*
> *His story is long with many brave deeds*
> *We shall sing of his valour forever.'*

He walked around the fire.

> *'A leader of men, so humble yet deadly*
> *For Rome, for Coel, for the Cymry*
> *He defended the Wall and slaughtered the Picts*
> *Selflessly defending so many.*
> *A hero no question, this fierce warring Bear*
> *Two queens and their broods he protected*
> *Duty abiding though tragedy stalked him*
> *Grim death could not be deflected.'*

He shook his head.

> *'A fosterling child, his wife and son murdered*
> *Brave Taly long questioned the strife*
> *Why was fate so hard on this eloquent bard?*
> *What purpose, what meaning to life?*
> *But the Lord does not plan the fortunes of man*
> *And to us Taly's role became clear*
> *This father to none was a father to all*
> *A life lived for everyone here.'*

He looked toward Martin who nodded approval.

> *'A father to Bryn, to King Gorwst and King Mor*
> *A bard who could soothe or amuse*
> *The father of Elfed and Reged too*

And for me the father of muse.'

He put his hand on his heart before grasping the pommel of Taly's
sword.

> *'His sword at my belt, and his stylus in hand*
> *A fair student, I hope not his worst*
> *But my wit is dull, my composition wanting*
> *I can see that he laughs at my verse.'*

The crowd laughed at Cian's humble confession.

> *'Ride forth eleven to the heavens above*
> *Where your friends all patiently wait*
> *Taly go follow that path through the stars*
> *For it's there you will find Peter's gate.'*

The final line was greeted with raucous cheering and clapping
from the crowd. Cian let out a deep sigh of relief and smiled. He caught
Bryn's eye as she wiped away tears in between clapping. Mor stood
and patted him on the back.

'Really good, Cian, really good. It was as if they were here with
us. I swear I saw them all for an instant.'

*

Arthwys turned to the seer.

'Did you see them, Myrddin?'

'Yes, they were all here, but they have left now. Did you hear that
distant bear's roar, Arthwys?'

'I think so.' Had he? Arthwys wasn't sure he had.

'That was the bear goddess, Artio, saying farewell to Talhaearn.'
Myrddin cocked his head, listening with a twinkle in his eyes.

'There, she roars again.' He paused. 'She says, "Welcome,
young Arthwys."'

XXXIX

Banna

Late Augustus 437

It had rained for nearly a week turning the yard between the great hall and Taly's old hut into a quagmire. Gorwst swallowed hard as he left shelter and plugged his way across to where his old mother now preferred to pass her days. The news was not good, and Brianna would take it hard, but it was his duty to tell her. Marchell had offered, but he did not trust his wife to be kind. Instead, he had waited a day, then another, for his own pain to ease enough for him to speak of the loss. Despite the pouring rain, he knocked and waited for the old lady to open the door. He could hear her shuffling inside despite his dogs howling indignantly at being left confined in the hall. She opened the door, shawl about her shoulders, and squinted at the light now illuminating her dingy abode.

'Mother.'

'Gorwst, you silly fool, you are soaked! You should have walked straight in; Marchell always does!'

Gorwst could see apprehension in her eyes. She knew he had come with important news.

'No grandsons or hounds today, I see?'

'No mother, this rain has us all taking shelter whilst it ruins the harvest.'

'Well, shake off the wet and sit by my fire.'

Gorwst gratefully accepted the offer and sat staring into the embers.

'You are here to tell me something?'

Gorwst looked on, his teeth gritted, tears welling.

'It's always been the same, since you were a little boy… I know that look – serious face, serious news.'

Gorwst rung his hands and started to speak.

'Taly is dead, killed in battle by Saxons. We hear it was a heroic stand.'

Tears welled, but Brianna smiled.

'Of course it was – he did those so well.'

She held Gorwst's hand. It was he who was supposed to be consoling her.

'He will be with them all now,' she reflected.

'If he had stayed with us, I could have protected him. I miss him, his wisdom, his wit.'

'You are lucky, Gorwst, you remember your father; Mor does not – the loss will have been all the harder for him.'

'Mor has become embroiled in Saxon wars. His fame as a warrior spreads like a wildfire.'

'Myrddin and Taly led him to that; he did not seek it.'

There was a silent moment, just the fire crackling and Gorwst's dogs still barking across the yard.

'He came to me.'

'Who, Mother?'

'Taly, he appeared over there, sat on his old bed smiling. I could *smell* him. I knew he had passed on.'

Gorwst shivered; he would not tell Marchell about the apparition for she would not believe it. 'The ramblings of an old woman already lost in herself,' she would say. But he believed it. Taly had always been there for them.

'Do you have everything you need?'

'Oh yes, everything.'

'Shall I stoke this fire?'

'No, don't worry about me, Gorwst; I'm just fine.'

Gorwst hurried back over to the hall.

It looked as if a messenger had arrived from Alt Clut, for a man was deep in conversation with Marchell. Gorwst's boys looked thoroughly bored; it was far too wet to play outside, and their tutor had failed to arrive for the second day. Marchell raised her hand to silence the messenger as the king strode through the hall.

'How is your mother?'

'She received the news better than I expected.' Then indicating the stranger in his hall, 'Who is this, Marchell?'

'A soaked messenger from my brother.'

'And what message does he bring?'

'My brother invites you to join him on an expedition to Hibernia. He will sail to Alauna so your keels may join his.'

'I thought we had discussed this?'

Marchell did not reply.

'Your brother is our strongest ally but a deeply violent man – he raids too often.'

'Does he scare the mighty Gorwst?'

'Marchell! Palladius counselled me upon his return from Hibernia. When your brother raids, the kings of that island believe it is us, that it is Reged, and they retaliate. Our losses outweigh our gains. The war band of Coroticus is strong, but his own territory does not produce sufficient wealth or sustenance for his wants. To him it is only sport. I do not wish to offend him unless I must, but this cycle of constant raids must end.'

'So now you will have your brother eclipse you as the mightiest of Cymry warriors?'

Gorwst controlled his temper at his wife's barbed jibe.

'Mor fights for survival. Reged is the mightiest kingdom in the Patria with an abundance of resources and a Christian heart. I did not understand my grandfather's designs as a young man, but I see them clearly now – as Taly did.'

'Talhaearn deserted you, Gorwst; I shall not mourn him.'

'Marchell,' he said firmly, 'send your messenger away. I raid only where retaliation is called for.'

Gorwst flicked his hand and the man understood, bowing as he left, but the king knew Marchell would allow him to return. Her brother seemed to matter more to her than her husband.

'So now he is dead, who will become the so-called Bear of the North?'

Marchell never failed to show her disbelief that Gorwst did not care about such things.

'Myrddin will know,' he replied, hoping that would be the end of the discussion.

'What!' screamed Marchell. 'That old crone. He has not visited Reged for years. He does not care for you, Gorwst, or he would be here.'

Gorwst sat with his boys, joining them in stroking their pack of dogs. It soothed them all when Marchell ranted.

'Look at the three of you. Reged, the most powerful kingdom in the land, you say, run by weaklings stroking dogs!'

Marchell stood then paced up and down in front of the fire speaking directly to her sons.

'My foolish husband missed his chance, but one of you should be the Bear. You, Meirchiawn, or perhaps you, Mordred, whosoever becomes the best warrior; it is your birthright, stolen from you by your father's brother!'

The boys gave knowing looks to each other but did not reply. A shaft of sunlight suddenly penetrated the hall. *God is merciful.* Gorwst had prayed the rain would stop because he knew his queen would not.

'Come boys, hunting.'

They ran out, hounds baying at their heels. He would show his sons where Coel hunted the best red deer, where Taly shot his finest arrow and where Mor fell in the river. As they escaped, he remembered Taly's amusing prayer.

'God grant me serenity to accept the things I cannot change,

courage to change the things I can,
and the wisdom to know when hunting is the better option.'

Glossary of place names and fifth-century terms

I have used authentic place names and terms wherever possible. These are gleaned from an array of sources, in particular the annals and monuments of the Romans and the Britons. By the early fifth century, Rome had dominated much of Western Europe for four hundred years. Latin became the language of the law, the military, religion and culture. Most ethnic languages endured, but the people who lived within or close by the Empire's frontiers came to adapt Latin terms much like the English language now pervades modern global terms. The written word was mostly Latin, and later, ethnic writing was influenced by the phonetics of Latin speech. The poetry of the earliest bards was likely composed in either common Brittonic or Archaic Welsh peppered with Latin. The 'Surrexit Memorandum' in the seventh century Lichfield Gospels is the best example of this hybrid writing that developed over two centuries. Christianity, in particular, was taught in Latin. In this book, the elites and their militias would have messaged and written in Latin but likely conversed in Brittonic.

Place names noted on the map

Afon Menai	Menai Straits
Alauna	Roman fort, just north of Maryport
Alt Clut	Brittonic fortress, capital of the kingdom of Strathclyde
Badon	Bardon Hill, Leicestershire
Banna	Birdoswald Fort, Hadrian's Wall
Bononia	Boulogne, France

Bremetennacum	Roman fort, Ribchester
Britannia	Roman Britain
Caledonia	Scotland, north of the Forth
Calleva	Silchester
Cambodunum	Barwick in Elmet
Camulodunum	Colchester
Candida Casa	Monastery at Whithorn
Cataractonium	Catterick
Causennis	Saltersford, Little Ponton
Clausentum	Bitterne, Southampton
Corieltauvorum	Leicester
Corinium	Cirencester
Corstopitum	Corbridge
Crecganford	Stamford Bridge
Criffel	Prominent hill, Dumfries and Galloway
Danum	Doncaster
Derventio	Little Chester, Derby
Deva	Chester
Din Eidyn	Edinburgh
Drumanagh	Headland, Loughshinny, north of Dublin
Dumnonia	Cornwall, Devon and part of Somerset
Dunnad	Scotti hillfort near Lochgilphead

Durnovaria	Dorchester
Durobrivae	Water Newton, Peterborough
Durovernum	Canterbury
Eboracum	York
Elfed	Kingdom of Elmet
Fortriu	Pictish kingdom
Gainnion	Stronghold, Gainsborough
Gaul	France
Glevum	Gloucester
Hibernia	Ireland
Hill of Tara	Seat of high kings of Ireland, County Meath
Isca Augusta	Caerleon, South Wales
Isca Dumnoniorum	Exeter
Isurium Brigantum	Aldborough, Boroughbridge
Lactodurum	Towcester
Letocetum	Wall, Lichfield
Lindinis	Ilchester, Somerset
Lindum	Lincoln
Londinium	London
Luguvalium	Carlisle
Maglona	Old Carlisle, Wigton
Mamucium	Manchester

Novomagus	Chichester
Orcades	The Orkney Islands
Pons Aelius	Newcastle upon Tyne
Reged	Northern kingdom: north-west England and south-west Scotland
Rutupiae	Richborough
Segontium	Caernarfon
Sorviodunum	Old Sarum, Salisbury
The Edge	Wenlock Edge
The Wrikon	Prominent hill near Wroxeter
Uxelodunum	Large fort, Stanwix, Carlisle
Vectis	Isle of Wight
Venta Belgarum	Winchester
Venta Icenorum	Caistor St Edmund
Verulamium	St Albans
Villa Octavius	Harley, near Much Wenlock
Vinovia	Binchester, Bishop Auckland
Viroconium	Wroxeter
Wippeds Fleet	Surfleet Seas End near the Wash
Ypwines Fleet	Swinefleet near Goole on the Humber
Yr Wyddfa	Snowdon

Other references

Aprilis	Month of April
Armorica	Brittany
Artio	Celtic bear goddess
Barus	Barons
Belgae	Large southern tribe
Brigantes	Large northern tribe
Bucinobantes	An Alemannic tribe in the region of the modern city of Mainz
Cena	Dinner
Chi Rho	Ancient Christian symbol
Cives	Citizens
Colonae	Areas of settlement (Lincolnshire in the story)
Cornovii	Large midland tribe
Crafen	Limestone region of Yorkshire
Culdeis	Partners of God, Church-appointed representatives
Cymry	A cultural grouping of Brittonic tribes who, prior to 410 AD, were Roman citizens. This included much of the west as far north as Dumbarton. The modern-day translation is 'the Welsh'.
Damnatio Memoriae	Latin phrase meaning "condemnation of memory", indicating that a person be excluded from official accounts, often executed usurpers.
Decurion	Roman cavalry officer in command of a squadron

	(Ala) consisting of three or more Turma of cavalrymen
Deisi	A tribe of people from ancient Ireland who settled in Wales
Dobunni	Large south-west tribe
Draco	Dragon
Flavia Caesariensis	Province of central England
Foederati	Barbarian tribes bound to provide military assistance to Rome
Gallic	The culture of ancient Gaul, Northern France
Germania	Roman province bordering the Rhine and the Danube
Gododdin	Celtic-speaking Brittonic people of north-eastern Britannia
Gorchan	Type of poem, commemorating a fallen warrior.
Great Forest	The largest forest in Britannia, incorporating Charnwood, Sherwood, Elmet and Galtres, stretching from Leicester to beyond York
Julius	Month of July
Kalends of Maius	First calendar day of May
Labarum	A Christian banner and the imperial standard of Constantine the Great
Legio VI Victrix	VI Legion who built Hadrian's Wall and were stationed in York
Legio XX Valeria Victrix	XX Legion , stationed in Wroxeter then later Chester
Lindsey	A large area of North Lincolnshire

Lorica	A prayer for protection, contemporary to St Patrick
Maius	Month of May
Mansio	A large house used as a hotel
Martius	Month of March
Pannonia	Roman province of the Balkans
Patria	Native country or homeland
Pontifex Maximus	Chief high priest of the College of Pontiffs in ancient Rome
Praetorian Guard	An emperor's guard
Publicani	Tax collectors
Ryknild	The northern end of the Roman road known as Icknield Street
Saturnalia	An ancient Roman festival and holiday in honour of the god Saturn, held 17–23 December
Seax	Saxon knife with a single cutting edge and a long, tapering point.
Siliquae	Small, thin Roman silver coins produced in the fourth century AD and later.
Solidus	A pure gold coin issued in the late Roman Empire.
Tanet	An area of land allocated for settlement
Turma	A cavalry unit of thirty strong
Vicus	Village or part of a town
Wealas	Anglo-Saxon term for Britons. Translates as 'foreigner'.

Senior Roman military and civil appointments

Dux Britanniarum   Duke of Britain

Comes Britanniarum   Count of the Britains

Comes litoris Saxonici Count of the Saxon Shore

Vicarius   Governor (Britannia)

The Descent of the Men of the North to c.430 AD

(Bonedd Gwyr y Gogledd)

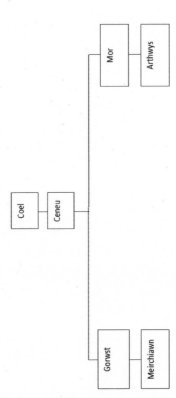

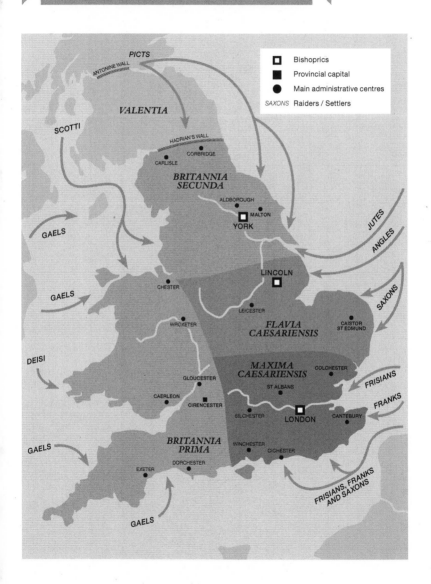

ROMAN BRITAIN'S ENEMIES AT THE CLOSE OF THE FOURTH CENTURY

Legend:
- □ Bishoprics
- ■ Provincial capital
- ● Main administrative centres
- *SAXONS* Raiders / Settlers

PICTS

ANTONINE WALL

SCOTTI

VALENTIA

HADRIAN'S WALL

CORBRIDGE

CARLISLE

BRITANNIA SECUNDA

ALDBOROUGH

MALTON

YORK

GAELS

GAELS

CHESTER

LINCOLN

LEICESTER

WROXETER

FLAVIA CAESARIENSIS

CAISTOR ST EDMUND

JUTES

ANGLES

SAXONS

DEISI

MAXIMA CAESARIENSIS

COLCHESTER

GLOUCESTER

ST ALBANS

FRISIANS

CAERLEON

CIRENCESTER

SILCHESTER

LONDON

CANTEBURY

FRANKS

GAELS

BRITANNIA PRIMA

WINCHESTER

CICHESTER

EXETER

DORCHESTER

FRISIANS, FRANKS AND SAXONS

GAELS